Draft com...
i

No Way Back

Kerry Costello

For my wife Lyn and my sons Andrew, Timothy and Alexander

ACKNOWLEDGEMENTS

Lyn Costello

Jasia Painter

By the same author

You Owe Me

The Long Game (Gibson series, book 1)

Florida Shakedown (Gibson series, book 2)

Florida Clowns (Gibson series book 3)

CHAPTER 1

I t's a Monday morning in late May; Jack Brandon is standing in a field with his dog by his side. The birds are singing, the sun is shining, the flowers are in bloom, and there's a body of a man at his feet.

Jack and his wife Rachel had flown back home the day before from the south of France, and this morning Jack was awake early, four-thirty according to his bedside clock. He was wide awake, and there was no way he would get back to sleep. He got out of bed, leaving his wife snoring softly and crept downstairs

'Shush girl.' said Jack putting his finger to his lips

The black cocker spaniel looked up at him and dutifully refrained from barking. They left the house quietly and Jack drove the half mile or so to the edge of the village, where he parked at the end of a small lane. Bess sprang out and bounced around like a puppy.

As they walked down the lane towards the river, Jack checked his pockets to make sure he had his phone, his car keys and the small canister of mace he sometimes carried these days. He'd bought the spray in a security shop in France after he'd been mugged at knifepoint, when drawing some money out of an ATM in Nice.

At the time, he hadn't felt scared, as much as foolish, for being taken advantage of so easily. So now he tended to take the spray with him whenever he felt the need.

Jack's walk took him down to the river, over a bridge, across a big field, then over a stile and down a metal road full of potholes, bordered by hedges and fields of crops.

Jack smiled at nothing in particular. It was turning into a beautiful spring day. He stopped briefly to watch the skylarks rising higher and higher into the sky singing their hearts out, then diving down to the ground in a spectacular display of aeronautical skill.

He could see Bess working the field on his right, nose to the ground looking for whatever she could find, rabbits, pheasant, maybe a partridge. Then went into a sort of trance as he walked along in the warm sun, *God it's good to be alive*.

About half a mile further on, he turned left into another field then through a small copse and over the motorway bridge, then along the path that took him out towards the hamlet of Briarley Bess worked the ground in a zigzag pattern as she followed her master.

Once across the bridge, Jack was obliged to walk through a field of shoulder high grass, bushes and brambles and towards a small wood. This was the most remote and isolated part of the walk. The path through the field was overgrown and the track narrow.

As Jack walked through the overgrown vegetation, he became aware of a thropping noise, loud at first then getting fainter - a memory. He stopped briefly to check his emails on his iPhone, but looked up when he sensed people approaching.

When Jack saw them, he thought there might be trouble, something about their demeanour. Had they seen him with his phone? He slipped it back into his pocket. *Two men out here walking, at this time of day, with no sign of a dog, hmm?* One of the men had a large rucksack on his back, *could have been camping? Unusual around here though.*

As they approached, Jack had a slight sense of foreboding, but he smiled as they got nearer. He made to move to the side to allow them to pass, the wet dewy grass immediately soaking through his trousers as they went by, uncomfortably close. Jack was more than able to look after himself, but the recent mugging experience in France, had demonstrated that even the most capable person can be caught napping.

'Morning' he said.

'Alright mate' said the first one, as he brushed past him. Jack got a whiff of a not very often washed body. The man looked to be in his late thirties, Jack estimated. He wore jeans, a tattered, faded blue tee shirt, dark, had unkempt hair and a round clown-like face complete with sad clown eyes. Jack sensed more fear than threat emanating from 'clown face', as he unconsciously christened him - *what was the man scared of?*

The second one was bigger, running to fat, but looked tough, arms decorated with elaborate tattoos.

Jack noted the obligatory 'love' and 'hate' words tattooed across his knuckles. *Jack's antennae registered violence.* This one was also unkempt and exuded a powerful stale smell as he passed by. He'd ignored Jack's greeting and seemed to be deep in thought. Jack waited a beat, turned and was about to continue walking when he sensed the men had stopped. He looked back and sure enough, the bigger one was standing still, looking straight at Jack.

'Ere' mate, I need to use your phone.'

Uh uh, here we go. I hand over my phone, and that's the last I'll see of that.

Jack hesitated and stood there, saying nothing. The man correctly interpreted Jack's inaction as a sign that Jack wasn't going to hand his phone over willingly, and started back towards him, his face now displaying undisguised aggression. The man suddenly produced a knife. Not a small knife but a large and nasty looking weapon.

Something about the way he moved and carried the knife told Jack he was practised at using it. The look in the man's eyes also made Jack aware he wasn't dealing with your average yob, but a much nastier specimen. Maybe high on something? A dangerous combination. He looked quickly at the second man who just stood watching, fear clearly showing on his face.

Shit! Is he just coming to just take my phone? No, this man uses any excuse for violence. Jack felt for the mace in his pocket *Jesus, I thought I'd left all this sort of violent crap behind years ago.*

The man got near, then stopped, put his left hand out, looked into Jack's eyes and almost screamed his demand.

'Give me that fuckin phone - now!'

His right hand was down at his side firmly holding the knife. Jack could see the other man in his peripheral vision; he hadn't moved and didn't look as though he was about to.

Jack hesitated. *If I do give him the phone now, he won't let it go at that, I'm fucked either way.* Jack made up his mind, his old training kicking in.

He put his left hand up in mock surrender and his right hand into his jacket pocket, trying to maintain a reassuring smile as he fiddled with the spray canister to make sure it came out pointing the right way. The man assumed Jack was going for his phone. They looked at each other, and in that instant, somehow the man knew whatever Jack was going to bring out of his pocket it wasn't going to be his phone.

The man's face contorted into a nasty snarl and he moved his knife hand backwards, ready to thrust it forward to stab Jack. Jack just about managed to get the spray out of his pocket as the man began to lunge. The man hesitated momentarily as he saw the strange little canister in Jack's hand.

'What the fuck?' said the man, before continuing the attack..

Jack pointed the canister at the man's face and pressed, sidestepping quickly to avoid the blade jabbing him in the stomach.

'You fucking bastard' Jack shouted as the man stopped in his tracks .

The spray had disabled the man instantaneously. Screaming with pain, he dropped the knife, then held both hands up to his eyes. Jack thought about spraying him again, but the man still had his hands over his eyes, and anyway he had obviously been rendered out of action for the time being.

The man dropped to his knees in front of Jack. Bess, who'd been quiet up to now, started barking from a safe distance, not sure if this was a game or a threat. The man was swinging his head from side to side, trying to shake out the substance that was causing him so much pain.

'You fuckin bastard, cunt. I'll cut your fuckin twattin head off you fuckin cunt, fuck, fuck fuck.'

He was screaming through his hands which were already dripping with saliva and snot caused by the mace. The screaming, sobbing tirade continued as the man tried to shake the pain out of his eyes.

Jack glanced quickly again at his sidekick who seemed mesmerised by what was happening. Jack had no idea how long the spray would incapacitate his attacker for, so had to think quickly about his next move. He decided in a split second that he wasn't going to let the man recover. *He'll probably try to kill me again if he does,* so Jack aimed a hefty kick at his head, but just at that moment, the man raised his head, and Jack missed his mark, catching him in the throat instead.

Jack had stout walking boots on, so the kick was effective. The man made a strange gurgling noise and fell sideways. Jack bent down quickly and picked up the knife. The second man seemed to come out of his trance, and looking terrified, turned to run away but was seriously impeded by the heavy rucksack on his back.

Jack was still very fit, and the man obviously wasn't. He gave chase and caught clown face after only a few yards, then grabbing one of the straps on his rucksack, pulled it towards him. The man toppled over and fell into a heap on the ground. Jack pushed him over and straddled him, bringing the knife to his throat. Bess ran up and tried to join in the fun. Jack shouted at her to go and lie down. She moved away and dropped to the floor in a funk. Jack turned his attention back to the hapless man he was sat astride.

'Do as you're told, or you'll end up like your mate over there,' he said in a way that left the man in no doubt about the sincerity of the threat. Jack was amazed at how quickly his mind had adjusted, he was all business now.

'I'm going to let you get up, but if you make one wrong move, you'll get a taste of this' Jack gestured with the knife, pointing it in the man's face. The man said nothing.

He stood up and let the man get to his feet.

'Get over there, sit down and don't move.'

Jack pointed at the body on the grass with the knife.

'And keep the rucksack strapped on.'

Jack was anxious to inhibit his prisoner's mobility. The man complied.

Jack moved over to the prone figure of his assailant and positioning himself so he could keep an eye on rucksack man, bent down and checked him out. The man's face had developed a grey pallor, and Jack couldn't see any sign of breathing. He put his two fingers to the man's neck but couldn't get a pulse. There was some nasty bruising starting to appear on his throat. Jack realised with horror that he'd killed the man. He knelt down by the prone form, stunned. *Surely he couldn't be dead?* Jack felt for a pulse again, he still couldn't feel anything.

'Oh shit' he said out loud, then rucksack man spoke.

'Is he dead, Ezra, is he dead?'

Jack couldn't believe the way the situation had spun out of control. One minute out walking the dog, the next... he answered.

'Maybe.'

Jack tried to keep his voice even. He'd killed before, but that was a long time ago, and in completely different circumstances.

'What's your name?' Jack continued while positioning himself to get the man onto his back.

'Alfie' came the reply.

'Well shut up Alfie as you can see I'm a bit busy here, just keep your mouth shut and stay still.'

Christ, what a mess, I should call an ambulance, call the police, tell them exactly what's happened, sweet Jesus! Jack rolled the man over on to his back and pumped the centre of the man's chest as he'd been trained to do, then he counted to ten and pressed again. The irony didn't escape him. Here he was trying to save the life of a man, who only moments earlier had tried to kill him.

He tried a few more times, but there was no response or sign of life. Jack took out his phone ready to dial 999, and then went through the story in his mind. *So this man asked me if he could use my phone and he had a knife. I sprayed him with a pepper spray, yes I know it's illegal. Then I kicked him in the throat and killed him. I didn't mean to kill him, but you had to be there. It was self-defence. I thought the man was going to knife me, kill me.*

Oh, in that case sir, you'll have defence wounds, you know the ones you got when he attacked you.

Well, it wasn't like that, I don't have any wounds as such.... He demanded my phone and... Oh, I see sir, he demanded your phone, tried to steal it did he? so you kicked him in the throat and killed him...

The cold realisation of how unlikely his story sounded was starting to sink in, despite it being the truth. *I'll probably be charged with manslaughter at best, found guilty and with a good chance of being put in jail.* Jack knew he couldn't go to jail. *It wasn't just the incarceration, though that would be bad enough, but Rachel and the kids, his life ruined because of this, not his fault…*

Jack took some deep breaths and concentrated. What he decided to do now he thought, would probably be one of the most important decisions he would ever make. He thought again about calling the police to say he'd simply found the body in the field, *but what about Alfie?, witness to the truth. Alfie would say it was me, no doubt about that. I'd also have to admit using the spray, an illegal weapon. Not a great start to trying to protest my innocence, then they'd bring up my army training. No, the risk was too great.* Jack weighed things up and tried to think; what were his chances of being prosecuted for manslaughter if he told the unvarnished truth? Quite high he thought, *especially as Alfie clown face here is unlikely to support any allegation I make about his mate Ezra attacking me first. Would I be found guilty? I think I probably would.*

Jesus H Christ, what have I got myself into? Jack wasn't going to put himself or his family through the pain and humiliation of being had up for murder, or manslaughter, or whatever. He decided to find out what these two were doing out here at this time in the morning anyway. Jack looked at his watch, it was still only 5.45 a.m. Time for some interrogation. He went over to the man..

'So Alfie, what are you and your mate here doing out here so early in the morning?'

'We've been er, camping, just making our way back home.'

Alfie wasn't very convincing.

Jack put the spray in his right hand and kept the knife in the left one.

'Take the rucksack off mister and no messing otherwise you'll end up like your pal here, understand?' Alfie nodded.

Jack made a stabbing motion with the knife to emphasise the threat. The man did as he was told.

'Stand with your back next to that tree and put your hands behind it, now!' shouted Jack.

The man jumped, plainly intimidated and fearful of what this lunatic would do to him if he didn't comply.

'What you going to do to me?' asked the hapless Alfie, his voice breaking as he spoke.

'Just shut up and keep your hands still.'

Still holding the spray, Jack moved behind Alfie, put the knife down on the ground, and took Bess's lead out of his pocket. He looped one end of the lead through the loop at the top to form a lasso, then slipped it round both of Alfie's wrists and pulled tight. This secured his wrists together tightly enough for Jack to drop the spray, enabling him to use both hands to make a proper job of tying Alfie up.

'What are you going to do to me?' the man asked again.

'Not decided yet, I'm thinking. Just keep quiet.'

Alfie, the witness, is the big problem here, If he wasn't alive to tell anyone what had happened? I could just kill him, walk away and no one would be any the wiser. The police find a couple of bodies body in a field and conclude it was some sort of gang killing, execution, happens all the time, just another unsolved crime. What am I thinking, even with my experience there's no way I could kill this man in cold blood. No, there'd have to be another way.

It seemed obvious that Alfie was a follower and not very brave or bright. Jack might have even felt sorry for him in different circumstances.

'Okay Alfie boy, what were you and your mate up to? and don't give me any of that shit about camping.'

'Er well just picking something up for someone and er, dropping it off to someone else.

'The rucksack?' He nodded.

'And what's in the rucksack?' Jack had a good idea what the answer would be.

'All sorts of shit, I don't know, drugs, don't know what kind of stuff though' said Alfie.

'Ezra was the one what gets the jobs, he just brings me along to help.'

Pack mule thought Jack and undid the straps to look in the bag. There were packets of stuff, and he took one out to examine it. He hadn't a clue what it was and didn't really want to know, so he put the packet back and tightened the straps up again.

'And where did you pick up the stuff?'

'Dropped from a helicopter,' Alfie said.'

Memories

'And where were you taking all this stuff to?'

'Don't know exactly, 'but somewhere over there,' he said nodding his head in the general direction of the motorway.

'You've obviously done this before so you must know where.'

'Honest I don't, they change the drop off place a bit, but it's always somewhere around here an' we, well Ezra, he has to phone to confirm we've collected the stuff. Then he gets told exactly where to drop it off, s'all to do with security an' that.'

Jack left Alfie, went to the prone body of Ezra and turned out his pockets. He found a wallet with a driving licence in the name of Ezra Madaki, s*trange name for a white* *man?* thought Jack, a huge wad of cash rolled up in an elastic band, a piece of paper with what looked like a telephone number written on it, and a phone which wasn't working, the battery dead. *So that's was why he was desperate to have my phone?*

Jack sat down on the grass beside the body and thought. A plan started to form in his mind, *but could I carry it off?*

Jack thought his plan through again, in as much detail as he could, but realised he had to act fast whatever he was going to do. He reckoned the body might not be discovered for days. He could tell, by the way the path was overgrown, that the path wasn't used that often. And there was another path that skirted the field which most other walkers used. *I had to be different?*

In all the confusion, Jack had forgotten all about Bess. He looked around and there she was, still sitting a few yards away, watching and wagging her tail.

Jack had concluded that if he was going to stand any chance of getting out of this, he had to turn Alfie, the witness, into Alfie, the suspect. *What was it his old captain used to say "if in doubt, blame it on some other poor fucker"* He picked up Ezra's knife and went over to Alfie who became very frightened when he saw the knife in Jack's hand. This was difficult for Jack, but he knew it had to be done to make his plan work.

Alfie screamed as Jack put the knife to his face and cut his cheek. Not a deep cut, but he bled a lot nevertheless. Alfie screamed.

'What the fuck you doin'?!'

My god, he'll be heard by people miles away, better get this next bit over with quickly.

Jack went around Alfie's back and made cuts on the inside of Alfie's forearms. Alfie started screaming and crying, pleading with Jack to stop, and writhing around to try to get free.

Jack steeled himself to ignore Alfie's pleas and held his arms still so he could continue to make wounds in a manner that would replicate defence wounds. An important part of his plan was to give the impression that Alfie had been cut defending himself in a fight with a knife wielding Ezra. Jack didn't make particularly deep cuts, but once again there was plenty of blood. In fact, there was so much blood that for a minute Jack thought he might have cut an artery.

Alfie was screaming even louder now, obviously convinced he had fallen foul of some evil sadistic fiend.

'Let me go, let me go you mad fucker, please let me go please, please, I won't tell anyone, honest.'

Alfie's pleas turned into cries of despair, and Jack couldn't help feeling sympathy for the man. But he gritted his teeth and finished the job as quickly as he could. Alfie was now whimpering and muttering something intelligible.

Jack knew the man couldn't stand much more and that he might have another corpse on his hands if he wasn't careful. He was finished now but gave Alfie a few minutes to calm down before releasing him.

'Okay Alfie, I'm going to untie you now, but you'd better keep still and do as I say or I'll spray you with this stuff and really go to town on you, okay?'

'Okay,' Alfie eventually said in a small voice.

Jack undid the lead and Alfie brought his arms around the front to see what damage Jack had inflicted on him.

Alfie stared at Jack, fear in his eyes, wondering what this sadistic madman might do next. He wiped his bloodied arms on his clothes never taking his eyes off Jack.

'Here take this.'

Jack handed Alfie the huge wad of cash he'd taken out of Ezra's pocket.

'What you giving me this for?' Alfie managed to say in a halting voice

'Cos you're going on the run.'

'What you talking about, why'd I go on the run?'

'Because you killed your mate Ezra'.

'But you killed 'im.'

'No Alfie, you killed him after a disagreement. You tried to take the drugs, and he went for you with the knife and cut you up, but you got the better of him, kicked him in the throat and killed him.

'You can't...'

Jack cut him off and shouted at Alfie to emphasise the message

'Look, go now. Piss off before I change my mind and kill you as well! Disappear, bugger off to Timbuktu or something, but don't even think of going to the police. If you do, I'll tell them I was out walking my dog and saw two men matching your descriptions, arguing and threatening each other and that I carried on my walk and that's all. They can come to their own conclusions about what happened next, but from those cuts on your face and arms it'll look pretty obvious to anyone what happened here.'

Alfie looked at Jack, and gradually it dawned on him that he'd been well and truly stitched up. He looked uncertainly at Jack for a couple of beats, then made his decision and stuffing the cash in his pocket, ran off down the path as if there were a pack of mad dogs after him.

So there Jack was, on a Monday morning in May, standing in a field with his dog Bess by his side. The birds were singing, the sun was shining, the flowers were blooming, and at his feet, the body of a man. The man was dead, and he'd killed him.

CHAPTER 2

J ack started to take on board the full implications of what had just happened. He was no longer the battle hardened soldier he used to be, experiencing violent death on a daily basis. All that was a distant memory, he was a different person now. *There was no war. I just went for a walk with my dog for Christ's sake!* He kept thinking how on earth it had happened, was it his fault? The stupidity and horror of it all in his mind. He felt as if he was going to be sick, but resisted the urge *That would make terrific DNA evidence.*

He took some deep breaths then shook his head to try to clear it, *think straight, there's a lot at stake here, it's too late now, and there's no way back, so get on with it you idiot.* Jack took the man's phone lying on the floor and holding it gingerly by the edges, wiped it on his shirt flap, which by now had worked its way out of his trousers, then slid the phone back into the man's pocket. He did the same with the wallet, then he stuffed the piece of paper, with the phone number on it, back in the man's pocket as well.

He bent down, took the knife by the blade, being careful not to wipe any of Alfie's blood off it, nor to get any of Alfie's blood on himself, then wiped the handle with the bottom of his shirt. He carefully laid the handle of the knife in Ezra's open palm and closed his hand around it, just like he'd seen in so many films. Despite all his unfortunate familiarity with dead bodies in the past, it still made Jack feel nauseous touching Ezra's dead flesh, but knew he had no choice, if he were to provide evidence in support of the conclusion he prayed the investigators would come to.

Gingerly picking up the knife by the very edges of the handle, he threw it into the long grass, then hoisting the rucksack on to his back, he set off walking. He thought he knew just the place where the drugs could be hidden, and where no one would ever find them.

He paused and looked around at the scene to check he hadn't left anything incriminating, well not anything that didn't fit with the scenario he hoped he'd created. Then he saw Bess's lead still at the bottom of the sapling he used to tie Alfie up to. He retrieved it and with one more look at the scene and the body of the man lying there, and left with Bess at his side, happily wagging her tail now the walk was back on.

Jack got home and was relieved to find that Rachel wasn't up yet. He took his walking clothes off, and got in the shower. He stood in it for a long time and turned the thermostat up to hot. He thought about the man he'd killed and how different violent death really is compared how such events are trivialised in movies. He knew, from his past experience in the military, that nothing could get near to the actual horror of killing someone in real life. His time in the Falklands was testament to that. He laughed involuntarily as he thought about the way people always assumed that once you'd killed once, it became easier. *Well, that might be the case for some people* he thought, *but unless you're a psychopath, if anything, it gets worse.* He desperately tried to rationalise what had happened, tried to convince himself he'd had no choice. *It was, after all, a tragic accident, a direct result of the violent act of a man who tried to steal my phone. And wasn't I just defending myself? After all, the man did actually try to stab me with a knife, and no doubt would have happily killed me without a second thought.* Jack had no doubt that the man intended to do him serious injury, probably worse. *Anyway, nothing I can do about it now, got to make the best of it.*

Jack got out of the shower, put on some clean jeans and a fresh shirt, then stuffed his soiled shirt into a plastic bag. Opening the front door quietly, he went to his car and put the plastic bag in the boot, then went back in the house and made some coffee. He drank it black, and as the hot oily liquid worked it magic, he started to feel a little better. Breakfast was out of the question, so he went into his study and tried to distract himself by sorting out the mail. As he read the mail he found it hard to concentrate and found himself going over what had happened, thinking through his plan again to see if there were any flaws, or if he'd missed anything. He thought about it all so hard that his mind swum and he could no longer think coherently.

'Jesus H fucking Christ, another speeding ticket!' he shouted out loud as he opened the fourth envelope.

'The fucking cretins. What's the matter with them, haven't they got anything better to do than trap people with their stupid fucking cameras? Why don't they get after real criminals instead of wasting all their time on....'

Jack suddenly realised what he was saying and stopped, just as Rachel walked past his study door in her dressing gown.

'My my, we are in a strop. All that profanity at this time in the morning. Not like you at all dear. Someone's really got you wound up.'

'Oh yes, sorry Rachel, I do seem to have let them get under my skin, sorry.'

'So are you going to tell me what's wrong?'

'Wrong? Nothing really, just another speeding ticket, so that'll be' six points on my licence now.'

'Jack Brandon, how long have we been married?'

'Em, not sure Rach, why?'

'C'mon Jack. That was what's called a rhetorical question.' You know very well what I meant. When did you start thinkimg you could fool me? I know something's wrong, and it's not just a speeding ticket. No doubt you'll tell me when you're ready. In the meantime, have you had any breakfast?'

'Yes I had some toast when I got up' he lied.

Rachel looked at him and sighed.

Jack opened the rest of his post, but he still couldn't concentrate. He wondered if he should tell Rachel what had happened, but decided against it. He didn't see any point. If he told her, she'd then be obliged to lie if he was to carry out his plan, and he wasn't sure she could carry it off, or even agree to lie. He knew she would do anything for him, but she might find being involved in the cover up of a dead man a bit too much to handle - out of the blue at any rate. He decided to think about it.

Jack sat down at the breakfast table. Rachel gave him another cup of coffee and put the morning paper on the table in front of him. She leaned over and gave him a peck on the cheek.

'Now just relax and read your paper.'

Jack pretended to read the paper, but he was lost in thought. From a fairly uncomplicated life just a few hours ago, he had, through no fault of his own, become what? *I don't even know what I've become. A fugitive from justice?* It was all too much, so he pushed it to the back of his mind and went back to his study. He had a lot of catching up to do now they were back home, all the domestic stuff, plus some business matters to sort out.

Rachel looked so relaxed, yawning and stretching after her lie in. Jack envied her and wished he'd done the same, but too late now he thought. Rachel popped her head around the study door.

'Sure you don't want any breakfast?'

'No thanks, the toast was enough, but thanks all the same.'

'You were up early weren't you?'

'Er yes, it was such a lovely day I thought I might as well get out there with Bess.'

'Well, what shall we do today Jack? I've got the unpacking and all the washing to do, but after that I'm free. So you could take me for a nice pub lunch if you were so inclined.'

'I would Rach, but I think I've got too much catching up to do, sorry.'

'Oh well, never mind, but there's no guarantee I'll accept an invitation tomorrow, so you may have to work a bit to get me to go then.' She smiled and, then busied herself getting some cereal for breakfast. Jack looked at her, still slim with a figure of a much younger woman, black shiny hair, cut in a bob and never too much makeup. She seemed to sense Jack looking at her and turned round.

'You're not okay are you?' she asked, 'you seem a bit distracted.'

'No, no I'm fine thanks just thinking about all the things I've got to do.'

'Okay, I can wait,' she said, 'as long as it's nothing to do with that busty blond who moved in across the road.'

Jack tried to smile at Rachel's attempt to cheer him up. *God, I love that woman.*

He was tempted to tell her everything that had happened, but he couldn't. If he was going to lie, which he definitely was going to have to do, in spades, he knew he couldn't involve Rachel in any deceit. He told himself it just wouldn't be fair putting that sort of pressure on her. And anyway, she might not be able to carry it off. *If my plan dissembles, and it was proved she'd lied for me, then she'll be guilty of something, perverting the course of justice or whatever, and lying to the police in such circumstances would be viewed as a really serious matter.*

'No Rachel, there's nothing honestly,' he said 'although I have been knocking off the blond off since she arrived, so maybe I'm just a bit exhausted.'

'Jack Brandon!' Rachel shrieked in mock horror. Then she cuffed him not too gently round the head.

'Ouch,' he said. 'That hurt.'

'It was meant to Jack Brandon.'

He rubbed his head.

'I'll be okay in a bit Rach, perhaps I got up a bit too early.' *Boy was that an understatement...*

CHAPTER 3

Tom MacBride ignored the chirping noise of his mobile phone. *They'll ring back if it's urgent.*

He was soaking up the sun at his luxurious villa in the south of Spain. He was half asleep on his lounger by the swimming pool, listening to the gentle swish of the water as a young woman swam up and down in a controlled, relaxed breaststroke. *Should have been a bloody mermaid* thought MacBride.

He could only manage a few manic lengths of the pool when he swam, which wasn't often. And when he did, the water would splash everywhere in response to his somewhat unusual and energetic style of the crawl. On the other hand, this girl could swim languidly for long periods, hardly disturbing the water at all.

He thought of all the years he'd been married and wondered at how remarkable it was that he still loved his wife as much as he did when they first met More, he supposed in some ways. He also wondered what she would do if she saw the young woman getting out of their swimming pool. She was blond, beautiful, tanned, and stark naked. Tom sat up admiring her.

'Don't you know it's rude to stare?' she said teasingly.

'Don't you know you could give me a heart attack walking around like that?

She laughed and started to towel herself dry.

'Need any help Tina?'

'Well, now you mention it....'

She'll kill me he thought, *but at least I'll die happy*. He was just getting up off his lounger to walk over to her when his phone chirped again. Ccursing under his breath, he grabbed it off the table and answered.

'Yes,' Tom MacBride barked.

'Hi Tom.'

It was his 'distribution' manager Tony Malone. Malone headed up the 'distribution division' as Tom MacBride euphemistically called one of his more dubious businesses.

'Hello Tony' he replied, 'what's up?'

Malone wouldn't normally disturb Tom when he was away in Spain unless it was something out of the ordinary.

'I think we have a missing person problem.'

'Oh' said Tom, 'I'll call you on a landline, the reception's not so great on my mobile here.'

The reception was, in fact, excellent, but Tom MacBride was aware that there were computers listening to mobile phone calls to pick up on any keywords that might indicate a call between terrorists, thieves, drug dealers etc.

Tom called Malone back on a landline.

'What's the problem Tony?'

'Well, we seem to have lost a couple of couriers and more importantly, the stuff they were carrying.'

'How do you mean, lost?'

'Well he, Ezra that is, didn't make the call to arrange the drop off and there's no sign of him, or that scroat Alfie.'

'What are we doing about it?' said Tom MacBride in an even voice. Tom MacBride didn't lose his cool, ever. That's what made him so frightening. If pushed, he could dish out the most appalling punishment without seeming to get at all angry or upset.

'The boys are out looking for him and his sidekick in the usual places. So far, we've been told that Alfie was around but then disappeared, but no one's seen Ezra.

'I thought you said those two tossers were reliable.'

'They normally are,' said Malone, 'I can't imagine what's gone wrong.'

'Well you'd better get it sorted, and soon. We're talking serious money here. If someone's nicked my stuff, I'll make them wish their mothers had aborted them. Tell the boys this is top priority!'

'On it now boss.'

'Call me as soon as you find the stuff or either of those two scroats.'

'Will do boss,' he said, but MacBride had already ended the call.

Malone put the phone down gently on to its cradle, then gave vent to his own anger.

'Shit shit shit,' he shouted, slamming his fist down on the desk, making all the bits and pieces of desk furniture jump.

'All my careful planning fucked, well and truly fucked! I'll kill that fucking pair of idiots'

When Tom MacBride replaced the phone receiver at his end, he stood still, looking out at the pool, and tried to figure out what was going on. *Typical, just as I was beginning to relax and enjoy myself.* He walked out to the pool where Tina was sitting on a lounger, applying some suntan lotion.

'What?' she said when she saw the expression on his face.

'Sorry Tina, something's come up. I've got to go back, but I'll come back out as soon as I sort things out.'

Tina sighed.

'When?'

'As soon as I hear back from the man who just called me, but I'd guess not till tomorrow at the earliest.'

'Well time for a bit more fun before you go. But you'd better hurry up back, or I might have to seduce Manuel, if you leave me for too long on my own.'

Tom MacBride laughed, Manuel was Tina's handsome personal trainer, who despite his rugged good looks and animal magnetism that turned women to jelly, was more attracted to Tom MacBride than Tina.

'Well if you do, give him a kiss for me!' he said before patting Tina on the bottom.

'Now how about that fun you were talking about..'

As he got older, Tom MacBride valued his time in his Spanish villa more and more. He enjoyed the sun and considered it much better for his ageing body. But he still had a serious business empire to run in the UK so could never spend as much time there as he'd like to.

MacBride owned a small chain of betting shops in Salford and Manchester, which he'd inherited from his father. He'd also established a very successful 'security' business in Manchester. Quadrant Security, provided door management personnel, or doormen and bouncers as Tom MacBride was more inclined to call them, to clubs, lap dancing bars, casinos, discos, pubs etc. It was a competitive business, but Tom MacBride liked competition. It enabled him to show the contrast between his well run outfit and the other less well organised and less well connected security firms.

Over the years, MacBride had gained the reputation for being a hard, but reasonable man. Liked by the police for his co-operative attitude, and feared by the bad boys for his ruthless ways, if he felt they'd had him over. He was a big solid man, good looking, or so Esther told him, sandy hair flecked with grey these days, but he still had a good muscular figure. Not the kind of guy you'd mess with, as some of his more foolhardy antagonists had found out to their cost.

At the age of thirteen, in the wake of the potato famine, his grandfather Michael MacBride, had left Ireland for England and settled in Manchester, eventually setting up an illegal bookmaking business in nearby Salford. Then, as the law changed, he went legit. *MacBride's the Bookies – Always a good bet!*

Tom's gambling and security businesses would have been enough for most people, but MacBride wasn't 'most people', and so he kept an eye out for any new exciting business opportunities. Waste recycling attracted him as a potentially lucrative business. Today's rubbish becoming tomorrow's gold appealed to him. As usual, he did his homework and recognised that China's growth alone would push up prices of raw material to previously unknown heights. Mind made up, Tom MacBride didn't hesitate.

'Rubbish,' said Tom MacBride when he'd walked into his office one Monday morning some two years previously.

'What's rubbish boss?' said Phil, his business manager.

'The future' said Tom MacBride.

Phil looked at his boss.

'I thought you were an optimist?'

'I am, and no I don't mean the future's rubbish in that sense, you plonker, I mean we're going into the recycling business.

'China!' said Tom MacBride.

'What?' said Phil again.

'China, we're off to China.' *Definitely flipped* thought Phil

'I've been boning up on this rubbish, sorry, recycling, and it seems that what we call rubbish, the Chinese call raw materials. Can't get enough of it.'

He bought some premises, a modest fleet of collection vans and spent a small fortune buying some sophisticated machinery that sorted waste into constituent parts, plastic, metal, paper, glass, you name it, it sorted it. The new business took off.

Tom MacBride enjoyed going to China, forging new business relationships and negotiating contracts. China appealed to his sense of adventure. There were few rules that the Chinese wouldn't break. They'd copy anything they laid their hands on and had little respect for brand protection or patents. Scotch Whiskey, Champagne, Coca Cola, Old Masters. Their talent for replication seemed to know no bounds. This amused MacBride, though he imagined the owners of the real McCoy wouldn't find it so funny. The place was buzzing with energy, and he found it exciting, intoxicating.

The Chinese also recognised the maverick in Tom MacBride, and they got along together well. He and they seemed to share the same philosophy on life - the need to sweep caution aside, and get on with it. *Life was way too short* he thought, and he would always say that the wrong decision on Monday was better than the right decision on Friday. *Make your decision and move on.*

The waste reclamation business expanded so fast, even Tom MacBride found it hard to believe it could continue indefinitely at this pace. It didn't. As the world recession bit, the re-cycling business slowed down, not disastrously, but it certainly wasn't the business it had been. However, the Chinese contacts that Tom MacBride had developed over the last year or so, proposed another interesting business opportunity.

MacBride had proved reliable and straightforward in his dealings with the Chinese, and they thought a lot of him. So when the recycling business took a downward turn, his Chinese contact Jun Shan suggested a possible additional business venture in which they could also become partners. And so began his most recent, and arguably his most profitable business venture. Importing illicit drugs from the Golden Triangle via China. Heroin, cocaine etc. MacBride was against using drugs on a personal level, but if idiots wanted to buy them, then let them. *No one forced the stupid bastards to take the stuff.* Perversely, if it were up to him, all drugs would be made completely legal, then the bottom would drop out of the illegal drugs market, *but who ever thought politicians were smart?*

The new venture proved a good fit with Tom MacBride's other interests. The 'security' business meant he had access to the club crowd, drug users to a man – and woman, plus the ability to launder the cash through his chain of betting shops – perfect!

CHAPTER 4

Jesus was a psychopath, whether by nature or nurture, his victims never knew, or cared.

His mother Mary used to tell him why she'd named him Jesus.

'Cos you were born in a shelter just like the other Jesus and his mother's name was Mary as well.'

But as he grew older, and found out a bit more about the Holy Family, he thought the fact that his own dad's name was Charlie rather than Joseph, spoilt the story a little bit. As for his ability to perform miracles, the only one, was to stay out of jail for as long as he did.

But it was true that Jesus Madaki was born in a shelter, albeit one run by the Salvation Army in Miles Platting near Manchester, a far cry from Bethlehem. His parents had fled to Britain in the nineteen seventies, following serious industrial unrest and violence in Durban. His father Charlie Madaki, had been involved in some dubious union strong-arm activities in the shipyards and had become the target of the opposition, so it was flee or be killed

When they arrived in Britain, his mother was heavily pregnant. They were sleeping on the streets, until the police alerted the local Salvation Army who took them in just in time for his mother to give birth. Mary was relatively well educated, and eventually found work as a teaching assistant in a Catholic school in Moss Side Manchester, an area that had gradually developed into a largely black ghetto area during the late fifties and early sixties. Charlie could only get badly paid part-time jobs and soon became involved in petty crime to make up his money, and to feed his drinking habit.

They rented a house in Moss Side, and four years after Jesus was born, Mary produced a second son. When the nurse presented Mary with her second newborn, she was shocked, but not as shocked as Charlie was when he came to visit.

'Some mistake here?' said Charlie when he looked in the baby's cot.

'I thought so too,' said Mary in a small voice, 'but the nurse checked and said this is definitely our son.'

'Our son, our son? but he's white!' exclaimed Charlie in a voice loud enough to wake the infant and several others in the adjoining rooms too.

Amid the wailing, Mary tried to explain to Charlie that she'd spoken to the doctor and he'd explained.

'Explained, I don't need no explained, you tryin' to make a fool outa me woman?' Shouted Charlie, now in a serious state of potentially violent agitation.

By now Mary was also in a state, and crying uncontrollably, trying to tell Charlie that she hadn't been unfaithful.

The nurse came running into the room to find out what all the shouting was about and eventually calmed Charlie down, then went to get the doctor. He explained to Charlie that it was very unusual but not unheard of for a black couple to have a white child. He said they used to call white children born of a black couple, or vice versa, Octoroons, and that this was thought to have been caused by one or more of their ancestors, having had children to a person of another colour. Charlie reluctantly accepted the explanation, partly because he knew Mary would have been too scared to have ever been unfaithful to him. Nevertheless, Charlie felt tremendous shame and never got over the child having pale skin. He was the butt of jokes by other members of the local black community, and this, in turn, made him despise his new son.

They christened the unfortunate child Ezra and Ezra didn't have a very nice life. As he grew up, Jesus began to realise the significance of his younger brother's condition and the combination of being called Jesus. Having a white brother proved also a serious disadvantage, giving everyone a reason to bully both brothers. Whereas Jesus was tall and rangy, Ezra by contrast, was smaller, always a bit overweight and looked as though he would go to fat rather than develop the fine physique of his brother Jesus.

Jesus was strong, violent and sadistic. When he was a kid, no creature was safe from his desire to inflict pain and suffering. Insects, mice, cats, dogs. Whatever creature came to hand, became something for Jesus to practice his sadistic nature on. Ezra was often the target of his brother's violence as well, and soon learned to keep out of the way.

Later, other children were the targets for Jesus's assaults, and he soon became feared for his brutal response to almost any situation. It wasn't long before Jesus ended up in Court and was sentenced to three months in a juvenile detention centre. He maintained his belligerent stance throughout the Court hearing, but when he was locked up, Jesus realised he'd badly underestimated how much he would hate confinement. The experience made him vow never to put himself in a position where he would be locked up again. To this end, he modified his behaviour to some extent, but the underlying violent nature remained.

Jesus had never made friends easily, in fact, he'd never really had any friends, or other kids to play with, other than his little brother, but one boy did manage to forge a friendship with him. Aaron lived in the next street. His family were originally from the Caribbean, and Aaron appeared to have the typical benign disposition of his race. But underneath this benign façade, he hid a cruel and mean disposition.

Aaron and Jesus got on well together. It was Aaron who suggested that the name Jesus wasn't cool.

'Hey man you don't want to go tru life bein' Jesus? You far too bad for that name.'

Aaron and Jesus both laughed.

'No man,' said Aaron, 'you goin' to be Jay for me man. Jay, now that's a cool name.'

And that was it. It was Jay from then on, for everyone.

A few weeks after Jay had been released from the detention centre, he was at home, upstairs watching the television with Ezra when they heard a commotion downstairs. It sounded like his dad was arguing with someone in the kitchen. Jay crept halfway down the stairs so he could hear better. On the other side of the kitchen door, Charlie was arguing with another man who sounded much younger.

'I ain't got no money see, so you just have to wait.'

'Charlie boy, you pay up now or else.'

'Don't call me boy, motherfucker, an' stop botherin' me I ain't scared of you or your punk brother.'

'You shouldn't be talkin' like that Charlie,' said the man

'Think I'm scared of a halfwit junkhead like you? what you gonna do – pussy, c'mon what you gonna do?' Charlie replied

'This,' said the man, and there was a loud shot, a moan, and the sound of someone falling to the floor.

Jay ran, and jumped down the last few stairs and burst through the door into the kitchen. His dad was on the floor, a large wound in his head, pumping out blood on to the floor. Jay was conscious of someone running out of the back door and caught a fleeting glimpse. He was followed into the kitchen by his brother and mother.

Mary gasped and scremed.

'Oh no, almighty God no.'

Ezra was dumbstruck and ran to his mother. They held each other, Ezra moved to go to his father, but Jay screamed at him.

'Stay away. Nuthin' useful you can do. The man's a gonner'.'

Jay's mother held tight on to Ezra and whimpered.

'Jay do something.'

Jay looked down at his father, eyes still open, looking at Jay with the fear and knowledge that he was dying.

Jay kneeled down by his father's side and muttered, so his mother and brother couldn't hear.

'You useless motherfucker. You sucked as a father, now look at you, gunned down by some piece a street shit cos you din't pay your way. But one thing. No one kills any of my family, even you, an' gets away with it.'

Charlie breathed one last big sigh, his breath rattled and he died.

By now, Mary had grabbed the phone and dialled 999. She couldn't speak at first, still too shocked, but recovered and with a gasping breath told the operator her husband was shot and they needed an ambulance right away. She was frustrated at the slow process, screaming and intermittently crying at the operator who insisted on taking seemingly unnecessary details before putting her through to the emergency services. Jay stood and knew Charlie was already dead, but said nothing, as they all waited for the ambulance to arrive.

The police arrived at the same time as the ambulance and immediately threw a cordon around the property. Jay and his family were made to feel more like suspects rather than victims. The paramedics pronounced Charlie dead at the scene, but the police had to wait for the doctor to come and formally confirm the death.

Jay's anger slowly simmered. He wasn't sure what he was angry at the most. His father, a no good weak loser putting himself at the mercy of some street dealer, or the dealer who'd shot him dead.

He vowed to himself that he would find who had done this - and do what? He'd think about that later. He went to the bathroom and stood there not knowing what to do. He knew he should feel grief, cry maybe, but he couldn't. He washed his face and thought about what difference it would make not having his father around. Apart from not feeling the back of his hand when his father was drunk, Jay couldn't think of anything that would alter his life very much.

CHAPTER 5

Harry Antrobus looked like a typical Cheshire farmer. Bucolic, red faced, big and loud. Only Harry didn't do any farming these days. His farm stretched to nearly seven hundred acres, all prime Cheshire agricultural land. Strictly speaking, it wasn't Harry's farm at all. It belonged to Tyford Estates, but his father and his father's father, had been tenant farmers on this land since the eighteen hundreds.

Crops were still grown on the farm, and sheep grazed from time to time, but Harry Antrobus had long since given up farming the land himself and sub-let it to neighbouring farmers, whilst Harry concentrated on his more lucrative business activities. Harry's current business had started by accident in the late nineteen nineties, largely due to the Farm's relatively remote location, and an enterprising proposal from a friend of Harry's son, Andrew. Andrew's friend Tim had asked Harry if he could hold a Rave in one of the barns on Harry's farm.

'And a Rave is?'

'Well we put up some lighting to create the right atmosphere, plus strobes and flashing lights etc., then we play music, very loudly, and people dance all night, simple as that really.'

But Harry still didn't quite understand. Tim went on to explain that there was very little risk or cost involved for Harry and that the barn was far enough away from his farmhouse so as not to be a nuisance.

'I'll just need some electricity to feed the music equipment and the lighting, plus somewhere for the revellers to park their cars.'

'And how many people do you expect?' asked Harry.

'Oh, at least a hundred' Tim replied.'

'And you say you'll charge £3 a head?'

'Yes.'

'And what will the costs be?'

'Well, just seventy five quid for the DJ and whatever you're going to charge me to hire the barn.'

'Which you expect to be how much, young Tim?'

'Suppose I give you fifty percent of whatever we get on the door, less the cost of the DJ?'

Harry did a quick calculation. No brainer.

'You're on' said Harry and spit in his hand then offered it to Tim.

Tim wasn't too thrilled about sealing the deal in this manner, but nevertheless, manfully spit in his own hand, and the two of them swapped spit. Deal done. As it happened, nearly two hundred people turned up, and the evening was a huge success, both socially and financially. Harry was agog at the antics and sheer energy exuded by the 'Ravers,' he was also impressed by their stamina.

Although the barn was a fair distance from his farmhouse the walls still reverberated with the pounding base vibrations from the music that went on well into the small hours. Not that it kept Harry awake, he just thought about it as the sound of money and slept like a baby. Harry was hooked. This was much better than farming, better paid, less work and you got to see all those scantily dressed young girls cavorting like exotic dancers, not that Harry had much experience of exotic dancers, just the odd stripper at the local rugby club on a Friday night in his youth.

Tim arranged another Rave and this time over two hundred and fifty people turned up. It became obvious this time that the barn was at bursting point. Harry asked Tim how many more Raves he might be able to organise that summer and he said maybe another two or three. At this second Rave, Harry stayed and watched the action for a while. Some people he noticed sneaked their own booze in, but they were in the minority. Tim had explained that it was against the rules.

This confused Harry who'd assumed that as they weren't going to sell booze at the raves, too complicated in terms of licences etc., that most of the young people would bring their own, but not so it seemed. *So what on earth got them into the manic state they worked themselves up to he wondered.* Harry watched carefully and soon clocked one boy, who looked slightly older than the rest, taking cash from a couple of girls and slipping a small paper packet into their hands. *Drugs* thought Harry, *of course!*

Harry became concerned, not at the moral aspect, just that he didn't fancy being raided by the police. He collared Tim and asked him for a quiet word outside.

'Sorry I didn't tell you' said Tim sheepishly, but I thought you'd refuse to let me hold these Raves if you knew about the ecstasy.'

'Ecstasy?' said Harry, please explain.

So Tim told Harry all about Ecstasy and how it was part of the culture, and it didn't do any harm, not like hard drugs, the pills just got you high so you could dance all night etc etc.

'And what about the money I saw passing hands?'

'Well, I get a cut of whatever he makes on the night.'

'I see' said Harry, 'but you didn't tell me about that either did you?'

'No sorry,' said Tim,'I should have, but if you let us carry on, I'll cut you in for a third - promise.

Harry thought. 'Does Andrew know about this?'

'Yes' said Tim.

Then Harry thought again. *Bugger it why not?* He spat into his hand, and this time Tim didn't hesitate. Another deal sealed with spit.

Harry and Tim discussed the next Rave and wondered if they should try to limit the numbers or find a bigger venue.

'But where?' asked Tim.

Harry was not up for asking any other farms around. He definitely wanted to keep this close, and under his control. Harry thought, but struggled to come up with a solution.

Then a couple of days later, the answer came to him, often as such things do, when least expected. He'd gone to the Cheshire Country Fair at Tatton Park, and as soon as he walked through the main entrance, he saw the big Marquee tent, and knew what the answer was. He didn't stay at the fair but went back and did some homework on the cost of hiring, and or buying a large marquee tent. Harry came to the conclusion that he'd buy a marquee for the Raves and hire it out when he didn't need it himself. *Perfect.*

Tim and Harry held two more raves that year using the Marquee, and they were both roaring successes despite the sometimes inclement English weather. At the end of that summer, both Tim, and Harry's son Andrew, went off to university. By then, Harry had learnt enough to be able to organise things himself. He'd also developed his own relationship with the boy who supplied the ecstasy.

The following year, Harry hired some people to help him, and organised the Raves himself. As the raves had got bigger, a little trouble occurred, and Harry felt the need to hire some security, to prevent his raves getting a bad reputation. Having found the golden goose, Harry was determined not to let it be killed because of a few nut cases.

He talked to a few people in the security game and eventually came across a company called Quadrant Security. He and Tom MacBride, who owned the security company, got on instantly, and so Tom MacBride's company supplied the security and doormen for all Harry's Raves. After a while, Harry realised that Raves on his farm had their limitations in terms of how often he could hold them, so when a friend of his told him about a big empty warehouse in Manchester that he couldn't find a tenant for, Harry went to see it. He chose to go in the evening first to see what kind of nightlife already existed in the area.

He parked his car in the Chorlton Street car park and walked the short distance to Canal Street. The warehouse was situated in a small street nearby. He found the pubs and bars nearby, buzzing with activity and decided to go in for a drink in one of the bars. Maybe pick up some more information on the area. He chose one called the Baa Bar, which as a farmer appealed to him.

'What can I get you handsome?' said the man behind the bar.

Harry was a bit taken aback.

'Oh, just half a bitter please.'

The barman laughed like a drain, in a high pitched giddy sort of way.

'You must be joking sweetie. Do we look like the Rovers Return? Now come on what'll it be, you can have a Becks, a Grolsch, a Bud or a Heineken?'

Bloody hell, thought Harry when he looked around. He saw now the bar was virtually all men and one couple in a corner booth were what Harry would describe as canoodling. Harry was by no means a prude, or naive, but this full on display threw him. Not wishing to cause offence, Harry said,

'Oh, I'll have a Heineken please.'

'No problem. There you are handsome,' said the man passing over a bottle, but no glass.

'That'll be five pounds please.'

Five pounds! thought Harry, *wow,* but he paid up. He noticed the other people were drinking straight from the bottle, so he followed suit. The barman served someone else then came back over to where Harry was leaning, still taking in the scene around him

'You in here on the pull, or looking for a rent boy, or did you wander in by mistake?'

The man was smiling as he asked the question and obviously meant well.

'Eh, I suppose wandered in by mistake, I mean I didn't know it was a, em, a gay bar.

'Well in this area, it'd be a novelty if it wasn't deary.'

'Oh' said Harry I didn't realise.'

'Not to worry. So what are you doing here if it's not trying to pick up some handsome young swain?'

'Well I organise rave parties out in Cheshire, and I thought I might try holding them in Manchester as well.'

'Oooh, said the barman, 'you'll do a bomb around here, they'll love it. Can I come and work for you?'

Harry was a little overwhelmed by the barman's enthusiasm, but he had to admit, he'd taken a bit of a shine to him.

'Well maybe someone with a bit of local knowledge would be useful,' he said.

'Does that mean yes then?' The barman gushed.

'Whoa, hold on a minute, I haven't got the place sorted out yet, in fact, that's why I'm here. You know, to have a look at the place from the outside.'

The barman shouted over to his colleague behind the bar,

'Just popping out with this man for a while, won't be long.'

Everyone turned to look at Harry, gave him the once over, smiled knowingly and turned back to their various conversations. Harry felt himself colouring up.

'Okay Robert,' said the other barman, 'don't be long we'll be getting busy in a bit.'

Robert had slipped around the bar and said to Harry,

My name's Robert by the way, what's yours?'

'Em, Harry' said Harry, wondering how he'd got himself into this situation.

'Harry, hmm, very manly. Well come on then, let's go and take a butchers at the gaff.'

Harry was about to object, but then thought, *Oh what the hell,* and they walked out of the bar together, Harry trying to find the piece of paper with the address on. He found it and Robert knew exactly where the place was.

'C'mon then' said Robert, and they walked down the street, Robert mincing slightly as he strolled along with Harry. Robert was quite tall, very thin, had blond curly hair and was dressed in skin tight white pants and a bright pink T shirt. Harry was sure he had makeup on as well. *My God, if my pals could see me now?* thought Harry, and started laughing until he had to stop walking, tears running down his face. Robert just stood there patiently, waiting for Harry to calm down.

Harry thought the venue looked fine from the outside. It also gained Robert's approval. Harry then bade farewell to his new found friend, and promised to be in touch if he went ahead with the deal. The next day he made an appointment to see the inside. Perfect, he thought. After checking with the authorities and finding that they were happy enough to give their permission for him to use it as a dance venue, he made an arrangement to hire it. At first, he used the place just for weekends, then eventually took a formal long term lease on the whole building.

Harry's first warehouse Rave in Manchester had gone very well. Illegal Fly posters around the city had been all they'd needed to promote the venue, and the village grapevine did the rest. With no small help from Robert, who now worked as Harry's marketing man. The kids loved it.

Harry's warehouse raves became more and more successful. The police turned a blind eye to the drugs aspect, content that Harry's security arrangements were such that they knew where a large number of kids were, who might otherwise be causing trouble elsewhere. They were all in one place, well supervised, getting high on illegal substances and dancing themselves stupid, but better that than the alternative they concluded.

Harry Antrobus was making serious money from his Rave business, both from the door money, but more from the sale of the 'dancing pills' as Harry called them. Harry had come to an arrangement with Tom MacBride to supply his security people for the Warehouse Raves for a share of the entrance money, and after some delicate negotiation between Harry and Tom MacBride, a share of the sale of the pills as well. Harry had been concerned that Tom may have taken a dim view of selling the Ecstasy, but he needn't have worried, Tom was a pragmatist and said

'If they weren't buying them from you Harry, they'd be buying them from some other bugger, so why not cash in? I'm up for it.'

Both parties were only too happy with the deal.

Another spin-off was Harry's marquee business, which was also doing very well. Over the years Harry added to his stock of marquees and now hired them out for weddings, fairs, private parties, exhibitions and all manner of events. The icing on the cake was the additional opportunity to supply certain substances to the guests. There was never any shortage of customers for alternatives or additional stimulants to alcohol. In fact, these days cocaine was cheaper than bubbly.

When Harry hired out his marquees, he always offered security service as well. Most people being aware of the problems of keeping out gatecrashers, were only too eager to take the additional services offered. This provided Harry with his distribution personnel, Tom MacBride's security men and girls, acting as his drug sellers to the guests, perfect. The man who provided Harry with the ecstasy in the first place, was only too happy to provide a further selection of other drugs at 'wholesale' prices, for Harry to 'retail' to his customers.

CHAPTER 6

Jay's father's funeral was held at the local crematorium, with only Jay, his mother, brother Ezra and Aaron in attendance, plus the obligatory policeman. Charlie hadn't been a popular man.

The coroner recorded Charlie's death as an unlawful killing. After a week, the police visited Jay's mother and told her they hadn't been able to make any progress in finding out who had shot her husband. No one had come forward, with information, and they had no clues. They asked her if she had any ideas about who might have wanted her husband dead, but she didn't.

They left, saying they'd keep her informed, and let her know if they made any progress. Jay wasn't surprised by the police's apparent inability to discover anything, but still felt offended.

We're just another bunch of niggers to them he thought, and it made him even more determined to sort matters out himself. Since Charlie's death, his mother had gone downhill. She didn't seem to care about anything anymore, and that only served to add more fuel to the fire burning inside Jay. His mother was the only person in the world Jay cared about, and it hurt him to see her in such distress.

He was now in his final year at school and had been doing well academically, but he found it difficult to concentrate on lessons or homework any more, spending less and less time at school. He thought about his father's death all the time, and he felt that letting it go without any response made him look weak and impotent – a nobody. The feeling gnawed away at him, and gradually but inexorably he developed a cold hatred for the people who'd killed his father, which crystallised into a determination to kill the person or people who'd done it. People already knew that anyone who messed with him or his, would pay a high price.

Aaron didn't much like school either and joined Jay hanging around cafes. They smoked weed then got into harder drugs, but Jay soon realised that this was the path to self destruction. He liked the buzz but didn't like the idea of being out of control. Drugs were okay, and he carried on smoking a bit of weed from time to time, but Jay didn't like to do anything that put him at any kind of physical or mental disadvantage. Aaron, on the other hand, was a serious user and just didn't care.

One evening, a couple of weeks after the police had been to visit, Aaron called and told him to meet him for a game of pool. He told Jay he'd been at Bakers the previous night, and heard some guy talking about Charlie, saying how he'd been playing out of his league, and had owed money to the Trojans. Everyone in the area knew about the Trojans, a serious local gang, involved in all sorts of illegal activities, prostitution, drugs, guns, protection.

When Jay arrived at the club, Aaron chided Jay.

'So you ain't gonna be able to do nothing 'bout them killin' your ole man Jay? There's no way you can mess with those guys. Those are some serious people.'

Jay felt overwhelmed. He'd always thought it would be a case of finding someone, who no matter how tough, and he could have taken them down by one means or another. But to go up against the Trojans was something well out of his league. As Aaron said, *unthinkable, or was it?* He had an audacious idea.

'Maybe I'll join the Trojans'

'What, you crazy?'

'Nope, well yeah, maybe I am.'

'An' how you goin' to do that?'

'Make friends with Jimmy the thief. He always claims his uncle Rocky is the big shit who runs the Trojans. Let's find out if it's true.'

The next night Jay and Aaron went to hang out at Bakers Cafe, and sure enough, Jimmy showed up later in the evening along with some of his crew. Bakers was a popular hangout for the kids in the area, had a couple of pool tables, served coffee, soft drinks, and although no alcohol, lots of substances changed hands, and a definite smell of something more than cigarette smoke hung in the air. It was originally the cellar of sort of bakery, which had gone out of business many years before.

No one knew if the occupation and conversion of the cellar was based on any legitimate arrangement, but who was asking? The 'cafe' comprised of one large dimly lit low ceilinged room, with a long bar along the wall opposite the entrance, a couple of pool tables and some tables and chairs that had seen much better days. The guy who ran the place was an ex con by the name of Little Mitch, and no one argued with Mitch. Mitch was also a dealer and well connected to the Trojans.

Jay started to buy hard stuff from Mitch to establish himself as a bad boy and to become noticed. He didn't use the stuff himself and sold it on for more or less the same as he paid for it, sometimes less.

Jimmy was playing pool with his pals, making noise as usual. His reputation was for doing small jobs, boosting cars, small time burglaries, post office robberies, and all that kind of stuff. He'd been caught a couple of times and done some time, but that didn't seem to stop him. He was jokingly known locally as Jimmy the thief, even by the cops.

Jimmy and Jay knew each other by site, and had played pool on opposing sides, but they had never been friends or even spoken to each other, but tonight Jay went out of his way to catch Jimmy's eye. This wasn't lost on Jimmy, and when the pool game was finished, he wandered over to where Jay and Aaron were leaning against the counter.

'You lookin' at me for a reason?'

'Yeah Jimmy, we a bit short of funds just at the moment and wondered if you had anything goin' we could join in maybe?'

Jimmy looked at Aaron and Jay for a long minute.

'You heard about somthin' I'm planning?'

'No Jimmy,' said Jay, 'why?'

Jimmy looked at them again and seemed to make up his mind

'Well as it happens, we doin' a mini-mart tomorrow night an' we need a driver an' some help. You up for this?'

'Yeah, we're in.' Jay spoke for both of them.

'Be here tomorrow at seven.'

'How much?' asked Jay.

'Depends on what we get, don't be late.'

They turned up on time as instructed. Aaron was told to drive, and Jay was given a baseball bat. There were three of them plus Jay and Aaron, so five all told.

'Okay' said Jimmy, 'first we get a car.'

There were no clever moves involved in stealing a car, no tricky stuff with steel blades being slid down the side of a car window to open it, then 'wiring' the ignition. No, they just drove along the main road into Manchester then making sure there were no police around, they simply drove in front of a car as it left the traffic lights and forced it into the kerb. Jimmy, who had a balaclava covering his face, jumped out and ran to the driver's door with a baseball bat in his hands.

'Get out now,' he screamed at the terrified couple.

The man had already wound his window down.

'Okay man, no worries, no problem,' the driver said holding up his hands in a gesture of compliance. He and his girl passenger got out of their respective car doors and came to stand on the pavement.

'Keys?' Jimmy said holding out his hand.

The man handed his keys to Jimmy threw them to Aaron, then got back into his car. Aaron drove the hijacked car away, leaving the hapless couple standing on the pavement. The two cars then took the first turn left off the main road into a labyrinth of small streets and parked up. Then with some white tape they changed the number plates on the stolen vehicle. 'L' became an 'I,' and 'U' became a 'J.' They'd done this before, and though it wouldn't stand close scrutiny, it was good enough to fool the cameras at night time, or any passing police vehicle check. The task completed, they drove away from Manchester for a few miles, towards the wealthy suburbs, eventually parking outside a smart restaurant. It was Saturday night just before midnight, when the takings would be at their maximum and customers at a minimum.

'This is it' said Jimmy.

'I thought you said a mini mart?'

'I did' said Jimmy, and laughed.

'Right, there's one security man on the door, and that's it. They don't expect much trouble in a posh joint like this. We walk in casual like we're expecting to get a late drink and you Jay, take out the doorman.'

'How?'

'How do you think? You hit him hard with the bat, right? Then Len and me go to the bar. Len has a replica gun, and he'll wave it about. No one'll have a go, but just in case they do, Joey here will go in with a bat and deck 'em. We should get a few quid from this one, but when I say leave, we leave, no messing about okay?'

The robbery went surprisingly well. Jay hit the doorman in the guts with the bat, and he went down, but Jay thought he was faking it so he wouldn't get hurt more badly. *Sensible. Surprise is so effective.* Thought Jay, *People taken off guard take a long time to react, and Jimmy played it well.* They went behind the bar and demanded the takings. Jimmy took a hessian bag out of his pocket.

'Open the till and put the money in here, no coins,' said Jimmy to the barman.

'Yes sir,' the barman said

'Sir?' Jimmy said and laughed, then started coughing, almost losing his composure.

'Quicker,' said Jimmy, 'Haven't got all night, fill the fuckin' thing up and don't forget the big notes under the draw.'

The barman complied, then when Jimmy judged he'd got as much as he was going to, he shouted to the others,

'Leave now.'

And they were all out of the door heading for the car when Aaron shouted.

'They got Jimmy.'

Jay looked round, and sure enough, the doorman had made a miraculous recovery. He had Jimmy round the neck, and it was obvious he was too big for Jimmy to handle. The doorman started hitting Jimmy in the face and blood spurted from Jimmy's nose, but despite the beating, Jimmy stubbornly hung on to the hessian bag. The others just stood there, but Jay ran back through the door.

The doorman looked around for help from the bar staff, but no one was moving. He put his leg across Jimmy and twisting his body, threw Jimmy to the floor to get ready for Jay's attack. He grabbed a chair as Jay ran at him swinging the bat. The doorman held up the chair high to fend off the blow, but Jay feinted, dropped the bat and dived for the doorman's legs, wrapping his arms tightly around them and pushing the doorman off balance, sending him crashing into the nearby furniture. Then Jay launched himself at the doorman before he could recover.

Jay was like a wild man punching him in the face. When the doorman tried to get him in a bear hug. Jay grabbed his ears, pulled his face forward into his own, then clamped his teeth on the doorman's nose and bit hard. The man howled in pain flailing his arms, trying to fend off this maniac. In the process, Jay untangled himself from the doorman's grip and kicked him squarely in the crotch.

The doorman went down, roaring in agony and holding himself between his legs. By then, Jimmy had recovered enough to get to a standing position, but had now dropped the bag. Jay turned and looked at the bar staff, but it was obvious no one was going to have a go, so he turned, retrieved the bag, got hold of Jimmy by the collar and manhandled him through the door and towards the waiting car.

'Put your fuckin foot down Aaron,' screamed Jay as soon as he'd bundled Jimmy into the car and jumped in on top of him holding the bag.

Aaron raced off.

'Man that was cool,' shouted one of the boys to no one in particular, but there was no doubt it was meant as a compliment for Jay and the way he'd retrieved the situation. The others all joined in laughing with nervous exhaustion and the need to break the tension of the robbery. They all joked about the way people had reacted in the restaurant.

'Did you see the look on the barman's face when I took all the money, then gave him a fiver tip?' said Jimmy, who had now recovered some of his composure.

They all roared with laughter, and even Jay joined in. Nobody mentioned that Jay had not only saved Jimmy but had also retrieved the money. Jay didn't care, he knew they'd all seen what had happened.

Jay had to admit, the adrenalin rush he experienced during the robbery was a blast. He and Aaron didn't know how much was stolen altogether, but all they got was a hundred each. Not much for the risk and effort he thought, but as far as Jay was concerned, he'd bonded with Jimmy and achieved much more than he'd set out to.

Rocky, the leader of the Trojans, was Jimmy's uncle by dint of Jimmy's mother being his sister. He had little time for Jimmy, who was too unreliable and didn't listen. He only allowed Jimmy to hang around the gang's headquarters as a favour to his sister, who thought Jimmy might learn something by osmosis. Jimmy was always trying to prove himself to his uncle, by doing stuff on his own account, like the raid on the restaurant.

Rocky tolerated this, but only because he was family. Normally, all activity was controlled by the gang leaders. They weren't that well organised but what they lacked in organisation, they more than made up for in their ruthlessness. Fear was their major weapon, and kept people from informing on them to the police, or snitching on their activities to other gangs.

Every now and then, they'd make an example of someone just to keep up the fear factor in the local community. This could range from a beating to more serious stuff if the person was actually guilty of an act of betrayal. In extreme circumstances, people had been executed, but that didn't happen very often as it brought too much heat from the police.

The gang's headquarters consisted of a scruffy apartment in a large, grand old turn of the century building called Clarence House, situated in Alexander Park near Moss Side. Alexander Park was a once prosperous area where large houses were built for the local wealthy cotton merchants, but the area had declined in line with the demise of the cotton weaving industry after the Second World War, and had become the black ghetto of Manchester. The large houses now either demolished or turned into flats.

Rocky sat behind an old Partner's Desk, which occupied a large area of the room that constituted his office. The room next door was where the gang members hung out. Jimmy sat uncomfortably on the other side of the desk. Rocky's assistant Vince, a large vicious looking man, sat in an old chair by the side of the desk and looked passively on. Rocky had heard about the restaurant robbery and how it had ended with Jimmy nearly being caught.

'You realise how the fuck that would've made me look if you'd been made by the police, you being family? Caught stealing a few fuckin hundred. You share the same surname as me so you embarrass me. I need respect boy and I earnt it, but you, you make me look stupid.'

Jimmy sat there head bowed.

'If you can't fuckin' handle it so you don't get caught, then you don't go on no more of your own little capers - got it boy?'

'Yes Rocky'

'If you ever embarrass me again I'll forget you're family, understand?

'Sorry Rocky, won't happen again.'

'Now, who was the dude who went back for you, got your ass outa there?'

'A new guy, Jay Madaki.'

'Madaki? I know that name, Vince?'

Rocky looked over at Vince. Vince got up, came over to Rocky and whispered something in his ear. Rocky nodded slowly. Vince went back to his chair and sat down.

'Well, you go find Mr Madaki and tell him I want to see him, okay? Now get the fuck out of my sight.'

Jimmy found Jay at Bakers playing pool and told him that his uncle the big man wanted to see him. Jay didn't waste any time and left right away.

This was what he'd hoped for. He walked to the house, about half an hour away. He knocked on the door which was opened by a small wiry guy who asked him his business.

'I'm Jay Madaki, Jimmy sent me here to see Rocky. I'm expected.'

The man showed Jay up the stairs and knocked on a door, opened it and told Jay to go in. He saw who he assumed to be Rocky sat at a large desk. Another man was sitting in a chair by the side of the desk.

'So you the hero?' Rocky asked as he waived Jay into the office chair on the other side of his desk.

Jay went to sit but nearly slipped out of the chair as it rolled away from him. It had castors on, and the floor, bare floorboards.

'This here's my, eh, my assistant Vince,' said Rocky, then laughed.

Vince and Jay nodded at each other. Jay had heard of Rocky but had never met him before. He was much younger than Jay expected, *only two or three years older than me maybe? Still, being a gang leader would be a young man's game he supposed.* Jay wasn't impressed with Rocky's office, the desk, in fact, anything he'd seen so far of the gang's headquarters.

'So come on 'hero', tell me all about it.' said Rocky.

'I'm no hero' said Jay, not liking the way Rocky asked the question.

'My my, modest as well.'

'No, not that either.'

'So why go back an' rescue my stupid motherfucker of a nephew? You can't like him that much, leastwise nobody else I know does, apart from his mummy.'

'Jimmy's okay, but I figured that if Jimmy was caught, then he might lead the police back to us. Or if not, then the police might at least be able to figure out where we all came from, an all that, so I thought it would be better all-round if I got him out of there, and the money too. Didn't seem right to make all that effort and leave empty handed.'

Rocky looked at Jay intently

'Hmm I'm impressed, especially such quick thinking from a hophead.'

'I'm not a hophead.'

'You a drugie though?'

'Nope, smoke a few splifs maybe, but don't do the hard stuff.'

Rocky raised his voice and pointed a finger at Jay.

'Listen boy I checked up on you, so don't lie to me, you and your pal buy stuff regular off that little shite Mitch, and you told him you needed a job to get money for drugs.'

'Not true' said Jay looking calmly at Rocky.

'You calling Mitch a liar? Now Mitch is a lot of things, but he ain't stupid enough to lie to me.'

'No Mitch didn't lie, but buying stuff off him was just a way to get noticed.'

'By who?'

'By you, by the Trojans.'

Vince who was still sitting in his chair, snorted.

'What the fuck you talkin' about boy?' Said Rocky, a quizzical look on his face.

'Same reason I went on the job with Jimmy, I wanted to get to meet you, get to be part of the Trojans, you know, join the gang.'

Rocky let out a huge laugh, and Vince snorted some more, stifling a laugh. Rocky stopped laughing and looked intently at Jay.

'Why?' he said at last.

'I want money, power all that shit. Same as you've got.'

Rocky sat there nodding his head in a contemplative manner.

'Well, you certainly ain't run of the mill boy. Anything else you want while we're playing this, "I want" game?'

Jay leaned forward looking Rocky straight in the eyes.

'Yeah, I want the person who killed my father.'

Jay hadn't intended to move this quickly in relation to his father, but somehow the moment seemed right. *Question is, what's going to happen now? Have I opened my mouth too soon?* He reckoned he was about to find out.

Rocky was silent for a few beats then said.

'Boy you don't beat about the fuckin bush, and that's for sure.'

Rocky and Vince looked at each other, and some unspoken intelligence seemed to pass from one to the other.

'Could you kill someone?' Rocky smiled as he asked the question.

'Tell me who killed my father, and I'll show you if I can kill someone.' Jay replied without hesitation.

'I remember your daddy, shame he was shot, yeah big shame, big shame.' Rocky leaned back and seemed to be deciding something.

Then he said to Jay.

'Now you just wait here and talk to Vince. I got a little errand to run.'

Rocky got up and left the office. Jay sat there and felt more like a captive than a guest. Vince didn't speak, and Jay kept quiet, thinking about what he might have got himself into. Rocky came back about ten minutes later with another man who Jay hadn't seen before. Rocky turned and locked the door. The new man looked pale and had a pinched, mean face, but was recognisable as a close relative of Rocky, similar facial features. Rocky sat down again, then said.

'Now we got a little situation here.'

The man who'd come in with Rocky had moved behind where Jay was sitting. Jay began to feel like a rat in a trap. Jay stayed silent and looked at Vince who just smiled. He looked back to Rocky who was looking at Jay as if expecting him to ask what the problem was, but Jay stayed silent and returned Rocky's stare with an equally hard look.

'See I've been checkin' up on you, and I think when you say, you're going to kill the man who killed your daddy, you're gonna to do it, sure as the fuckin' sun rises every day.

Word on the street is you're a stubborn fucker who won't give up. Is that right?'

Jay was silent.

'I said is that right?'

Jay nodded, never taking his eyes off Rocky.

'Well, I have a small problem, which is now your big problem. That is, the guy who offed your daddy, is my little brother Stevie, and he's standin' behind you with a gun.'

Jay twisted his head round to see the mean-faced man with a gun in his hand complete with silencer. They were serious.

'Now you heard the expression about blood being thicker than water Jay? Well, it's true, so as much as I've gotten to like to you in the short we've been acquainted, family comes first. So don't take it personal Jay, just takin' care of business.'

As Rocky was giving Jay his farewell speech, Jay sensed the mean faced man coming up close behind him. If he was to get out of this alive, he had to get the gun. Jay was familiar enough with handguns. You don't grow up on the streets where he did without getting to handle guns from time to time. And though he was no expert, he knew enough to use one if he had to. Time seemed to stand still. Jay did some quick calculations. His chances of getting out of this, with the three of them against him, were close to zero. But the alternative of doing nothing, wasn't an option. Jay pretended to be getting out of his chair slowly, then put his feet square on the floor, and pushed it back as hard and fast as he could.

Thanks to the bare floorboards the chair flew backwards, castors screeching on the wooden surface. Jay's tactic achieved the desired effect of surprise, but more importantly, the chair hit Stevie hard in the legs, knocking him backwards to the floor. Jay moved like lightning, spun around and launched himself at the fallen man, as he was trying to recover and scramble on to his feet.

Jay grabbed the arm holding the gun. The man tried to resist, but Jay was too strong. He rolled them both over, jammed his knee in the man's back and twisted his arm against the joints. With a yelp of pain, the man let go of the gun, and it clattered on the floor. Jay grabbed the gun, rolling away to minimise the opportunity for any of the other two to shoot him, and at the same time chopping with the side of his other hand at the man's throat.

Jay got to his knees in a flash pointing the gun at Rocky, but Rocky already had a gun in his hand waiting to get a clear shot at Jay, and was now in the process of pulling the trigger. The bullet hit Jay in the thigh, just before he heard the silenced 'phut' from Rocky's gun. But the impact of the bullet wasn't enough to stop Jay pulling the trigger on his gun. He fleetingly prayed the safety was off.

A large hole instantly appeared in Rocky's forehead, and he dropped like a puppet whose strings had been cut. Jay went down on one knee, gun still in hand and switched his attention to Vince. *Why hadn't Vince done anything?*

Vince stood there looking at Jay and smiling. The brother was beginning to recover and was trying to get to a kneeling position. Jay looked at Vince again. People had obviously heard the commotion and were hammering on the locked door. Vince went over shouting through the door as he opened it a crack.

'Calm down brothers, nothin' to worry 'bout,' he shouted to whoever was on the other side of the door.

'We cool here, so stand down. I'll call you fuckers if I need you. Anyone comes around you heard nothin' okay,' silence.

'Okay?' he asked again.

'Yeah sure' said an anonymous voice, sounding unconvinced.

Jay didn't know what was going on with Vince, but he knew he'd find out soon enough. In the meantime, he wasn't going to let his father's killer off the hook. If it were the last thing he did in this life, it would be to kill this man. He got hold of the man and dragged him to the chair that Jay had propelled across the room and had fallen over on its side. Jay grabbed the back of it, and put it upright, then threw the man into it. If there had ever been any fight in Stevie, it was all gone now, he was sobbing.

'You killed Rocky' he blubbed.

Jay held the gun, pointing it at the man, but looked at Vince, who stood there just looking back at Jay. He'd just killed a man, and although he knew his life had changed forever, he didn't feel any remorse. Why should he? The man was trying to kill him. In fact, he enjoyed the experience. The blood was beginning to spread from Rocky's head wound, forming a deep red pool under the desk. Vince said.

'Are you gonna kill that drugged up dipshit or what?'

Jay found his voice.

'Did he kill Charlie?'

'Oh yeah, he killed your daddy all right.'

The pain in Jay's thigh suddenly registered, and he realised he needed to do something about it, like sit down for instance. Stevie had a strange look on his face, perhaps suddenly realising what was about to happen. His eyes opened wide in terror, but before he was able to speak, Jay brought the gun to Stevie's head.

'Die you motherfucker', he said, and pulled the trigger.

The man slumped in the chair dead. Jay looked around at Vince. Vince looked back at him and nodded. Jay pulled the inert body of the man out of the chair on to the floor, then sat in the chair himself.

He looked at Vince again, and they both sat for what seemed an age, but was probably no more than ten seconds. Jay was the first to speak.

'So Vince, what's the score, why didn't you help Rocky?'

Vince said nothing, but went over to Stevie's body, rolled it over, and taking the jacket off the dead man, took the shirt off the body and ripped it into pieces. He selected a long piece, came over to Jay and wrapped it round his thigh above the wound, twisting it and tying it to make a tourniquet.

'And now?' Jay asked.

'I'll call in the brothers in and tell them I'm the new boss.' Vince looked at Jay and smiled.

'You my friend, just did me a big fuckin favour, the biggest. I been wonderin' how to get rid of Rocky and his badass shit for brains brother, then you come along and bang, you blow them both away, awesome just fuckin awesome.'

Then Vince's face creased into a huge smile, and he began to laugh till tears ran down his face.

Jay stood rooted to the spot, not sure of what was going to happen next.

Vince gathered himself together, drawing a deep breath and said

'Now we got to act fast here.'

'We,' said Jay.

'Yeah we,' said Vince looking Jay straight in the eye.

'You said you wanted in, so now you in. What's more, you're gonna be my, what's it they say in the army, my 2IC, my second in command. Yeah, I like the sound of that. That is unless you want me to just call the brothers in and let you explain how you just popped by to shoot Rocky and his brother, and now you'll be goin' home now thank you very much - I don't think so.'

There was shouting at the door and a voice asking if everything was alright.

Vince shouted back.

'Yeah, no problem brother, nothing for you to get fussed about.

Turning to Jay, Vince said.

'Now I'm gonna have to call the brothers in and tell them about the new arrangement. You say nothing, but watch out for the big guy with the attitude.'

'How do you mean, watch out?'

'Well, when the brothers come in here, the one likely to give us trouble is a guy called Duke, he always had ambitions. You know him?' Jay shook his head.

'Well he'll be the one with the mouth and when he opens it you gonna have to make it three.'

'Three?'

'Yeah three, you still got the gun don't you, and you can count, no?'

Jay looked down, and he was still holding the gun in his right hand.

Vince didn't give Jay time to react. He stood up went to the door, opened it and bellowed

'All you motherfuckers come in here now an' meet the new boss.'

There were about a half a dozen gang members, Jay recognised some faces. They all came in and took in the scene. No one showed any emotion. Vince stood to Jay's right while Jay sat in the same chair with the gun in his lap. The men were all stood behind Rocky's chair. *Too late to bottle out now* thought Jay.

'Okay boys, Rocky and his brother had a little accident, and now I'm takin' over as boss.'

Vince looked at the men, letting them take in what he'd just told them, then said.

'Anyone got a problem with that?'

A thick set man moved forward.

'Yeah, I got a problem.'

Jay assumed this was Duke talking. The man continued.

'What makes you think we're just gonna let you take over?'

Vince looked over at Jay eyebrows raised as if to say *I told you so* and Jay knew it was now or never. He quickly raised the gun and shot Duke in the face. Duke's face exploded scattering flesh and brain tissue around the place. The bullet, having passed through Duke's head, made a big hole in the wall behind him, narrowly missing another of the gang. Duke's virtually headless body collapsed on the floor. Silence

'Any more questions?' said Vince looking at each of the faces in front of him.

'No? Okay, then let's get this mess cleared up. You know what to do with the bodies. I'll tell you when we're meeting later, but sometime tomorrow, so be around.'

Vince helped Jay up from the chair and just as the men were about to leave, he said

'Just one more thing brothers, this here's Jay, and he's gonna be helpin' me run the show from now on, so what he says goes, understand?'

The men looked across at Jay, and no one dissented. They all walked out of the door without saying a word.

Vince helped Jay down the stairs and into his car.

'I think we'd better get you patched up Jay, you've lost a bucket full of blood boy.'

Jay took his hand away from the wound, looked at the blood, leaned back into the seat and passed out.

CHAPTER 7

Harry Antrobus became a very wealthy man. His wife lived high off the hog and never asked questions. Elevated from farmer's wife to one of the local socialites, was a transformation she could only have dreamed of. Harry was enjoying life to the full as well, and spent a lot of time at the local golf club, where in the past, he wouldn't have got through the door, let alone be feted as one of their most valued members.

Then out of the blue, Harry had a call from Tom MacBride.

'Fancy a bite to eat at the Midland French?'

'Pushing the boat out a bit aren't we Tom? But the answer's yes. Although I'm sure my wife will use it as an excuse to buy yet another frock.'

'It's dress, not frocks these days Harry. But don't worry about that, it's just going to be you and me. I want to talk to you about something.'

'Oh, okay, sounds interesting can't wait, when do you want to go.'

'Tomorrow?'

'Fine by me.'

Tom MacBride's chauffeur driven limo picked Harry up from his farmhouse. Harry still lived on the farm, from where he managed his marquee hire business, and where he was able to store all his equipment, delivery vans, flatbed trucks etc., in the old disused barn buildings. He liked the old place. It was very convenient to be able to keep an eye on his now not insubstantial investment.

They made good time into Manchester. On the way, they discussed the latest signings for Manchester United and Manchester City. Tom MacBride was a serious United fan, and had a box at Old Trafford. Likewise, Harry was a City supporter to the core, and also had a box at the new posh Manchester City stadium. They swapped friendly insults and banter till they got to the restaurant. Once they'd got their aperitifs and ordered their food, Harry said.

'Come on then Tom, what's this all about?'

Tom told Harry about the proposal from the Chinese about 'importing' drugs into the UK. Harry knew about Tom MacBride's involvement with the Chinese, in relation to his waste company, but this development was a bit of a surprise.

'So' said Harry, 'what's the angle as far as I'm concerned, apart from the obvious that is? I assume you want to replace my current supplier, yes?'

'No, well yes, but there's more to it than that, I've a more interesting proposition. See, my Chinese pal Jun Shan, says I can have the drugs in a finished state. And if I take that option, I'd like to talk to you about storage and distribution anyway But he also says, I could make much more money by buying the stuff in its raw state, and making it up over here, processing it. It would cost less to buy and by getting the raw stuff, I'd be able to import larger quantities each time.'

Harry sat and thought through what he'd just been told. 'And how will you get the stuff into the country?'

'Well, there's a China Airways Jet comes into Manchester twice a week. The stuff will be brought in on that. One of the stewards will be paid to transfer the gear in a suitcase to anywhere within the airport perimeter, avoiding security, customs and all that.'

'And how do you get it out of the airport? It'll have to be taken out by someone and go through customs at some stage.'

'Now that's where the clever bit comes in,' said Tom.

'A pal of mine runs a flying school at the airport. He has a few light planes, and a couple of helicopters. His school is located inside the airport perimeter, across the tarmac from where Air China planes park. He's bent as a nine bob note, and always up for earning a few quid on the side. So he's willing to take the stuff, then drop it off in a field, or any other remote location. You know, when he's out on a 'training flight'? Tom said,

'A location or field, not too far from the airport, such as, a field near your farm, for instance? No need to smuggle stuff through customs, with all the atendent risks. No security, nothing, just a few sheep to negotiate with.' Tom laughed.

'Right,' said Harry, 'but I couldn't have a helicopter landing at my farm. Once might be okay but a regular drop...'

'Yes, I realise that so I'd choose a place where no one would see anything. Early morning, when no one's around. And I arrange for someone to collect the stuff and drop it off at your place, nice and discreet.'

'And what does making it up, or processing it entail?' asked Harry.

'I haven't a clue Harry, but Jun says that they'll send someone over to set it all up and train people. He says they'll even supply us with illegals, Chinese people who are over here already, who will work for buttons.'

Harry weighed things up, then said.

'So what's the deal then Tom?'

'Well, your farm is so remote, and you've got a lot of disused buildings, it'd be ideal for storing and processing the stuff, plus you've got transport. Making regular trips all over the place, perfect cover. You could transport the illegals to and from Manchester, or wherever they stay, to your place. I can get my security lads in all the clubs and bars to distribute the finished products, just like they've been doing for you at the Raves in Manchester, and when you rent out your tents.'

'Marquees please, if you don't mind?' said Harry taking mock offence at Tom MacBride's remark.

Just then, their first course came, and they were silent while they tucked in.

'Any bread please?' said Tom and the Maitre de apologised profusely sending over one of the waiters who donned white cotton gloves to serve the bread.

Tom MacBride loved this archaic touch of silver service. When they'd finished the first course, Harry wiped round his mouth with his napkin and looked at Tom.

'Can't see a problem in principle Tom. I'll have to come up with some story for the wife, not that she gives a bugger as long as I keep her in posh frocks and champagne.'

'So it's a yes?

'Yes, I guess it is.'

'Brilliant.'

'Okay' said Harry, 'what do I do now?'

'Well you'll need to clear one of your big barns out and make sure it's secure, and the roof doesn't leak, then I think we can leave the rest to Jun.'

'Sounds simple enough. Now where's that wine waiter?'

And so another deal was sealed, not with spit this time, but with vintage Moet Chandon Dom Perignon, and a handshake.

CHAPTER 8

Jack woke up to find Rachel all in one piece.

'Are you okay?' She said, 'you were thrashing around like a madman. Muttering and shouting. I had a job waking you up.' Relief flooded over him.

'Sorry Rachel, had a nightmare.' Then he remembered, he really was living a nightmare.

'I'll make you some tea,' said Rachel.

Jack fell back on his pillows and thought. *What I'd give to be able to turn the clock back.*

He didn't take Bess out for a walk that morning. Jack not going out for his morning walk, even for one day, was enough for Rachel to be concerned. When he went downstairs, Bess wagged her tail expectantly. She looked confused, looking up at him with adoring, pleading eyes, then slumped to the floor, in a deep flunk, when she finally realised they weren't going out.

Jack made a few excuses to Rachel, but he knew they all sounded lame.

'C'mon Jack what's up? You've not been yourself lately, what's going on? No morning walk.'

'Nothing's going on Rach,' said Jack 'I'll be okay, just strained my ankle a bit. Don't want to put pressure on it too soon.'

No matter what it took, Jack felt he had to try to go on as normal. The next day, Wednesday, Jack braced himself and took Bess in Rachel's Jeep and parked in his usual place. Then took his normal route, towards Bycroft Farm. Sure enough, there was a police incident van parked in the gateway of one of the fields, positioned so they could speak to anyone who walked down the road.

'Good morning Sir,' said a constable wearing an ingratiating smile.

'Morning officer' said Jack.

'We're investigating an incident, and I wonder if you'd mind answering a few questions for us sir?'

'Yes of course' Jack said as nonchalantly as possible.

'Were you by any chance walking your dog in this vicinity on Monday?'

'Yes I was, it's my usual walk. I normally do the walk every weekday, although I was much earlier than usual on Monday.'

'I see. Did you notice anything out of the ordinary on your walk on Monday?'

'Not really' he replied.

'Do you always take the same route?'

'Yes,' he replied, 'pretty much always the same.'

'And where would that take you – normally?'

'Well,' he began, and told them the route he normally took.

'That's a fair stretch' said the policeman when Jack had finished talking.

'Em yes I suppose it is, but I like to keep fit, and I enjoy walking anyway.'

Jack decided it would look suspicious if he didn't inquire what this was all about.

'Excuse me officer, but why are you asking these questions, I mean what's happened?'

The policemen completely ignored his question and ploughed on.

'I imagine you see a lot of regulars on your walk? Most of the people we've interviewed today walk through here every morning, though most of them do a shorter walk than you, it would seem.'

'Yes, I do see a number of regulars.'

'And did you see anyone different on Monday; I mean people who you might not normally see, strangers as it were?

Jack didn't hesitate.

'Funny you should say that, but I do recall an odd couple of men, when I say odd, I mean they didn't seem to have a dog with them. And they seemed to be arguing.'

The policeman stiffened

'And where abouts were these men - arguing?'

Jack had practised this answer in his head a million times already.

'Oh, they walked past me going the opposite way, just as I reached the stile that takes you on to the road, near to Talton Park.'

'I see sir, 'er Mr?'

'Brandon – Jack Brandon.'

'Well Mr Brandon, did you hear what they were arguing about?'

'Oh no, it wasn't like that., I couldn't actually hear what they were saying, it was just an impression. They walked past me and didn't say good morning and were obviously having some sort of intense discussion. I didn't really take much notice. It was only that they didn't have a dog, that made me remember.'

The policeman tapped his teeth with his pen waiting for Jack to continue.

'Very unusual for anyone to be out walking without a dog, especially that early' Jack added.

The policeman looked at Jack and said.

'Well we'd be grateful if you'd take a seat in the car sir, then we can write down as much as you can remember. And we can take your contact details as well if you don't mind.'

'Fine' said Jack, and did as they asked. Bess waited outside the car looking glum.

The officer wrote, as Jack repeated what he'd said previously. When he asked for Jack's contact details, he took out his wallet and handed him a personal card with all his contact details on. The policeman thanked Jack, and told him that he wouldn't be able to go on his usual walk, as they were investigating an incident in that area, and he should choose another route.

'For today at least,' he said

Jack tried not to look too relieved as he left, and even managed to wave a cheery goodbye Then he turned back through the farm gate and back to his car, via a shorter and different route.

Jack made his way home. He felt he'd entered into a time warp, where everything slowed down to a snail's pace. He waited for the inevitable announcement of the police finding a body. *Will the police ask me to "help them with their enquiries" and grill me till they find some inconsistency in my story?* Thoughts went round and round in Jack's mind until he felt his head would burst. *Why would I be a suspect?* He answered his own question, *because you're possibly one of the last people to see the guy alive as far as they're concerned, that's why.*

Then there's the press, would the press come around if the police released the information that I'd seen these people? The thought of being interviewed by the press did nothing to make Jack feel better. He felt he was under enough pressure as it was without being in the press or on the news. Plus, Rachel would hate being in the public eye.

Jack had got himself so wound up by the time he'd got home, that he had to make a huge effort not to tell Rachel the whole story. But he steeled himself, and realised it would serve no purpose at this stage. Nevertheless, he had to tell her about the police stopping him, and interviewing him about "a possible incident". He told her, and with some difficulty, he managed to make light of it. Rachel showed only mild curiosity.

Jack showered and had some breakfast. He could tell Rachel knew he wasn't his usual self, but said nothing. He made an excuse about having some work to catch up on, and went to his study. Jack sat in his office chair, put his feet up on the desk, and thought through his plan again. Its main weakness, he concluded, was Alfie. The only other witness to what had actually happened. He'd tried to compromise him as much as possible, by getting him to take the money and cutting him, to make it look as though he and Ezra had had a fight. That was fine, he thought, other than Alfie would tell the police about Jack using some sort of spray on his pal. Surely the police would find it hard not to believe him. *How could a person of such obvious limited imagination, possibly concoct such a story if it wasn't true?*

Jack decided there were no really good answers to this aspect of the story, and he'd just have to wing it, brazen it out. Maybe suggest that Alfie had seen something like that happen in a film or on the TV, or maybe even in real life in some other encounter? *God, what a mess.*

He went over his story again and again in his head until his mind was confusing fact and fiction. The facts were becoming so blurred, he just had to stop. He closed his eyes and tried to empty his mind, then he thought it through again, *Okay, whatever happens, I just stick to my story. There's no way that anyone can prove different, I was simply out for a walk with my dog as usual, saw a couple of men who seemed to be arguing, and I carried on with my walk as usual. As far as the police are concerned, hopefully, it will appear that Alfie and Ezra had had a serious disagreement. Somehow Alfie had got the better of Ezra and killed him in a fight, kicking him in the throat, accidentally or otherwise.*

Evidence? knife found in the undergrowth with Ezra's prints on it, knife cuts on Alfie's face and arms, and on the inside of the forearm to indicate defensive posture – and, Alfie in possession of Ezra's money. Perfect, if only, thought Jack.

One thing Jack kept telling himself, was not to underestimate the police. They may be the butt of criticisms and jokes at times, but they were formidable people at this level of crime, and not to be thought of as fools. *Nevertheless, I just have to keep my nerve, stick to my story, then the police will simply have to conclude it was "Alfie what done it", or find some alternative explanation.*

Seen from another perspective Jack thought, it was galling that he was the one who could be cast as the guilty party. *Hadn't he just been just out for a walk, minding his own business? Wasn't he the one who was attacked?* Jack wondered how long he could keep up the conviction that he was the one who'd been wronged. The bottom line was, he wasn't the one who'd been killed. The feeling of guilt was overwhelming.

CHAPTER 9

Vince drove Jay to the gang's unofficial medical man. He worked as a paramedic at the Manchester Royal Infirmary, and lived a few streets away from Clarence House. The man was well paid for his occasional services to gang members, but wasn't too thrilled at being woken during the day, as he was working nights that week. Nevertheless, the man was very professional.

Jay had recovered from his faint, and the man soon had the wound cleaned and bandaged up. He didn't inquire about how Jay had got his wound, just said it wasn't too bad, that the bullet had gone right through his leg, and should heal by itself without any problem.

'Just keep it clean and come back to see me every four or five days for the next week or so to have the dressing changed.'

On the way to get his wound treated Jay had recovered sufficiently to speak, and was about to ask all the questions that had been piling up in his mind after he'd gone through the whirlwind of the last couple of hours, but Vince began talking anyway.

'Okay so why did I want rid of Rocky and Stevie? Well see, Rocky used to be okay, but he was starting to take too much of his own product. So he, and his shitfaced brother, were draggin' the business down. Anyway, he was never a great businessman, an' these days you got to be more, you know, sophisticated. The gang's losing business all over the place to the competition and on the 'protection' front too. We got sloppy, so we needed a change and now we got it.'

'So where do we go from here Vince?'

'You go rest, then come along in the mornin' and have a look how things are. Business is fallin' apart, and that means trouble from the brothers if we don't fix it soon.'

Jay had a flair for organisation and after a while, could see that one of the problems with the gang's activities was that they were too diverse. They were involved in selling drugs, prostitution, gambling, protection, extortion, pirate videos, music and illegal imports of booze and fags. Virtually any form of criminal activity. After a month of looking into the gang's activities, Jay sat down with Vince and told him his conclusions.

'We in too many marketplaces man. We got fingers in every pie, but no control and we got individual gang members eatin' some of the pie too, moonlightin'.'

'Yeah I know,' said Vince, 'we got some of the boys take a bit on the side, but that's only natural man an' we ain't ever goin' to be able to stop that.'

'We got to stop it, I done some rough calculations an I reckon we losin' nearly fifty percent, give or take, that's before we get our share.'

'Jeez, that much? So how do you think we can stop it Jay my man?'

'Easy, we cut down the number of activities to get better control, more focus on the things we do well.'

'Yeah okay. And so what do we cut out?'

'Well, I think we should cut out everything except gambling, drugs and protection.'

Okay, but how do you stop the moonlightin'?'

'Well, we'll operate what they call a 'carrot and stick' policy. The carrot will be a share in the increase profits the gang make. I think I can work out a simple way of doin' that.'

'And the stick?

'That's where you come in Vince. The stick will be that if you get caught moonlightin', you get shot - dead.'

'Whoa man, that's some stick' Vince laughed, 'you serious Jay?'

'Never been more serious Vince, an' we need to find someone now to make an example of. Benny is definitely running his own little side-line so let's use him an' make it very public. Don't hide the body, leave it on the street, so the brothers know. Let it sink in.'

'Man you don't mess about do you? You realise leavin' the body around will attract a lot of heat from the flith.'

'Yeah, I know, but we need this to be as public as possible, so it's worth the aggro.'

Benny's body was found two days later, and the rest of the gang were left in no doubt as to why he was shot.

He had a hard time at first convincing the men that the gang needed to cut down on their range of activities.

'We need to work smarter and be more focussed,' he told them.

'We all over the place. We could be makin' more and workin' less, see?'

They muttered and hummed and harred, but he finally persuaded them, and they went along with the idea. Pretty soon, as more money rolled in, Vince and the gang began to realise that Jay knew what he was doing.

The protection business thrived in direct proportion to the increased violence meted out by the Trojans. Object lessons were given to those resisting payment to encourage other businesses in the vicinity to pay up without putting up any resistance. Most people coughed up without too much trouble. Jay also introduced a new harsher regime in relation to anyone defaulting on gambling debts or drug dealers who didn't pay up on time. Vince left all the strategic planning to Jay realising that he was very good at it. Jay suggested to Vince that they also adopted a new strategy towards expanding their territory and mapped out what physical territory he thought they could adequately handle and control.

Jay proposed that they concentrate on an area just north of where they were based, which was just south of the city centre. He drew a line across the city map using Piccadilly as the northern-most border of his proposed operations area. He said to Vince that they would probably get some aggravation from some of the smaller gangs, but that didn't bother Vince, he felt they had enough troops to handle any problems in that department. But he warned Jay that they shouldn't cross the line into the other big Manchester gangs' territory. The Trojans might be strong, ruthless and violent, but they weren't big enough to go to war with any of the other larger well established gangs in certain areas of the city just yet.

Things went well for the first year then Jay made a serious error of judgement.

'Vince my man, I suggest we take our operations into some new territory. We're missin' out on all those new bars an' clubs openin' up on the edge of that Castlefield area. Hell, the council are givin' licences to anyone who can pull the top off a beer bottle, and we ain't joinin' in, 'bout time we did.'

'You know my view on expandin' into someone else's territory Jay, 'specially them Salford boys. They left us alone so far, but this is pokin' them with a stick man. They ain't goin' to take kindly to us movin' in on what they consider their sacred turf, no Siree.'

'Don't be a pussy Vince. You more than a match for those jerks, we established now. It'll be fine, let's do it. Worst off we get a serious warnin', an' if we do, maybe we back off, but no harm in pushin' the envelope, as they say.'

At first, it seemed that Jay had been right. The Trojans were able to expand their territory without too much trouble, and with no apparent resistance from other gangs. Vince's concerns seemed to have been unfounded.

Seemingly unopposed, Jay decided they needed to blitz the new area and make an impression on their prospective clients. He ordered the gang to carry out some brutal beatings and break a few places up to set an example. Jay said they needed to make sure everyone knew who they were and that they meant business. There was still no resistance from any other gangs, and no one complained to the police, so it looked as though they would have a fairly easy time establishing themselves as the new extortionists on the block.

Two weeks into the new venture Vince went missing. Jay asked around, and none of the gang knew where he was. Vince always checked in with Jay every day and vice versa, so Jay was getting concerned when he didn't hear from Vince for a whole day. He asked around if any of the gang had seen Vince's minder, Leroy, One of the gang told Jay he'd talked to Leroy that morning and he'd told him that he and Vince had met a couple of hot chicks in a bar the previous night and got lucky. *That explained it.*

Later in the morning, Jay got a text from Vince asking him to come and pick him up from outside the new Hilton hotel in the city centre.

Jay asked Mickey to go with him just in case. Since their recent expansion into another gang's territory, Jay rarely went anywhere without Mickey, He'd become Jay's right-hand man over the last few months and watched Jay's back in all situations. Jay trusted him completely, or as completely as he could trust anyone. Mickey was of mixed race, not quite as tall as Jay, but still tall and looked younger than his forty five years. He was reliable, intelligent and very tough.

They drove up to the entrance of the Hilton and left the car on the forecourt, giving the flunky on the door the keys to the car and a twenty pound note, saying they'd only be there a few minutes.

Jay and Mickey stood to the side of the hotel entrance waiting for Vince to show. The text had said twelve thirty, and it was just coming up to that time. Jay didn't know which came first, the woman's scream or the sickening thud as Vince's body hit the pavement. He winced at the sudden realisation of what had happened and why one of the highest buildings in Manchester had been chosen for him to pick Vince up from. *How could Vince have fallen for one of the oldest tricks - a honey trap?*

Mickey was the first to recover.

'C'mon boss let's go.'

He got hold of Jay's arm and pushed him towards the car, and took the keys off the doorman who'd turned as white as a sheet. They got in the car without another word and watched the large crowd gathering near to where Vince's body lay. As they drove away, they could hear the sirens of the approaching emergency vehicles.

The experience of Vince's death had a serious effect on Jay. He became moody and withdrawn. Mickey and the other gang members were worried. They took it upon themselves to cease all activity in the new area of operations. The message had been clear enough, and they didn't need telling twice. After a few days, Jay seemed to recover, much to the relief of Mickey in particular, as the gang were turning to him for direction. Mickey told Jay that he must speak to the gang and re-assure them. They were all getting twitchy It was obvious, Jay had to take over as the new gang leader.

Jay asked Mickey to call the gang in.

'You all know 'bout Vince, and though I don't back down from a fight, I don't commit suicide either. I unerstand you already pulled back from the new operations area, an' that's good. Like I said I don't back down, but I do choose my time an', this ain't over.'

There were murmurs of approval.

'Unless any of you guys want the top job I'm takin' it, any objections?'

Jay stood up from his chair, and Mickey moved nearer to Jay.

One of the gang broke the silence.

'You the boss now Jay, no argument here.'

'Okay, we meet tomorrow at ten to discuss some new tactics. We bin too soft on the existing clients, so the new game is to squeeze them for more protection money. We gonna squeeze till they really hurt.'

And with that Jay left the room and Mickey following in his wake.

From then on, Jay was more inclined to get involved personally in any opportunity to mete out punishment to anyone resisting paying their protection money. He told his men to let him know if anyone objected to paying protection or defaulted on payments, then he'd take some of his more violent people with him and make an example of any individual who dared to resist payment, whether they were able to pay or not. He would beat people with a baseball bat, or sometimes with his bare hands. The beatings were vicious, and the level of cruelty he was prepared to inflict on someone wasn't lost on the gang members, something Jay relied on.

Jay went much further than Vince would have done. It was obvious to everyone that Jay enjoyed violence even more, these days. He seemed oblivious to the pain and misery he caused. On a couple of occasions, Jay got carried away, went too far, killing people in front of witnesses. The witnesses would be found and warned off from making any statement to the police. If they couldn't get directly to the witnesses, they'd make sure they knew that their families would be targeted, if they informed on Jay or the Trojans, or showed any inclination to agree to be a witness in any police action. One or two brave souls had ignored his warnings, and Jay was arrested and charged with murder on three occasions. But the cases never came to trial as witnesses, no matter how well protected by the police, were eventually intimidated enough for them to clam up.

Jay's new brutal policy seemed to be paying off, and all was going well for the Trojans. Takings were up, but then a new pattern of resistance seemed to be emerging with an increasing number of establishments refusing to play ball.

Jay questioned his men about this, and why they hadn't taught the owners of these places a lesson? If it was a pub or a club, the gang members would normally go in when it was crowded and break the place up, punch a few of the customers and generally cause mayhem. This usually broke down any resistance and payments would resume, but this wasn't happening. Jay realised that the common denominator in most of these cases was that the establishments in question had taken on legitimate protection by way of a company called Quadrant Security.

Unfortunately for Jay, his policy of turning the screw on his clients and targeting even more establishments had a negative effect on business, and an increasing number of bar and club owners now employed more formal security services, not the least to protect themselves against the huge financial demands now being made by the Trojans.

Jay's response was to tell his men to become even more ruthless and violent and to warn their 'customers that they would pay a heavy price if they stopped paying their protection money to the Trojans. And so the pendulum swung back, having the effect of suddenly reducing the amount of business going to Quadrant Security and in some cases resulted in the cancellation of their contracts.

It didn't take long for Tom MacBride's manager at Quadrant Security to understand what was going on and why. He told Tom that some of their relatively new clients had cancelled their contracts, and that potential clients weren't signing up either. That this was happening due to intimidation by the Trojans and they were losing out big time as a result. Tom MacBride knew he had to do something. Apart from the loss of income, there was the risk of seriously damaging the firm's credibility and reputation.

He knew about the Trojan's violent reputation and had heard about Jay Madaki, but he hadn't had any reason to take much notice before. This was the first time the'd ever encountered the gang head on. He told his men to collect as much information on the gang as they could, and arranged some surveillance on Jay Madaki. Before you attack, get to know your enemy, was one of Tom MacBride's rules.

Quadrant Security had its own specialist department to conduct surveillance on behalf of some of its clients. It was headed up by Gerry Naylor and Pete Smith, two of the best people in the game. Gerry was great with long range camera stuff, and sound as well, if such recordings were required. Gerry had persuaded Tom MacBride to spend a fortune on electronic surveillance equipment, long range mikes, telephone tapping gear, expensive telescopic cameras and so on. Although dubious at first, Tom MacBride had seen a good return on his investment.

Gerry was also a wiz at being able to find out huge amounts of data on someone by using the internet and other less legitimate means. He was able to access supposedly confidential data. Pete was no less talented in his speciality. Being an ex-burglar, he could get into most any premises, without detection. He knew all there was to know about disabling alarms and other security equipment. Tom MacBride was glad they were on his team and not with the competition.

MacBride called Gerry and Pete to his office.

'I want you to find out all you can about a character called Jay Madaki, he's the boss of the Trojans, and he and their activities are getting in our way.'

'Yeah boss we've heard about this guy,' said Gerry.

'How long do you want us to spend on him?'

'A week should be long enough. Go and talk to some of our boys and see what information they can give you. Let me have your report on my desk when you've finished. I want to know everything about the man, where he lives, where he goes, day and night. Who he meets, his family situation, girlfriends, boyfriends, what he has for breakfast, you know the drill.'

'We do,' said Pete

'Impress me with all those bloody expensive surveillance toys I bought you.'

The pair laughed as they left Tom MacBride's office.

Just over a week later, MacBride had a report on his desk detailing the results of their surveillance on Jay. He sifted through the stuff which comprised of mostly predictable movements and patterns of behaviour. There were a few surprises though. Jay's father had been shot in a gang related incident some years ago, but no one ever caught for the crime, Mother still alive but in a home somewhere. A brother called Ezra who apparently Jay despised. The brother was white, but had the same parents, some sort of throwback from the gene pool. *Wow*, thought Tom MacBride, *not heard of that one before, I don't suppose he's had an easy life.*

There was more stuff on Jay's background. A story on the street that Jay eventually found out who'd shot his father and killed him in turn. *Not surprising if it was true, but you could never tell if these stories were street myths. A lot of these guys had little grasp on reality.* There were photographs of Jay with his bodyguards, visiting nightclubs and other establishments during the day and night, no doubt collecting their protection money. There were other photographs of Jay in nightclubs with some very pretty girls, dancing and having a good old time.

Then Tom MacBride found some very interesting photographs. Jay was sitting on a park bench talking to a tall white man dressed in an anorak. The man looked wrong somehow. Not at all like a typical associate of a person like Jay. Then it clicked. It was the clothes. It took him a few seconds to realise who it was. *It's that dodgy Assistant Chief Constable, the guy who tried to put the arm on me for a handout, bloody hell. Colin someone, Colin Neale that's it.*

He hadn't recognised him as he'd only met him the once and then the man had been wearing a dress police uniform. *All that bloody police regalia, brass and buttons. Well bugger me*, he said to himself again. MacBride was fascinated. He looked through the rest of the stuff to see if there were any sound recordings. He found an envelope with a small bulky item in it. He took it out, and it was a memory stick for a computer. He turned around to his PC and stuck it in the USB slot. Up came the folder on the screen called *Jay Audio*. In it were displayed several separate files. The first was called *Athenaeum*, presumably the club. The next was the one he was looking for, called *The Park*. He clicked on the file, and the speakers came to life. Too low to hear, so he turned up the volume and put the track back to the beginning. The voices were a bit muffled, but clear enough to be able to decipher what was being said.

'I'm having a hard time trying to persuade my boss that it would be a waste of time.'

'Man, what's the point? The dude won't testify anyway, I'll see to that.'

'Well, I wouldn't be too sure Jay. This guy says he saw what happened and he will testify.'

'But it's over six months ago, and man he was askin' for it.'

'That's hardly the point Jay, and you know it.'

'So you goin' to give me this witness?'

'It's risky, so it's going to cost Jay.'

'Look we're in this together.'

'Oh no we're not my friend. You try to implicate me in any of your dealings and its goodnight Vienna. There isn't any record of my taking anything from you, so don't push it Jay or I'll come down on you and your friends like a ton of bricks, and don't think I can't do it.'

'Okay man don't lose your cool. But I ain't goin' to prison, so what's it gonna cost?'

'Ten k.'

'What?'

'Ten K, and that's not negotiable.'

The recording ended, and Tom MacBride looked back at the photographs again. There was one of Neale walking away from Jay, who was still sitting on the bench looking distinctly angry.

Tom MacBride looked through the stuff again but found nothing else of particular interest. *Well*, he thought, *Colin Neale on the take, no big surprise there,* not after my experience when I met the man. *Bent coppers aren't exactly unheard of, but catching an Assistant Chief Constable in the act. Now that's something else. Better keep this stuff very safe, never know when I might want to use it. And didn't this cretin try to threaten me, albeit a veiled threat. Well Mr Colin Neale, I might well cook your goose one of these fine days. Teach you to try it on with Tom MacBride.*

CHAPTER 10

As MacBride was leaving his office that evening, he thought about the witness they'd talked about and who would no doubt be getting a visit from Jay or one of his men soon. Although he made it a rule not to get involved in other people's problems, the thought of Jay Madaki getting away with murder, literally, and it got to him. He tried to shake it off, but it kept coming back to him, then he had an idea. *He could find out details of the murder Jay had been accused of easily enough, but could he find out who the witness was, and offer to protect him?*

The police would no doubt arrange for protection of witnesses anyway, but they were useless at stuff like that - notwithstanding people on the take, like our Assistant Chief Constable Neale, he thought. In MacBride's experience, the police force was as leaky as a colander, *If I could look after the witness and Jay ended up going to jail, then bingo, the Trojans would be greatly weakened, and they'd be out of my hair, at least for a few years. Chop of the head of the monster and all that. And what pleasure I'd get from seeing a toe rag like Jay doing time.*

Tom MacBride considered how he might be able to arrange to provide protection for the witness. *Go to the top,* He and Eric Parr, the Chief Constable were only social acquaintances, but they did get on very well. He hesitated for a moment, and then made the call.

'Hello Eric, Tom MacBride here, yes Quadrant Security, yes that's right, very well thanks.'

After the initial pleasantries, Tom MacBride got straight to the point and asked if Eric was aware of the allegation of murder against Jay Madaki and the possibility of a new witness who was prepared to testify.

'How on earth do you know about that?'

'Rather not say Eric, but it illustrates a point I was going to make anyway, leaks from your lot.'

'Yes, well. So what's all this to you?'

'Well, truth to tell, I have a vested interest in getting Jay off the streets as well. He's demanding protection money from some of my clients, and I can't let him succeed. So I thought if I could help in any way to get Jay convicted, then it would do us all a favour.'

'And just what are you suggesting?'

'Well, as I've just demonstrated, there isn't much confidentiality in the police department. And too many people know too much for things not to leak out.'

'Well I'm not sure I agree with you on that but go on.'

'So, how about you let me protect the witness, Quadrant Security that is. No charge of course. He'll stand a much better chance of getting to Court in one piece, if my boys are looking after him.'

'Well Tom MacBride, you must want this Jay character put away pretty bad.'

'I do, he's going costing me money, and more importantly, my reputation, unless I get him off my clients' backs.

'Hmm, well I suppose it would save the taxpayer some money. If I do Tom, don't let me down.'

'I won't Eric. You know me, reliable as they come.'

'I hope so. Come to the office tomorrow at eleven, and I'll get the information you need. I'll also need to contact the witness and tell him what's going on, oh and the victim's widow.

'Thanks Eric. You won't be sorry.'

'Make sure I'm not, see you tomorrow.'

When Tom MacBride got the details of who the witness was, he put Gerry and Pete back to work again, but this time to check up on the witness. He didn't want to end up spending time and money on someone who turned out to be a nutter, or a flaky witness who would lose his bottle at the last minute. He needed, as far as possible, to be sure this guy was the genuine article, and that he had the guts to go through with it. Tom told Gerry to check up on Jay's brother Ezra as well while they were at it. He had the germ of an idea on that subject as well.

The witness turned out to be a solid guy called John Wilson, aged forty five. He was single with no immediate family, which made him much less vulnerable. Tom MacBride called him to make an appointment and went to visit him personally to make sure he was as reliable as he seemed. Tom took Andy and Ged along with him. Two very capable members of his security outfit.

John Wilson lived in a fashionable apartment block in Manchester city centre. He worked away in Saudi Arabia a lot, using Manchester as his base in the UK. Tom MacBride had telephoned ahead, and Wilson had been expecting his call, the police having advised him of the new arrangement.

John Wilson welcomed Tom and his men into his apartment. Tom introduced Ged and Andy.

'I think you know why we're here but I'll go over it again, so there's no confusion, okay?'

'Okay' said Wilson.

'You witnessed a violent act, and as I understand it you're willing to testify in Court that the man who stabbed another man to death was Jay Madaki?'

'Well obviously at the time, I didn't know who he was, but yes I now know the man who knifed the guy, killed him, is this Jay Madaki.'

'I assume the police have told you this man is vicious and has previous, for intimidating potential witnesses?'

'Yeah they told me all about him, but don't worry I don't scare easily. I know how to look after myself.'

'Okay, well I own a private security firm Quadrant Security, and I've volunteered our services to the police to protect you until the trial, and after if needs be.'

'That's okay by me.'

'Good,' said Tom, 'as a matter of interest what did you actually witness?'

'Well, I'd been out for a meal with my accountant. He had to get home to his wife, but I fancied a nightcap, so I went to the Merry go Round club to see if there was any action. I had a couple of drinks but then decided I'd go home myself. I was on my way out, and there was a ruckus just outside. At first I thought it was just a brawl, but then I saw this guy with a knife and the other guy who looked terrified and well out of his league.

The doormen didn't seem to want to intervene, so I jumped in, only these other two thugs grabbed me and held me back. Turns out they were this Jay guy's minders. It was sickening, and the guy who got stabbed had no chance and was pleading with this Jay not to hurt him, but he just went ahead, showed no emotion, even when it became obvious the guy who was stabbed was in a really bad way. Then he legged it with his pals. The police rolled up eventually, and I told them what happened.'

'I was going back to Saudi the next day, so that was that as far as I was concerned, but when I came back a few weeks later, there was a letter waiting for me from the fuzz asking me to call. It seems that I was the only one willing to say what had happened and all the other witnesses had developed galloping amnesia.'

'And why are you willing to testify?'

'My brother was killed in a knife attack, and no one was ever convicted for it, so I know what it's like. And anyway, I'm not the kind of guy who's easily intimidated. Neither do I have any close family that can be threatened. So if I can help nail the guy who did it then I'm more than happy to help.'

Okay, but I'm going to have to keep you out of harm's way until the trial, and that means you living with these two jokers for a couple of months,' Tom pointed at Andy and Ged. John said he wasn't too bothered and told Tom that he had plenty of spare room in the apartment, so it wouldn't be a big deal.

'The boys should be comfortable enough.' He said

Tom said that Andy and Ged would work in shifts to provide twenty four seven cover, and that he would use what influence he had to get the police to try to move the case up the list. He knew they were anxious to get a conviction against Jay this time round.

'They've had Jay in their sites for a long time now and this time, thanks to you, they think they have a good chance of putting him behind bars,' said Tom.

'It'll be my pleasure to help then.'

The two men shook hands, and Tom MacBride left Andy and Ged behind, to make arrangements for moving into John's apartment.

CHAPTER 11

Jay answered the phone.

'Me' said the voice at the other end.

'Have you got the information?

'Yes'

'Great.'

'But I've got bad news as well.'

'Shit, give me the good news first,' said Jay.

'The witness is a John Wilson, lives in some fancy apartment block in Manchester. I can get the address.'

'Okay, and the bad?'

'He's being protected by Quadrant Security.'

'Quadrant Security, you mean as in that twat, MacBride?' Jay's voice changing to a feral growl, as his anger increased at the news.

'Yep, 'fraid so, he's a pal of the Chief Constable, and he offered his services for free.' It took Jay a moment to work it out.

'The dirty motherfucker bastard. He's trying to make sure I go away so's I'm out of the game.'

'I think that's the plan my friend. You should have maybe left his clients alone. MacBride's no fool.'

Jay was silent, then spoke between gritted teeth

'I'll get the fuckin witness, and teach MacBride a lesson as well. No fucker jerks me around.'

Colin replies in a calm voice.

'Look Jay, this isn't like going up against the police. If you try to intimidate the witness, while he's under the protection of MacBride, he can do things the police wouldn't be able to.'

'Such as?'

'Well, I can think of quite a few things, such as wiping you off the map, permanently.'

'He wouldn't be so stupid,' said Jay, knowing full well that MacBride would come after him given the least excuse.

'What's he got to lose Jay? We certainly won't be looking too hard if you have some sort of fatal accident. Think about it.'

'You bastard,' Jay began.

Neale raised his voice in anger.

'Look Jay, don't think you can speak to me like one of your rubbing rags. If you're not careful, I'll walk away now and leave them to it.'

Jay realised he'd gone too far.

'Okay, cool down bro, I'm just sayin'.'

'Well show some respect Jay.'

'Yeah, sorry. Shit man, what do I do?'

'Well, looks to me like you've got two choices.'

'Go on,' said Jay.

'If you try to get to the witness, you might succeed. But either way, you'll start a war with MacBride, and he'll have us, the police, on his side. And although we won't actively support him, we won't be trying too hard to interfere either.

My boss won't get involved directly, but he will try to make things as difficult as possible for you, to do anything against MacBride.'

Colin could hear Jay's breathing down the phone as he reluctantly asked the question.

'And my other choice?'

'Take the rap.'

Jay's voice screeched down the phone.

'What me, go to jail? You must be joking motherfucker!'

Colin kept his cool.

'Well, you're definitely going to be arrested and charged. Then if you plead not guilty at trial, but get convicted, which is probably what will happen from what I've heard about the witness, then they'll put you away for a good long time. But if you plead guilty, put up a good story about it being a fight that got out of hand, you might get away with a lesser offence, and spend a lot less time in jail.'

Jay was silent for a long time.

'Jay, you still there?'

'Yeah, what would I get, d'you think?' asked Jay in a sullen voice.

'Don't know. Depends on the judge, but a lot less than you'll get if you plead not guilty, then get convicted.'

'Fuck - fuck fuck fuck!'

'Look Jay, you've had a good run. You've got away with murder, literally, so take the hit. You'll probably only serve half the time anyway. Up to you, but this is the last time I can help you. You're on your own now, you're poison, and I'm putting plenty of distance between us.'

'You can't do that.'

'Just watch me. And don't forget, if you think it's bad now, just think how bad I can make it if you piss me off, by trying to implicate me in anything.'

'You fuckin...'

Jay didn't get to finish his threat.

'Careful Jay. Oh, and don't forget to tell one of your boys to call me to arrange to drop off the ten grand you owe me.'

'You....' Jay began to protest, but Colin cut him off.

'Jay, we had a deal, and I expect you to pay up okay?'

The phone went silent as Jay considered his predicament. Jay was lots of things, but he wasn't stupid. He knew the odds were well and truly stacked against him this time. He needed Colin, more than Colin needed him, so he made his decision.

'Yeah okay, bastard.'

'That's the boy. Now go and think about what I've told you. Use your head boy.'

CHAPTER 12

Jay talked to Mickey and told him what Colin had said. After looking at the alternatives, and despite Jay putting up a token show of defiance, Mickey eventually looked at Jay and said.

'Man, I hate to say this, but that policeman fucker is right. You take the gamble, and you could spend a whole chunk of your life in prison dude. A good lawyer and maybe you get the minimum. With the pull you got Jay, you can make prison a walk in the park. If you keep your cool, you could be out after a couple or three years. You only a young man, and better that, than takin' the big chance.'

And so reluctantly Jay took the advice and looked for a lawyer. Jay and Mickey asked their pet solicitor, John Gower-Jones, who told them that Harvey Wickersham was the top man for this sort of thing. He was a QC and had a reputation for getting minimum sentences for criminals who should have gone down for longer. Sometimes he got people off completely, on some obscure legal technicality. *Sounds like the man for me* thought Jay.

The first meeting with Harvey was a tense affair. Jay and Mickey went to his chambers. Jay was in a defensive mood and didn't like being talked down to by anyone. Although he wouldn't admit it, Jay was intimidated by Harvey, who was a large rotund man, impeccably dressed in a three piece, pinstriped suit. He welcomed them into his office, asked them to sit down. Sitting behind his large desk, he adjusted his glasses, took out a yellow legal pad and pen, then adjusting his glasses again, said.

'Okay, now tell me the story from the beginning.'

'Well I was in the club, you know the Roundabout, mindin' my own bidness when some motherfucker punk dissed me, so I put his lights out. End of story okay? Now what you gonna do to get me off?'

'Yes well I'm afraid that won't do Mr. er, Madaki, did I pronounce that correctly?

'Yeah, you pronounced my name right, but forget the Mr Madaki shit okay? Jay, call me Jay.'

'Yes well, then er, Jay, you need to tell me the whole story properly. As it happened, from when you entered the nightclub, to when and how the altercation started.'

'Like I said man, this mother....'

Wickersham stopped him.

'Look Mr, er Jay, you need to understand that when I ask a question, you need to answer it properly. Please understand, either do it my way, or find another lawyer.'

Jay looked shocked at being talked to like this and was about to tell the brief to take a hike, then he glanced at Mickey, who had a tight look on his face and shook his head just enough to signal to Jay that he should do as he was told.

Jay hesitated then smiled, and the tension broke.

'Yeah man sorry 'bout that.'

Jay did his best to describe what had happened, being careful to slant the story in a direction that meant he wasn't to blame for the man's death, but when Jay said something that might have put him in the wrong, Harvey carefully coached him to re-phrase the way he described a particular event. It was skilfully done and by the time they'd finished the story had some semblance of having a defensible position. It was obvious nevertheless that Jay was a vicious thug and no matter how well the story was slanted, Jay would still be found guilty of a serious crime.

The only question was, what charge he would be found guilty of, and how long a jail term he would serve.

'Okay, I'm going to write this up now, and you and your friend here are going to read it over and over again and make sure you agree with it. You can read can't you?'

'Yeah we can read, being a nigger don't mean we're stupid.' Jay glared at the barrister.

'Yes of course, forgive me,' Wickersham coughed, then continued.

'I need you to understand the necessity for you to confirm that my version is exactly what happened, got it?'

'Yeah got it.' Jay said sullenly.

'And, there's something very important that you need to remember.'

What's that man?'

'Lose the fucking attitude, and lose the look if you don't want to go down for a nice long stretch.'

Jay was momentarily taken aback by the use of such language by someone so apparently respectable.

'What the fuck you talkin' about?'

Wickersham continued, pointing his finger in Jay's face.

'I'll spell it out for you, so there's no misunderstanding. If you go into the Court and look at the judge or the jury in that defiant threatening way, I can't help you. Whatever I say, and however eloquently I put the case for the defence, they will hand out the harshest punishment possible, just to teach you a lesson. So you'd better start practising looking ashamed and sorry. Unless you come over as showing sincere regret and remorse for the victim's death, you'll be put away for a long time. So, get that into your thick fucking gangster head, or face the consequences.'

A tense silence followed. Jay's first instinct was to grab the lawyer by the throat and beat him to a pulp. *Nobody talked to him like that, nobody.* But his fear of prolonged incarceration was enough to quell his violent response, on this occasion. He recognised what was at stake, looked at the lawyer and nodded his head in reluctant compliance.

Jay said he had kept away from his usual haunts, ever since he became aware that a witness was willing to testify against him. So the police hadn't been able to find him to make an arrest. Harvey was pleased, and told Jay to turn this to his advantage and go immediately and voluntarily with a solicitor, and give himself up to the police. However much this was against Jay's natural instincts, he could see the tactical sense of it and soon convinced himself that he was in fact, the one who'd been attacked and had only acted in self defence.

To the amazement of the police, Jay showed up at the main police station in Manchester with his solicitor, who asked to see the detective in charge of the case in question. They were duly shown into the interview room where they sat for ten minutes or so before a detective, who introduced himself as Derek Brady, sat down with his assistant and began to ask Jay about the incident at the nightclub. Jay answered giving the version drummed into him by Harvey Wickersham. The police saw through the tactic, but had little choice but to play their part, by the book.

Tom MacBride learned of Jay's arrest and intention to plead guilty, and had to grudgingly admit to himself that he was impressed with Jay facing up to reality. He was told by the Police Chief, that he should nevertheless remain protective of the witness until the trial. Jay was still considered a serious danger to the witness, especially if he was let out on bail. Through less official channels Tom MacBride was told that Jay had promised he would be settling the score when he finally got out of prison, and Tom MacBride would know what that meant. MacBride laughed, but knew that Jay had killed before, so he wasn't foolish enough to ignore the threat altogether, though there was plenty of time to think about it. One way or another Jay would be out of the way for some considerable time, *and maybe a more permanent arrangement could be made*, thought MacBride.

The trial went largely as predicted. Jay's defence team presented him as a victim of circumstance, whose father had been murdered while Jay was still young. How Jay had had such a hard time etc. That he was good at his studies at school, before the shooting of his father etc etc. As for the incident itself, Jay deeply regretted the outcome of what had been an argument, which had got out of hand. The knife, had not been brought into play by Jay, and there had been no intention to kill the victim. It was all a terrible accident and so on. Jay played his part, burying his pride and playing the judge and the jury as he'd been told.

The prosecution tried to blacken Jay's name saying he was said to be a gang leader involved in questionable activities including drugs and protection rackets, but they couldn't bring any evidence to support their claims. The case turned entirely on the death of the man, which Jay had already admitted to. In the end, the Crown Prosecution realised that Jay had played the case to his best advantage, and that at least he would do some time, but not as long as he deserved, as far as they were concerned.

There was no requirement for any witness to give evidence, and the judge recommended that the jury find Jay guilty of manslaughter and they did. The judge then made his speech prior to sentence.

'The crime of which you have been found guilty is a serious one, and a life has been lost. But I believe that you didn't set out that evening to kill the unfortunate victim. I've listened carefully to the evidence and the mitigating circumstances put forward by the defence. I have also taken into account your exemplary behaviour in coming forward of your own accord, to give yourself up to the authorities and. Given what I've heard, I am inclined to give you the minimum sentence of two years in jail.'

Jay knew that he'd got away with murder, literally. And that the fool judge had fallen for all the bullshit in giving him the minimum. Nevertheless, Jay was horrified by the sudden reality of it all. He'd been assured by Mickey that everything would be done to make sure things were as good as possible in jail and all Jay had to do was behave and keep his temper. But the prospect of being locked up was already having a severe impact on Jay. He vowed to get even with anyone who had been instrumental in putting him away. It never occurred to Jay for one moment, that he himself, bore any responsibility whatever, for his predicament.

CHAPTER 13

A nnabelle had let Lady off the lead. Lady, initially, trotted diligently at Annabelle's side. Then, as soon as she felt her mistress's attention wandering, Lady ran off down the lane and into a field. Annabelle shouted after her dog. Sometimes Lady would have a bit of a run then go back to Annabelle, but this morning, there were sheep in the field and they looked like good fun to chase.

There were notices pinned to the trees and posts saying that sheep were grazing in the fields and that "dogs should be kept on a lead or risk being shot if they chased the sheep." Annabelle had ignored these notices thinking, mistakenly as usual, that she could control Lady without a lead. Lady could hear Annabelle calling her but she was quite a distance away now, so she ran at the nearest sheep. At first, the sheep seemed to mistake Lady for some distant relative. Then when Lady began to bark, the sheep realised "dog," and it ran away, spooking all the other sheep in the process. Mayhem followed.

The field was next to the motorway, but well fenced off. It wasn't a big field, so the chase went around the field one way, then as the sheep tried to manoeuvre out of Lady's way, they ran around the opposite way. Annabelle finally got to the stile, and remembering the potential consequences to her dog should the framer see what was happening, went into a blind panic screaming at the top of her voice

'Lady stop Lady.'

Annabelle finally managed to coral Lady into a corner of the field, and held the lead ready to slip over the dog's head, but Lady was having none of it, and ran under a stile in the corner of the field and into a little copse, then up some metal steps and over a bridge that crossed the motorway into another field. Annabelle, who was now shouting and crying at the same time, ran after Lady and over the motorway bridge.

On the other side of the bridge, there were two paths. Lady took the one immediately opposite, through the tall grass, nettles and bushes and was quickly lost to view. Annabelle followed valiantly, shouting after Lady. Annabelle thought she would never catch up, but then she heard Lady's bark, and not too far away.

She came to a little clearing in the path and saw Lady standing over what looked like a pile of rags. She went closer, all the time concentrating on getting the lead, ready to slip the lead over Lady's pretty bobbed head. The she saw, that what she'd thought was a pile of rags, was in fact, a body. Annabelle fainted.

She came to with a wet tongue licking her face and couldn't remember where she was for a moment, then she screamed. Even Lady jumped at the noise. Annabelle got to a kneeling position, and trying not to look at the body, managed to get the lead on Lady, who by now had had enough fun and was getting hungry.

Her legs felt they would buckle under her, but she finally got to her feet. Finding her way back to the Motorway Bridge and slowly crossing over it, she thought how strange it was to be so close to so many people driving past her, on the motorway beneath, but her not being able to summon any help. She and Lady made their way back, through the field with the sheep in it, Annabelle firmly holding on to her dog's lead.

They walked up the lane and came across another dog walker who Annabelle recognised, and with whom she would normally exchange a cheery "good morning," or "lovely day" or some such greeting, but on this occasion, the man saw that Annabelle was somewhat dishevelled and distressed. He asked what was wrong and she managed to tell him about the body, then promptly fainted at his feet. He took out his mobile phone and called for an ambulance and the police.

Police headquarters Trafford Greater Manchester, Tuesday.

'Sarge, just been passed a message from communications. Someone's called 999 claiming they've found a woman, who says she found a body in a field out in Briarley, you know, out Alderham way? There's a patrol car bobby on the way to see if it's a genuine call, but sounds as if it is. The woman's in a bit of a state by all accounts, but managed to give her details, and so did the man who found the woman.

'Shall I tell CID?'

'Yes Prentice,' came the reply.

CHAPTER 14

Alfie was still trying to take in the fact that Ezra was dead. Although Ezra had bullied him and generally gave him a hard time, Ezra was nevertheless the nearest thing Alfie had to a friend. All his life Alfie had wanted to have friends like other people, but somehow it just never happened. He tried to be liked, but even from a very early age, it became obvious that he was just one of life's unfortunate victims.

Alfie looked dirty, even when he'd been washed. Many times he was scrubbed raw by teachers in the infants' school, who were invariably disappointed, that no matter how much they tried to make Alfie look clean, he always looked dirty. He had a hangdog expression and unruly dark brown hair.

He was small for his age, and was bullied in the infant's school, battered by his dad when he came home from the pub drunk, and usually ignored by the other kids when they picked a football team or a gang.

Alfie finally found a sort of salvation in his junior school. He would often stand alone in the schoolyard, frightened of being picked on. Then one day one of the older lads, Johnny Evans, who was considered to be one of the toughest boys in school, asked him to go and steal some fags for him from the local newsagents during the lunch break. Alfie didn't know if he was more terrified of being caught stealing, or of coming back empty handed, and suffering the inevitable punishment that would be visited on him for failing to deliver.

Alfie went to the newsagents and waited till the owner was serving someone else, then launched himself over the counter and grabbed a carton of twenty cigarettes off the shelf behind the long counter. The newsagent, used to such attempts to steal cigs, was quick to react. He pulled out a baseball bat from under the counter, then putting one hand on the counter, leapt over it, hot on the tail of poor terrified Alfie.

Alfie almost made it to the door then looked around to see the man swinging the bat towards his head. Alfie ducked sideways and was spared a blow that would probably have split his head wide open. Having missed Alfie's head, the bat continued its course and hit the armoured window in the door with a resounding thwack. The Window cracked in all directions but didn't break. The distraction was just enough for Alfie to gain the extra distance he needed to get away.

Fuelled by fear and adrenalin, Alfie ran like the wind around the corner, down a back alley, finally collapsing in a heap when he couldn't run any more. He shook with aftershock, but still had hold of the carton of twenty ciggies. Once his legs worked again, he gingerly looked round the corner to make sure there was no one looking for him, then made his way back to school with his prize. He was rewarded with a friendly, if somewhat painful smack around the head, when he handed the cigs over to Johnny.

'Well done er, Alfie ain't it?'

'Yeah Alfie.'

'Well Alfie, I think you can run a few more errands for me in the future, so stick around.

Alfie had found his niche, and with it, some measure of protection from his new lord and master. Alfie had a series of such 'masters' from then on, and had hooked up with his latest one, Ezra some two years, before when, they'd shared a prison cell. Ezra was in for GBH and Alfie had been nicked, yet again, for burglary. As usual, Alfie had been caught while the other man involved in the theft, got away with the goods, leaving Alfie to take the rap. *Nothing changes* thought Alfie at the time.

Alfie sat in the pub and thought back to what should have been a straightforward, simple earner. *How could it have all got so messed up?* He didn't know what to do without Ezra to tell him. He realised he shouldn't have taken Ezra's money from that man, but what else could he have done? *Ezra had made a right bollocks of things. It was all his fault, everything would have been okay if his phone hadn't run out of battery. Stupid fucker forgot to charge it the night before, cos he was so rat-arsed. Then that man came along an all Ezra had to do was to ask him nice like if he could use his phone. Tell 'im it was an emergency, but no, out with that fuckin knife. Couldn't resist cutting someone, any excuse. Well, the man well and truly fucked Ezra. What the fuck was in that spray? Then that kick, who'd have thought someone like him ad it in 'im?*

Alfie had a few more drinks to try to calm himself down. Like the man said, it would look like he'd done Ezra and nicked the gear. *Shit,* thought Alfie and decided to make himself scarce.

CHAPTER 15

'Sammy, call for you. Seems that they've found something.'

'Thanks Sarge, put 'em through, 'Pownall here,' he said.

'Constable Walker here sir, down at the search site in Briarley. We've found a body, looks like a middle aged male.'

'Okay Walker, the usual. Secure the scene. I'll get SOCO there right away. Eh, what's your first impression? Sorry Walker, don't know your first name.'

'Pete Sir. The body's a few yards from a footpath. Could have been missed easily, but a woman's dog found it. When she went to look why the dog was making such a fuss, she stumbled across the body. The only visible injury seems to be some nasty bruising to the throat, but I haven't gone too near the body. We've kept well away, not wanting to mess things up, you know? We'll put tape up and secure the scene till the SOCO gets here and we'll make sure we cordon off a large area. Anything else you need me to do sir?'

'No thanks Pete, just keep any rubberneckers and the press boys well away.'

CHAPTER 16

J ay sat in his cell thinking about the outside. It was stiflingly hot, and the air conditioning, such as it was, made little impression. Still, it was better being back in his normal cell again. Jay had been in jail for four months now and already had had spells in solitary for violent behaviour. Bastard screw, he deserved the kicking he got thought Jay, *taken the bribe then laughed in my face when I asked him when he'd deliver.*

They'd taken his cell apart while he was in solitary, but had found nothing. *As if I'd leave anything in my own cell? Just hope that soppy git, butter wouldn't melt, Martin, doesn't say he's holding it for me.* The first few days in prison had been difficult for Jay. Any new prisoner is tested when he arrives, but in Jay's case, his reputation preceded him, so he presented a challenge to the top dogs, who saw him as a potential threat to their dominance.

Anticipating such a situation, and before Jay went to Court, Mickey had taken him to see an old prison hand who'd seen it all. He told Jay that if he was going to be targeted, it would be in the first couple of weeks, and the three likely places the attack would happen. He told Jay the showers were the most unpredictable, and Jay would need to rely on his wits and obvious physical strength.

If it was going to be the prison yard or the canteen, then he said, Jay was to look out for a diversion such as a fight breaking out. Jay could expect an attack then. Sure enough, on the third day in, Jay was in the prison yard when a fight broke out on the other side. It drew the attention of everyone, prisoners and guards alike, but Jay kept alert and readied himself. He saw the knife man coming from his right but pretended not to notice till the last moment, then turned and kicked the man just below the kneecap. Jay's shoes were not prison issue and had steel toecaps hidden beneath the canvas covering.

The sound of the bone snapping was audible. The knifeman screamed in agony as he went down, but no one was taking any notice. Jay looked around just to be sure, then bent down and twisted the knife out of the man's hand. The man immediately knew his fate, but before he could utter any sound, Jay stuck the knife under his ribs and into his heart. He pulled out the knife and wiped the handle with an old rag he'd brought with him, then threw it on the floor and slowly walked away towards the fight, which was now being broken up by the guards.

The top dogs got the message, and Jay was left alone from then on, free to develop his own small fiefdom within the unofficial prison structure. Jay needed to catch up with events, now he was out of solitary. *Tomorrow morning at grub up will be the time.* Despite his familiarity with the seamier side of life, even Jay was amazed at just how much went on in the confines of a prison.

A whole world of racketeering, politics, bribes, drug dealing and sex. Before too long, he was running a smaller modified version of his protection racket, right there in jail.

With so much time on his hands, he would often sit and think about his family, or what was left of it. His mother was the only person Jay ever really cared about, and he would do anything for her. She was in a nursing home now, paid for by Jay. She'd never recovered from Charlie's death and had gradually become more and more distanced from the real world.

Jay used to go to see her every now and then, but he found it too upsetting when she didn't recognise him, which was most of the time. He went to see her again, just before he went to jail and she didn't seem to know who he was at first. Then she became quite lucid, and as she recognised him, she pulled him towards her and kissed him saying.

'My beautiful little boy Jesus, all growed up now, a fine young man. Where's your brother Ezra? Is he with you?

'No Mama, Ezra's not here, just me.'
He didn't add that he hadn't seen his fuckwit brother for years. He'd always hated him, and though it was Jay who'd driven his brother away, Jay as usual re-wrote history in his mind to make Ezra the one who'd caused the relationship to fracture.

'You looking after your little brother Jesus?'

'Yeah Mama, I'm lookin' after him okay.' Jay felt bad lying to his Mama.

'You promise?'

'Yeah Mama, I promise.'

'You're a good boy Jesus, I know you won't let your Mama down.'

'I won't Mama, I swear.'

CHAPTER 17

The SOCO's team had worked through the afternoon and late into the evening, then gone back again early the next morning. Sammy decided to visit the crime scene, assuming that the SOCO had had plenty of time to reach his initial conclusions. Sammy's old pal Mike Beauchamp was the senior officer at the scene. He'd just finished making his verbal record. He turned to Sammy, and they shook hands, exchanging pleasantries as they did so.

Mike sent an officer to ask Allen Appleton to join them, and they made small talk while they waited for him to join them. Allen walked over, peeling off a pair of plastic gloves as he did so.

'Nice to see you Sammy,' said Allen.`

'Likewise' said Sammy as they shook hands.

'Okay, overview and first conclusions,' said Mike

'We have a male body, been here for two days approximately, appears to have died more or less where he was found. Some evidence of a fracas, some trodden down grass, which was starting to recover. The weather's been warm and dry so no muddy shoe prints.

Mike looked at his notes again.

'Age of deceased, thirty seven years, two months and three days on the day of death.

Sammy raised his eyebrows at Mike's nonchalant accuracy, then smiled.

'Wallet' Sammy said 'with driving licence in it.?'

'Correct,' said Mike returning the smile.

'C'mon then, who is he?

'One Ezra Madaki, it says on his licence, unusual name.'

'It certainly is Mike, brother of one Jay Madaki, notorious Manchester gang leader. Now that is interesting.'

'Could it be anything to do with the brother then?' Mike asked.

'Might have been, but as Jay is currently incarcerated at Her Majesty's pleasure, there's unlikely to be any direct connection, but you never know. The brothers weren't particularly close by all accounts. Ezra is known to us as a regular, but relatively minor stuff compared to his brother. The last couple of years, he and his pal Alfie Campkin seemed to be joined at the hip.'

'Wonder where Alfie is?' said Sammy more to himself than anyone else, then addressed Appleton directly 'Cause of death?'

'Well, there's a nasty bruise around the larynx, which would indicate he died as the result of a severe blow to the neck. The bruising isn't typical of strangulation, so like I say, probably the result of a blow to the neck. No other obvious marks found so far.' Appleton replied.

'Any weapon found?' Sammy asked.

'Yep, hunting type knife found in the long grass about fifteen yards away. Looks like dried blood on the blade. No great attempt to hide it, perhaps thrown away in a fit of temper or panic,' said Mike.

'A knife case was on the deceased so reasonable to assume it was the vic's own knife'.

'Anything else on him, apart from the wallet I mean?'

'A mobile phone, dead, out of battery. The boys will get it charged up then record all the calls and, or, messages etc. There was a piece of paper with a phone number on it. We've tried the number, and it's not being answered. Initial checks with the phone company, indicate a throwaway.'

Then Alan chipped in.

'As for the definite cause of death, 'fraid you'll have to wait until the post mortem. I'll have a lot more for you in about twenty four hours' time.'

Sammy thanked them for their time, said his goodbyes and drove back to the station. Okay thought Sammy as he drove, we need to talk to Alfie *so where are you, you scroat?* Sammy called the station and gave instructions to find Alfie Campkin.

'The boys will know his usual haunts, pubs mainly, so get them on it straight away George.'

'Will do Sammy.'

The next morning Sammy bumped into the desk sergeant.

'Any news on Alfie yet?'

'No Sammy,' said the sergeant, 'he's been seen around then disappeared. Been spendin' a few quid though, by all accounts, nothing outrageous, but a bit over generous buying everyone drinks etc.'

Sammy stroked his chin as he absorbed the information.

'Okay George, get someone to find out where his bolt-hole is. He's not the sharpest knife in the box so it shouldn't be difficult. Get a line on his friends and relations, any close family. From what I remember of Alfie he won't have many places he can go to hide, so let me know as soon as.'

'Will do,' said the sergeant.

'What about the press?' asked George.

'Are they on to it yet?'

'Well, the local newspaper guy called about us, about questioning people walking their dogs, near Bycroft Farm. He'd heard there was a restricted area set up in Briarley, so it won't take long for the rest of that lot to cotton on that there's something serious going on.'

'Okay, set up a news conference for fifteen hundred hours today, and tell all the usual media bods to be there. Nothing they like more than a juicy suspicious death to help them pedal their rags.'

George reached for his pen.

'Calling it suspicious death formally are we Sammy?'

'Yes, and that's what it is until we get the post-mortem report tomorrow. We really need to smoke Alfie out, so the press and television might help us there. Have we got a picture of Alfie?'

'I'm sure we can find a recent mug shot. He's been photographed by our lot enough in the past. I think he's only been out about a year.'

'Okay George, I'll leave all that to you - and get someone to clear out the briefing room will you. The last time we had a press conference in there, it looked like a pig sty – no pun intended.'

'Yes sir, very good sir,' said George in mock obsequiousness.

'Oh and George, better try to find out if Ezra's mother's still around And send someone out to tell her before we brief the press. We know his dad was murdered when he was a kid, and his brother Jay's in prison. We'll arrange to tell Jay in due course, but what we don't need is a grieving mother, saying the first she knew of her son's death was when she read about it in the paper.'

Later that afternoon, Sammy walked into the briefing room and looked around. All the usual suspects he thought. He looked across at George who stuck his thumb up to signify everything was in place, and Sammy was good to go. Sammy walked across the small room and stood behind a lectern facing the assembled journalists.

'Good afternoon ladies and gentlemen, and thank you for coming here today. For those who don't know me, I am Chief Inspector Pownall. I know you've all been wondering what's been going on out near Briarley, so I'll read a statement and then take questions.'

The journalists stopped talking.

'Working on information received, yesterday we found the body of a man in a field near the M60 motorway in Briarley, near Hallerton in Cheshire. The corpse has been identified as thirty seven years old Ezra Madaki, a small time serial criminal who was released from prison about two years ago. This incident is being treated as a suspicious death. Until the post mortem results are in, we can't say any more at this stage.

'Was he murdered'? one of the reporters shouted out. Sammy smiled and repeated the line about it being a suspicious death for the time being.

'Are you looking for anyone in particular in relation to the death?'

'Well, that's an interesting question. We think he may have been in the company of a known associate by the name of Alfred Campkin, or Alfie Campkin as he's known to his friends. We are currently unable to locate or contact Alfie Campkin, so anyone knowing his whereabouts should contact the police on the number I've given in the printed handout, which you will be handed to you as you leave.

'Is Alfie Campkin a suspect?' asked another.

'No, we would just like to talk to Alfie to see if he can help us with our enquiries.'

'That's police speak for yes he definitely did it!' shouted a wag and they all laughed, including Sammy, who couldn't help himself.

'As you well know, that isn't the case, so I'd appreciate if you wouldn't re-interpret anything said, to try to make the story more exciting. Not that you would ever dream of doing such a thing?' More laughter.

'Well ladies and gentlemen; I don't think I have anything more to add at this stage. The sergeant here will keep you informed of any developments as they occur, so thank you for coming today and goodbye for now.'

The reporters all filed out of the room.

Sammy went to see the sergeant.

'George, have we managed to find Alfie Campkin yet?'

'No Sammy, Perris and Hughes have been looking round his usual haunts, but nothing so far. Looks like he's done a runner.'

'Well tell them to keep at it and let me know the minute they get anything on him. We need to speak to him yesterday!'

'Will do Chief Inspector.'

CHAPTER 18

News travels fast and bad news travels faster. Malone called Tom MacBride again in Spain and told him about Ezra's body being found.

'When did you find out?'

'It was just on the six o'clock news.'

'Did it say how he died?'

'No, just that it's being treated as a suspicious death.'

'I'll bet it is,' said MacBride.

'We need to find his mate Alfie, and fast. Find out what the fuck's going on. No one knew about the drop so how's this happened, and more to the point, what's happened to the stuff? If the police have got it, we can say goodbye to the best part of two mill And if they get to Alfie, he might be able to tell them enough to drop us all in the shit – big time! Get Andy to pull out all the stops and find Alfie Campkin before the cops do. Make it top priority and tell Andy he gets a ten grand bonus, if he gets Alfie before he talks to anyone. That should do it.'

'Will do boss.'

Then Malone thought about how he was going to get to Alfie before any of the others did, including Andy.

CHAPTER 19

J ay was looking through the reinforced plexiglass screen at his visitor, a look of disbelief on his face as Mickey told him the news about his brother.

'What the fuck! The stupid shit for brains getting himself topped. He always was a fuckin' disaster.'

Jay had raised his voice attracting the attention of the prison officer who looked up from his magazine as if he was going to come over.

'Keep your voice down Jay' said Mickey, 'they'll cut the visit short if you don't.

'Yeah okay,' then Jay made a choking noise, his face suddenly contorted with a mixture of emotion Mickey had never seen before.

'Everything all right there,' the prison officer shouted in Jay's direction.

Jay straightened up and raised his hand in a gesture that said I'm fine.

'Just a coughing fit mate,' Jay managed to shout back.

'Mate!' said the screw to himself. 'I'm not your fuckin' mate, an' that's for sure.' He went back to his magazine.

'Tell me what happened.'

'Don't really know, but seems he was found dead in a field in Briarley, that's out in the country, north Cheshire.

'And what the fuck was he doing out in the country? Never thought of my stupid brother as a fresh air fiend.'

'The word is that he was on some sort of pick up.'

'Pickin' up what?'

'Yeah, well I asked around, and all I could find out was that Ezra and his mate, a man called....'

Mickey took out a piece of paper from his pocket and looked at it.

'A man called Alfie Campkin.'

'Never heard of him.'

'Anyway, Ezra and this man were on some sort of drugs pickup and delivery job.'

'For?' asked Jay

'I was afraid you'd ask me that.'

'Well?

'Well I'm told, he's been doin' some work, off an' on, for a guy called Tony Malone, who works for that MacBride guy.'

'What?!' Jay exploded.

'Keep your voice down, or the screw'll be on you. And calm down, you'll give yourself heart failure.'

Jay took a deep breath.

'That stupid fuck of a brother. I can't believe it.' Jay was silent, then said.

'You mean to tell me that MacBride's involved in drugs?'

'Don't know, could be. But if he is, it's been a well kept secret. Having said that, MacBride's a big pal of the guy who does the raves in Manchester. Does his security. Lots of opportunities to sell plenty of the stuff at those venues, that's for sure.'

'That fuckin MacBride playin' the white fuckin knight, protecting witnesses for the police, so I'll go down. And all the time, he's a fuckin drug dealer. Man, he's just as bad as us. I'll fuckin kill that bastard if it's the last thing I do. When I get out of here I'll be callin' on Tom MacBride, and I'll get mine, I fuckin swear.'

Mickey kept his mouth shut waiting for Jay to calm down. Jay went on.

'So Tom MacBride helps get me convicted and gets my brother killed. He's dissin' my whole fuckin family. I'm goin to settle that motherfucker's hash if it's the last thing I do. I'm goin' to make that fucker suffer so much before I top him, he'll be beggin' me to kill him by the time I'm finished.

Mickey had his head down. When he thought Jay had finished, he looked up. Jay was deep in thought, then he said.

'This Alfie, Ezra's mate, where is he now?'

'He was hangin' around, then disappeared. The police are looking for him, but as far as I know, they haven't found him yet.'

'Right,' said Jay. 'I need to call in a few favours. Get hold of Rick Cooper and tell him to take Mo and find this Alfie. Tell him to get hold of the guy before anyone else does and tell him to find out what happened. Tell him I don't care what he does or how he does it, but tell him I ain't asking here, I'm tellin'. If he doesn't get a result, tell him he's in for a serious kickin' hisself– got that?'

'Yes,' Mickey said 'I got that,' looking into Jay's eyes and not liking what he saw there. He knew that Jay would turn his anger into something really very nasty. You wouldn't want to cross Jay even if he was locked away in prison. Jay still had enough pull on the outside to do most anything he wanted, short of getting himself out of prison. But even that wasn't out of the question.

The bell rang, and Mickey got up to leave. Jay just sat there until the screw came over and dug him in the ribs. Jay turned and glared at the screw, but got up and walked back to the cells.

CHAPTER 20

Detective Sergeant John Carter hadn't been to Blackpool since he was a kid, when their family, his mum, dad, older sister and younger brother, used to go on day trips. They always checked the weather forecast beforehand to make sure it was good, but inevitably, when they got there, it was blowing a gale or at least, raining. Nevertheless, they always enjoyed themselves.

His Dad was fond of monologues, and could, and would, recite Albert and the Lion, by heart on the drive there. It drove them scatty when he started the recital, but they all ended up laughing by the time he'd finished. Now Carter remembered those times with a great fondness. Even now he could see and hear in his mind's eye

There's a famous seaside place called Blackpool, that's noted for fresh air and fun, and Mr and Mrs Ramsbottom went there with young Albert, their son. A grand little lad was young Albert, all dressed in his best; quite a swell, with a stick with an 'orse's 'ead 'andle, the finest that Woolworth's could sell.

He was woken from his reverie by the booming voice of the desk sergeant at Blackpool's Central Police Station in Bonny Street.

'Please follow me Sergeant Carter' said the sergeant in voice, almost reminiscent of a Gilbert & Sullivan character.

I'll take you to see Detective Sergeant Poole who's handling the matter.'

After the introduction formalities, Poole began.

'Well Sergeant Carter., as requested we visited Mrs Campkin's house to ascertain if her nephew was staying with her, or if she'd had any contact with him recently and it turned that he'd stayed there for a few days recently, but went out on Friday night and never returned. She's been worried about him since, but not overly so, as she says he's always been like that. Appears out of the blue, then he's off again without a by your leave. So bearing in mind the high level of importance we were told you attached to matey, we decided to check around further.

Then I came across a report at South Shore Police station about a man found under the pier on Saturday morning. He'd been beaten up. In a very bad way, by all accounts. Funny thing though, he still had his wallet, which is how they identified him as Alfred Campkin. And a wad of cash in his pocket. So I think we can rule out robbery as the motive. He was taken to hospital, so we went to see if we could interview him, but he was in far too bad a condition, and the prognosis was very poor for any prospect of us getting anything out of him in the near future. Maybe never, according to the Doc.'

Great, thought Carter, *Sammy will be pleased. The only potential witness to whatever went on in Briarley, and he's out of the game.*

'Could it have been random? Do they know how it happened?' he asked Carter.

'We checked the likely bars and pubs nearby, and it turns out he was drinking in the White Horse Friday evening. Then around nine, a couple of men turned up. The barman says that Alfie went white when he saw them, then added that he wouldn't want to be on the wrong side of these men. That they looked very professional, if you get the drift?'

'Did you get a good description?'

'Yes, it's all in my report, but there was nothing remarkable about them, other than the barman's comments about their demeanour, which was just his impression. He said they were "all business" and not out for fun. Alfie apparently went with them without finishing his drink and left looking terrified.

CHAPTER 21

The police phoned Jack just as he was about to leave home for a board meeting.

'Mr Brandon, we're sorry to bother you, but we'd be grateful if you could pop into the station at Collingham Road sometime, to go over the statement you made to officer Brindle last Monday?'

'Yes, of course.'

Jack knew it would be odd if he didn't ask why, might imply he knew something if he didn't.

'Has something happened? I mean the officer I gave my statement to said there'd been an incident.'

'Well sir, a man's body has been found near to where you went for a walk that morning, so we need to get as much detail as we can in about anything you may have seen.'

'Oh right' said Jack not knowing how he was expected to respond.

'Are you still there sir?'

'Yes still here, when do you want me to come in?'

Jack tried to sound confident, and hoped he'd given the impression of someone happy to help the police – as an innocent man would.

'Well as soon as you can, tomorrow morning?'

'Yes, fine, okay, tomorrow morning it is then.'

'Okay sir, say ten thirty. Just tell the officer on the desk you've come to see Chief Inspector Pownall.'

Jack said goodbye and put the receiver down, he felt angry.

All this because of some drugged up tosser trying to steal my phone, I know what I'd like to tell this Chief Inspector when I meet him. Jack took some deep breaths and tried to calm down.

Later he went to his board meeting but couldn't concentrate. He was largely unaware of the proceedings, concentrating instead on rehearsing his lines for his interview with the Chief Inspector.

When he got home, Rachel had made dinner, but Jack was preoccupied with meeting the police the following day and sat at the table moving his food around the plate, rather than eating. Rachel was talking to him, and when he didn't respond to a question she asked, Rachel got annoyed.

'Sorry Rach what was it you said?'

'You haven't listened to a word I've said all evening, and you've hardly eaten, what's wrong Jack?'

'Nothing, sorry, just thinking about the board meeting.'

'Well please leave business matters at the office. You're home now, and I don't like being ignored.'

'Sorry Rach. Oh, by the way, the police called this morning. They want me to go in tomorrow, to go over the statement I made. Seems they've found a body of a man near to where I walk the dog.'

'A body, my God?'

'Yes, shocking isn't it?'

'Did they say how he died?'

'No they didn't, but they did say it would be on the news so maybe we'll learn a bit more then.'

Jack would have given anything to be able to tell Rachel what had actually happened, but he couldn't. He couldn't put her in a situation where she might have to lie. He knew she wouldn't stand up well to any kind of interrogation. Not that she was weak, far from it, but Rachel always insisted on telling the truth and taking the consequences. Jack agreed in principle, but on this occasion, Jack thought his chances of getting out of this situation, and staying out of jail, would be much better, if he just kept things to himself.

The next morning, he skipped breakfast and got to the police station twenty minutes early. He went into the desk and asked for Chief Inspector Pownall.

'Ah yes,' said a young constable, 'he's expecting you. Follow me please, and I'll take you through to his office now.'

He lifted up the counter flap to let Jack through.

The inspector's office was neat and tidy. The inspector himself was well dressed in a grey suit, light blue shirt and a dark blue tie. He looked slim and fit, unlike the scruffy slobby detectives you saw on television, thought Jack. He was just finishing a phone call and waved Jack in, then gestured for him to take the seat in front of his desk. Jack saw he had a copy of his statement on his desktop with his personal card clipped to it.

The inspector finished his call.

'Mr Brandon I assume? Thanks for coming in. Sorry to trouble you.'

They shook hands, and he introduced himself as Chief Inspector Sammy Pownall.

'Not at all,' Jack said, always happy to help if I can.'

'I know you've spoken to one of my colleagues and already given your statement about what you saw that morning, so I'm sorry to trouble you again, but I presume you've now seen the news about the body we found?'

'Yes, I heard it on the news this morning.'

'Yes, well Mr Brandon, it looks as though the person we found may be one of the two men you saw on your walk on the morning of the 25th. Last Monday.'

'Oh really?' said Jack, hoping he had given the right impression of shock and surprise.

'Yes' the inspector carried on

'We think the two people you passed on your walk may have been a Mr Ezra Madaki and a Mr Alfred Campkin, the former being the one whose body we found. So apart from Alfie, sorry Mr Campkin, you might be the last person to have seen Madaki alive.'

'Oh,' said Jack again, thinking he'd better try to establish if they'd found Alfie, and what he'd told them about the events of that morning.

'Didn't I hear on the news that you were looking for his friend, er, this Alfie person? Have you managed to find him yet?'

'No sir, not so far, but we will, you can be sure that we will.'

'Right' Jack said, thinking what to say next.

The inspector then picked up his statement from his desk and asked if he'd mind if they went over it together. It merely stated that he'd seen these two people very early in the morning while out walking his dog and that they looked as if they might have been arguing. Jack had said he didn't take that much notice, but had given them a very vague impression of what they had looked like, approximate ages etc. The inspector asked a few more questions and seemed satisfied with the answers. Jack felt relieved, then the inspector said.

'I see you have a place in France?'

'Yes,' Jack said, realising that he'd seen his French address on the card he had handed to the policeman who'd first interviewed him.

'Yes,' Jack repeated, 'we'd only just come back from there the day before I went on my walk. You know, when I saw these two men.'

'Oh, right,' the Inspector said in a disinterested way. He went on.

'We haven't talked to Alfie Campkin yet, but we have managed to talk to some of his drinking pals, and he told them a really strange story.'

'Oh really,' said Jack, not wishing to be told the story. He had a good idea what it might be.

'Yes,' he went on, stroking his chin in a thoughtful way.

'Apparently, Alfie told them that that morning, Ezra tried to take a mobile phone off a man who was out walking through the fields with a dog. And that the man sprayed Ezra with some stuff that blinded him, then Kung Fu kicked him in the throat.'

Jack felt hot, then cold. He hoped the inspector couldn't see his discomfort. *Hold on,* he told himself, *this is the time you need to hold your nerve. Just think, prison, Rachel, the kids.*

'Are you feeling okay sir' asked the inspector.

'Yes I'm fine thanks,' Jack managed, 'been feeling a bit under the weather lately, and we had a very long business meeting yesterday, all takes its toll.'

'Yes, I'm sure it does Mr Brandon. So what do you make of this version of events?'

'Er, sorry, what version? Oh someone, what did you say, spraying them with something? I'm afraid I have no idea inspector.'

I take it you're not an exponent of the art of Kung Fu either?'

'No, couldn't box my way out of a paper bag, if the truth be told.'

Jack thought the less you say the better, so he said no more. He looked at the inspector and he held his gaze for a moment longer than felt comfortable, then the inspector said.

'I think you're being a bit modest on that score Mr Brandon.'

'Modest inspector?'

'Well, we naturally did a background check on you. Routine in such circumstances. And you have quite a distinguished military record it would seem. Saw action in the Falkland's, commended for exceptional acts of bravery in rescuing a unit in trouble, according to the records.'

'Yes, well, that was all a long time ago inspector. I'm afraid I couldn't knock the skin off a rice pudding these days, and as for the commendation, it was all a bit exaggerated. You know, just didn't realise what I was doing until I'd done it.'

The inspector looked at Jack thoughtfully.

'I assume you own a mobile phone Mr Brandon?'

'Well, yes I do, doesn't everyone these days?'

'And did you take it with you on your walk that particular morning?'

'Erm, can't recall particularly, but I always do unless it's on charge. One of those things you do without thinking isn't it?

'What's that Mr Brandon?'

'You know, pick up the phone when you go out.'

'Yes, I suppose it is.' The Inspector looked thoughtful again, and Jack prayed silently - no more questions, please.

His prayer was answered, and the Inspector seemed to come to a conclusion. He stood up and said.

'Well, thanks for coming in Mr Brandon. Sorry to have troubled you. We may need to talk to you again, and there may be some formalities to go through, depending on how this case develops.'

'How do you mean?' he asked.

'Well although it's formally described as a suspicious death at the moment, due to the nature of the injuries, it's likely to end up as either manslaughter or murder. So, if and when we charge someone, then you may be called as a witness. But nothing to worry about Mr Brandon, it'll all come out in the wash.'

They shook hands, and Jack left the station. He managed to drive home without causing a major traffic incident then went straight to the drinks cabinet and poured himself a large cognac, and gulped it down in one.

Back at the station Inspector Pownall pondered the interview he'd just had. *Rattled, Brandon was definitely rattled. The story about the boys being sprayed seem to bother him. If they had been sprayed with something, it could be Mace or a pepper spray, hard to buy in this country and illegal, but you can buy it over the counter in other European countries, and Brandon has a holiday home in France. Hmm,* thought Sammy, *wait till we get hold of Alfie, check out this story and then I'll maybe have another conversation with Mr Brandon.*

In the meantime, Sammy called forensics and asked for Alan Appleton.

'Hi Allen, Sammy Pownall here, yes fine thanks. The body in the field in Briarley, yes, I was wondering if you could tell if the victim had been sprayed with a pepper spray, or mace or something like that, residue on the face or eyes, that sort of thing?'

Appleton laughed.

'What's so funny?'

'No I shouldn't laugh, but our friend had been lying there on his back for over forty eight hours, in mild, if not warm weather, and there are a lot of hungry birds and rats, even insects that love soft tissue and the eyes are a particular favourite.'

'Okay' said Sammy, 'I get the picture, forget I asked.'

Gruesome buggers, wouldn't have that job for all the tea in China thought Sammy as he returned the phone handset to its cradle.

CHAPTER 22

arter stood at the end of the bed looking at the doctor as he read the clipboard. Alfie was drifting in and out of consciousness. *He couldn't move, but he didn't want to, he just wanted to stay in this nice warm blanket for the rest of his life.* It all went black again. The doctor began to read out loud.

'Severe head trauma caused by a blow with a blunt instrument, something like an iron bar. The patient also has severe bruising on seventy percent of his body, plus burns that appear to have been inflicted with a lit cigarette. My informal assumption is that he was tortured. The torturer or torturers beat him, probably with fists to begin with, by the look of the bruising. Then they burnt him repeatedly, with cigarettes, and finally hit him, again repeatedly over the head with a blunt instrument, and left him for dead.

That he survived at all, is a miracle. However I think that this man will never be able to function in any way that might be called normal. And for your purposes, he is extremely unlikely to ever be able to provide any information or evidence to you in the future. He'll be lucky if he ever wakes up, let alone speaks. In fact, if he's lucky he won't wake up, he'll die. I certainly wouldn't want to wake up in his condition. We've put him into an induced coma to alleviate his pain.'

Carter started to thank the doctor, but stopped as he saw some hesitation in the doctor's eyes.

'What?' said Carter.

'Well' said the doctor, 'he also has some other recent injuries, but they're not new enough to be attributable to this attack.'

'Go on.'

'He has lacerations on his arms and some on his face. They look like knife wounds, not very deep, but still nasty. From the state of the healing process, I'd say they were inflicted a week or so ago. And as the wounds are mostly on the underside of his forearms, they're consistent with defence wounds, when you hold your arms up to protect your face, that sort of thing. Anyway, perhaps not really relevant now for this poor devil, but I thought I'd mention it.'

'Thanks Doc.'

Carter called in.

'Hi Jim, Carter here, put me through to Sammy Pownall will you?' Carter waited.

He didn't relish telling Sammy about the state of their one and only potential witness. Sammy answered.

'Carter?'

'Sir.'

'I hope you're going to tell me you've found Alfie, or else I'll...'

Carter cut him off.

'Sir' yes sir, we've found Alfie but...'

Sammy's heart sank.

'But what Carter?' Sammy asked in a weary voice.

'Well sir, he's in hospital, someone used him as a punch bag. Well, it was more than punches, they tortured him with lighted cigarettes, then bashed his head in with an iron bar or similar.'

'And what state is he in?' asked Sammy.

'As bad as it gets sir, without actually dying. In fact, the doc said if it were him, he'd prefer not to be alive having sustained such damage.'

'Can he speak?'

'No sir, best guess is that he's going to be a human vegetable from now on. Might survive and still be alive, but only in a very limited meaning of the word. They've also put him into an induced coma to relieve the pain.'

'Shit – poor sod,' said Sammy, 'there goes our potential witness, *well the only witness we know about* thought Sammy.

That it?'

'Pretty much, although the Doc did say he had some other recent wounds as well, on his arms mainly, but some on his face. Could be defence wounds from a knife attack he thought.'

'Hmm, how old?'

'Bout a week, or so he reckoned.'

'Okay Carter, well done. Keep in touch with the hospital and let me know of any developments.'

'Will do sir.'

CHAPTER 23

Tom MacBride liked the Beatles, who didn't? He was playing the White album on his IPod, *but not with those silly bloody things stuck in your ears*, as Tom MacBride would say. No, he had it on full blast on his IPod docking station with some very expensive speakers attached. Lying by his pool in Marbella, with a large gin and tonic to keep him cool. The music transported him back to Manchester in the nineteen sixties. He was mentally singing along with the record *When I wake up early in the morning … Still missed that John Lennon. Bit of a funny bugger, different, bit caustic with the wit, but nothing wrong with that. Too much smarm these days.*

There was a gap in the music, changing to the next track. Tom heard the phone. He turned the volume down and answered.

'Tony, I hope you're calling to tell me you've found Alfie.'

'Yeah sort of, fact is, someone else found him first and beat the living shit out of him. The police found him in hospital in Blackpool and from what I've been able to find out so far, he's not going to be any help to them or us.'

'How so' asked Tom MacBride.

'He's only just alive. They say if he recovers he certainly won't be speaking. Serious brain damage.'

'Great,' said MacBride, 'any idea who did it?'

'None at all. The police were looking for him, and obviously, we were as well. Can't think why anyone else would, unless they knew about the stuff, but I'm sure we're watertight on that. I'm one thousand percent sure we have no leaks in our organisation. They all know the price for double crossing us. And, they know what the Chinese can do. I can't think who might have tortured Alfie.'

'Torture?' You didn't mention torture.'

'Sorry Tom, as well as being beaten, he was burnt with ciggies, and in some very interesting parts of his body by all accounts.'

Hard as Tom MacBride was, he winced.

'That changes things Tony.'

Apart from the information on our little operation, what else would Alfie know that would be worth torturing him for? Have you still got your friend in the filth' Tom MacBride asked.

'Certainly have Tom, I was out with him only last week. We had a great night out, met some very expensive girls, and you paid for the lot.'

'Well its payback time now, so get on to him and find out all they know about Ezra and Alfie, and anyone else involved, then we'll decide what, and possibly who, we're going to do!'

CHAPTER 24

The next few days were uncomfortable for Jack. He was losing weight at a rate of knots. Previously he'd tried everything to slim down, and just about kept to being what they used to call "portly". Now he felt he could start a new dead cert diet trend, - *"Want to lose weight? Easy, kill someone, and the pounds just drop off!"* His clothes felt they were a bit big for him now, and his face had thinned down. When he looked in the mirror, he caught a glimpse of the slim young man he'd once been, albeit now, somewhat more haggard.

Rachel was worried. Jack was short tempered and snapped at the least thing, then felt guilty and apologised. He woke up in the night and wondered if it had all been a nightmare, but realised it was real. He still went on his morning walk with Bess, but took her to the football fields instead. Not as enjoyable as his country walk, but he just didn't feel like going anywhere near that place.

The call came in the late afternoon. Rachel answered the phone. Jack had been absorbed by the monthly figures his business. For a brief spell, he'd mercifully about it, and even though he'd been police to call again, the shout fro go weak at the knees.

'A chief inspector Pownall wants to know if you're home.'

'I'll pick it up here Rach,' Jack said, picking up the extension in his study.

Sound as casual as you can, he told himself.

'Hello Chief Inspector.'

'Oh hello Mr Brandon, sorry to disturb you again so soon, but there's been a development and I wonder if you could come down to the station Or I can come to see you at your home, if that's more convenient.'

'No no,' he said. The last thing he needed was to have his private space invaded by the police.

'When would you like me to come in?' he asked.

'Well, I was hoping you could come right away You see, we've found Alfie Campkin.'

Oh shit no, just what I need. He sat down with a thump in his office chair.

'Are you still there sir?'

'What, oh yes, sorry, the dog just jumped up at me. Er, yes I'll come down now.'

'Thank you Mr Brandon, much appreciated.'

Jack put the phone down, and tried to pull himself together. He wondered if they'd have Alfie there to ontradict his version of events. My God, he thought, could

"ly stand there and claim that I was telling the truth in

meone who knew I was lying through my teeth?

ry hard about lying in front of someone who knows

ought, and Jack wasn't sure he could

pull it off. *Maybe he'd be better off telling the truth and taking the consequences. But, am I prepared for the consequences?*

'What was that about Jack, why are the police calling you again?'

'I don't know, they say there's been some sort of development, and they'd like to speak to me again.'

'Jack, is there something you're not telling me?'

'No of course not Rachel, you know what the police are like? Perhaps it would've been better not to have said anything to them at all.'

Rachel looked at Jack.

'There's something going on here, I can feel it, but I'll wait till you're ready to tell me.'

'Honestly Rachel, there's nothing I promise.'

Rachel gave him a look and left the room muttering about emptying the dishwasher.

Jack felt distraught. He hadn't fooled Rachel, and he was going to have to tell her, but not just yet.

CHAPTER 25

Jay sat looking through the armoured screen at his visitor. Vince was on edge, and it showed. A small nervous tick twitched by his right eye as he told his story.

'Rick's boys found Alfie before anyone else did.'

'How do you mean anyone else? I thought the only others looking for Alfie were the filth?'

'Well it seems that there was at least one other party asking around, maybe two, and they definitely weren't the police.'

'Hmm' said Jay 'guess that would be MacBride's boys?'

Mickey went on.

'Well the boys gave this Alfie man a hard time, and they're sure they got everything out of him.

'You absolutely sure they got everything?'

'I'm sure.' They roughed him up pretty bad, in fact, I think they may have gone a bit over the top.'

'What do you mean, "over the top"?'

'Well' said Mickey, 'they nearly killed the man.'

'So what?' said Jay, 'did they find out who killed my little brother or not?'

Little brother now? He was 'shit for brains' before he knew he was killed.

'Well yes and no.'

'Don't give me that fuckin yes or no shit,' shouted Jay.

The guard came striding over.

'Careful' said Mickey, 'stop raising your voice Jay, you know what they're like, they'll take you back to the cells'

'What's all the noise about?'

'Sorry,' said Jay, 'man here just told me some bad news, personal stuff.'

'Well, any more noise and you go back down, pronto. You got five minutes left, so I'd make the most of them if I were you.'

'Right, sorry mate, eh, sir. Now Mickey, no more fuckin word games.'

'Okay, he told the boys that they were on some sort of job, him and Ezra. Simple stuff but well paid. Just had to collect some stuff and drop it off. Nice job and no hassle, but Ezra's phone went dead, and he went mad. Said he needed a phone otherwise they were in the shit, then they came across this man out walking his dog, and Ezra tried to nick his phone, but the man knocked him out with some sort of spray, then kicked him in the throat and killed him. That's what Alfie said, and the boys swear he wasn't lyin'.'

Jay was quiet for a while.

'So who's this man, the man who did Ezra?'

'Don't know Jay, but after he'd offed Ezra, he cut Alfie on the face and arms, then gave him Ezra's money wad and told him to piss off and disappear. I know it sounds funny, but the boys worked on him for hours, but couldn't get him to change his story.'

'So you're telling me that some fucker out walking his dog, sorted out two hard lads, and killed Ezra?'

'That's what Alfie said, but I've been thinkin' an' what's really peculiar is the man cutting Alfie like that then givin' him the money. Seems to me he was setting Alfie up, makin' it look like he an Ezra had been in a fight. Can't think why else he'd do what he did.'

Jay sat in silence while he thought about what Mickey had said.

'And what were they picking up, as if I couldn't guess?'

'The boys didn't get much more than I've said. This Alfie said that Ezra regularly spoke to a guy called Tony Malone, presumably MacBride's guy, and he thought he was the person who organised the job, but that's all he knew. He said Ezra just took him along to help. He said he thought it was drugs of some sort, and plenty as well, all in a rucksack. But then the boys went a bit overboard, and the guy ended up not being able to speak anymore after a while.'

Jay sat in silence thinking.

'Did the pigs say anything about the drugs?'

'No, that's the funny thing, they usually say if they've found stuff, you know "Body found and drugs recovered with a street value of a million quid", and all that sort of shit.'

'Then the man walking the dog had to be a pro,' said Jay 'nothing else makes sense. Ezra might not have been the hardest or brightest man in the world, but he could look after hiself, so it had to be a pro, and that makes sense about the stuff not being found. The dog man knew about the drop, offed Ezra, took the stuff and framed this Alfie man. I almost like this guy, stealin' MacBride's shit an all, however, he did kill my little brother in the process, and that was his big mistake. You find out who the dog man was that killed Ezra and we might even get our hands on MacBride's shit as well. Now that would be sweet. We need to put this on contract. I don't want it coming back to my door, I'm in enough shit trouble already, so find out who we can get and what it's gonna to cost. You'll need to tell whoever, that this man sounds like a pro and is probably connected. But whatever happens, I want him topped for killing my bro, right? The drugs come as a bonus, got that Mickey?'

'Got that Jay.'

The bell rang to signal the end of visiting time. Jay got up and walked towards the door leading to the cells.

CHAPTER 26

Chief Inspector Sammy Pownall put the phone down after speaking with Jack Brandon and sat at his desk contemplating. Brandon seemed rattled by the news that they'd found Alfie, why? And he had the distinct feeling that Brandon hadn't told him the whole truth about what he saw that morning. But how could Brandon be involved in Madaki's death?

He just couldn't imagine any previous connection between Brandon and Madaki or Campkin. *There is, of course, his admitted sighting that morning of two men fitting their descriptions, so was there more to it than just a vague sighting, but what? How could Brandon have become involved with them and why? Could Brandon be the killer? No it's too ridiculous, but then what about Alfie's story, the spray, the kung-fu kick, why would Alfie make up such a story.*

On the face of it, Alfie and Ezra had a fight, evidenced by the wounds on Alfie's arms definitely the most likely explanation and yet…. Just as well not to have told Brandon that Alfie wasn't going to be any use as a witness. No, let him sweat a bit, there's still an outside chance that Brandon was involved in some way, so let's see how he stands up to some more interrogation.

Pownall greeted Jack amicably when he entered his office, and waived him into the same chair he'd occupied previously. No Alfie on show so far thought Jack.

'I've asked you to come in to tell you about the findings of the post-mortem and the pathology reports before we release them to the news media people. It seems that Ezra Madaki, the man whose body we found, suffocated, well that's what killed him in technical terms. But the pathologist says that the suffocation was probably due to a blow to the throat, which caused severe swelling that damaged the larynx and blocked the airway, thereby causing death by suffocation.

He's not absolutely certain, but with the available evidence, that seems to be the only logical conclusion. Ideally, we need a sound witness who can tell us precisely what happened that morning, and why. Until then, it will remain as a suspicious death until we can prove what went on, one way or another.'

'I see,' Jack said, trying to keep his voice steady

'I also wanted to ask you again about this story that Alfie is supposed to have told his pals about. If you remember, he claimed that some man spayed Ezra with something that blinded him.'

Pownall looked at Jack intently.

Jack was about to answer, but suddenly thought about the way the Inspector had phrased the question. *If he'd got the story directly from Alfie, he would have said Alfie's told us, or Alfie claims that you sprayed Ezra, or something like that, so it sounded as if for some reason Alfie hadn't made such a claim yet, at least not directly to the police, how peculiar. Something not right.*

'Sorry Inspector, as I said the last time you mentioned this. I don't know anything about anyone spraying anyone with anything. I've told you all I know about seeing those two men, and...'

Pownall cut him off.

'Yes Mr Brandon, I remember what you told us, it's just that the story strikes me as a bit odd, doesn't it strike you as odd Mr Brandon?'

'Well I suppose so, but then again farmers do a lot of spraying of crops and things at this time of year, so perhaps someone's got their stories muddled up.' *Where on earth did I get that from?* Jack could see he'd managed to put some doubt in the inspector's mind about the story, to maybe even enough to discredit it.

'Hmm, interesting theory,' said Pownall.

Jack decided to go for broke and spoke with a confidence that amazed himself.

'Presumably, you've asked this Alfie, so what does he say?' Hoping against hope that the inspector wasn't about to march Alfie in and tell Jack to ask him himself. The Inspector sighed inwardly and knew he had no choice but to reveal the state of play. After all, it wouldn't be too long before it was on the news and in the papers.

'Yes, that would be the obvious thing to do', said the inspector, 'but, well, I'm afraid Alfie isn't in a fit state to speak at the moment.'

'Oh,' Jack said, trying to understand what he was being told, 'Can't speak?'

'Well,' said Pownall, 'can't do anything at all much, except breathe. Beaten to a pulp, poor soul.'

'What, why would he be beat him up?' Jack asked lamely.

'Don't know yet,' said Pownall, 'but for the time being, it seems we've lost our witness to what went on in that field. So we're no nearer knowing why, and how Ezra Madaki died. That is, unless you know more than you've told us already Mr Brandon?'

Jack felt hot and his heart rate accelerated. He hoped his discomfort at the question wasn't too obvious. *Keep calm and summon up some righteous indignation or you're lost, but don't overdo it.*

'I'm sorry Inspector, what did you say?'

The inspector looked meaningfully at Jack.

'I'm asking you if you've told us everything you saw, everything you know about that morning Mr Brandon?'

'You're suggesting that I'm lying Inspector?', if so could you tell me why you think I would? I simply told your officer what I saw that morning, in an effort to be helpful, and now I'm sat here being accused of telling lies. Quite frankly, Inspector, I don't know what to say, should I get a lawyer, what exactly are you suggesting?'

'Calm down Mr Brandon, I have to ask awkward questions, and I'm not suggesting anything or accusing you of anything. I just have to be sure as I can, that you've told us everything you know.'

'Do I take that as an apology?' said Jack trying not to sound too haughty.

'I'm sorry if I offended you. But the fact is, I have a dead body and no satisfactory explanation as to how this man died. Apart from Alfie Campkin, you may be the last person to have seen him alive.'

Jack was thinking on his feet now and decided he might as well find out when this Alfie character was likely to recover.

'Well presumably, you'll be able to find out more when this unfortunate man Alfie recovers, so when do you expect that to be?'

The inspector knew that Jack would get to know about the extent of Alfie's injuries, once the news leaked out to the press etc., so he decided to come clean.

'Well, it may be that Alfie never fully recovers I'm afraid, not sufficiently to be of any use as a witness anyway.'

Jack tried to contain the euphoria he felt, and immediately felt guilty at benefitting from the beaten man's condition.

'Oh I see,' was all Jack could think of to say.

'But that's not all I'm afraid.' The Inspector continued.

'Oh' said Jack

'there's more?' *What now?*

'Yes, I'm afraid I have some disturbing news for you.'

'What, what news?' Now Jack was confused and not a little scared again.

Jack felt he was on a roller coaster, one minute he was off the hook and the next he was back in trouble.

'Well, my lads have picked up on some talk amongst the criminal fraternity, suggesting there's some sort of contract out on you.'

'What!?' this time Jack got up out of the chair, then slowly sat down again.

'Yes, it looks as though someone is blaming you for Ezra Madaki's death, and is out for revenge.'

'Why would anyone blame me? I mean....' Jack ran out of words.

Of course, they would blame me. I'd killed Ezra. But how did they know. No one knew what actually happened, other than Alfie. The penny dropped.

'Who beat Alfie up?' Jack asked.

'Don't know but they didn't just beat him up, they tortured him as well.'

So, thought Jack, *whoever tortured Alfie now presumably had the real story, at least enough of the story to know it was me who'd killed the man. They wouldn't know it was an accident, or self-defence. I'd been the cause of his death, and someone wanted revenge.*

The inspector continued.

'The contract could be something to do with what they were doing that morning. The only other thing I can think of, is that Ezra's brother Jay Madaki, might have some sort of revenge motive. It's well known that the brothers weren't exactly close, in fact, it's said they detested each other, but you can never tell where families are concerned, blood thicker than water and all that sort of stuff.

And I don't suppose he'd have been too pleased at hearing his brother had been killed. Now if Ezra was bad, he was a saint compared to his brother Jay. Jay Madaki personifies the word psychopath. However, he's locked up in prison at the moment, but that wouldn't necessarily stop him putting out a contract on someone, if he really wanted to.'

Jack sat there in horror. *This wasn't happening. All because of his decision that morning to get up early instead of turning over and cuddling up to Rachel.* Jack had rarely felt so low in his life. Pownall gave him a minute then said.

'Are you sure there isn't anything else you want to tell me?'

Jack shook his head, looked up and said.

'Surely you can help me? Surely you can't just let people pay someone to harm someone, or murder them, without doing anything about it? Why don't you arrest somebody or something?'

'Well unfortunately Mr Brandon, we don't have any real evidence that there is a serious threat, nor does a "contract", necessarily mean murder. It's just street talk at the moment and believe me. If we had any credible evidence of anyone arranging such a thing, we would investigate and make arrests as appropriate, but at the moment there's far too little to go on.'

'What about witness protection and all that sort of stuff?' Jack asked hoping he didn't sound too desperate.

'Yes I've thought about that, but at the moment, you're not a witness in a case against anyone. You're just a chap who happened to see someone shortly before his death, but you're not a witness to a crime as such. So there's no legitimate way you could enter a witness protection programme.'

'Isn't there anything you can do?' Jack asked.

Pownall looked sympathetically at him.

'Yes, of course, we'll do our best, arrange regular patrols past your house, keep our eyes and ears open for any unusual activity and try to establish just how real the threat might be. We'll also put the word around, so the bad lads will know that we know, and we'll let it be known that if you do come to any harm, we'll know who to come looking for. We don't, but they won't know that. And remember, emotions cool down, and people re-evaluate what it's going to cost them if anything is traced back to them. So if the threat is real now, then given time, we may find that it's, in effect, withdrawn, or at least reduced.'

'What do you mean 'reduced?'

'Well, let's say someone at the moment is, and this is only speculation at this stage, but, that someone wants you dead, then they may well consider that it's not worth the candle and be satisfied with a bit of rough stuff.'

'You mean a beating?'

'Well yes, I suppose I do.'

'And that's what Alfie got is it, a little mild beating and now by the sound of it he'd be better off dead.'

'I'm really sorry about this Mr Brandon, we do our best, but we can't make everything as it should be, Lord that we could. Don't you have a place in France?'

'Yes,' Jack said miserably.

'Well, why don't you go there for a while, at least until things cool down? Might be the best thing in the circumstances. We'll keep in touch and let you know any developments of course. I assume your house here is well secured, burglar alarms, security light and all that?'

'Yes' said Jack, still trying to evaluate what he'd just been told.

There was nothing left to say so Jack left the inspector's office and went to his car, already looking over his shoulder.

He went home and decided he couldn't keep it from Rachel any longer. Apart from anything else, she had to know now that there was a threat against him – and not just him he realised. Any 'contract' would include his nearest and dearest, he knew that.

He asked Rachel to sit down and told her everything, well not quite everything, but all the bits that mattered. He told her about the confrontation with the two men and how he'd badly injured one of them in self defence.

Rachel stood up.

'Badly injured? How badly injured?'

'Well about as badly injured as you can be.'

'You mean dead don't you, you mean you killed a man?'

'It was self-defence Rach, I didn't mean to kill him but he was coming at me with a knife, and I kicked him. I didn't mean to kill him but....'

Jack didn't finish the sentence as Rachel had collapsed into the chair with her head in her hands sobbing. He found a box of tissues and handed them to her. Her makeup was streaked with tears but she recovered her composure enough to speak.

'I don't understand any of this, what were these men doing out there, why would they pull a knife on you?'

'It was something to do with drugs,' Jack started to explain, but Rachel interrupted.

'Drugs! In the middle of the Cheshire countryside at that time in the morning?'

'I know it all sounds crazy Rachel, but this man demanded my phone, and he wasn't taking no for an answer. He came at me with a knife.'

'Why didn't you just give him the fucking phone?' Rachel's voice was raised to almost a scream.

'It was just one of those spur of the moment things, I thought he might kill me even if I did give him the phone, I don't know Rachel, it all happened so quickly. I suppose my old army training isn't quite as dead as I thought it was, I just reacted on instinct.'

Rachel was silent for a few beats.

'Go on.'

'Well, I sort of made it look as though the other one had done it. You know, as though the two of them had had a fight, then I let this other one go.'

'Made it look as though the other one had done it?' Rachel said her voice rising as she tried to comprehend what Jack was telling her.

'What on earth, why didn't you just call the police and tell them what had happened?'

'It wasn't as simple as that Rachel. The way it happened, I'd used one of the pepper sprays, you know one of the ones I bought after we'd been mugged in France? so I thought I'd be in trouble, serious trouble. I thought I might go to prison, murder, manslaughter whatever. You know what they're like these days, criminals have more rights than ordinary people. What about that man who shot the burglars, that Martin guy, they sent him down for years. I'm not going to go to prison for something that wasn't my fault Rachel, I was only out walking the fucking dog!'

By now, Jack had become angry at the injustice of it all. He looked at Rachel and saw how shocked she was. He went to her and put his arms around her, she put her head on his shoulder, and he stroked her hair, his voice now gentle.

'If I could turn the clock back Rachel I would, but I can't, and I have to deal with things as they are. If I go to the police now and tell them the truth, I'll go to prison for sure.'

'So what did you tell the police?'

'I told them I saw these men when I was out walking the dog and that they were arguing, that's all.'

'Is that it, have you told me everything.'

Jack hesitated.

'You haven't, have you? There's more, I can tell.'

'Well the police say that someone thinks I might have killed the man, and they've.., well they've put some sort of contract out on me.'

Rachel's face had turned a deathly white.

'Contract? You mean someone's being paid to kill you?! I can't believe this, it's like we've been transported into some nightmare gangster movie. Who is it? I don't understand, how did you find out there's this "contract" out on you?'

'The police told me when I went to see them this morning. They said that someone must think I was responsible for killing the man they found in the field. They said they didn't know who might have arranged it, and it was just a rumour at the moment, but they thought I should take it seriously. They even suggested we consider going away, until things blow over. The detective says that the dead man has a brother who's in jail, but he might have arranged the contract. He didn't know for sure though.'

'Can't the police do anything?'

'Apparently not. I've been over that with them, and they say if they knew who it was they'd sort it, but for now, all they can do is try to increase patrols near our house and keep their ears open, that sort of thing.'

'What are we going to do Jack?'

Rachel's distress was hard for Jack to take. He felt guilty for having put his wife in harm's way. Thankfully, he thought, the children were far enough away not to be in any danger.

'We're going to go away Rachel, and hope things blow over. The police say that given time, whoever it is may cool down and decide it's not worth it, so let's hope they're right.

'Where will we go, France?' asked Rachel now a bit more composed,

'That's what people will think. But I think we should go a long way away from this nightmare and in time I'm sure it will all pass.'

Jack wished he genuinely believed what he was saying.

Rachel managed a faint smile.

'When should we go?'

'As soon as we can pack and sort out the plane tickets. I'll book it on line direct with the airline then no one will know where we're planning to go. Let's hope Mrs Anderson's free to look after the house and the animals.'

Mrs Anderson was a no fuss Scottish woman. A widow, who lived in the next street, but moved into the Brandon's house whenever they went to their home in France. She loved looking after the house, and she loved Bess and the cat Angel. She also liked the cash Jack paid her, and he felt she was worth every penny, especially when they decided to go away at short notice.

'You make the arrangements with Mrs Anderson' Jack said to Rachel, 'and I'll tidy up things here, make sure we don't leave anything with names and contact addresses in. And don't tell anyone where we're going, not even the kids, let Mrs Anderson think we're going to France and tell her we'll email the kids when we get to where we're going.'

'Okay Jack, but I can't tell anyone anyway, you haven't even told me where we're going.'

CHAPTER 27

They cleared immigration at Orlando Airport, and went to wait for their bags to appear on the luggage carousel. While they waited, they watched as customs officers wandered through the baggage hall with sniffer dogs. They eventually claimed their bags from the carousel, walked through customs then put their bags on to a conveyer whilst Jack and Rachel went on the monorail for the short journey to the main terminal.

Reunited with their luggage, they went outside and after a short wait, boarded a courtesy coach which took them to the Hertz car hire collection point on Butler Avenue. The rental car was waiting for them, and with the minimum of fuss, they were on their way.

Once they were in the car and driving Jack felt they were safe. They'd flown direct from Manchester on Virgin. Jack had booked them in Upper Class. One, because he wanted Rachel to have the best. And two, because, as there were relatively few people in Upper, it would be much easier to spot if anyone was following them. Jack didn't think whoever was supposed to be after him, would really follow them to Florida, but, he thought, better to be safe than sorry. He hadn't seen any sign of anyone showing any particular interest in them on board and had gradually relaxed and enjoyed the rest of the flight as best as he could in the circumstances. *Can't see how anyone would know our travel plans anyway.*

Jack was absolutely sure they weren't followed to Hertz but still felt a huge relief when they got into their car and drove away from the car hire depot. He hadn't booked any accommodation in advance to eliminate any possibility of anyone knowing where they were going to stay.

They drove for a while and were soon heading towards Naples on the west coast of Florida. As they drove, Rachel said

'I think I can guess where we're going to stay.'

'Sorry I didn't tell you before, but I thought it best to keep my options open in case things changed.'

'I assume it's the Moonlight Inn' she said smiling broadly.

'Correct.'

They'd stayed at the Moonlight Inn a few times in the past, and its relaxed familiarity was just what Jack thought they needed. He also knew all the escape routes should they need to get away fast, but he hoped that all his planning, or lack of it as far as booking a hotel was concerned, meant they were safe and that no one could trace their whereabouts.

Jack had booked their airline seats and car hire directly online, so that there was no travel agent to tell anyone about their booking. But then he realised that if someone gained access to his credit card records, they might be able to find out which airline and car hire company he'd booked with, and it wouldn't take much more effort to discover where they'd flown to. So Jack had taken what cash he could lay his hands on, about seven thousand pounds, so he didn't have to use his credit cards once he got to Florida.

Maybe I'm being over cautious he thought, but he suspected that people with the right resources and clout could monitor his credit card transactions, providing them with a virtual road map of their journey and destination, something he was desperate to avoid.

Once they were out of the city limits of Orlando they drove west towards Tampa Bay, then turned south, passing by Sarasota, Venice then Fort Myers and on down to Naples. The sun was shining, and the traffic was light. They listened to the radio and temporarily forgot about the trouble they were in. They talked a lot about their first trip to Florida when they took the kids to Disney World - happy, uncomplicated days.

They arrived at the Moonlight Inn and presented themselves at the reception desk. The desk clerk remembered Jack and Rachel and greeted them warmly. He was a bit perplexed about Jack paying cash and not having made a reservation in advance, but he was happy enough. They asked for an Efficiency room, overlooking the Naples Bay. That meant they could cook simple meals in their room and had less need to go out. Jack felt able to relax a little for the first time in a while. When they got into the room, he set up his laptop and emailed their children to tell them that they'd decided to take a last minute holiday to

Florida. Then, exhausted by the journey, and the added tension of worrying about being followed, they both went to bed and slept soundly for nearly twelve hours.

The next day after breakfast, Jack checked with the front desk to make sure no one had enquired if they were booked in. No one had. He went back to the room and made coffee for them both, then he and Rachel went to the beach for a long walk. The sea air and the early morning sunshine were a tonic, and they felt refreshed and ready to think about how they might move forward. Jack had developed an idea of what he thought they should do next.

'I think we need professional help, someone with experience.'

'And where are we going to find someone like that Jack?'

'Well, I was thinking a private detective. We can't go the police, there's no crime committed yet anyway. And they'd think we were just nut cases or paranoid. Let's start with Yellow pages, call someone and see what we come up with, we've got nothing to lose?

Rachel wasn't convinced, but she agreed they needed to do something.

Jack looked through the phone book and was spoilt for choice. He called several detective agencies, but most of his calls were answered by receptionists who invariably wanted more details, before putting him through to anyone. Jack didn't feel able to explain their predicament to a receptionist, so he kept calling until he came across one where the detective himself answered.

'Ramsay Investigations, Dave Ramsay speaking, how can I help you?'

Jack liked the voice, a bit weary but it had a nice timbre. Funny how you can instinctively know you're likely to get along with someone just by listening to their voice thought Jack.

'Hello,' said Jack 'we're over here from the UK and we need some advice on a personal security matter. Is that something you can help us with?'

'Well that depends on a number of things, and I'll obviously need some more details, but I'm not overly busy at the moment, so why don't we meet up, and you can tell me what it is I might be able to help you with?'

'Okay,' Jack said, 'I'll come to your office if that's all right with you,' not wishing to reveal where they were staying, not yet anyway.

'You in Naples?' he said.

'Yes,' Jack replied

'Then come to 1156 Pine Ridge Boulevard. You coming now?'

'Yes' said Jack, 'I'll be there in half an hour.'

'Okay, you'd better tell me your name.'

'Brandon, Jack Brandon.'

'Okay Mr Brandon, my name's Dave Ramsay, and I'll see you shortly.'

Jack related the conversation to Rachel, and she agreed it would be better for Jack to go to meet with this man on his own, to begin with.

The weather was lovely and sunny, so he suggested Rachel stay and sunbathe. He walked with her down to the hotel pool and left her in the company of a stylish elderly couple they'd exchanged greetings with that morning. She should be safe enough there thought Jack.

The couple must have been in their eighties, possibly nineties. The wife was quite slim and very glamorous despite her great age. Her slightly rotund husband was sat at the table with a glass in his hand, contentedly smoking a huge Cuban cigar. Jack told Rachel he'd be as quick as he could and waved as he left to find Mr Dave Ramsay. As he walked away, he wondered if he and Rachel might live to be that old and to still be able to enjoy life as much as the old couple seemed to.

CHAPTER 28

The plane touched down at Manchester, and Tom MacBride looked out of the window through the pouring rain. A bit different to the warm Mediterranean sunshine he'd left behind. He could see the Air China jet parked on the tarmac and smiled.

'Thank you for flying Monarch today, we know you had a choice of airlines....'

MacBride tuned out of the stewardess's voice prattling on and wondered if Malone had made any headway with his couple million quidsworth of gear they'd lost, or hopefully only temporarily lost. The next shipment from China was due in three weeks' time, and they'd had to find a new location to make the drop. Same plan, just a bit of a problem finding another big field remote enough, but not too far from the airport, and not too far from the farm.

Tom had devised the original plan. It was just so simple, it really tickled him every time he thought about it. Malone met him in the arrivals hall, took his luggage and they walked to the Bentley. Malone drove, and Tom sat in the passenger seat. When they were out of the airport and on the motorway, Malone relaxed and started to give Tom an update on the situation.

'I assume you're up to speed on the Betting Shop business, and the security outfit?'

'Yes thanks Tony, everything looks fine. I've got board meetings this week to go through the figures and stuff in more detail, but generally speaking the betting business and Quadrant Security look to be in good shape.'

'And the recycling business?' Malone asked.

'Well' said Tom MacBride, 'looks like we're going to have to downsize it for the time being. It'll all come back in time, but this recession's going to last another year or so at least, and it's having more impact on recycling than the other two businesses. Funny, but with money short, you'd think gambling and nightclubs would suffer, but no, the good old British public have got used to having a good time and they ain't stopping 'cos of some pesky recession.'

The rain was coming down so hard Malone felt obliged to slow down as the spray from the road was limiting his vision.

'Good old Manchester weather,' said Tom MacBride, then continued, 'okay, so give me an update on the main event, any progress with your pal in the police?'

'Not much. He says they don't really know any more than they did before. Madaki's death is still officially described as a suspicious death, but they know he was killed, but they don't know why. They can't call it murder yet as they haven't got enough definitive evidence yet. They know he was with his mate Alfie, when whatever happened, happened. And, that Alfie did a runner. They eventually found Alfie some time later, in Blackpool of all places, but he'd been beaten and tortured, and by all accounts was as good as dead. My pal told me that they've been told by the doctors, he's unlikely to recover at all, and if he does, it's unlikely he'll be in any condition to say what happened. So, the police don't have any information about what the two of them were up to, but they don't think they were out walking for the good of their health. They also found some wounds on Alfie, which might suggest that Ezra and Alfie had a fight, and that Alfie might have killed Ezra, but they don't really buy that.'

Tom MacBride listened and nodded as Malone talked.

'The one witness they do have, is a guy called Brandon, Jack Brandon. Says he was out with his dog and that two men matching the description of Ezra and Alfie passed him on his walk. No mention of a rucksack or anything. The cause of Ezra's death was,' he consulted his notes, 'suffocation or asphyxiation due to severe trauma to the neck. That's about it.'

'Hmm,' said MacBride, 'this witness, Brandon, what's he do for a living?'

'He's in the property business, respectable, and my pal says, he's never been in trouble. Has a military background, Captain in the army, clean as a whistle on the face of it, no record or anything.'

'But,' said Tom MacBride sensing some hesitation.

'Well, this is where it gets interesting. Someone is gunning for Mr Brandon. Some serious people are looking for him.'

'How do you mean, who's looking for him?'

'Don't know who, but word on the street says there's a contract out on him.'

The traffic was getting busier as they got nearer to Manchester and Malone slowed down some more. *No need to rush in a Bentley anyway, unseemly.*

'Interesting, why would anyone put a contract out on an innocent witness, unless maybe someone's found out he's not so innocent? The only people who would have reason to go after this guy would be us if we believed he nicked our stuff, but we don't have any reason to think that do we?'

'Nope we don't,' said Malone, 'but if he didn't, who did?' *It just doesn't add up. I've checked every way I know how to, and there's no way this Brandon guy is a player.'

'So where is our Mr Brandon now?'

Malone braked to avoid a boy racer who'd slipped in between him and the car in front.

'Well, my man tells me that DCI Pownall tipped him off about the possibility that someone was out to do him some harm, and he's very sensibly scarpered.'

'And do we know where he's scarpered to?'

'No' said Malone, 'according to my friend, he's got a place in France, so he's maybe gone there. We managed to speak with the old bird who's looking after his house, but she says he didn't say where he was going, just that he'd be gone for quite a while.'

'Well,' said MacBride, 'you'd better see if you can find out where our Mr Brandon's gone to.'

Tom MacBride looked out of the window again.

'Looks like the rain's easing off,' he said, then stroked his chin, thinking.

After a while he said.

'Who would put out a contract on Brandon, and why? It has to be business or personal, and we know it's not business, 'cos we're the only ones involved in that respect. So it has to be personal. That being the case,' Tom MacBride continued as if talking to himself,

'The only one who might be thought of as being personally involved is Jay Madaki, 'cos it's his brother Ezra who was killed, right?'

'Right,' said Malone.

'So it was probably Jay's goons who worked Alfie over, and whatever they beat out of him, made Jay believe that it was this Brandon man who killed Ezra.'

'Could be, makes sense' said Malone.

Tom MacBride thought some more.

'So if Jay's decided, despite treating his brother like shit all his life, that someone has to be punished, for knocking him off, then however unlikely it is, maybe our Mr Brandon does know where our stuff is. Maybe he's not so innocent after all?'

'You could well be right Tom,' said Malone, 'seems unlikely, but hard to see it any other way. What do you want me to do?'

'Well, try to find out where Brandon is, obviously, and find out who the hitmen are. Maybe play follow the leader and see if they lead can lead us to where Brandon is?'

'I'll get on to it right away Tom.'

They'd arrived at Tom MacBride's betting shop headquarters. Malone pulled into the kerb. It had stopped raining.

'Okay Tony anything else I need to know about?'

'Just that Harry was on to say, he'll see you and Esther at the Lord Mayor's Ball tomorrow night.'

'Okay, I'll take a taxi back home after I've finished here, so keep the car for tonight and pick me up from home in the morning, eight thirty.'

Tom MacBride got out of the car and Malone drove off deep in thought.

CHAPTER 29

The business arrangement between Tom MacBride and Harry Antrobus had thrived, and Harry had taken to the 'processing' business like a duck to water. Security at his farm was tight but discreet with the processing area located well away from his Marquee Hire business. The only problem Harry had was how to hide the wealth the drugs business created, but this was overcome by some clever accountancy work which laundered the illicit funds through the marquee hire business.

Tom MacBride and Harry socialised on a regular basis, and much to the pleasure of their wives they had become sought after guests at many of the notable social events in Manchester, and the fashionable suburbs. As both men had now become seriously wealthy, they decided it would be only proper to contribute to the less well off in society, and both made generous donations to various local charities and the police charities.

The fact that such apparent unstinting largess had the effect of developing valuable personal relationships with many of the leading movers and shakers in the local business world, was, after all, just a spin-off, but extremely useful. From time to time, at various charity dinners and balls, they would be introduced to visiting dignitaries as "leading Manchester businessmen" and "pillars of the community".

Tom and Harry had taken particular pleasure in becoming friends with the Chief Constable Eric Parr, though they were less enthusiastic about his new Assistant Chief Constable Colin Neale, who was introduced to them at the Lord Mayor's Ball.

'These are a couple of our esteemed Manchester businessmen Colin, this is Harry Antrobus, tent hire isn't it Harry?' The Chief Constable said winking at Harry as he said it.

'Marquee hire if you don't mind Eric,' he said back, in mock offence, and shook Colin Neale's hand.

And this is Tom MacBride, who amongst other things has a bookies business and a security business.'

Tom shook hands with Assistant Chief Constable Neale.

'Yes I've heard about your outfit, Quadrant Security isn't it? You have quite a presence in the city,' said Neale.

'Yes we do,' said Tom, surprised that the ACC knew about his business.

'Been checking up on me have we?' Tom said in as jovial a manner as he could muster.

'You could say that Tom,' said the ACC in a meaningful way.

What on earth does he mean, he can't know anything about our other activities. The man's just fishing, I can guess what's coming next.

The Chief Constable moved away, talking to Harry. As soon as they were out of earshot, the new ACC made his play and suggested that he was "always available" should Tom need any "consultancy" work doing. Tom said he'd think about it, and moved away feigning the need to visit the loo. Later on in the evening, it became clear that the man didn't intend to take no for an answer, and cornered Tom by the side of the bar as he went for a top up. The ACC dived straight in.

'The matter we were discussing before Tom.'

'What matter is that Mr Neale?'

'Colin please. You know Tom, I can be a very useful person to know, especially in your line of business.

'I'm sure you can, er Colin, but I don't particularly need any consultants at the moment, but if I ever do....'

'Yes well, perhaps I didn't make myself clear. What I mean, is I'm a very useful person to be friends with, but not a very nice person, not to be friendly with, if you get my drift?'

Tom could hardly believe the cheek of the man, only known him for five minutes and was coming on strong for a bribe.

'Yes well, I've got the message, so let me have a think about it, will you, er Colin?'

'Okay Tom, no rush. Great pleasure to meet you and I'm sure we'll meet again before too long.'

'Yes, I'm sure we will Colin.'

Tom MacBride was by no means averse to greasing the wheels when it was appropriate, but couldn't see what Colin could do for him, other than if he was implying that he knew something of Tom's other business activities. *No* thought Tom, *someone like him would have said so. He's just trying it on. Still I don't like being threatened by anyone, even by implication. I'll have to see if I can think of how to teach Mr ACC Colin Heale a serious lesson.*

Maybe he could be useful if Tom or Harry ever got themselves into a situation with the polic? thought MacBride, but he disliked the man so much he didn't try too hard to think of a good reason to justify a handout. And anyway, his relationship with the Chief was solid, and based on a natural affinity, which meant they were genuinely good friends, and enjoyed each other's company. *So, why pay the monkey when I'm friends with the organ grinder?*

He put the matter to one side in his mind, went back to his table, gave his wife a big kiss and tried to enjoy the rest of the evening. Unfortunately, they were sat next to a couple of charity junkies, as Tom called such people. He was a lawyer, and she worked the charities to climb the social ladder. They were a pain. She'd obviously had a serious face job, and her rictus smile made Tom feel slightly queasy. He asked his wife for a dance, found the table that Harry was on, and decamped to it.

CHAPTER 30

Jack took a cab from the Moonlight Inn to the address he'd been given. The detective's office was located in a low rise building sandwiched between a laundrette and a pizza parlour. By the door was a plaque simply saying; Dave Ramsay Confidential Private Detective Agency. Jack knocked, the door opened.

'Mr Brandon I presume, come in.'

'Thanks, and it's Jack please.'

'Okay Jack, well I'm Dave Ramsay, but everyone calls me Ramsay.'

Ramsay showed Jack through to his offices. They consisted of a small reception area and two separate office rooms. The decoration was plain and simple, with some family photographs on the walls. Jack followed Ramsay into one of the offices.

'Take a seat Jack, coffee?'

'I will, milk no sugar thanks.'

Ramsay made coffee then sat down opposite Jack, placed a pen and notebook on the desk and sipped his coffee. Ramsay was dark, but ebony rather than black, about five ten, had a lived in but open face and smiled a lot. He had shiny straight dark hair slicked back, piercing intelligent eyes, stocky, but looked tough and agile nevertheless. He was wearing jeans, a very fancy leather belt, a plain white cotton shirt with a button down collar and a bolo tie with what looked like a buffalo's head as the centrepiece.

Jack looked at him trying to decide his origins. Ramsay spoke answering Jack's unasked question.

'Pure Navajo Indian, Jack.'

Then Ramsay laughed, making Jack feel slightly uncomfortable. *The man knew what I was been thinking?*

'It's okay Jack, most people can't figure out my origins when they first meet me. I could see the same quizzical look in your eyes. Don't worry I can't read your mind.'

Jack smiled, but despite the explanation, felt a little unnerved.

Ramsay told Jack what he charged, gave him a sheet with his terms and conditions on, and said he would need a cash deposit equal to two days hire, if Jack wanted to take him on. He then said that Jack had thirty minutes, free of charge, to tell him what he wanted him to do. After that, he would decide if he would take the case, and Jack could decide to hire him or walk away without any charge or obligation.

'And with no hard feelings,' he added, then said 'I won't do anything to break the law, but I don't mind bending it a bit if I think it's necessary. I carry a gun as a matter of course, and I'm licensed to use it. I have killed in the past, but it was justified.' He didn't go into any more detail on that subject. 'Okay Jack,' he said, 'now tell me what your problem is.'

Jack told him everything, well almost everything. When he'd finished, they sat in silence for a few minutes, and Jack felt uncomfortable again. It was obvious that the man was weighing up the pros and cons. Perhaps looking for lies or inconsistencies. He wasn't the sort of person you'd interrupt thought Jack, so he sat and waited. Eventually, Ramsay seemed to make up his mind and looked at Jack straight in the eyes.

'Did you kill this man – this Ezra?'

Jack looked him straight back and said.

'I'm not a murderer.'

He considered his answer.

'Not quite the answer I was looking for. But maybe it'll do for the time being. I go a lot on instinct, have to in this profession, so I'll take the job and see where we go. You've asked if I'll try to make sure you're not being followed, but the first and most important thing is, to find out who it is. If anyone is actually looking for you that is. So, I propose I hook up with a limey friend of mine, who can work the UK end. He's good, not cheap, but he'll find out what's going on I guarantee. Any objection to that?'

'No, I can't see what there's to object to. I do obviously have a limit on funds, but I'm not a poor man. And, I need a way out of this nightmare.'

'Understood,' said Ramsay. 'I'll get on this right away and call you as soon as I have something to report. In the meantime try to relax and enjoy the sun. Go fishing or something, and give yourself a break. Don't worry, you're in good hands now, and we don't want you dyin' of a heart attack now, do we?' and he laughed again.

Jack felt a great sense of relief at having an ally at last. Someone well and truly on his side. He hoped his faith wasn't misplaced.

'You'd better give me your cell number and email address. Are you still using your English cell phone?' He asked.

'No' Jack replied. 'I bought two here when we arrived. One each for me and Rachel. And I pre-paid for calls. Paid cash for everything.'

'Good' he said, 'you're learning!'

Jack laughed nervously.

'I need to pay you some money' Jack said, and gave him a thousand dollars as an advance, which was more than the minimum he'd asked for, but he wanted to express his confidence in Ramsay. Jack figured he had to trust the man. He had to trust someone other than Rachel, and he had a good feeling about this Ramsay character.

Jack left Ramsay's office, and felt that at last, he'd found someone who could help. For the first time since that fateful morning, he felt he was making some progress. He just hoped his instincts were good, and that he wasn't placing too much faith in someone who he didn't know existed until a couple of hours ago. Jack got a cab back to the Moonlight Inn and felt hungry. Wow, there was an improvement already he thought. *I could murder a couple of beers, a pizza and some red wine.*

The next morning broke with a copper red sky then as the sun rose, the sky turned a cloudless cornflower blue.

Jack sat on the small balcony watching the palm tree fronds swaying in the warm breeze blowing gently off the bay. He watched the seabirds wheeling about the sky, their strident cries mixing with the tinkling noise of the rigging of the boats moored on the pontoons just outside their balcony. It felt good. He asked Rachel what she wanted for breakfast then called room service and ordered eggs, bacon and coffee. They ate on the balcony. Everywhere, they could see activity, people preparing their boats to go out fishing or sailing. There was nothing to do while they waited for Ramsay to come back to them with his initial report, so they tried to relax and spent time by the pool, sunbathing and reading, but the tension was still there, and the day passed slowly.

Jack woke the next morning form a deep sleep, and momentarily forgot about the fix he was in, and then it all came back to him. It was now over two weeks since the 'incident', and he wondered how long it would take for whoever it was who wanted to take revenge on him, to start to calm down and call off the dogs.

He figured he and Rachel could stay in Florida for quite a while, at least until the cash ran out, then maybe they could go to France. Mrs Anderson would be happy to mind the house and the animals for as long as they wished. His business would run quite happily without his input. There were four other main board directors to manage it, so he'd emailed them to say he'd decided to take a sabbatical.

After breakfast, they went for a walk down to Naples pier and watched the people fishing. There were lots of fish being caught with the ever hungry seagulls and pelicans watching on. They sat on a wooden bench, and watched for a while, grateful for the distraction.

They spent the rest of the day on the beach, but Jack could sense that Rachel was becoming anxious and tense again after the brief respite. Jack felt the same.

As they walked back to their condo, Jack's cell phone rang. It took him a while to recognise the unfamiliar ringtone as he'd only heard it once when he and Rachel had initially tested their new phones. He struggled to get it out of his pocket, finally opened it, and pressed answer.
'Hello.'

'Hi, this is Ramsay.'

'Oh hi, any progress?'

'I think so; but it's better if we meet face to face to talk, rather than do it over the phone? You can come to my office, or I can come to your hotel.'

Jack felt he had to put complete trust Ramsay now, so he suggested they meet at their hotel, and told him where they were staying. Ramsay knew the Moonlight Inn and said he'd be there in about twenty minutes.

Sure enough, in twenty minutes the front desk called to say Jack had a visitor. He went down and met Ramsay at the reception. They shook hands, went to the room and Jack introduced him to Rachel. Jack felt that Rachel was taken with Ramsay immediately and he felt grateful that they were all comfortable with each other. Rachel made coffee, and they went out on to the small balcony.

Formalities over, Ramsay was all business now. He checked the balconies either side to make sure there were no flapping ears around, and then began.

'Okay, well, my man Freddie, in the UK, asked around. He's got good contacts in the police and some on the other side of the fence as well. And yes someone is trying very hard to find you.'

Jack's heart sank. He looked at Rachel, who looked back at him in a resigned sort of way. Ramsay carried on,

'Well someone isn't quite accurate. I'm afraid that apart from the police who are a bit annoyed that you didn't tell them when and where you were going, there are possibly three parties looking for you. You seem to be very popular Mr Brandon.'

'Three!' Jack was up on his feet. Rachel reached for Jack's hand.

'Who are these people?'

'Freddie says that the brother of the guy who died,' Ramsay consulted his notes, 'Ezra Madaki, has a brother, Jay Madaki. Who incidentally, is in prison himself for killing someone in a knife fight. He thinks you killed his brother Ezra, so he's hired a couple of guys to find you.'

'To do what exactly?'

'Well, according to Freddie, the guys he hired are both professional hit men, so it doesn't sound too good. Sorry Jack, but there's no other way to tell it.'

Rachel audibly drew her breath in, and put her hand to her mouth

Ramsay held his hands, palms upwards, and shrugged his shoulders in an expression of helplessness.

'And is there anything we can do to stop these men, I mean, can't the police do something? asked Jack.

'The problem is,' said Ramsay, 'no one is going to give the police, either here, or in the UK, any information for them to act on. So the answer, unfortunately, is no. But don't forget, that all the time they're looking for you, their costs will be racking up, so there may come a point where this Jay character calms down a bit and decides it's not worth it to keep paying out.'

'And how long do you think that will take and what do we do in the meantime?'

'Depends on the guy and how much patience and dough he's got. Freddie says he's a nut, a psychopath, so maybe it just comes down to how much money he has stashed away. The longer you can't be found, the better chance there is that he'll get sick of spending money and cool off. These hit guys don't work for peanuts, so who knows?'

Rachel spoke.

'And who else is looking for Jack?'

'Freddie isn't sure, but one of them has connections. The third one, Freddie thinks maybe looking for you, seems to be just one guy. Freelancing maybe? Just one guy, asking a lot of questions. Freddie's not sure if he's a real player, so maybe we should forget him.'

Ramsay took a long sip of his coffee.

'Any idea what these other people want from me?' Jack asked, but he was pretty sure he knew the answer to that question - *the drugs he'd hidden.*

'Nope, Freddie couldn't find out, but they are serious people, so Freddie's trying to get more information. Says he'll get back to me soon as he knows more.'

Jack got up and paced around the room thinking.

'So what do we do now Ramsay?'

'Yeah, been thinking about that Jack. First thing is to make you hard to find, preferably impossible to find, then we'll think of the next move.'

Jack sat down.

'I don't think anyone can find us Ramsay. I purposely didn't tell anyone where we were going. And I've paid in cash for everything since we arrived. So I think we're okay in that regard. I mean someone might know we're in Florida, but the chances of them finding us would be like trying to find the proverbial needle in the haystack.'

Ramsay gave Jack a pitying look.

'You booked you fight online with your credit card, so anyone with good connections will know you flew to Orlando, and with which airline. Did you buy a return ticket or one way?'

'One way' Jack said.

'Good. Now you said you also booked your car online with your credit card, what rental company?'

'Hertz' said Jack, 'but I'm absolutely certain, beyond any doubt that no one followed us. Not on the plane over, and not from Orlando airport to the Hertz depot. Once we were in the car, no one could know where we went, so I think we're clear there.'

Ramsay looked at them both again and said,

'Ever hear of satellites, GPS and all that stuff Jack?'

'Yes' but so what? We don't have a GPS in the car we hired.'

'Well GPS, in this case, doesn't mean GPS in that sense. You see, these days, rental companies install trackers in their cars, so that if someone steals or abandons one of their vehicles they can locate and recover it.'

'Yes' said Jack. He had a horrible thought of what might be coming.

Ramsay went on.

'So assuming your pursuers are prepared to follow you to Florida, how much do you think they would need to pay someone at Hertz in Orlando to tell them where your car is at this very moment?'

'Oh shit' said Jack 'Someone could know our hire car is sitting in the car park here in Naples, and hasn't moved for two days?'

'Yup' said Ramsay, 'they just might.'

Rachel put her head in her hands momentarily, then said.

'God this is impossible. We're just not up to this sort of thing, we've got to tell the authorities.'

Jack looked completely defeated.

'What the hell do we do now?' he asked, and looked at Ramsay who was smiling confidently.

'Well you could go to the authorities as Rachel suggests, but you still have the same problem I mentioned before. Look I haven't finished telling you what Freddie's discovered. There's what you might call bad news and good news.'

Rachel and Jack looked at each other, and Jack wondered how much more bad news Rachel could take. Ramsay carried on.

'The bad news is that according to Freddie, a couple of guys, who could well be the boys the brother hired, boarded a flight to Orlando this morning. My guess is that they'll go to the Hertz depot, hire a car, then ask around and find someone who's willing to sell them the information they need, to locate your car. Anyone senior enough is likely to have access to that information.'

Ramsay smiled, then went on.

'Least that's what I'd do, and if these guys are any good, that's what they'll do.'

'Okay, so that's the bad news, what's the good news?' Jack asked.

Ramsay's face cracked into a grin.

'The good news is that I have a plan. And there's nothing as good as a man with a plan.' Ramsay said with a laugh, 'especially this man' and he laughed even louder.

His laugh was infectious, and both Rachel and Jack began to relax a little. Ramsay seemed so confident, Jack prayed to God he was as good as he seemed. Ramsay stopped laughing and assumed a serious face.

'Okay so here's what we're going to do. These guys should be arriving in a few hours, so you take my car, it's parked in the bay outside the hotel, here's the keys. It's a white Buick sedan index MG6 3NU. Check out of this place and book in somewhere else, preferably another town, say Marco Island. Then drive my car over to Orlando airport but don't actually go to the airport. Find a hotel or a Mall, somewhere you can park, not too far away. Say, three or four miles from the airport. Lock the doors, don't want you to get mugged do we? And wait there till I call, okay?'

Jack and Rachel agreed, still unsure what Ramsay was up to, but he seemed to know what he was doing. *And what other choice do we have*, thought Jack

'Gimmie your car keys, and all the docs for the rental.'

They did as Ramsay asked, and walked out to the car park with Ramsay so they could show him where their rental car was parked. Ramsay got in, adjusted the driver's seat, then started the car up wound the window down and said.

'Don't worry, you'll be okay, see you in Orlando.'

And with a wave, he was off.

They went to reception and said they had to leave unexpectedly and could they pay the bill. Jack paid then they went to the room, packed, went down to the car park and found Ramsay's big Buick car in the hotel car park, loaded their luggage in the boot and drove to Marco Island where they booked into a small anonymous looking motel.

As soon as they'd checked in, they went to the room, dumped their luggage, left the hotel, got back in Ramsay's car and took the road north towards Orlando. It was one o'clock when they left, so they reckoned they should make Orlando airport for around five in the afternoon. *What was Ramsay going to do* they wondered?

Ramsay's car was very comfortable and had a soft suspension that could rock you to sleep if you weren't careful thought Jack With such a powerful engine, he found it was all too easy to build up his speed to over the limit without noticing, so Jack had to watch it. *I can't afford to be pulled over by the highway patrol, on this journey of all journeys.*

The drive was uneventful, and as they got nearer to Orlando airport, they looked out for somewhere convenient to stop. Jack knew the roads around the airport didn't lend themselves to stopping at will, and you really have to see well ahead in order to be able to leave the road and the traffic without causing an accident. Jack eventually managed to pull into a shopping Mall and parked next to a huge Walgreen's pharmacy store. It was hot outside, so they kept the engine going and the air conditioning on. Rachel decided to go into Walgreens to find a restroom and to buy some soft drinks. Jack stayed in the car waiting for Ramsay's call. It had been over four hours now since Ramsay went off in their hire car. Just as Rachel got back in the car with the drinks, Jack's cell phone chirruped. He answered and heard Ramsay's voice.

'Where are you guys parked?

CHAPTER 31

The two men, identified by Freddie as having flown into Orlando from the UK, were indeed looking for Jack. They were a study in anonymity. Dressed in nondescript clothes, beige slacks, white short-sleeve shirts with ties, nothing flash, and nothing to make them stand out. They were both average height and looked like insurance salesmen. If you'd been asked to remember what they looked like you'd have said average and nothing out of the ordinary, that is if you could remember them at all.

They never spoke each other's names when around anyone else. They were professionals. It hadn't taken them long to find out about Jack's online booking for the flights and car hire. They'd watched the Brandon house until the house minder left, then one of them phoned the other on his mobile, and they left their lines open. One followed the minder, and the other one got into the house. Entry was easy, the rear French doors had two locks, but only the Yale lock was engaged, which meant the man could get in without too much trouble, and without leaving any trace of entry.

Once inside he soon found the small study off the hall with a desk, chair and filing cabinet. The lock on the cabinet was a breeze. He rifled through the suspension files and found one marked personal credit card statements. *This is just too easy* he thought. He took the last few statements and slid the draw back into place. He left the way he'd come in, making sure there was no trace of his entry. Outside now, the man spoke to his partner and told him he could stop following the old bat and come back to the car.

They called Jack's credit card company posing as police. With some persuasion, they managed to get the manager to confirm that there was a record of an online transaction with Virgin Airlines for £2,450 and another on the same day with Hertz rent a car. Thanking the manager for his co-operation they then phoned Virgin airlines again posing as police. Getting the information here was more difficult, but they managed to impress the reservations manager with the wealth of information they had on Brandon, his credit card number, address, the date, time and value of the transaction. So in the end, the manager gave way.

'Mr Brandon purchased two tickets from Manchester to Orlando in Upper Class. One way,' he said, then told them the date and time of the flight.

Armed with this information, they called Mickey to ask if he wanted them to follow Brandon to the USA. Mickey told them to go. They booked on the next available flight from Manchester to Orlando. They slept on the flight and drank nothing stronger than tea. When they arrived, they did as Ramsay had expected, and went to Hertz rental counter and talked to the depot manager, a small balding wiry man whose name badge said Stan.

Stan wore a permanent world-weary bored expression on his face. He was uncooperative at first and not interested in listening to what they had to say. They said they were Inland Revenue inspectors from the UK and that a Mr Jack Brandon had fled the country to avoid a tax tribunal. *Good luck to him* thought Stan. They went on saying that Mr Brandon would almost certainly end up being jailed for tax offences. They said they were empowered to pay a substantial cash sum to anyone who could help locate the Brandons. At this, the manager suddenly began to pay attention. They said they knew the Brandons had rented a car from this depot a few days ago.

The manager wasn't sure he believed their cover story, but he didn't care. He was willing to go along with it for the money. The substantial sum turned out to be $500, and he would have sold his granny for that much at the moment, such was his current personal financial situation. He explained to the "Inland Revenue Inspectors" that he could locate the car the Brandon's had rented using their GPS tracking system. Stan did some checking on the computer, then made a phone call and was able to tell them that the car was stationary at the moment in Naples on the west coast of Florida, about a three to four hour drive away from Orlando. He took the GPS details and then went on to Google where he managed to identify the precise location as the car park of the Moonlight Inn Hotel and also the street address of the hotel.

The two men thanked the manager and said they needed to make a call, but would be back in ten minutes and not to go away.

The manager said he wasn't going anywhere for the moment. They called Mickey and gave him an update, then went back to the manager's office. When they came back the manager told them that the car seemed to now be moving away from Naples. They waited a while, to see if it was just a local journey or if the car looked as if it was on the way to a new destination. The manager said it wasn't practical to keep checking every few minutes so maybe they'd like to go for a coffee and come back in half an hour or so and he could tell them if it looked as though the car was on a longer journey.

They decided to take his advice. When they returned, Stan told them that the car had covered a considerable distance and looked as though it was heading in a northeasterly direction, probably back towards Orlando in fact. Though it was still quite a distance away, they felt they had no choice but to wait until the car stopped travelling, before they could make a move, but the manager was due to go off duty, so it cost them another hundred dollars for him to stick around for a while more.

They went for some food and gave the manager their mobile phone number and asked him to call if the car looked as though it had stopped at a destination. The manager didn't call so they went back to the depot an hour later, and the manager told them that the car had continued travelling towards Orlando. Tedious as it was, they had no choice but to wait and went back to a nearby bar keeping in touch with the manager by phone. The manager had asked for another hundred as this was taking a lot more of his time than was first agreed. They had no choice and handed over another hundred.

They couldn't get tea at the bar and alcohol was not acceptable, so they drank coffee until they just couldn't drink any more.

It was now nearly four hours since the car had left Naples. In his last telephone call, the manager said he was fairly certain that the car was coming back to Orlando airport. It was in the vicinity, and on the road leading to the depot.

'In which case,' he said, 'it was reasonable to assume they would return the car to the depot within the next fifteen to twenty minutes. Then, if they're taking a flight out of Orlando, which seemed likely, they would drop the car off, and take the complimentary Hertz shuttle to the airport.

The men looked pleased. All that waiting had been a ball ache, but it looked as though their patience had paid off. Brandon was about to deliver himself into their hands. The manager told them that the Brandons had hired a blue metallic Toyota Avensis, index number 885 XRK. The men decided they would wait in their own rental car, then when Brandon drove into the depot, they'd grab him and his wife as soon as they parked up and bundle them into their car. One of the men nudged the other in the ribs.

'Never mind the luggage. The manager can have that. Those two won't need any luggage where they're going, that was for sure.' The second man laughed.

'Too right,' he replied.

The manager looked again and estimated the car was about ten minutes away from the depot. Sure enough, ten minutes on the dot, a metallic blue car drove through the In Gate, and over the metal and into the depot. The men double checked the index number. It was the right car, but there appeared to be only one person in it, and he didn't look Caucasian. They looked at each other, then at the manager, who looked confused.

The car got nearer, and the guy driving stopped and parked it up, and got out.

'What the fuck's going on?' one of the men said to the manager. The manager shrugged his shoulders and grimaced. They all looked at the driver as he walked away from the car.

He was dark skinned and certainly didn't fit the description of Jack Brandon the men had been given.

'You sure that's the car the Brandons hired?' the other man asked the manager.

'One hundred percent,' he replied

The two men ran out of the door of the Hertz office and chased the driver as he walked towards the exit. They caught up and spun him round. He looked surprised, but not intimidated.

'Hey, what's going on?' he said.

'Did you hire this car?' one of the men asked aggressively.

The man looked back at the man who'd asked the question and took his time answering.

'No man I didn't hire it, okay?'

He started to walk away again toward the exit. The manager was out of his office now watching the scene.

'Hey,' one of the men shouted at his back, 'just wait. How come you were driving that car? Why did you bring it here?'

'Look man, Ramsey said, 'I was standing at the airport, waitin' for the bus, just finished my shift. When this guy drove up, took out his luggage and shouted *anyone take this car back to the Hertz depot for two hundred bucks?* Man, ten minutes work for two hundred, those are my kinda rates.'

The grey suited man opened his mouth to ask another question, then threw his hands up in a gesture that said he realised they'd been had – big time. The dark guy pretended not to know what was going on, shrugged his shoulders and walked away.

Once out of sight of the depot, Ramsay flagged down a cab and dialled Jack's cell phone to find out where he should tell the taxi driver to drop him off. He arrived at the Mall ten minutes later, paid the cab, walked over to his own car and got in the back. He laughed like a drain when he described the looks on the faces of the two men he'd encountered at the depot.

'Those guys were spitting mad' he said in between fits of laughter.

'It was just so cool playing the dumb ass Indian. If they weren't mad enough to kill you before, they sure are now,' he said still laughing.

Rachel and Jack were now laughing too, a well needed moment of levity.

'What do you think they'll do now?' asked Jack.

'Well assuming they believe what I told them – and why wouldn't they? I think it's safe to say they'll assume you've taken a plane to somewhere, and if they try to find if you bought tickets with your credit card, they'll come up with zilch and assume you paid cash. So they'll further assume the chances of finding out where you've gone are between nil and zero. You're free of them for the moment my friends, so relax. Now I'll drive us all back. Which hotel did you folks book into?'

On the way back Ramsay told them the next part of his plan.

'I suggest instead of hiring another car, you take mine for a while, at least while we decide what your longer term plans are.'

When they said they couldn't possibly inconvenience him in that way, he laughed said it wasn't a problem, he had another two cars.

'In any event, I got a Harley too, and any excuse I have to ride it instead of driving a car, is okay by me.' He drove them back to Naples and to his office, where he got out, then waved them off. As they drove to their new hotel in Marco Island. They were too keyed up to make any rational decisions after the sort of day they'd had, so they delayed any thoughts about their next moves until the folowing day. Ramsey told them, they should lie low for a while, to see how things panned out.

'Maybe the two guys tailing you will take the bait, and return to the UK. Don't really see they've any choice, unless they've rumbled our little scam, which I doubt. We need to wait a few days at least, so that my Limey friend can try to find out.'

Jack and Rachel had agreed with Ramsay's suggestion, and they drove off to their new accommodations on Marco Island. It was late when they got back to the hotel, so they had a pizza delivered, and a couple of beers. They went to bed exhausted, feeling a little relieved for the moment. They had a breathing space, Jack thought, just before nodding off.

CHAPTER 32

'You what? You lost 'em! You fuckin lost them. I don't fuckin believe it, you went all the way to fuckin Florida, got within a few fuckin miles of the mark, then fuckin lost em? Jay will go fuckin apeshit an my life won't be worth livin'.'

'Look Mickey' said Eddie, one of the hired men, 'there was nothing we could have done. It was just unlucky. We nearly had them, but they must have been late for their plane or something and went straight to the airport. There's no way they could have known we were waiting, it was just bad luck, could have happened to anyone.'

'Well bad luck or not Eddie, Jay will be really pissed, and you know what that means for me? lots of serious fucking shit.'

The two men looked miserable and shamefaced, in stark contrast to their normally cocky assured attitude. Their reputation was now in serious doubt, *So much for professional,* thought Mickey,

'Look you two fuckin morons, do whatever you have to, but find the Brandons and finish the job. Don't come back to me until you've got a result okay?'

'Yeah okay' said Eddie, 'no problem,' but thought to himself, *but how the fuck are we going to pick up their trail now?*

Edie and his sidekick weren't used to failing. They were both intelligent guys and streetwise. They knew every trick in the book and then some.

'Let's go for a coffee' said Eddie, 'something stinks here, I got a feeling we're being had over somehow, but I need some time to think this through.'

'Like what, how?'

'Dunno, just all too pat, too smart. That guy, the guy who drove the car in, it's almost like he was expecting us. Couldn't keep the smile off his face. Something's not right, I know it.'

'Okay, but if it was a set up, then someone would have to know we were there, waiting.'

'Yeah, and we were able to find out where the Brandons were, so why couldn't someone be able to find out about us?'

'Yeah, okay but who?'

'Fucked if I know, let's go get that coffee.'

CHAPTER 33

J ack woke the next morning from a deep sleep and wasn't sure where he was for a moment. Everything was so unfamiliar, and then it all came back. He got out of bed, closed the bedroom door behind him quietly sat down on the sofa in the tiny living come kitchen area, to think.

Eventually, he heard Rachel get up and go to the bathroom. He made some fresh coffee. Rachel kissed him good morning and sat at the breakfast counter. Jack spoke.

'I've been thinking. We might have fooled those two guys for now, but I think we need to keep on the move rather than stay here. So maybe we should drive down to the Keys, stop a few nights here and there, maybe Islamorada for a few nights, then down to Key West and plan our next move?'

Rachel agreed they needed time to think things through properly, and not rush any decisions. They decided to leave the following morning. Jack called Ramsay to tell him what they'd decided. He said it sounded like a good idea and would keep in touch by phone, to update them on any developments as they happened. Jack asked Ramsay if he could pay him what he owed him so far and Ramsay said he would swing by tomorrow morning before they left and asked for the name of their motel.

The next morning Jack was looking out of their first floor window. The motel was only three stories high, and on the water, overlooking a sort of river along which a continuous stream of boats were sailing out into the gulf. Big boats, small boats and expensive looking cruisers, all setting out for a day in the Gulf to fish, sail and generally soak up the glorious Florida sunshine. Jack's reverie was broken by the unmistakable sound of a Harley Davidson riding into the motel car park. Jack craned his neck and could see Ramsay on his bike, no helmet, cool. The bike looked like a retro work of art.

Jack went down to reception to meet him and took him up to the room. Rachel made the coffee, and they sat down and talked things through. Jack said they needed a few days to get their thoughts together and they would take Ramsay's advice and just lay low for a while and see how things panned out. Jack asked him how much they owed him to date. Ramsay said it came to $2,800 all told, which Jack thought was a bargain considering how he'd got rid of the people following them, at least for the foreseeable future.

Jack paid him, and they told him their plans and that they would like to take up his offer of the loan of his car, for which of course they would pay him a hire fee. Jack said they wouldn't make any decisions about their next move without consulting him. Jack paid up, and they said their goodbyes. Ramsay told them to let him know where they were staying each time they moved then raised his fist in the air as he roared off on his Harley.

They checked out of the motel then drove along the Tamiami Trail, highway 41, through the Everglades skirting Miami, and down to Homestead where they picked up the US 1, where the road to the Keys starts in earnest. Jack loved driving through the Keys. They passed through Key Largo, and on to Islamorada, a narrow key, with the Atlantic Ocean on one side and Florida Bay on the other. In places, just a short walk separating each body of water. Jack and Rachel had spent many holidays in Islamorada, and felt they might be able to relax for a few days in the familiar surroundings.

They went to the Islamorada tourist information office where they asked for any good deals on budget motel type accommodation. The receptionist was helpful, as they'd found in the past, and suggested the Island Beach Garden Motel, which had a couple of rooms left the last time she'd checked. She told them the rate and called ahead for them to check they still had vacancies.

'Go ahead and have a look at the room before you commit yourselves. The lady who owns the place is expecting you. Oh by the way, could I have your name, for my records.'

'Yes sure' said Jack it's… Brown, John Brown.'

They expressed their thanks, got into their car and drove down to the motel. The hotel come motel was modest. A typical understated Keys clapboard building, painted a cornflower blue, with a grey metal roof. The room was perfect for what they wanted, and the place looked nice and quiet. They told the lady they'd book in for three days for the moment, but might extend their stay later. Formalities over, they moved their luggage in the room then called Mrs Anderson at their home in the UK. Everything seemed okay at her end. She said the police had been round a couple of times and asked her if she knew where they were, but she quite honestly, told them she had no idea. True, as they hadn't told her where they were going in the first place. They still didn't reveal where they were.

They spent the next morning sunbathing, and reading by the small motel pool. Then went for lunch at the Islamorada fish company and tried to relax, but found it difficult. They were both constantly on alert, always looking over their shoulder to see if there was anyone in the vicinity who looked the slightest bit suspicious. They gave up on lunch without finishing their food or drink, and as they walked towards where their car was parked, a man came after them, shouting Jack's name. Jack looked at Rachel.

'Open the car, quick Jack.'

In an effort to open the car doors quickly Jack dropped the keys. Rachel looked as if she was going to faint as the man closed the gap between them. Jack realised they weren't going to be able to get in the car in time and turned to face the man, *ready for what?* At the same time he looked for a second man, *surely they always worked in twos?* The man stopped short and pointed at Jack.

'You Jack Brandon?'

Jack realised the man was quite a bit older than him, overweight, and not at all aggressive. Hardly looked like your average assassin, thought Jack. He also noticed he was holding Jack's wallet in his hand, which he realised he'd left on the bar in their unseemly hurry to leave. A sense of relief, accompanied by a feeling of foolishness swept over them both, and they looked at each other not sure whether to laugh or cry. Jack found his voice.

'Yes, I'm Jack Brandon. Sorry, I thought, well I don't know what I thought,' he said.

Jack looked at Rachel who had tears forming in her eyes.

The stranger was still holding the wallet out to Jack. He took it.

'Look thanks, thanks very much, here', said Jack taking a ten dollar bill out of the wallet, 'let me buy you a beer.' He tried to hand it to the man. The man looked at them obviously confused at the emotion of the moment.

'No siree, no need. Happy to help. Y'all have a good one now.'

Jack thanked the man again. They got into the car, and both sat in silence for a few moments, then Rachel burst into tears. Jack leaned across and put his arm around her shoulder, and she sobbed uncontrollably. After a while, Rachel stopped crying and wiped her eyes.

'Sorry Jack, but it just got to me. We can't even go for a meal without thinking someone's there looking to get us.'

'I know,' Jack said not really knowing what else to say. In truth, he felt guilty at having brought this on them both.

'Look, let's move on. Let's go down to Key West for a few days. At least it's busier, and we won't feel as though we stand out as much, then we can decide what we should do next.'

'Okay Jack and don't worry I'm not going to turn to jelly, just got to me a little bit that's all.'

'Look we need to try and relax. Ramsay was quite sure that the men following us think we flew out of Miami to who knows where, so we're safe for the time being. So let's try to enjoy the good weather and take time to re-charge our batteries.'

They went back to their apartment and bumped into the lady owner.

'Hi,' she said 'were you expecting anyone to visit?'

'Visit?' said Jack perplexed.

'Yeah, I didn't think so.'

'Sorry' said Jack, I'm not sure what you mean..'

'Two guys asking if we had a couple staying here, description sounded a lot like you folks.'

Jack and Rachel looked at each other thinking the same thought *how on earth…* Jack recovered first.

'And did you tell them, I mean, are they here?' Jack began to look around.

'No don't worry, I told them nothin' Been in this business a long time and I can tell decent folks when I see them. And, I don't like snoopers of any kind, for whatever reason. I also mind my own business and expect others to mind theirs, so don't go frettin' about me. Don't know if they believed me though. They were real cute with their questions, so maybe they'll come back. So you take care now.' And she went back behind the reception desk, busying herself with some paperwork.

Jack looked at Rachel.

'Oh sweet Christ' whispered Rachel, 'what do we do now, and how did they know we were?'

Jack said nothing for a minute, then went to the desk.

'These men, what did they look like?'

The lady looked up and took off her glasses.

'Grey, they looked grey, sorta nondescript I think you'd say. But I could tell they were no good, the eyes it's always the eyes.'

She put her glasses back on and went back to her paperwork, humming quietly.

Jack turned away, took Rachel by gently by the arm and started to lead her to their room.

'I did, however, get a look at their car as they drove away,' she said, 'a black Chevy.'

Jack looked around, and the lady was back into her paperwork, humming away as if she hadn't spoken.

'Thanks' said Jack but the lady ignored him.

They went to their room, he closed the door, and they both sat down on the bed.

'What now Jack?'

'Well, obviously, Ramsay's plan didn't work out. At least, not enough to convince them completely, but they still may be working on a hunch, rather than being certain that we haven't already skipped. So, I reckon we still have a chance to lose them. We've got to stay calm, contact Ramsay, tell him what happened and then disappear. I just can't figure out how they'd know where to look for us. They probably went to The Moonlight Inn. They'd know the car was parked there for a few days, so they'll have assumed we likely stayed there and they'll have talked to the people there to try to find out where we went when we left. Can you remember what we said to them, why we were leaving earlier than we thought? I'm sure we didn't mention where we were going, so how could they know to look for us?'

Rachel looked thoughtful.

'It's my fault.'

'Sorry Rachel, your fault what?'

'My fault they know where we are. When you went to meet Ramsay that first time, I got chatting to the guy on reception at the Cove, you know, the funny one who's always cracking bad jokes. I'd gone to ask for fresh towels, the cleaner had forgotten to leave any that morning. Anyway, he was asking what our plans were and I told him we'd probably go down to the keys as we usually do when we come to Florida. It was just conversation, something to say, I thought it was best to pretend we were on holiday, like normal, and that's what we normally do, so…'

'So that's what he would have told the people looking for us - shit!'

'I'm sorry Jack, I didn't think I …..'

Jack was silent for a moment, thinking.

'It's not your fault Rach, you couldn't have guessed how it would work out. The main thing to do now, is to try to think where they'll look next. Did you say where we might go in the Keys?'

'I think I mentioned Islamorada and said we might go to Key West as well.'

'Well it looks as though our funny friend's memory at the Moonlight Inn is good, so we might as well work on the basis that they'll look around Islamorada then head south to Key West if they don't find us here. At least we have the advantage.'

'We do?'

'Yeah, they don't know what car we're in, but we know what car they're in.'

'They must have looked for us at every accommodation place in Islamorada.'

'I don't think so,' said Jack. 'These people are real pro's so they probably concentrated their first efforts on booking agencies, and of course the Tourist Info place. Okay, so let's think this through. They think that maybe we're staying here, even though the lady on reception told them we weren't, but they won't be sure, so what will they do? C'mon Rach what would you do if you were them?'

'I can' think straight Jack. I suppose if they didn't fully believe the lady when she said we weren't staying here, then if I were them, I'd assume the lady would warn us about them looking for us.'

'I agree, and what would they expect us to do then?'

'Make a run for it?'

'Yes, and they'll park somewhere where they can see us leaving this place. If they're already in place, then they might have even have watched us coming back from lunch just now. And if they did, then they'll know what car we're driving.'

'How can we be certain Jack?'

'We can't, but we need to think like them if we're going to have any chance of getting away. I'm certain they won't want to do anything in public, so whatever they do, they'll wait for the right opportunity. They certainly won't want to get caught, that's for certain.'

'Do what, Jack, kill us, this is crazy why can't we just go to the police?'

'And tell them what, what proof do we have, why do we say they want to kill us?'

'There are two men following us officer, and they intend to kill us, we've got a contract out on us.'

Oh, and why is that Mr Brandon?

'Oh well you see I killed this man's brother, in the UK, I didn't mean to but..'

'Presumably, you reported this to the British police Mr Brandon?'

'Well, actually no, I didn't, you see I didn't want to get arrested for murder….'

'Okay Jack,' yelled Rachel, 'you've made your point So what the fuck do we do now?'

Rachel was good and angry and looked as if she could kill Jack herself.

'You got us into this mess Jack Brandon, so you get us out of it,' she screamed.

They looked at each other, and neither of them spoke for a beat, then Rachel sat down on the bed and lowered her head, weeping quietly.

Jack sat down by her side and put his arm around her shoulders, she didn't resist.

'Look I'm sorry, you know that, and it's just me they're after anyway, so why don't we split up. I'll go, and they'll follow me.'

'And you think they'll just leave me alone Jack? They won't. We're in this together, and we'll just have to figure a way out, together.'

Jack felt a lump in his throat, and it took a few breaths before he could recover and speak.

'Right, well first off I'm going to have a look out front and see if I can see a black Chevy parked anywhere nearby. You put the coffee on, and I'll be back in a minute.'

Jack donned a baseball cap, put his sunglasses on, and pulling the peak of his cap down over his eyes, walked out of the room. The motel car park fronted the property, so Jack walked across the car park towards a red Toyota. He stood at the door of the car, then patted his pockets as if looking for the keys while surveying the road. It was busy as unusual, being the only road running up and down the Keys. This one road ran from Homestead in the north to

Key West, the southernmost point of the USA. After that, it was just ocean. As Jack scanned the opposite side of the road, he spotted the car parked in the forecourt of a roadside restaurant. From their vantage point, the men had a clear view of the exit from the Island Beach Garden Motel. Jack made as if to curse at forgetting his keys and as casually as possible made his way back to his room.

'There's a black Chevy parked across the road, so coincidence apart, it looks as though they're waiting for us to leave.'

'Great, so now?'

'Now we think. What time is it?'

'Three o'clock, why?'

'I've got the bones of an idea. We just need to get a bit of a start on them, but I think I know how we can lose them, and this time for good.' Jack was smiling now.

Rachel looked intently at Jack 'Well are you going to share this idea?'

'Still thinking it through, but let's get the laptop out.'

Jack stated the laptop and typed away for a few minutes, Rachel looking over his shoulder.

'Perfect' said Jack. Right, the Key West Express leaves Key West at six this evening.

'So your plan is?'

'Okay, we book ourselves on the Key West Express leaving tonight. We create a diversion; that is we phone the local police and tell them about a suspicious car, a black Chevy parked along the highway etc., you get the picture?'

Rachel nodded, 'and that gives us time to drive off while they're detained answering questions. It won't take long for them to convince the police they're not up to anything, but that'll give us enough of a head start on them. We drive south to Key West, and we know that they're unlikely to be able to catch us up, overtaking places are just so limited, and so we'll keep our head start.

'Go on.

'It takes about an hour and a half to two hours to drive to Key West from here, so we leave with just enough time to catch the Express to Fort Myers. It's a jet-propelled catamaran, and it's fast. We need to leave in the next fifteen minutes to be safe. So, we need to book our tickets and be thinking about making that call to the police.'

'Just before we do that, and don't take this the wrong way Jack, why is this such a good plan?'

'Well, our friends will assume we're going to Key West to try to hide from them, but if they know anything about the place, they'll know we could be virtually boxed in, with just the one road out of there. So, they might reasonably assume they'll eventually find us. It's not exactly that big a place to hide. What they won't realise, at least I don't think they will, is that we will have scarpered by sea, on the catamaran to Fort Myers, and by the time they do, they won't be able to do anything about it.

'They couldn't just drive to Fort Myers and meet us off the catamaran?'

'How could they? The drive from Key West to Fort Myers would take them five to six hours depending on traffic, the Catamaran only takes three hours forty five minutes.'

'They could charter a plane.'

'Yes they could, but first they'd have to figure out we'd taken the Express, then go to the airport, find someone to charter the plane from, who's willing or qualified to fly at night in the dark?   And that's going to take time. Then they'd fly to Fort Myers airport and have to get a taxi from there. I just don't think they'd have a prayer.'

'What about Ramsay's car?'

'Yeah, well we'll just have to leave it in the car park at the dock and pay for Ramsay to get someone to collect it. In the scheme of things, we should worry too much about that. Come on Rach, the clock's ticking.'

'Okay, call the Express and book us on, then look up the phone number of the local sheriff. I'll make that call, it'll sound better coming from a woman. Then you pay for the room, and I'll get our stuff in the car. I think we should divide the luggage into two lots, bare essentials which we can carry easily and the rest we'll have to leave in the car. Ramsay can get it back to us if possible, but I think we have to be able to travel fast and light.'

'I'm on it.'

CHAPTER 34

The sheriff's car drove up behind the car with the two men in it. The sheriff got out and approached the black Chevy, hand on the handle of his gun. The driver of the Chevy had seen the arrival of the sheriff's car in his rear mirror. When the sheriff got out, the Chevy driver opened his door to get out, already wondering what game the Brandon's were playing. Whatever it was, they had no legitimate reason to call the police. *None that anyone would believe anyway.*

'Stay in the car sir,' the sheriff shouted as the driver started to get out of the vehicle. 'Wind your window down, and put your hands on the steering wheel where I can see 'em. Passenger, put your hands on the dashboard where I can see 'em.'

The driver put his leg back in and closed the car door. Both occupants of the car complied with the sheriff's orders. The sheriff drew his gun and came to the driver's side window.

'Now sir, please show me some ID and your driver's licence, take it nice and easy, no sudden moves okay?' The driver complied.

'British, okay. Now we've had a report that you've been parked here for some time now, and that you're involved in some sort of surveillance activity. So, would you kindly explain why you're here, and exactly what you're' up to?'

Jack had seen the arrival of the sheriff's car from his vantage point in the car park across the way. As soon as he saw that the sheriff was engaged with the two men, he signalled to Rachel. They both got into the Buick and drove out of the car park on to the highway and headed south to Key West. Jack couldn't help smiling as they picked up speed. He looked at Rachel, and she was grinning.

'That was great Jack. Almost fun, if it wasn't so serious. But at least I feel like we're doing something positive for a change and not just acting like a pair of sitting ducks.'

'I know exactly what you mean Rach, I wonder how long it'll take them to convince the sheriff to let them go?'

'I should think anything from ten to fifteen minutes, which gives us a good start on them, but they'll try like hell to catch up, so step on the gas Jack.'

'Will do Rachel, what time is it?'

'Two forty five, are we okay?'

'Well the Express leaves at six, but we have to be there to board at least half an hour before so it's going to be tight. But the upside is, it leaves no time at all for our friends to get on, particularly as they won't have booked a ticket.' Rachel smiled for the first time in days.

The journey was anything but relaxed. The road was mostly single lane with plenty of traffic, so there were few opportunities to overtake. Jack kept a constant look out for the black Chevy in his rear mirror and Rachel counted off the mile markers, and when they got to mile marker 47 the road became a four lane enabling overtaking. Jack overtook as often as possible knowing that the driver of the black Chevy would make the most of this opportunity to close the gap and catch up. As the four lane became a two lane again, some three miles further on, Jack sighed with relief and began to relax a little, but as they drove to the top of the incline on the seven-mile bridge, in his mirror, Jack could see a black Chevy in the distance. He assumed the men would also see their car so 'game on' thought Jack.

'Rachel, I hate to say this, but I've just spotted the Chevy.'

'Oh shit, how far behind?'

'Far enough, providing he doesn't get to overtake more cars. Have you got the instructions I printed off for how we get to the ferry terminal?'

'Got them here Jack, but I've been thinking. It says the terminal is walking distance from downtown Key West, so why don't we dump the car in the first convenient place we see downtown, and walk to the terminal? That way they won't know we caught the Catamaran.'

'Good thinking Rach, Ramsay's going to love us.'

They were a few miles from the outskirts of Key West when the Buick suddenly slowed then stopped dead. Jack tried the starter, but the engine wouldn't kick in. Rachel looked horrified. Then they were nearly rear ended by a big silver coloured truck traveling behind them. The driver had just stopped in time, but was now hooting his horn loud and long. Jack got out and spread his hands wide in a gesture of helplessness. The guy threw his hands up too, but stopped pressing his horn. Jack got back in and tried the starter again. The engine turned over but then died. They were back to a one lane, so the traffic behind them had nowhere to go.

The oncoming traffic was heavy as well, so gave no opportunity for anyone to overtake. The man in the truck behind them, tired of waiting, jumped out of his truck, came up to Jacks window and told him to put the drive in neutral. Jack couldn't say no, but realised what would happen if they pushed the car off the road. The two men in the Chevy would be on to them in less than five minutes. *Think quick or it could be a disaster, we could be killed, Rachel could be killed.* Jack made a decision. He played stupid and pretended he couldn't find neutral.

'I'm sorry, but I'm not used to automatic cars.' Jack said to the man who'd come to help. By now Jack had his window wound down. Drivers behind the truck couldn't see the cause of the delay and were beginning to hoot their horns, the angry sound adding to the panic that he and Rachel felt. The frustrated helper spoke.

'Geddout of the fuckin thing and push, I'll drive'
Jack looked at Rachel and spoke. He just hoped the man didn't speak French. Jack's French wasn't brilliant so he hoped against hope it would be sufficient for the purpose.

'Rachel, descendre de la voiture, et en va vole son camion, comprendes?'

'D'accord'

'Vous evez les passports dans ton sac.'

'Oui, Jack l'argent aussi.

'Bon'

The man looked at them both.

'I was just explaining the situation to her – she only speaks French.' *Unknown to the man, Jack had told her they were going to steal his truck and also made sure she had their passports in her handbag.*

'Yeah well let's push this fucking heap of junk out of the way in any fucking language you like, I'm fuckin late as it is, so get behind the pair of you and push.'

By now a couple of people from further behind the truck had turned up to see what the problem was and seemed ready to give a hand to push the car off the road.

Once the other people started to push the car, and the truck driver was fully engaged in steering the Buick, Jack looked at Rachel and nodded slightly to give her her cue. They both moved quickly to the Truck. It was high, and they struggled a little to climb into the cab. Jack breathed a huge sigh of relief to see that the keys were still in the ignition as Rachel climbed into the passenger seat.

Jack started the engine, put it swiftly into reverse, then when he felt it bang against the car behind he manoeuvred the vehicle out to pass the Buick which was now thankfully more or less off the road giving them a clear way to move forward without having to face the oncoming traffic. Jack put his foot down hard on the accelerator, and the truck responded with a surprising turn of speed. He looked in the rear mirror and saw the mayhem they'd left behind. People were stood out on the road watching them flee, effectively blocking it for any other traffic to drive after them for the moment. Couldn't have planned it better thought Jack. He looked in the mirror again and saw what appeared to be a man doing a jig in the middle of the road. He guessed that would be the truck driver.

'I can't believe we just did that.'

'Neither can I,' said Jack, and they both burst out laughing. Jack had to get a tissue from Rachel to wipe his eyes so he could see to drive. The laughter soon evaporated into a serious silence.

'Look, mile marker two, just one more mile to go to Key West. It won't take long for the cops to put out an APB or whatever it is so we need to ditch the car as soon as we can. I reckon we've got a few minutes left before the police get to the man we stole this from, then a few more minutes for them to get organised, so what, ten minutes at most, probably less.'

'Looking at the map Jack, we need to keep right at the next junction on to Roosevelt Boulevard and keep on that road until it becomes Truman Avenue. Then we're near enough to walk to the terminal. We could get nearer, but that might tip them to where we're going. Look, Roosevelt, keep going.'

They got a red at some traffic lights and braked. No sign of any police cars. The tension was unbearable. The lights turned green, and Jack had to resist putting his foot down and screeching the tyres as he drove off. They encountered no more delays and were soon on Truman Avenue proper. Jack turned right on to Windsor Lane and immediately became part of a funeral cortege.'

'Oh shit, I don't believe this.'

'Calm down Jack we still have time, look there's the cemetery gates, follow them in then find somewhere to park and let's go.'

They followed the funeral cars which moved frustratingly slowly but Jack thought, the flip side is, who'd look for a stolen truck in a funeral cortege? Eventually, the mourner's cars slid into parking spaces, the official cars and the hearse drove on, taking the deceased to his final resting place. Jack and Rachel exited the stolen truck and waited until the rest of the mourners were walking towards the graveyard, then walked swiftly through the gates and on to Angela Street. They navigated their way towards the ferry terminal and could hear the sirens of a police car in the near distance.

'We pick the tickets up at the terminal, so we just have to keep or nerve for a short while, and we'll be out of this mess. What time is it now Rach?'

'Twenty past five, so we need to get a move on.'

They arrived at the terminal with a few minutes to spare, picked up their tickets and followed the man's directions to where to board the catamaran. Rachel looked at Jack and smiled, then as they got closer to the departure gate, they saw a police car parked, its roof light flashing ominously. Jack and Rachel looked at each other.

'Too late now Rach, we'll just have to tough it out, course it could be something else entirely and nothing to do with us?'

'Who you kidding Jack? not me. C'mon let's do it.'

They joined the short queue to board the ferry. The man collecting the tickets was talking to a policeman.

'Yeah okay. So, I'm looking for this couple, he speaks English and she speaks French. That right?'

'Yeah, the guy says the man definitely had an English accent, but had to speak to her in French, 'cos she only spoke French. Anyway just in case, make sure anyone who gets on board speaks with a proper English accent. I mean English or American, you know what I mean? We got no reason to think they're takin' the Express. Just covering all the bases see. So anyone who don't speak proper English, stop 'em and let me know, okay?'

'Yeah okay.'

'I'm just gonna sit in my cruiser over there. Haven't had a break all day. Just let me know if this couple try to board, okay?'

'Yeah okay officer. Next please.'

Jack and Rachel were next in the queue and approached the ticket collector talking to each other continuously, and pretending not to notice the ticket collector until the last minute.

'Ticket's please,' he asked. Rachel handed the tickets to him, then spoke to him in a clear English accent.

'Excuse me, but will the boat leave on time do you think?'

'Yes, ma'am it will, but strictly speaking, it ain't a boat it's a catamaran, okay?'

'Oh, I see. Yes, sorry, I'm sure.'

The ticket collector raised his eyes to heaven.

'Next please,' he said, and they boarded. They made straight for the bar, where Jack ordered two Jack Daniels. Neither of them normally drank spirits, but both of them downed the drinks in one.

'Celebrating?' the barman said.

'You could say that,' said Jack, and ordered another two.

CHAPTER 35

The two men were incandescent with rage. They'd made good progress and were only a few cars behind the Brandons when the traffic came to a sudden stop. They knew Key West was a very small place and felt confident they would find their prey easily. There was one road out of the place and water all around it. Boxed in was the phrase they used when they talked about getting their hands on them. Payback time for the stunt played at Orlando airport, and the latest one involving the sheriff in Islamorada. Nobody made fools of these two, they were the best. The Brandons would pay heavily for trying to make idiots of them.

As soon as the men realised the traffic wasn't going to move any time soon, they pulled over and ran up the line of vehicles just in time to see a big silver Dodge truck pulling away from the front of the queue of traffic. A gawping crowd of people stood by the side of the abandoned white Buick the Brandon's had been travelling in. A man was now running down the road after the truck, swearing and cursing at the top of his voice and gesticulating wildly at the disappearing truck.

'What happened?' said one of the men to one of the onlookers.

'Seems the car in front of that guy's truck broke down.' He pointed at the now forlorn figure walking back down the road towards them. 'And while we were all helping push their car out of the way, the couple from the car stole his truck. French people by all accounts, leastwise, that's what the guy whose truck they stole said. Yellin' about French fuckers takin' his truck an all...'

Just then a cop car arrived, lights flashing and sirens wailing. Two overweight police officers got out and while one went to talk to the man whose truck was stolen and began taking particulars, the other officer started to get the traffic moving. At that point, the two men jogged back to their car to continue their pursuit of the Brandons. The fact that the Brandons had stolen the truck made no difference. They still felt confident they would be able to find them in this so called town. They just had to make sure they got to them before the cops did, easy.

Ramsay's phone rang as he was coming through the door of his house. His key stuck in the door and by the time he's managed to get it out, the phone was taking a message. He heard his own voice 'Ramsay here leave a message,' then a short beep. He decided to listen rather than pick up just in case it was a sales call.

'Jerry Johnson here from the Key West police department. Message for Dave Ramsay. Please call 305 809 1111 as soon as you get this message. Subject a white Buick sedan index MG6 3NU registered to you. This vehicle has been involved in an incident in the vicinity of Key West. Thank you.'

Uh-uh thought Ramsay and looked for the Brandon's cell number.

Jack Brandon answered on the first ring.

'Hello'

'Hi Jack, what's happening?'

'Hi Ramsay, we were just about to call you. I'm afraid we've had a problem with your car, and we had to ditch it near Key West, I'm really sorry, but we had no choice. I'll fill you in on the details later, and obviously we'll pay for any costs etc., but can you meet us at Fort Myers ferry port tonight, I think the catamaran gets in at nine forty five?'

'Well I would if I had a car, just kidding. I'll borrow my wife's car and meet you there, and you can tell me what's going on. But in the meantime, I need to call the Key West police department. They called me as the registered owner saying there'd been an incident, so just give me the short version and I'll make up some story to suit. See you at the ferry port.'

Jack told him briefly what had happened, Ramsay listened without interrupting, then said.

'Okay got the picture. You can give me the long version later over a beer, sounds like you're having an exciting time.'

'I think we'd settle for unexciting, if given the choice. See you later Ramsay and thanks.'

Ramsay picked them up from the ferry terminal later that evening.

'So before we get to what happened, where do you guys want to go?'

'Good question. We don't have any luggage, just the clothes were wearing. We do have our money and passports, but not much else.'

'Well, it looks like you're gonna have to stay at my place for the time being.'

Jack and Rachel thanked him, and Ramsay waived their thanks away.

'So, tell me all.'

Jack and Rachel told Ramsay the whole story as they drove. Ramsey laughed a lot as they told their tale.

'You two are getting pretty good at this fugitive game,' he said when they'd finally brought him up to date. 'So, it seems the two guys weren't quite as dumb as we thought they were,' he continued. 'Still, looks like you've really given them the slip now. Have you decided on your next move?'

'We have, we had lots of time to think things through on the crossing. We've been doing some calculations, and we've decided to go to France. We were going to have to do something soon anyway, we're running out of cash. We can't go to an ATM without the possibility of alerting someone as to where we are, so that's out. Also, we have to pay the rest of what we owe you, plus two air tickets to France, and that's going to take up pretty well what cash we have.' Jack continued, 'Like you say, it's reasonable to assume that we've lost the two men following us for the time being, so we'll probably be okay to go to Miami without them knowing, and catch a flight to Paris, then on to Nice. We also think that anyone trying to find us has probably already checked out our place in France, and satisfied themselves that we're not there.

'Okay, a reasonable assumption,' said Ramsay.

Jack continued,

'We think it's too soon to go back to the UK, but maybe it'd be safe enough now for us to go back to our apartment in the south of France, just for long enough to organise ourselves, then we can then disappear for quite a while. Maybe go to another part of France, it's a big country and it would be hard to find us. We could tour round a bit, then when we feel it's safe, go back and stay in our apartment for a while. Then eventually think about going back to the UK when enough time has passed for things to have cooled down. What do you think?'

'Sounds like a plan,' said Ramsey.

He slowed down as they approached a bar by the side of the road and suggested they stop and have a beer.

They found an empty table, and while Jack went to the bar to get their drinks, Ramsay asked Rachel about their apartment in France, and how secure they would be when they were there. She told him it was in a small gated complex called Le Jardin d'Eze, just fifteen minutes' drive from Nice. It had beautiful views over the Mediterranean. There was a guardian, and to enter the property you had to have an electronic device to open the gate, or ask the guardian to let you in. It was secure, but someone could enter the complex without too much trouble if they were determined enough.

Jack returned with the beers, and they discussed more details of their plan to go back to France. They said despite the number of years they'd had the apartment, they hardly knew anyone on the complex apart from the guardian Jean-Pierre, so he would probably be the only one who would know they were there, and they might not even bump into him if they only stayed a night or so. Once they were in Eze, they would have access to the funds in their French bank account in Nice and they could make arrangements to draw cash out directly from banks in France whenever they wanted to, rather than use cash machines. Plus, they would be able to collect some clothes and their own car, which they kept in the underground garage in the complex.

They'd thought about just staying at the apartment, but decided it would be too great a risk, until a few more weeks had passed at least. If they felt the need, they could stay elsewhere, they had the whole of Europe to hide in.

'Okay, well you two must be exhausted let's get home. I'll call and tell Mrs Ramsay she has house guests.'

The next morning they went to a local travel agent where they paid in cash and booked a flight from Miami to Paris with an onward connection to Nice. That done, they went shopping for some essentials. In the meantime, Ramsay called the police in Key West and convinced them that his car had been stolen by joyriders and they agreed to let him have it back. They'd recovered the truck Jack and Rachel had stolen, and returned it to its owner, so they were happy enough to let the whole thing slide. In theory they were still looking for Jack and Rachel but Ramsay knew it wouldn't be a priority. He made arrangements with a local garage to collect the car, have it repaired and said he'd send someone down to collect later that week.

In Key West, two men were trying to find the Brandons. It was obvious from the incident on the road into Key West that the police would be looking for them as well. Now the Brandons had ditched their car, the men had nothing to identify where the Brandons might be holed up. Plus, the Brandons now knew the men were back on their trail, so the job of finding them had got much harder. Still, the men thought, we're very good at finding people.

They'd started to visit the car rental agencies to check if the Brandons had hired a car, but soon established that the

Key West police had issued instructions to all the rental agencies to report to them, if the Brandons attempted to rent a car. Likewise, the police had issued similar instructions to the taxi firms and hotels. With that kind of pressure, the Brandons would have a hard time hiding anywhere in Key West. The men decided to check with the police and went to the headquarters on North Roosevelt Boulevard. Posing as insurance agents acting on behalf of the owner of another vehicle involved in the 'incident' in which the Brandons stole a truck, they asked if there had been any progress in finding the couple who'd ditched their car and stolen the truck.

'No sir,' the man on the information desk said after checking with colleagues.

'Surprising in the circumstances,' He said, 'this is a small place and we have everything covered, so maybe they've managed to get out of KW without being seen, but unlikely.

'Course they could've left last night on the Key West Express, but they'd have had to have pre-planned. That, or been extremely lucky with their timing. I know sergeant Bramowski was looking into that possibility, hold on I'll give him a call.'

'Just a minute,' said one of the two men, 'what's the Key West Express?'

'Oh, it's a ferry, well a catamaran, jet powered, it goes from here to Fort Myers, left last night at six, so if they were on that, they're long gone.'

The two men looked at each other. The policemen finished speaking and put his phone down.

'Well there were quite a number of couples who fit the general description, and who were booked on the ferry last night, but we can't say as we don't have any names, but leave me your contact details and I'll let you know if anything develops. The two men went to the ferry terminal and found the ticket office. Unlike the police, they did have a name. After a conversation involving the ticket clerk telling them such information was confidential, and then agreeing that anything was available at a price, they finally got confirmation that a Mr and Mrs Jack Brandon travelled on the Key West Express at six the previous evening.

They called Mickey and gave him the bad news. Eddie held the phone away from his ear as the tirade of insults spilt from it. The phone call over. they looked at each other and Eddie said.

'I don't know about you, but I've had enough of this shit, I'm going back, and they can keep their fuckin contract, money and all.' The other man nodded in agreement.

That same day Ramsay drove Jack and Rachel to Miami across Alligator Alley. Thunder rumbled, and then the rain came in such quantities, Ramsay had to slow down to a crawl. Nevertheless, the journey seemed to go quickly. Jack and Rachel felt excited at the prospect of getting back to more familiar territory. They arrived at the airport and had to say their goodbye's quickly in the drop off lane. Ramsay saying he'd be in touch with them soon, with any updates from Freddie, in the UK.

CHAPTER 37

They arrived in Paris Charles De Gaule Airport in the early morning, tired and weary. Jack had suggested they fly economy to preserve their funds. They had quite a reasonable amount of money in their French bank account in Nice, but they weren't sure how long they'd have to stay away from the UK. After clearing immigration and customs, they had just over an hour to kill before their connecting flight to Nice. When they finally landed in Nice, it felt like coming home thought Jack, and by the look on Rachel's face, he could see she felt the same.

Jack exchanged some of their dollars for Euros at the airport then they took a taxi to Eze. The journey took them along the familiar route on the motorway round the back of Nice to the La Turbie exit then down the Moyenne Corniche towards their apartment complex. They asked the taxi, to take them right to the door of their apartment to avoid anyone seeing them arrive. Jack paid the extortionate taxi fare, and they sneaked into their apartment. The plan was to spend just the one night there, then pack what they required for the next part of their imposed exile.

Managing to get to their apartment door without meeting anyone, Rachel stepped through the door and raised the electric shutters. The light streamed in, through the patio windows. Jack went to his computer, started it up and began loading and updating his various programs. There were plenty of new emails waiting to be read. He quickly went through them to see if there were any that he should be concerned about. There was one from Mrs Anderson who said that the police had him to contact a Chief Inspector Pownall when convenient. That didn't sound as though the police were too bothered thought Jack. While Jack was on his computer, Rachel cleaned the apartment. Having each finished their tasks, they made a list of groceries and Jack drove down to Eze village to buy the essentials.

On his return, Jack was just driving into the complex when Jean-Pierre, the guardian came out of his little office situated next to the entrance. Jack returned Jean-Pierre's wave, but Jean-Pierre walked the short distance to the car, so Jack was obliged to stop and wind the window down to greet the man.

'Cava Jean-Pierre?' Jack said.

'Ahh, cava bien, merci monsieur Brandon,' Jean-Pierre replied greeting him obsequiously.

'Jack, 'ow are you, 'ow nice to see you and where is the beautiful Rachel? 'ow long are you 'ere?'

Jean-Pierre continued to ask lots of questions, without stopping for an answer. Jack managed eventually to get a word in

'Oh not long,' Jack said, 'as a matter of fact we're leaving tomorrow.'

'Tomorrow? but surely, you 'ave only just got 'ere?'

'Yes well we're going on a bit of a trip. Want to see some more of your beautiful country.'

'Ahh I see,' said Jean-Pierre.

Jack asked,

'Has anyone been asking about us in the last few weeks?'

'As a matter of fact, you know there was a man who came and asked if you were 'ere, but I told 'im no, I 'adn't seen you in weeks. Friend of yours maybe?'

'Er no, not exactly, er, someone we met in the UK probably, nuisance really. He said he also had a holiday place not too far from here and would drop in and see us sometime, but we'd really like to avoid him. So, if by any chance he comes back, would you tell him you haven't seen us this time? And, if he or anyone else comes again, and even if we are here, please tell them the same thing, that we've not been back for ages, okay?'

'Ahh, I understand,' said Jean-Pierre tapping his forefinger against the side of his nose in a Gallic gesture of complicit understanding.

Jack then took out a hundred Euro note from the money he'd exchanged at the airport and handed it to Jean-Pierre. As usual, when Jean-Pierre was offered money, they had to go through the performance of him pretending he couldn't possibly take it.

'Non, non, that is not necessary Jack,' while at the same time putting the money into his pocket, a little too quickly for his feigned protest to have any credibility.

Jack played his part insisting that he deserved it for all his help etc. He thanked Jean-Pierre for his understanding. Then they wished each other well.

'Av a good trip Jack, what time will you be leaving?'

'Oh probably about lunchtime, by the time we've got everything sorted.'

'Well let me know when you get back,' he said.

'I will,' said Jack, and drove to the door of the underground garage.

Jack pointed the electronic remote, pressed the button, and the garage door opened slowly. This underground garage always reminded Jack of the Thunderbird programme the kids used to watch. The door opened, and he drove into the dark interior, then the door closed behind him. He drove further into the garage, which had all manner of cars parked in individual spaces on either side. Jack's garage was the last one from the end. He parked, locked the car and walked up one flight of stairs to the ground floor level to their apartment. *Was Jean-Pierre just a little more obsequious than normal* thought Jack? *No, maybe just glad to see us probably,* he concluded.

Jean-Pierre went back inside his office, looked for the piece of paper with the number on it and dialled.

'Hello?' the voice said.

'Yes, 'allo, this is Jean-Pierre from Le Jardin d'Eze in France. Is that the gentlemen who left me his number?'

'Yes it is,' said the man, 'are they there now?'

'Yes they are 'ere,' said Jean-Pierre 'but they are leaving again tomorrow.'

'Tomorrow, tomorrow, shit.' The man was not pleased.

'Why didn't you call me before?'

'They 'ave only just arrived, last night I think.'

'Do you know where they're going?'

'Ah yes, to Provence, touring around.'

'Okay, well at least that's something. Any idea what time they're planning to leave?'

'Well, Jack said about lunchtime.'

'Fuck!' said the man. Jean-Pierre did not like people using obscenities to him in any language, and he grimaced at the phone, holding it away as if to recoil from the man's temper.

The man calmed down.

'Have they hired a car or do they have their own?'

'They 'ave their own little car, a fiat I think, a white one.'

'Do you know the number?'

'Yes I think I do, all the cars 'ave to be registered with the management for insurance and fire department, so let me see here, ah yes 'ere it is 237 AB 06.'

'Okay, thanks I'll make sure you get the rest of the money.'

'Thank you monsieur and 'ave a nice day.'

One thousand Euros for one phone call, mais oui, not bad. He could buy his wife a nice little something and his son could now have the bike he wanted for his birthday.

It wasn't his fault that someone was looking for Jack, he should pay his debts like respectable people, and then no one would be after him.

CHAPTER 38

Jack took the groceries back to the apartment and told Rachel about bumping into Jean-Pierre.

'I suppose it was unrealistic to think we could have got away without him seeing us,' she said.

'Yes I suppose it was, but at least it gave me the chance to ask if anyone had been asking about us, and I'm afraid they have.'

'What - who was it?'

'He didn't know, but anyway I made up a story about having met someone recently who said they might call in on us. I greased his palm and told him if this person returns, or if anyone else asks about us, he should say that we haven't been here for ages, so that should sort that.'

'I hope you're right Jack. But I was wondering on the flight, we've been so pre-occupied with avoiding the men sent to, well, sent to, to kill you.' Rachel stopped and swallowed trying to regain her composure.

'I still can't believe all this.' she said, 'what I mean is, we've forgotten about the other people Ramsay said were looking for you, at least I had. If revenge isn't their motive then what do these other people want from you Jack?'

Rachel looked at him.

'There's something you haven't told me, isn't there?'

Jack sat down.

'Well, I didn't want to compromise you in case the police started asking you questions. I thought if you didn't know then you wouldn't have to lie.'

'Lie about what Jack?'

'Well, the guys who I had the, the, erm, problem with that morning, were carrying drugs, a lot of them. They'd collected them from somewhere, a helicopter drop, and they were delivering them to somewhere, I don't know exactly, but somewhere not too far away from where I came across them.'

'I still don't understand.'

'Well after I'd been attacked and, well you know what happened, I decided to make the other guy the scapegoat, you know make it look as though they'd argued and had a fight.'

'Yes you told me that before.'

'Yes well, I took the drugs, they were in a rucksack, and I hid them.'

'What on earth did you do that for?'

The incredulity in Rachel's voice made Jack wonder at his actions himself.

'I thought I had no choice. If I'd left the drugs there, then the police would have found them, and there would be no chance of them coming to the conclusion that the two men had fought. Why would one of them kill the other, then leave the drugs, it wouldn't make sense?'

'Oh Jack, what have you got us into? Presumably, these "other people" who are after you, after us, are the people who own the drugs and they want them back?'

'It's a reasonable assumption. The only one that makes any sense,' said Jack

'Well, why don't you simply give them back? Tell them where the drugs are.'

'I would Rachel. Believe me, I've thought about how to do that a million times, but how do I contact them? I don't have a clue who they are, or how to find out who they are. I can't ask the police that's for sure. And don't forget that Ramsay said there may be two other parties looking for me, so maybe there are two lots of people who want to get the hands on the stuff?

And if I told them where I'd hidden the drugs, there's no guarantee they still wouldn't want to punish me for killing their man, mule, courier, or whatever the correct term is. Even if I was able to convince them it was all an accident, self defence.'

'My God I didn't think it could get any worse' said Rachel, struggling to hold back the tears. 'Is there any more you haven't told me? If there is, tell me now because I don't think I could stand any more surprises.'

'No Rach, nothing more I promise. Look, let's try to make the best of it now, and I'll try to figure out how I might be able to give the drugs back when we get back to the UK. Maybe Ramsay's friend Freddie can help us?'

'Rachel nodded her head in agreement. Jack put his arms around her and kissed her head.

'We'll sort this all out, and one day....'

'Don't say it Jack Brandon, just don't say that one day we'll laugh about this, because I certainly won't. Once this is over, I'll wipe it from my mind forever, assuming I have a functioning mind left that is.'

'Okay Rach, sorry. Let's try to relax, maybe have a walk down to Eze later, then a couple of hours by the pool this afternoon, and an early dinner. We've a long journey to do tomorrow, so we might as well make the best of today and try to relax. Rachel looked up at Jack,

'Sorry I shouted just now, I don't know I....'

'I know' Jack said 'I keep thinking I'll wake up and this has all been a nightmare. C'mon let's go for that walk.'

The next morning they loaded the car up with all they thought they'd need for a few weeks away. Jack reckoned they didn't need all that much.

'The weather will be good,' he said, 'so jeans and shorts are all we need Rach, plus don't forget our sandwiches for the journey.'

By the time they'd locked up the apartment and got all their stuff loaded, it was gone one thirty, and they were finally ready to go.

CHAPTER 39

Tony Malone had to move quickly. It was two o'clock in the afternoon UK time when the guardian from France had phoned him. First things first, go and see Tom MacBride and ask him if he would let him go on holiday, then play the sympathy card and borrow some money off him. Malone liked the idea of Tom MacBride funding him to nick his own gear. He was confident he could finesse Tom. Like all hard men, Tom MacBride had a soft centre if you knew how to find it.

He put on a performance, telling Tom MacBride how he needed a break but he was broke etc etc, and sure enough, Tom MacBride fell for it. The trick now was to get to Nice then Eze, and be in place in time to follow Brandon and his wife, then plan his next move. He couldn't do what he needed to do without help, so he called Kamal Petrovic, a Bosnian Serb who came over to the UK in the seventies, illegally.

Kamal was not particularly tall, but wiry and fit. He was hard as nails, the result of a harsh upbringing. Brutal, but could lay on the charm if needed. He worked under Malone in Tom MacBride's 'security business' and proved to be reliable and utterly ruthless. He was extremely loyal to Malone, who he admired as being even more ruthless than him. He knew that Malone had done things in the IRA that even a Bosnian would find a bit extreme.

Malone had also paid personally to get Kamal some new papers, good ones, but ones that gave him a hold over Kamal. Malone wasn't so stupid to trust Kamal completely, so he told Kamal that he'd lodged certain papers with a lawyer, only to be opened in the event of him dying in suspicious circumstances. Included in the papers were details of Kamal's origin and his forged papers etc, so he explained to him that it was in Kamal's very best interests to watch his back, and make sure that nothing bad ever happened to him. It had proved to be a good insurance investment so far.

He called Kamal and told to get packed. He needed him to come with him to France for a couple of weeks, right away.

'Tell anyone who wants to know where you're going, that you're going to visit your dying Aunt in Bosnia.'

'Okay Tony' said the Bosnian, 'life was getting boring round here anyway, and I could do with a change of scene.'

'I'll collect you in about an hour,' said Malone, 'there's a flight from Liverpool at nine thirty tonight. I've booked us both on it.'

Malone packed a few clothes in a small case, plus his shaving gear and a box of Zolpidem sleeping pills. He collected Kamal, and they drove to Liverpool airport. The flight was on time and arrived in Nice at one o'clock in the morning, local time.

Malone had taken the one credit card he possessed, that still had some emergency funds on it. They went to the car hire counter and completed the formalities. As luck would have it, they offered Malone a free upgrade to a BMW. Nice car and a lovely shade of unremarkable grey. Perfect. Malone drove while Kamal dozed in the passenger seat.

They arrived in Eze just before four in the morning. Malone found a nice quiet corner of the car park, and left the Bosnian snoring in the passenger seat while he curled up in the back to catch up on his own sleep.

So far so good, he thought as he dozed off. He woke as dawn broke, shook Kamal awake, and they waited for the Café in the square to open. They took a table outside in the early morning sun and ordered orange juice, coffee and croissants. Malone retrieved his toiletries from the car had a good wash in the café's toilets, brushed his teeth and had a shave. He felt remarkably fresh and alert. He sat down again at the table and ordered more coffee, while Kamal went to the toilets to freshen up. He came back to the table, and they sat in silence watching the coaches arrive, bringing tourists from the cruise ships in Villefranche, for their sightseeing visit to the village of Eze.

Malone got up and went to the small Casino supermarket located at the corner of the square and bought a roll of wide sticky tape, some plastic straws, plastic knives and forks, a tube of paper cups, a pack of bottled water and some tins of beans, *Heinz beans in a French supermarket – seen everything now*. He paid in cash, put the items in the boot of the BMW and went back to the table to finish his coffee. He explained to Kamal what they were going to do. He didn't give him all the details, just that they were going to follow this couple, the Brandons, who were going on a car journey and that he would tell Kamal more as they followed them.

Malone said they should leave and drive up to the gates of this apartment complex called Le Jardin d'Eze, to suss out where they could park later, so they could follow the couple when they left. He said that would be about midday. They drove up the road, and Malone found a convenient little lay-by which afforded them a good view of the gates, but would also enable him to turn either way, depending on which way the Brandons decided to go when they left the complex. He was careful to avoid being seen by that oily little guardian who would be looking for his five hundred Euros blood money.

In the meantime he decided to have a drive around the immediate area to familiarise himself, then park up nice and early in anticipation of following the Brandons when they left. It was eleven when he parked up. He sank down in his seat and waited. Kamal got into the back and snoozed.

CHAPTER 40

Once they were in the car, Jack and Rachel were anxious to get on their way. They drove out of the gates of the complex and turned right taking the Moyenne Corniche to Nice where they could draw some cash out of the bank.

The road was busy, the high season was kicking in, and as usual, the roads were blighted by mad French drivers and motorcyclists competing for who could be the most the most suicidal road user. They got to Nice unscathed, parked up and went to Credit Agricole where they asked for Gille, their 'personal manager'. Jack and Rachel were kept waiting but eventually were shown into Gille's office. He showered Jack and Rachel with elaborate apologies for making them wait.

Jack explained that they were going on a trip, possibly for a few weeks, and that they wanted to draw some cash out now. He explained they'd never requested a credit card as they always assumed they would use their UK credit cards. But this time they might want to draw funds from some of the bank's branches, depending on how long they stayed away for, and could they do that without a credit card as they didn't have one? Gille said that was fine, but to make sure they took their passports and driving licences with them and to call him if they encountered any problems.

'And how much would you like to draw out now Jack?'

'A thousand Euros should be enough to get us going.'

'No problem,' he said and telephoned one of the cashiers to bring the money through to his office. The money arrived. He handed it to Jack, stood up and shook Jack's hand, then Rachel's and showing them out of his office, wished them bon voyage. Malone had picked them up easily enough when they'd left their apartment complex. He'd been dozing, but Kamal alerted him as the gate opened and the Brandons drove out, turning right in their white Fiat, towards Nice.

They followed at a discreet distance, letting a couple of cars get in between the BMW and the Brandon's Fiat. They were sure the Brandons had no idea they were being followed and weren't they taking any precautions. *This would be a doddle.* He nearly lost them in Nice when they drove into the underground car park at Cours Saleya. He followed and eventually found them parking their car, spotting a place to park not too far away. He decided to stay there rather than risk following them on foot. They were bound to return to the car. The heat and fumes in the car park were unbearable, both inside and outside the car. He figured that if he kept the engine going he could keep the air conditioning on, but then he thought that the fumes would probably give them both carbon monoxide poisoning. He turned the engine off.

They waited and sweated like pigs. Just as Malone thought he might pass out with the heat, the Brandons came back, got into their car and drove out of the car park. They followed. Once outside the Brandon's car turned left, then right and along the Promenade Des Anglais. The beaches were in full swing and crowded. The turquoise sea looked so inviting to the two men after spending the last hour in that oven of a car park. They followed the Brandons past Nice airport, then they turned right, on to the A8 autoroute, taking the westerly direction towards Cannes and beyond.

Malone slotted in behind a vehicle a couple of cars back and settled in for what might be a long motorway drive. As they drove along, Malone explained his plan to the Bosnian, well at least the part that needed his input The Bosnian nodded, taking in the details with an implacable look on his face. This would be easy, thought the Bosnian. A real holiday, and the woman was a looker, from what he could see through the car windscreen, not bad at all. He might have some fun with her later he thought, then closed his eyes and dozed off.

Jack drove along the A8 beyond the Cannes turnoff and on towards the Luberon. *French motorways are great* thought Jack, *lots of room, not that much traffic once you leave the big conurbations behind.*

He was musing to himself, thinking about the French outlook on life. *Would you rather be driving manically on a crowded English motorway, more than likely in the rain, stopping briefly to grab a quick sandwich for your ten minute lunch break, giving yourself indigestion and working yourself to a frazzle? No, the French have the right idea, quality of life, a two hour lunch break.....*

'Whoa!' Jack shouted, jolted out of his reverie by a lunatic French driver who'd suddenly chosen to move out of the inside lane without warning, and nearly hitting the side of their car. Rachel screamed, Jack stamped on the brakes, and swerved and avoided a collision.

'The bloody idiot!' Jack screamed as he concentrated on getting the car back under control. He manoeuvred the car into the middle lane and put lots of distance between him and any other cars.

'Bloody French drivers,' he said.

Then Jack laughed, thinking how just a minute ago he was admiring the French for their quality of life. He'd forgotten about their shortcomings as drivers. Rachel looked at him with a quizzical look on her face.

'Sorry Rach, I'm not going mad, I was just musing about the quality of French life when that jerk tried to end our lives altogether. Listen, why we don't stop at the next picnic place and eat our sandwiches? Here's one coming up now.'

Rachel agreed, and Jack signalled to pull off the motorway.

Malone had seen the near miss, and thought how ironic it would have been if Jack had been killed and he'd been deprived of the chance to get his hands on the drugs. Now they were turning off the motorway into a rest area, come picnic-park. This could be tricky thought Malone, but he turned off after them and managed to park well away from their car, while still keeping them in sight. Watching all the other people tucking into food made both Kamal and Malone hungry and they hadn't had the foresight to buy any food for the journey.

The Brandons got out of their car and took their food and some cans of drink to a picnic table. Malone and the Bosnian took the opportunity to get a good look at them both, to make sure they would know them again, without their car to identify them.

Jack and Rachel rejoined the motorway after having their sandwiches, and settled in for the next stage of their journey. No matter how many times they made this trip, they still found the countryside fascinating. Rachel noticed Jack was looking in the rear mirror quite a lot. Rachel turned in her seat to look at the road behind but couldn't see anything amiss.

'What is it Jack?'

'What's what?'

'You seem to be looking in the rear mirror quite a lot.'

'Nothing really, it's just that there's a grey BMW behind us, and I'm sure we've seen before, earlier in the journey, before we stopped for our lunch.'

Rachel turned round and spotted the car Jack was talking about.

'Yes I can see a grey BMW. But there must be literally thousands of grey BMWs in Europe. So, unless you think it's exactly the same one, I don't think we should worry. I mean how could anyone be following us? Think about it, they'd have had to have someone watching our place in Eze since we left for Florida. I can't imagine any organisation doing that, can you?'

'Yeah, good point Rachel, just my paranoia getting the better of me, let's try to relax and enjoy the rest of the journey.'

As they drove along, they passed the big red coloured mountain range on their left, which Jack remembered was called the Massif des Maures. A little further on, vineyards started to appear along the side of the motorway, then the famous landmark mountain, Mont Sainte Victoire, hove into view on their right hand side. Every time they saw the mountain it looked to be a different colour. It even seemed to change colour as they drove past it. No wonder Cezanne was so fascinated by it, or was it Van Gogh? Jack could never remember. What he did know was that the artist, whichever one it was, was obsessed by it and painted it numerous times.

'Stop day dreaming Jack Brandon, you're supposed to be concentrating on your driving.'

'Sorry Rach, miles away, listen we'd better decide where we're going, and where we're going to stay, so where do you fancy?'

They both loved the Luberon and had decided to head in that general direction, then choose where they fancied staying once they were a bit nearer.

'How about the little hotel we stayed at in Fontaine de Vaucluse' Jack suggested.

'Yes 'said Rachel, 'La Mimosa?'

'That's the one, what do you think?'

'Sounds good to me, let's call and see if they have a room.'

They stopped in a lay-by, and Jack found the hotel's number on his IPhone, called and booked a room, then they set off again trying to remember how to get to the hotel.

They came off the motorway at Cavaillon passed through a semi industrial area, then along roads lined with plane trees, and as they got nearer to their destination, the countryside changed again with vineyards and cherry orchards appearing on either side of the road. This was what Jack considered to be the real Provence, the one that Peter Mayle wrote about. *There's nowhere quite like it* thought Jack, *so many mountain villages with stunning views, cherry orchards laden with fruit, fields of sunflowers, lavender fields that go on forever, and so many vineyards you wonder if there are enough wine drinkers to consume that much wine. We'll try and help out later* thought Jack and smiled to himself.

'What are you smiling at Jack Brandon?'

'Sorry Rach, just told myself a joke that's all.'

'You're cracking up Jack.'

'You could be right Rach. Now, isn't that the turn to Fontaine de Vaucluse?'

They followed the Fiat to where it veered off, just before coming into a village. They stopped as they saw the car parking up outside a hotel. The hotel was in a sort of cul de sac making it impossible for Malone to drive by, but they had fortunately stayed back far enough for him to take the alternative option of stopping and turning around without being noticed.

Malone drove back round and out of site. Kamal got out of the car and wandered down the road far enough for him to make sure that the Brandons were staying. They were, they were unloading their luggage.

CHAPTER 41

Rachel loved these small boutique hotels. They'd first found La Mimosa by accident as they were driving to see the source of the river Sorgue a couple of years before. The gin clear water gushes out of a sheer rock face at the back of the pretty village of Fontaine de Vacluse, and a tributary of the river it created ran through the La Mimosa's grounds. The hotel had been converted from an old water mill. Jack loved the place too and liked watching the wild brown trout swimming in the crystal clear river that flowed past, and virtually through, the hotel.

They rang the bell on reception and a lady appeared out of an office door behind the small reception desk and greeted them. They went through the formalities, got the room key and went to their room. Jack was tired after all that driving, but Rachel said she needed some things from the pharmacy in the village, and said she could do with stretching her legs anyway. And it was only a short walk. She pecked Jack on the cheek and left.

Malone and Kamal sat in the car deciding how to achieve their objective. It would involve a great deal of patience and waiting, but there was little choice. The first thing they had to do was get some food and drink. So, knowing their quarry was here for at least the night, they found a parking place and went to a small shop which sold sandwiches and soft drinks. They were heading back to the car when they spotted Rachel Brandon walking on her own through the village.

This presented an opportunity, but much sooner than anticipated. Malone had learnt, you should take your chances when you can. He told Kamal what he intended to do. Kamal went back to the car with the sandwiches and drinks, started the car and waited. Malone saw Rachel go into a pharmacy, so he waited outside.

This was going to be tricky. He would have liked more time to plan the kidnap, but improvisation was his necessary in situations like this. Anyway, risk fired him up. It was why he did what he did. Rachel came out of the pharmacy, and he went to make his move. He was going to approach her, pretending to ask her something, then planned to tell her, very forcibly, that she had better do as he said, as his friend was in their hotel room and was holding a gun at Jack's head, waiting for his call. Malone was just about to make his approach, when Rachel stopped in the doorway, holding the door open for another woman leaving the shop at the same time. They had obviously struck up a conversation while in the pharmacy and were now walking off together in the direction of the Mimosa hotel, talking away ten to the dozen. *Damn damn damn* he thought, as he stood there trying to calm down after the adrenalin rush he had had in anticipation of the snatch.

He gave himself a minute then headed back to the car, but as he turned the corner, there was Kamal leaning on the open rear car door, talking to Rachel pointing at a map in his other hand. The other woman was nowhere to be seen and had obviously left Rachel trying to help this poor foreigner find his way to somewhere. Malone looked around. Not too many people. He nodded at Kamal as he approached Rachel's back. Rachel was concentrating on the map. Suddenly she felt a hand close across her mouth, then her legs went from under her as she was bundled into the back seat of the car.

Malone got in quickly beside her and told to behave, or he'd do her some serious harm. The other reversed the car then drove away from the village. Rachel was too shocked to speak or think properly, then screamed and started to flail her arms at the man in the seat next to her.

'Stop it you stupid bitch,' the man said. And holding her wrists with one strong hand, he slapped her hard across the mouth. Rachel's head shook at the strength of the blow. She felt faint and dizzy and slumped in her seat. *The grey BMW, I should have listened to Jack.*

Kamal drove at an even pace, so as not to attract any attention, while Malone sat in the back with Rachel. She had a small handbag which she'd stuck hold of despite the attack. Malone now took it away from her. He told Kamal to find a nice quiet place where they could park up without being disturbed. A million thoughts were racing through Rachel's mind, *who were they, what were these thugs going to do to her, how had this happened? Were they something to do with the people chasing Jack, they had to be, it was too much of a coincidence to be anything else, oh please God don't let them touch me.* Rachel felt too terrified to say anything.

Malone spoke.

'Listen to me, and listen good. No harm'll come to you, providing we get what we want. It might be uncomfortable for you for a while, but providing everyone plays ball then you'll be released, none the worse for wear.'

'What are you talking about?' Rachel said, finally finding her voice, 'What do you mean play ball?'

'Nothing for you to worry about, we're not perverts or anything like that. This is just business.'

He looked up, and through the rear mirror, saw the expression in Kamal's eyes. He wondered about what he'd just promised. Kamal turned down a smaller road that led to a derelict building, which had once been some sort of farm or barn. Kamal got out and had a good look around. He gave the okay and got back in the car. Malone took Rachel's bag and emptied it out on the seat beside him.

'Ha!' he said when he saw the phone, 'perfect, I was hoping for that.'

He scrolled through the names in her phone until he came to Jack's mobile number. He pressed call and Jack answered after the third ring.

'Rachel?' he said, 'where on earth are you? It's nearly seven o'clock?'

'Listen carefully Brandon.'

'What - who's this?'

'Never mind who it is, just shut up and listen. We have your wife, but as long as you give us what we want, you can have her back as good as new. But if you tell anyone about this, such as the police for instance, she's dead.'

Malone closed down the connection just as Jack was saying

'Who the….?'

Okay, he said to himself, *move number one. Now move number two.* Indicating to Kamal, he said,

'You just hold on to Missy here while I get her a drink.'

Kamal got out of the driver's seat and got into the back seat of the car on the other side of Rachel. She looked perplexed and afraid. Malone got out and went to the boot and opened it. He split open the tube of plastic cups and got one of the bottles of water; he then delved in his case and found the sleeping pills. He crushed two of the pills in his fingers and let the pieces drop into the cup, then filled it half full with water from the plastic bottle, got one of the plastic spoons and stirred the water to make sure all the contents had dissolved. He walked back to the rear door, opened it and said to Rachel.

'There are two ways we can do this, the hard way, where Kamal holds you, and I force you to drink, or the easy way where you just drink it all up yourself.'

Rachel was white with fear.

'Take it easy, this will just make you sleepy. We need to keep you in good shape, otherwise, you're of no value to us, so don't worry we won't harm you. So what's it to be, easy or hard?'

Rachel nodded. Malone held the cup to her lips, and she drank. She filled her mouth up with water then spat it back out all over him.

'Fuck you! When my husband gets hold of you two, you'll be sorry you were born.'

Malone looked at Kamal, then dragged Rachel out of the car.

'Hold her a minute.'

Then he went to the open boot of the car, grabbed some tissues and wiped himself as dry as he could, then came back. He stood in front of Rachel and backhanded her across the face. Rachel screamed in agony at the powerful blow. Blood running down her cheek, a cut from the signet ring he was wearing.

'Now I'm going to get another cup, and you're going to drink it, or I'll just beat your face to a pulp here and now, understand?'

'Rachel nodded, and this time she didn't resist when she was offered the paper cup.

They all got back in the car, Malone got back in the back with Rachel and Kamal got into the driver's seat.

'Okay Kamal, drive around a bit till the bitch gets sleepy, then we'll eat those sandwiches and decide on our sleeping arrangements.'

CHAPTER 42

Jack had been on the bed, dozing and thinking about where they would go for dinner, and then fallen into a deep sleep. He'd woken up with a start when his mobile phone rang. They were now back to using their UK mobile phones. Jack looked at his phone's display panel and saw it was Rachel.

Strange, how long had she been gone and why is she ringing me? He looked at the clock it was nearly seven. How long had he been asleep? He answered the phone.

'Where on earth you have been Rach, it's nearly seven o'clock?'

A man's voice replied, and Jack was momentarily shocked.

'Listen carefully Mr Brandon.' said the voice.

'Who's this?'

'Never mind who it is, just shut the fuck up and listen. We've got your wife, but as long as we get what we want, you can have her back, as good as new. But if you tell anyone about this, like the police for instance, she's dead.'

Jack started to ask who the hell it was but the connection was broken. Jack sat back down on the bed, the nightmare was back, and worse this time. Jack sat there not knowing what to do. *They've taken Rachel, she'll be terrified.* He couldn't bear the thought of her being distressed or frightened, *she'd be terrified.* He would change places with her in a heartbeat if some higher power could arrange it.

Jack felt totally and utterly distraught, but then Jack pulled himself together and got mad. His distress turned into burning anger. *If they harm a hair on her head, I'll kill them with my bare hands. Whatever it takes I'll get you back Rachel, I promise on my life.* Jack ditched his emotions and started to think about the situation, as he'd been taught in the army. Apply cold logic, plan without emotion or anger, outwit the enemy. Try to think as they do. *They have no idea what they've started.*

He tried to recall all the details of the phone conversation. The man said something about giving him what they wanted. This was no random kidnapping, and it had to be the missing drugs they were after. He comforted himself with the thought that they would need to keep Rachel alive to trade her for the drugs. That was something positive. He recalled the conversation with Ramsay when he said that Freddie had found there were possibly three sets of people who wanted to find him.

One set were presumably the two guys they'd assumed had been hired by the psychopath brother of the dead man. The men they'd lost in Key West. This phone call didn't mention anything about Ezra the dead man, so this wasn't the same people. The obvious people in this instance were the ones who'd arranged the drugs collection, but why two more parties looking for me, not one? *Okay, put that on one side for the moment. This lot want to exchange Rachel for the drugs, and they'll obviously want to arrange some sort of exchange or something. But the drugs are in the UK, so how can I handle the situation, to guarantee I end up with Rachel back unharmed?*

Jack realised he needed help. On his own, he was unlikely to succeed against the people holding Rachel. Knowing your own limitations was part of the key to succeed in any situation. He couldn't risk telling the police, how would he explain, especially to the French police, *and anyway how would I explain away the drugs connection?*

With my French language ability, I'd probably confuse the hell out of the police and end up in jail for some drugs offence. No, I need help. Ramsay, would Ramsay come and help? He was the only one who could. What time would it be now in Florida? let's see, five hours or so behind, so that's three o'clock in the afternoon. When Jack and Rachel had gone back to using their UK mobiles, Jack had put Ramsay's phone number in it, assuming he would talk to him when this whole thing was over. Maybe arrange to meet the next time they went to Florida.

Jack found his number and pressed the dial button. Answer machine.

'Damn,' He started to leave a message.

'Ramsay, its Jack here I know you didn't expect....'

Ramsay's voice broke in.

'Hi there Jack buddy, how you doin'?'

'Ramsay, sorry, look they've taken Rachel.'

'What, I thought you'd got rid of those guys.'

'No, these are some other people. I think they may be the people whose drugs I hid.'

'Drugs, what drugs?'

'They said they'd kill her if I told anyone or don't give them what they want. I didn't know who else I could ask Ramsay, but I need help. I don't care what it costs'.

'Hold on there Jack, slow down, now, take your time and tell me the whole story.'

Jack told him about getting back to Eze okay, then coming to the Luberon, then Rachel going to the shops and him falling asleep, then the phone call.

'And what exactly do they say they want from you Jack?'

'They didn't say exactly, but it has to be the drugs. When I had the run-in with the two guys I told you about. Well, what I didn't say, was that they were carrying drugs, some sort of collection from a drop off. I took the drugs and hid them after I'd accidentally killed the guy. I only did it to make it look as though the two men had fought. I wasn't interested in the drugs. I've never taken anything stronger than aspirin in my life. As far as I'm concerned, they can have their drugs. In fact, I'd told Rachel I would try to give them back, but I didn't know how to. So, we were going to ask you to ask Freddie if he could help us to do that when we got back to the UK. But now they've taken Rachel.'

There was silence at the other end, and Jack wondered if he'd hung up, upset about not being told about the drugs.

'Ramsay, are you still there?'

'Yep still here. You should have told me about the drugs Jack.'

'I realise that now, but it didn't seem important at the time. And I thought you might have thought I was involved in drugs myself. All I was worried about then was the death threat against me. I see now it was stupid of me not to tell you the whole story. It wasn't that I intended to lie to you Ramsay. Please can you help? I can't get Rachel back by myself, the odds are too much in their favour. I can't tell the police either, not that they'd be much use in this situation.'

Ramsay was silent again. Jack waited..

'Okay, they took her how long ago?'

'Well just over an hour ago, but they could be miles away by now, and heading in any direction.'

'Whoa, slow down buddy, give me space to think. Okay, if you've only just arrived in the area and only decided to go there at the last minute, it's obvious they were following you. That means they haven't got anywhere already set up as a base. So, the first thing they'll need to do, is find somewhere they can stay, and keep Rachel without anyone knowing. They're going to have their work cut out organising that for the next few hours at least, What time is it over there now?' he asked.

'Just gone eight p.m.'

'Hmm, that means they probably won't be able to find anywhere till tomorrow. That gives me at least some time to get moving.'

Did I hear right? thought Jack.

'Ramsay, you till there?

'Yeah just thinkin'. Listen I need to call my travel agent and find out how quickly I can get to France. What airport would I come to?'

'Er.. Marseilles is probably the nearest, but Nice if not.'

Jack had to spell Marseilles for Ramsay. H he promised to call Jack back in five minutes.

'Obviously, I'll pay for everything,' said Jack

'We'll get to that later, but for now, let's get me over there and sort out the scum who've taken Rachel.'

He cut the connection, and Jack felt grateful relief. Suddenly things didn't look completely hopeless.

Half an hour later, Ramsay called him back and told Jack he'd booked a flight from Fort Myers, with connections via Atlanta and Paris. It would take about fifteen hours in all, so could he meet him at Marseilles airport at four thirty the following afternoon French time. He gave Jack the flight number, and Jack said he'd be there.

'Now they'll probably call you again when they've settled into wherever they're holed up, so whatever they ask you to do, you'll have to stall them till I get there. Best thing would be to switch your phone off altogether. They'll be annoyed but better than you trying to lie to them. They can think what they want, maybe you have no signal, maybe you've run out of battery, lots of reasons they might not be able to contact you.

In the meantime, move out of your hotel, make sure you're not followed, and book into another hotel a few miles away. Book me a room in the same place as well. Try not to worry, eat, rest and keep your strength up. You'll need to be firing on all cylinders if we're going to get this sorted – and we will. See you tomorrow buddy,' he said.

CHAPTER43

hey ate their food and discussed options. They had little choice in the circumstances, so it was another night sleeping in the car. They decided to go back to the abandoned building they'd just left. It offered cover from the road and was remote enough for their purposes. Rachel was spark out in the back, so Malone altered the front passenger seat to make it as flat as possible and shuffled around to get as comfortable as he could. The child and window locks on the back doors were on, so escape wasn't an option for the woman, even if she did wake up. It was a very warm night, so Kamal elected to sleep outside on the grass, a few yards from the car.

The next morning dawned bright and warm. Malone was already awake as the sun came streaming through the car window. He had to wake Rachel and gave her some water to drink

'Don't worry' he said, 'no sleeping pills this time.'

Rachel needed to pee so Malone led her to the side of the building. He warned her about trying to escape and turned his back to give her some privacy but stayed near, then put her back in the car and soon she was asleep again. *Just as well* thought Malone, *too early to make the next move yet.* They waited until eight o'clock, then drove a few miles until they came to a medium sized town called Isle sur la Sorge.

They found an Immobiliere that was open. Malone parked the car. Kamal stayed in the back of the car to keep an eye on Rachel who was stirring, slowly waking up again.

Malone went into the agency, found one of the staff who spoke passable English, and camping it up a bit, said he was looking to rent somewhere cheap, small and remote for a week, or maybe a little longer. He said he needed somewhere where he could find peace and quiet. Somewhere he would not be disturbed while he was writing his book. Nothing suitable she said, but wished him well in writing his book. Malone went through the same process with another agency, nothing.

Then just as he thought they'd have to try the next town, he found a third agency, Exploreimmo, offering something in the window that looked ideal. "Une petite maison pres del la riviere, trois piece," which he translated as being a small house near the river, with three rooms. The lady in the agency said the path to the house was very bumpy and full of pot holes. Not very good for the car and a long way off the road. Not very convenient for the shops and restaurants, but very quiet, or as she said "tres calme."

As it was a last minute booking, she said the price could be "very good" and she could let him have it for three hundred and fifty Euros for the week.

He said he'd take it. The lady went on to tell him that there was fresh linen, and that a cleaning lady could come to clean each day if Malone wanted. He declined the cleaning lady's services, reminding her that he and his friends didn't want any disturbance at all, as he was writing his book. Told her the couple he was with, would do any housework that was needed.

She asked for payment up front for a week's rent, and a refundable breakage deposit of two hundred Euros, which would be returned to him providing nothing was damaged during their stay. She insisted on them following her in her car as she said they would never find it by themselves. Malone asked her if he could first of all go to the supermarket to stock up, then return to her office and they could then follow her to the house.

Less than an hour later, Malone returned. They followed her to the place which had been quite accurately described as remote. *Perfect*. Rachel was fully awake by now, so Kamal stayed with her in the back of the car, until the agent handed over the keys and left.

'Stay with her, and I'll look the place over.'

Malone went into the small house and looked around. He checked upstairs which had two bedrooms then the ground floor comprising a small kitchen and two other rooms. He noticed another door near the stairs, with a large key in it. He opened the door, found a light switch and went down the stairs, into a cool, dark cellar, *a wine cellar, great!* He checked for any windows, and found just one, which was boarded up. He tried to move the boards, they wouldn't budge. The floor was dusty, and there were empty wine racks, a table, but no other furniture. He went outside and spoke to Kamal.

'You can bring her in now Kamal. We have a little room for you missie, a place of your very own, he said to Rachel, smiling.

Kamal looked at Malone, and they all went into the little house. Malone pointed at the open cellar door and gave Kamal the key. Stick her in there, but don't damage the goods. The stairs are a bit steep so be careful she doesn't fall. I'll bring a chair down, and we can tie her to that.'

Kamal, who had never spoken a word to Rachel since he asked her for directions, just before they'd kidnapped her, took Rachel down the stairs.

'Stand there and don't move.' He said.

Malone brought a chair down the stairs and told her to sit on it. They tied her hands behind the chair. Satisfied she was secure, Malone went back up the stairs, but the Bosnian lingered behind, looking at Rachel.

'Maybe we can get to know each other a little better later?' He said, once again, looking her all over.

'Get lost you imbecile, you snivelling coward. Picking on a helpless woman is all you can do. Just wait till my husband catches up with you. In the meantime, go fuck yourself. Off you go now, and mind you don't scrape your knuckles on the floor on your way out.'

The Bosnian slapped Rachel with his open hand with such force, he knocked both her and the chair over.
Rachel cried out involuntarily. A raised voice came from the open door of the cellar.

'Kamal, I won't tell you again, leave the fucking bitch alone. We concentrate on getting what we need. Till then, she stays untouched. Afterwards, you can do what you like, but until we find out where those drugs are, keep your fucking hands off her, and keep your mind on the job.'

Kamal looked at Rachel, then roughly pulled her upright He spoke to Rachel in a whisper.

'You'll pay big time for that. No one talks to me like that and gets away with it, I'm going to have some fun with you later, and then I'm going to kill you, slowly. I'll probably your husband too. Have a nice day.'

With that, he went up the cellar stairs switched off the light, then closed and locked the door.

When she was sure they couldn't hear, Rachel cried for a while, then thought about what the Bosnian had said. *He's going to kill me, and he isn't lying, so that makes it easy, I've nothing to lose, I rather die trying to escape than go through whatever it is he has planned for me.* She tried to control her emotions and think logically. *Until they get the information they need from Jack to find the drugs, they won't kill me. They won't risk doing me too much damage in the meantime. Without proving to Jack I'm okay, they won't get what they want, so even if they catch me trying to escape the worst they'll do is beat me.*

Rachel could hear them bringing in their bags and groceries. She was sure Jack would be devoting every living breathing moment to finding her. Any cost, any way, legal or not. He would rip bricks out of a wall with his bare hands to rescue Rachel, *but how will he find me?*

Malone made coffee and put croissants out on the kitchen table. Rachel heard the cellar door creak and the Bosnian came down, untied her and took her upstairs to the kitchen, then sat her down at the table. Despite resolving not to eat or co-operate in any way, Rachel found she was so hungry and thirsty that she ate the offered food and drank two cups of coffee. There was virtually no conversation between the two men during the meal. The man called Malone was absorbed, looking at a map he'd bought in a garage when they'd stopped just outside the town to refuel the car.

When she'd finished eating, she asked to be allowed to go to the toilet. The Bosnian stood outside the door until she came out, then took her back down the stairs tied her up again, and left her in the dark. She heard the key turn in the cellar door lock.

'Time for the next move,' Malone said to the Bosnian, 'but first, we need some good quality sleep. Tired minds make mistakes. I'll sleep for four hours, then wake me up and you can have your four hours, while I plan our next move. And keep your hands off the woman, got it?'

'Got it, you don't have to keep telling me.'

Malone went upstairs and lay on the bed.

Rachel tried to undo her bonds. They'd been tied just tight enough so as not to cut off the circulation but not loose enough to be undone. She tried shaking the chair with the body, but it was too well constructed and stayed firm. Her eyes had become accustomed to the dark, and the little slivers of light coming through the small gaps in the planks boarded over the solitary window helped some.

She looked around for anything that might help her get free. She spotted the remains of a broken bottle near to the now empty wine racks. She leaned over and pushed on the floor with her right foot and managed to topple herself and the chair over on to the side. It made a noise, clattering to the floor. It was also painful. She wondered if she'd done herself any damage, but nothing seemed broken. She stayed still on her side and listened - nothing. She tried her bonds again, they were still tight, maybe a bit looser?

`If she stretched her legs out, she could almost reach the pieces of broken green glass gleaming in the limited light. Although painful, she used her shoulder and knee against the ground to manoeuvre herself nearer. She managed to get her big toe behind the largest piece which had formed part of the neck of a wine bottle, and with a sideways motion, something between a kick and a flick, the piece of glass skittered over the stone floor, away from the rack and into the space in front of her.

Now she gradually turned herself round again using her upper arm and knee. It was all very painful, and the chair made scraping noise on the floor, so she stopped every now and then to listen, and to gather her strength for the next effort. Finally, she moved to a position where the piece of glass was behind her hands, and she was able to get hold of the neck part, and with a sawing motion she started to cut through the rope.

Kamal shook Malone awake.

'How is the woman?' Malone asked.

'Quiet,' said Kamal, 'but I suppose I should go and have a look.'

Malone followed the Bosnian down the stairs to the kitchen, and started to make more coffee. He told the Bosnian that he planned to call Jack, as soon as he'd had his shuteye. It was two o'clock in the afternoon now, so he'd call later after Kamal had slept. He took Rachel's phone out of his jacket pocket and noticed the battery was nearly out.

'Damn, the phone's running out of battery, look in the bitch's bag and see if she's got a charger.'

The Bosnian found Rachel's bag.

'No charger here.'

'Fuck, I'll have to go see if I can get a phone charger. Jesus that's all we need. You'll have to wait till I get back before you get your head down.'

'No worries' said Kamal, 'I can have a cat nap while I'm babysitting if necessary, I can sleep with one eye open. You learnt to do that in Bosnia, or you wake up with your throat slit from here to here,' he made a gesture of a knife across his throat.

'Go and get whatever it is you need, and let's get moving, I'm getting bored again.'

'Okay, but before I go, just check on the woman.'

The Bosnian shrugged, got the key and unlocked the cellar door. He was tired and badly needed some sleep. He switched the light on and went to the bottom of the steps.

The woman was sitting where he'd left her, her head on her chest, asleep. He went back up the steps, turned off the light and locked the door.

'It's okay, she's asleep - go get your battery charger.'

Rachel breathed a sigh of relief. She let her eyes adjust to the darkness again, then looked around the cellar for something to prise the planks off the window. In the corner, she found the remnants of an old metal hinge, presumably from the original window shutters. It was heavy and rusty but might just do the job. Rachel stuck the pointed end in between the bottom two planks and heaved. The bottom two pieces of wood splintered. She could see that although the wood looked solid, it had been eaten away and was quite fragile. She stopped and listened again then started to pull off the wooden pieces by hand. There was some resistance but not much. Within a few minutes, she'd removed nearly all the pieces of wood from the window. The window was floor height with the outside and there was no glass in it, nothing to stop her crawling out. She moved the chair under the window, and stood on it. Then she heaved herself up, through the window, and on to the ground outside. She rolled on to her back on the grass, and closed her eyes against the bright sunlight.

She opened her eyes slowly and saw two legs. She screamed as the Bosnian got hold of her by the hair and hauled her up on to her feet. She beat her fists against the Bosnian's chest and face, but he didn't let go. While holding her by the hair, he struck her in the stomach with such force, she thought her insides had collapsed. She was badly winded and had to fight to start breathing again

'Now we have ourselves a situation here. And we're all on our own this time.'

He dragged her back round the building and through the open door of the house, kicking it shut behind him. Then he threw Rachel on the floor. She rolled up into a ball to try to protect herself, while trying to recover from the vicious blow.

'Now we're going to have some fun, at least I am.'

She felt a hefty kick at the base of her spine, and she screamed in agony. The pain seemed to radiate through the rest of her body. Then she felt the man get hold of one arm then the other, and her wrists being tied together behind her. She was lifted up and thrown over his shoulder. He walked towards the stairs to the upper floor. There was little doubt in her mind what he intended to do next. She used what strength she had left to try to wriggle off his shoulder on to the floor. It was hopeless. As he took the first step up the stairs, he put his hand on the bannister to help him climb the stairs. As his arm came up, she managed to get her teeth into the back of his upper arm, and bit down as hard as she could on the flesh behind the muscle. The man screamed in agony. At the same time, a voice came from behind them.

'What the fuck…?' said the Bosnian turning and dumping Rachel on the stairs in a sitting position. Whether in response to the bite, or the voice of the man who'd just shouted, she didn't care. The man dropped the stuff he was carrying, and came over to where the Bosnian stood, trying to rub the pain away on his arm.

'The fucking bitch bit me.'

'I thought I told you not to damage the goods. I can't leave you for five minutes without you forgetting, so it looks as though I'll have to make sure you don't forget next time.'

'Look Tony…' That was as far as the he got. Rachel watched as the man called Malone grabbed the Bosnian by the throat with one hand. He squeezed. The Bosnian tried to wrench the man's hand away, as his eyes bulged out of their sockets. His face contorting in agony as the pressure continued. He soon lost the capacity to breath and slowly sank to his knees then on to his side. Malone kept the pressure up. Finally, just at it looked as if the man was finished, Malone let go. There was a rasping retching sound as the injured man tried to gulp in some air, then he started to cough uncontrollably. Malone came over to Rachel.

'You okay?'

She nodded. He left her hands tied behind her back and guided her to a kitchen chair and sat her down. He poured some water into a cup and placed it in front of her, then untied her hands. He went and retrieved the bags he'd put on the floor, laying the contents on the table. There were sandwiches and some soft drinks. He put a sandwich on the table.

'Eat, it might be all you get for some time.'

The Bosnian had recovered sufficiently to get up into a sitting position. He looked defeated, humiliated.

Malone took Rachel's phone out of his pocket and connected it to a charger he'd just taken out of a box.

'Look, I got carried away, I won't do it again, okay?'

'No you won't. Believe me, if you do…' Malone didn't finish the sentence.

'When she's eaten, let her get cleaned up then take her back down to the cellar, and make sure she can't escape this time.'

The Bosnian nodded and went to the sink, put his head under the tap, bathed his face then slurped some water noisily. He turned round, wiped his face and motioned for Rachel to get up. He pointed for her to go upstairs towards the bathroom and followed.

'Don't be long,.' he said roughly, then in a low voice added, 'and don't think that's the end of it, next time there'll be no one to save you from what you've got coming.'

Rachel looked at him with unalloyed hatred.

'You've no idea what's coming to you either,' she said, 'you can only fight helpless women. You're a coward, an insult to the human race, and when my husband gets hold of you, you'll wish you'd never been born.'

And with that, she spat in his face, ran through the door into the bathroom and locked it. She heard the man laughing, but there was a hollow ring to it. She'd never spat at anyone in her life, nor had she felt she could kill another human being. But if given the chance, she would happily kill this man.

When the phone was fully charged, Malone called Jack's number. A female electronic voice answered saying, *I'm sorry but calls cannot be taken by this phone at the moment please try later.*

'What the fuck! What does he think he's playing at? Does he think we're playing games?'

Kamal looked at Malone enquiringly.

'What?' he asked, his voice still croaky from his near strangulation.

'He's switched his phone off, the stupid fucker.'

'Are you sure?' asked Kamal.

'How do you mean?'

'Well maybe he hasn't got cover, no signal, or maybe his battery's run out, that one did.'

'He had a signal before when we spoke.'

'Yes, but you know what it's like. Try again a bit later.'

CHAPTER 44

Jack arrived at Marseilles airport early, to make sure he could find the car park and get to the arrivals lounge in plenty of time. Sure enough by the time he was at the arrivals barrier, the display board confirmed that flight AF 392 had arrived five minutes early. *Perfect* he thought, Ramsay'll be out any minute, but it took a little longer than Jack expected before he saw the unmistakable figure of Ramsay striding along, pulling a suitcase behind him.

They shook hands, and Jack said.

'Am I glad to see you?' Ramsay grinned

'Likewise buddy.'

Ramsay followed him out to the car. They didn't speak until after they'd cleared the airport itself and were on the road to the Luberon.

'It took you a while to get through customs,' Jack said, 'problems?'

'No' said Ramsay 'I had to wait for my luggage. I would've just bought just hand luggage, but there were certain items I wanted to bring that wouldn't be allowed in hand luggage.'

'Oh, I see, yes of course.'

'So,' said Ramsay 'any update?'

'No' said Jack 'I did as you said and shut the phone down, but I'm worried Ramsay, what if they get angry because they can't contact me and take it out on Rach?'

'Yeah, said Ramsay 'that's a possibility. So switch your phone on now. I only wanted you to be out of touch until I got here.'

'What do I say when they call?'

'Just go along with anything they ask, but ask to speak to Rachel first. And don't give them anything until they let you speak to her. Tell her not to worry we'll get her back, but say you and not we. We don't want to alert them that you have help.'

'How can you sound so confident?' asked Jack.

'Well, all that time on a plane gives you plenty of time to plan. And now I have a plan for your friends?'

'You do, already?

'Well, I assume these boys want you to tell them where the drugs are?'

'Yes, I can't think of anything else that makes sense.'

'And I also assume that you hid the drugs somewhere in the vicinity of the original incident?'

'Yes, correct.'

'Okay, in that case, my plan will work.'

'Are you going to tell me what the plan is?' he asked, but before Ramsay could answer, Jack's phone rang.

He pulled over and skidded to a stop. Fortunately there were no cars immediately behind them. Jack grabbed the phone out his pocket and answered. The same voice as before.

'You switched your phone off,' said an accusing voice.

'No no I didn't,' Jack said, 'my battery ran out and then I couldn't find the charger. I've only just been able to switch the thing on.'

Silence.

The man at the other end obviously decided to accept the excuse. Ramsay signalled for Jack to hold the phone away from his ear so he could hear what was being said.

'Listen, I know you have the drugs, or you know where they are, and I want them. D'you understand?'

Jack looked at Ramsay, who nodded, giving Jack a thumb's up..

'Yes' he said, 'I understand.'

'Okay, so the only way you get your wife back, is if you tell me where the drugs are. Once I've got them, you get her back.'

'Okay,' Jack said, looking again at Ramsay. Ramsay mouthed.

'Rachel, ask to speak to Rachel.'

'I want to speak to Rachel, before we discuss anything further.'

'Hold on.' The man hadn't hesitated, obviously anticipating the demand. *Kidnapping protocol* thought Jack.

He heard footsteps, then the man's voice saying.

'Here talk to your husband, make it quick.'

304

Rachel's voice came on the phone, and Jack's heart lurched.

'Jack, Jack, please get me out of here.'

'Have they hurt you?' Jack started to say, but the phone was back with the man again.

'Now listen up. Here's what we're going to do. Your wife is going to stay here with my friend, and when I confirm to him that I've got the drugs; he'll release her, simple as that.' Ramsay leaned over, took the phone out of Jack's hand and pressed the 'end' button.

'What on earth are you doing?'

'It's okay, switch it off for a minute, he'll call back, just say you lost the signal. I need to tell you what to say before you agree to anything. Say you've been thinking about this, and you'll tell him the general area where the stuff is hidden now, but he'll have to go to the UK. Tell him, once he's near to where the drugs are, you'll guide him to the exact spot by phone. But say that for you to give him that final bit of information, you want his friend to drive Rachel to a pre-arranged spot over here, where you can see her in the car, alive and well. Then you'll call him in the UK to tell him the final details. Once he gets his hands on the drugs, you'll expect his friend to let Rachel get out of the car, then he drives away, leaving Rachel unharmed. Tell hi, they get what they want, and you get what you want, understand?'

Jack nodded.

'You sure you're okay with that Jack?

'Yes sure.'

'Okay, switch the phone back on.'

The phone rang almost as soon as it was switched back on.

'Are you playing games?' the aggressive voice said.

'No, look I just lost the signal, it's not my fault.'

'Okay, so what's your answer?'

Jack repeated the conditions as well as he could remember it, with Ramsay giving him encouragement and nodding as Jack dictated the terms. The man was not pleased with being told how it would play out, but Jack insisted that was the way it had to be. 'Otherwise,' he said, 'if I just tell you where the stuff is, how would I know you won't just kill Rachel and go get the drugs?'

The man said he needed time to think about it, and rang off.

'Well done Jack,' Ramsay said with a smile.

'The guy'll think about it, see if there's any snags. He might even think it's a better way of doing it? This way he has the chance to make sure he gets the drugs, before he double crosses you and kills Rachel.'

'You think that's what he's planning to do?'

'I'd say it's a racing certainty.'

'The bastards, the evil fucking bastards' was all Jack could say.

'Don't worry Jack, we'll get Rachel back safe and sound.'

The man rang back and agreed. Jack told him that assumed he knew the general area where Ezra and Alfie had picked up the drugs that morning. He said he did. Jack told him to go back there, and he could then guide him to where he'd hidden the drugs. The man said he would fly back to the UK that night if possible, and should be in place the following morning sometime. He told Jack he would call him once he was in the immediate area, then give Jack instructions where to go to meet his colleague, who would bring Rachel to a pre-arranged location in his car.

'What pre-arranged location, what time?' asked Jack.

'I'll let you know tomorrow morning, early.'

He went on to say, the man in the car would release Rachel once he confirmed to the driver of the car that the drugs were in his possession. He warned Jack to park well away from the car, just close enough to be able to see Rachel, who would be in the passenger seat. But not too close. He said if Jack went too near, the man would just drive away with Rachel, and he might never see her again. Then he gave him another warning.

'If you try anything tricky, your wife will be killed, not quickly, but slowly and in great pain. Just remember that, in case you think up any clever moves, okay?'

'Okay' said Jack, and the man cut the connection.

Jack looked at Ramsay.

'Drive on Jack, we have our own plans to make.'

Jack drove back towards the hotel with a heavy heart. He could hardly believe he'd just been told by someone holding his wife that she may well be killed. Jack found it unbearable, gut wrenching. He swore to himself that if anyone hurt Rachel, he would find them and kill them, or die trying. Ramsay looked out of the window, and Jack was grateful for the time to regroup and find his calmer centre. Ramsay sensed what he was going through and offered some advice.

'Jack old buddy, I know this sounds corny, but you're no good to Rachel if you let them get to you. You fold, and they've won, remember, and channel your distress into controlled anger against the enemy. Have no doubt, we'll get Rachel back, unharmed, I promise.'

Jack said nothing but felt grateful for the confidence booster. They were both silent for the rest of the journey, apart from Ramsay's occasional exclamations on the beauty of the French countryside.

CHAPTER 45

Malone put the phone down. He'd already talked it through quickly with Kamal, immediately after Jack had put forward his demands for the exchange. Neither Malone nor the Bosnian could see any particular problem with the terms Jack had demanded. They were just a little perturbed that Jack seemed to know how to organise things, and it didn't fit with their image of him. Still, maybe he was just a bit more switched on than the average punter. *Could he be a player, could they be walking into a trap? Would Brandon have contacted the French police and risked them killing his precious wife?* No, definitely not thought Malone. Anyway, Kamal would still have the woman when he got his hands on the drugs, and Malone himself would be in the UK, far from any harm. As far as Kamal was concerned, they'd make sure that whatever handover location they arranged, Kamal would have an escape route planned.

They'd already agreed to kill Rachel once they had the drugs in their possession, so why not let Kamal have his fun, once they were sure of getting the stuff? The bitch had to die anyway. They certainly couldn't let her go, and risk her being able to identify them.

They discussed the finer details of their plan. Malone would go with Jack's demand regarding where the drugs were hidden. He'd use Rachel's phone for that purpose, but as Malone got near to where the drugs were hidden, he would call Kamal's mobile on his own phone, then keep the line open so Kamal could hear his on-going conversation with Jack. When he found the drugs and checked they were all there, he would say to Jack that he couldn't see any stash of drugs and there was no rucksack. The word "rucksack" was the signal to Kamal that Malone had, in fact, found the drugs, and had them safe in his possession.

Malone would accuse Brandon of double crossing him and Kamal would immediately drive off with Brandon's wife, take her back to the cottage and remove all traces of them having been there. He would then kill the bitch and hide her body, maybe have his bit of fun first. If Brandon tried to follow Kamal, Kamal felt confident he could lose him easily, but on the other hand, he might let him follow him all the way to the cottage, then kill them both. Kamal would then make his way back to Nice airport, return the hire car, and fly back to the UK, simple.

Malone got his map out, and they planned where to make the rendezvous for the "release" of Brandon's wife. Kamal pointed to a place where the D28, Route de Avignon, crossed the D31 Route De Velleron in an area called Saint-Joseph. Only about fifteen minutes' drive away from where they were, possibly less. There was a little side road that came off the D28 and back on to it again a hundred yards or so from the roundabout where the roads intersected. It looked on the map as if it could be an unmade road or track, *ideal.*

Malone stayed to keep an eye on Rachel, while Kamal went to check out the location to make sure it was suitable for purpose. He came back and confirmed it was.

'The side road runs in a banana shape off and back on to the road, just a short distance from the roundabout, giving me a choice of four directions when I make my getaway from the place. There's also some sort of crop growing between the road and the dirt track, which provides good cover between it and the main road, so it's perfect. I tell you Tony, this is going to be so easy.'

Jack drove Ramsay to the hotel he'd booked. The Mas De Senecole was a typical French farmhouse conversion into a country hotel. As they reached the hotel, they drove into its short gravel driveway, flanked on either side by beautifully manicured cream green conifers. Tall, but fat at the bottom with pointy tops. The hotel building had been constructed using roughhewn local cream coloured stone, and aged wooden plinths, which contrasted with the terracotta pantile roof. It looked like something out of a fairy tale.

Despite its modest size, the hotel had a swimming pool and gourmet restaurant. It was located just down the road from the mountain village of Gordes, and despite the seriousness of the situation, Ramsay couldn't help but wonder at the beautiful Provence countryside. This was Ramsay's first trip outside the USA, apart from when he was in the army, and it was only luck that he had a current passport, due entirely to his wife insisting that he take her on a trip to Europe to celebrate their next wedding anniversary.

Jack asked Ramsay what the plan was for the next day, but Ramsay would only tell him part of it. Ramsay explained that Jack would have enough to think about, guiding the man to the drugs. That if he knew what Ramsay had planned, it might distract him. Ramsay then asked Jack to think of an alternative location where he could have hidden the drugs.

Jack wondered what this was all about, but he'd learned to do as Ramsay asked, rather than question his motives. He thought hard and told Ramsay that there were some derelict farm buildings on the farm on the left, just past Meadowcroft Hall. That was an alternative place he considered hiding the drugs. Ramsay asked him if he would draw a map and specify one building in particular. Jack did as he was asked. Ramsay took a long look at the drawing, then said.

'Ideal, this is where you're going to guide the man to tomorrow.'

'Not where the drugs really are?'

'No, definitely not to there. I have to go to the reception desk now, so could you order some room service for both of us? Steak for me, nice and rare please. After we eat, I'll explain what we're going to do tomorrow at the meet.'

Jack ordered steak for both of them, even though he had precious little appetite. But he knew he needed to be strong, both mentally and physically, if they were going to get Rachel back safely. Ramsay came back, and they went to Jack's room. The food arrived shortly afterwards, and over the meal, Ramsay outlined how they were going to play things the next day.

'First, they will have already decided on the location for the meet, and it will have features to their advantage, not ours. When the man calls you tomorrow morning, he'll tell you where to meet his accomplice. Then once you've arrived, and been able to see that Rachel's in reasonable shape, he'll expect you to guide him to the drugs as agreed. Now I'm going to hide in the back seat of your car, and when we're nearly at the rendezvous point, I want you to stop briefly just before we get there so I can slip out of the car. As near as possible to their car, but without me being seen okay?' Jack nodded.

'We'll be a little bit late to make sure their car is there first. Now I'm going to have to rely on your judgement as to when you stop to let me out, as I won't be able to see anything, okay?' Jack nodded again, Ramsay continued.

'As soon as the man in the car with Rachel, sees you arrive, he'll call his buddy in the UK. The man in the UK will then call you, so you can guide him to where the drugs are.'

'So what happens when he finds there aren't any drugs there?' Asked Jack

'Don't worry about that, just leave that to me.'

'Anything else?' said Jack

'Yes, make sure your phone is fully charged before we leave tomorrow.'

Then Ramsay suggested they get an early night and said he'd see Jack early for breakfast. They bid each other good night, and Ramsay went to his room. Jack sat on the bed and tried to think positive thoughts.

Jack didn't sleep well that night, but eventually dozed off. He woke with the dawn, the early morning sunlight, finding the gap in the curtains, sending a laser beam of light across his room, lighting up the dust motes doing a slow dance in the sun's rays. He lay there watching the display trying not to think about what sort of a day was in front of him.

Eventually, he kicked out of bed, showered and thought about what Rachel might have gone through these last couple of days. He tried not to dwell on it, as it upset him too much. He recalled what Ramsay had told him, about channelling his distress into nailing the evil bastards who had taken his precious wife. And concentrating on getting her back unharmed.

He went outside for a wander, and found he was too early for breakfast, but he couldn't just lie around in his room. He walked out the back of the hotel into the early Luberon morning. It was pleasantly warm. The sky was blue with just a few wispy clouds hanging there, as though for decoration. The morning had a quiet, intense tranquillity that produced a feeling of peace and calm. There was hardly a sound to be heard as he walked past the swimming pool, through the small hedge bordering the hotel perimeter and into a field where a squat stone tower stood.

He imagined it had originally been used for grain storage, and though now obviously redundant, nevertheless looked right just being there. The ground level here was higher than the surrounding area, and Jack could see across the whole floor of the valley. Opposite, in the distance, were mountains, coloured light purple in the early morning light. He stood there almost in a trance looking over the fields of crops, small copses and occasional rows of tall, thin cypress trees. It all looked so perfect, as though it had all been newly manicured.

He was about to walk back to the hotel, when he saw something out of the corner of his eye. Gradually, a hot air balloon came into sight, gently wafting across the valley, noiseless, apart from the occasional and barely discernible whoosh of the propane burner, re-heating the air in the balloon, enabling it to stay suspended, whilst drifting across the sky. The vivid colours of the balloon contrasted starkly with the backdrop of mountains, meadows and sky. Jack sighed and wished Rachel was there to share this unexpected magical moment and tried to comfort himself that it wouldn't be long before he got her safely back again.

Reluctantly, he walked back to the hotel, then out through the front entrance where he met Ramsay coming in from his early morning run, his ebony bronze skin bathed in sweat.

'Hi Jack, ready for the day?' Ramsay asked breathlessly.

'Ready as I'll ever be,' he replied.

Ramsay got his breath back into a regular rhythm.

'Don't worry, remember, Ramsay has a plan, and this time no hitches, I promise!' He laughed, and his confidence lifted Jack's spirits.

Ramsay went to shower, and half an hour later they had breakfast which was laid out, self-service style, on tables alongside the hotel's swimming pool. Ramsay was fascinated with the breakfast buffet. Cold meat, cheese, croissants and jam, a boiled egg option, fruit, pastries, orange juice and coffee.

'Great coffee,' Ramsay said, but he was a bit perplexed with the rest of what was on offer. Nevertheless he tucked in, explaining that he needed the fuel and that Jack should make sure he ate lots as well.

'Lots of nervous energy to expend this morning,' said Ramsay.

He suggested they go back to their rooms, pack and check out and ready themselves for the call. It was just after eight thirty French time, so an hour earlier in the UK.

As they were making their way back to their rooms, Jack's phone rang. It was the man. He told Jack to get his map and a pen. Jack asked him to hold on while he went to his room. Jack and Ramsay sat on Jack's bed, and he got the map out, Ramsay making sure he made no noise.

The man on the phone told Jack to look where the D28, Route de Avignon, crossed the D31 Route De Velleron in an area called Saint-Joseph. Ramsay found it and pointed out where it was.

'Found it,' Jack said to the man.

'Okay, a short distance from the roundabout is a small dirt road that comes off the D28 and back on to it a hundred yards or so further along.'

Jack could just make out the thin line of the track on the map.

'Yes, I can see it.'

'Be there at nine o'clock this morning, make sure you're alone. If my man sees anyone with you, the deal's off. Drive into the track from the direction of Pernes les Fontains,' the pronunciation was excruciating, but Jack had no problem understanding him.

'I'll be there' he said.

'Remember, don't get too close,' said the man, and Jack responded,

'And don't you forget, that I won't tell you anything unless I see Rachel is okay.'

Then Jack broke the connection, feeling slightly more empowered. Ramsay smiled at Jack.

'Way to go Jack. Make 'em realise it's not all one way traffic.'

Ramsay went back to his room to collect his luggage, and Jack made sure his phone was fully charged before he left his room. He met Ramsay at reception, and they checked out of the hotel. Jack felt nervous. They drove out of the hotel car park and drove along in silence, other than Ramsay telling Jack when to turn right and left, until they got within a mile or so of the rendezvous point and stopped. They were too early Ramsay said, and they needed to wait.

'Timing,' said Ramsay 'is everything.'

While they waited, they looked over the beautiful Provencal countryside, and Jack found it hard to believe that they were embarking on such a potentially violent and dangerous mission, in such a peaceful looking place.

It was time. Ramsay got out of the front passenger seat and into the back of the car. He was dressed in a dirty looking green shirt and trousers, and wearing some old soft looking leather boots. He also had a wire in his ear, which Jack assumed was connected to his mobile phone. Jack drove towards the meeting place. Within a few minutes, he spotted the entrance to the dirt track, specified as the rendezvous point. He stopped briefly just before turning right into the start of the road and heard the rear door close quietly as Ramsay slid out of the car. Jack looked in his rear mirror, but couldn't see any trace of Ramsay.

The track was shielded from the busy main road by some high growing crops, and Jack could see why they'd chosen this spot. They were now a few minutes late, but as Jack turned into the track, he could see a car parked at the other end, facing towards the road, no doubt ready for a quick getaway.

Right from the start, it occurred to Jack that there was really nothing, to stop this man driving away with Rachel once his pal had got his hands on the drugs. *Did they think he was stupid enough, not to have considered that?* He supposed they relied on his desperation to get Rachel back, and anyway, what other choice would he have, but to accept that they would keep their word? And, if the man took off with Rachel, they knew he would follow them, and that Jack could then be desperate enough to call the police. *It's all academic now*, thought Jack, *now that Ramsay's involved.* He'd told Jack not to worry, just play along.

Jack flashed his lights to signify he was there and a few seconds later his phone rang. He answered, Rachel's phone name showed on the phone's display panel. The same man's voice spoke. Jack assumed the man in the car had called the man in the UK to tell him he'd turned up as instructed.

'Okay Brandon, the voice said, 'take a look at your wife then start talking.'

The man got out of the driver's door, went round the other side of the car and pulled Rachel out by her arm. He held her where Jack could get a clear view. She looked okay but not particularly alert, thought Jack. And she seemed to be leaning against the car. They'd obviously drugged her, to avoid her trying to run away. At least she was alive, and he was grateful for that.

Jack started giving directions to the man. He asked where the man was at the moment and pictured the geography in his mind.

'Okay, from where you are, you'll see a lane with a gate across the entrance and a stile. There's a sign saying to Meadowcroft Farm, no bikes, no horses or something like that.'

'Yes, I see it,' said the man.

'Go over the stile and walk down the cobbled lane for about a quarter of a mile. Tell me when you come to some old farm buildings on your right.'

'Okay, I'm walking.'

The road through Meadowcroft was a public right of way, but not many people used it. There was access for walkers, but no horses, or cyclists and definitely no cars other than the farmer's family. The other end of the road finished at a padlocked gate with a stile for walkers to get through.

Jack could hear the man's laboured breathing as he walked up the lane, as fast as he could by the sound of his breath down the phone.

'Okay, I'm coming up to some old buildings, and there's what looks like big piles of compost type stuff in the yard, it stinks.'

'Okay, sounds like you're in the right place. Now turn right into the yard and then walk towards the first derelict brick building on the left. There's an old rotten door hanging off its hinges. Pull it aside, and you'll find the drugs in a rucksack in the far left corner, under some old tarpaulin.

The man kept saying okay, every time Jack gave him some instruction, and repeated what Jack said, which seemed unnecessary. Then he said.

'I'm pulling the door aside and walking into the building now...'

Suddenly, the connection went dead!

'Shit,' said Jack and sat there not knowing if he should wait or try to call the man back.

'Shit, shit, shit!' Jack was starting to panic.

He looked at the car at the other end of the track and Rachel had disappeared. Presumably, the driver had put her back in the car. Jack didn't know what to do, but he felt he had to do something, and quick, but what?

Then to Jack's amazement, he saw Ramsay launch his attack, coming out of the field to the right of the car, wrenching the front passenger's door open and diving in. The man tried to escape out of the driver's door, but Ramsay was on him like a wild animal. They both tumbled out of the car on to the floor. Then the man, somehow managed to break free, rolled over and got to his feet. He reached behind him, and a large knife appeared in his hand. Jack sat there fixated by the scene.

The man was smiling now moving quickly towards Ramsay, his knife at the ready. Ramsay seemed to just stand there, hands by his side. The man lunged at Ramsay who still didn't seem to move. He looked frozen to the spot, then in a movement that defied anything Jack had ever seen, Ramsay moved sideways at a speed that seemed impossible, while at the same time clamping his hand over the man's wrist and turning the knife towards the man's throat. The man resisted, and then overwhelmed, tried to avoid the knife as it went into the side of his throat. He tried to turn away from the inevitable, but he hadn't got a chance. Blood spurted out of the wound. He collapsed on to the floor, body convulsing, then it stopped. He lay there lifeless on the dusty dirt track, a knife sticking out of his neck.

CHAPTER 47

F reddie didn't do violence himself, far too messy. But, unfortunately, in his line of work, it was sometimes necessary. So he'd taken his man Albert along, who was very adept at dealing with such matters, being an ex-wrestling champion. Albert was not interested in all that fancy judo, karate stuff. No, Albert was what Freddie called a force of nature. He was also a lot quicker than his bulk suggested. Many had sorely misjudged his agility, to their serious disadvantage.

Freddie and Albert had been camped in the dirty old farm building since the early hours, waiting to hear from Ramsay as to when the mark was likely to turn up. Once Ramsay told them, they simply waited for the poor wretch to walk into the trap. Albert had positioned himself behind the partially open doorway, and as the mark stepped through, he felled him with a single blow to the back of the neck. As the mark went down, Freddie grabbed both phones from his prostrate body and took the batteries out, just to make sure. Then he spoke into his clip-on mike, advising Ramsay that the mark was down, telephones cut.

Although Jack obviously knew there was a plan to get Rachel away from the kidnappers, he wasn't aware of the detail of how this would be achieved. And Ramsay was right, if he'd have told Jack what he had planned, he'd have found it difficult to keep calm, when directing the man to the false hiding place. So when he lost the connection to the man in the UK, he just sat there panicking and wondering if he should try to call the man back, or leave the line open so he could call him back.

Once Jack saw what Ramsay had done to the man, he realised that Rachel was no longer a prisoner. He ran towards the car. Ramsay was getting Rachel out of the back seat and walking her towards Jack. He grabbed hold of her and hugged her. She was very dazed. Jack didn't let go of her for a long time. Rachel was tearful and still a bit dozy. Jack clung on to her, and she held him as if she'd never let go.

Then Jack realised they had to get away quickly. As he disentangled himself from Rachel, he saw Ramsay putting on some thin rubber gloves, then getting hold of the body of the man on the floor, manhandled him into the boot of the BMW. Jack couldn't see the knife, so assumed Ramsay had taken it to dispose of later. Ramsay closed the boot lid and went over to where the man's blood had stained the dusty track dark red Grabbing a handful of tall grass, he made a crude switch and swept the blood into the dust.

Then he came over to where Jack and Rachel were standing.

'Okay Jack, we need to get away from here before anyone comes by. Get Rachel in your car and find another hotel. Don't rush, but get a good distance from here and don't book a room for me. You've got my cell number so call me when you're in your room. I need to get my kit out of your car now. I have a long journey ahead of me.'

There were a million questions Jack wanted to ask, but he realised they'd have to wait for now. Ramsay got his stuff, loaded it into the kidnapper's car and drove off in a cloud of dust.

Ramsay called Freddie as he drove along the motorway towards Nice. He'd checked the papers in the glove box and found out that the car had been hired from Avis at Nice airport, in the name of Anthony Malone.

Freddie answered on the first ring.

'Morning Ramsay.'

'Morning Freddie, what've we got?

'One Anthony Malone, according to his documents. He very kindly brought along his passport and driving licence to prove it. What do you want us to do with him?'

'How old is he, and how fit?'

'About forty five. Looks fairly fit other than suffering from Albert's little smack.'

'Okay then, he needs a lesson. Don't kill him, but make sure he doesn't forget to keep away from my client. Make sure he understands that if anything happens to my client in the future, I'll find him and kill him. While you're at it Freddie, find out if he and his buddy were working alone, and how they picked up the Brandon's trail. When you're done, take all his ID away, break his legs and arms and dump him outside some hospital, then call the emergency services, you know the drill.'

'Will do Ramsay old boy. Bye for now. and Albert send his regards.'

'Bye Freddie, likewise to Albert.'

Ramsay settled in for the long drive, checked that he had enough fuel, hoping he wouldn't need to stop to fill up on the way. Thankfully the tank was full. Ramsay was still wearing the rubber gloves. He didn't want his fingerprints in the car, but he didn't want to wipe anyone else's. He realised that Rachel's would also be in the car, but there wouldn't be any connection to her, so no worries there. He'd made sure to wipe his prints from the passenger door handle and anywhere else he may have touched when he launched his attack against the guy holding Rachel. He hadn't planned to kill him, but Ramsay's rule was live by the sword die by the sword, so he didn't feel any guilt. The guy had played his hand and left Ramsay no choice.

Ramsay made good time along the A7, then on to the A8 towards Nice and on to the airport. Nice airport was well signposted, so he had no problem finding it. He drove on past the Airport to find somewhere to park, where the car wouldn't be found for a few days, and where there were unlikely to be any CCTV cameras. He figured that if the car wasn't reported until it started to stink really bad, forensics might not be able to say for certain, precisely when the car and body were dumped.

The police would certainly discover that it was an Avis car, and eventually make the connection. between Mr Anthony Malone, who flew from Nice to the UK only a day or so before, and the corpse in the trunk. *A ticklish problem for Mr Malone*, thought Ramsey, when the French police contacted the British police, and caught up with him.

It was getting on for two o'clock in the afternoon when Ramsay turned left off the promenade. He drove round the back streets of Nice and found a spot he could park the car, next to some large industrial looking rubbish dumpsters. Ideal. He couldn't see any snooping CCTV cameras, so he quickly got out of the car, shielded his face with his hands as an extra precaution. He collected his suitcase from the back seat, locked the car, then took off the gloves, and stuffed them in his pocket, before walking away towards the promenade, and on, into the centre of Nice.

The sun was up, and it was hot. Wouldn't take too long for the body to start to stink in this heat, he thought. He hoped the locals blamed it on the rubbish containers before they realised where the smell was really coming from. Ramsay walked along the Promenade des Anglais. It was crowded with tourists and beach people, and had a carnival-like atmosphere, joggers, skateboarders, cyclists and people of all ages, sitting, reading, sleeping, and walking.

The promenade was a feast for the eyes. Ramsay turned and looked at the turquoise sea with foaming waves crashing on to the shore, the white spume dissipating as it raced up the stony beach. Ramsay was hot and sweaty and wished he could rip his clothes off and run into the sea. He envied the people on the beach.

As he walked along he saw that there were public beach areas, and private beaches with restaurants with smart sun loungers and waiter service. Across the other side of the promenade, he saw a small modest looking two story hotel. The Hotel du Flore. It looked ideal. He crossed the road and enquired at the quaint reception desk. A room was available. Ramsay booked in. It was simple accommodation, with an old fashioned bathroom and toilet, but the bed was comfortable, and the sheets were crisp white cotton. *What more could a man want* thought Ramsay. Air conditioning came to mind, *but what the hell.*

Ramsay took a nap for half an hour then showered, put on some clean clothes and feeling refreshed, went for a walk along the promenade and into the centre of Nice. He made his way from the promenade, and into the heart of the city. Soon he came to a huge square with fountains and gardens. With no particular aim in mind, he wandered across the square and into what was obviously the old part of town, with narrow streets with a variety of shops and restaurants.

He enjoyed the tourist experience, but decided he'd better get back to the promenade and get some food. He hadn't eaten since breakfast, and he'd seen plenty of restaurants not too far from his hotel. It had been a long and eventful day, and fatigue was beginning to set in. He found a restaurant with a view of the promenade and ordered some veal escalope with pasta. When he'd finished his meal, he called his wife on his cell phone. She asked what he'd been up to and how his client was. He told her things were going well. *If only she knew*, he thought.

'I'll be leaving in a couple of days to come home hon,' then told her he missed her and loved her. He paid the bill then walked back to his hotel. He unlocked the door to his room. Exhausted, he threw his clothes on the chair, got into bed and fell asleep as soon as his head hit the pillow.

CHAPTER 48

The emergency services contacted Waterfield hospital, in south Manchester, to say they'd had a call that there was a seriously injured man in their A&E car park. The porter was sent out to see if it was a crank call, but soon came rushing back to ask for medics and a stretcher. When they got to him, they found the man was comatose, but that was the least of his problems. They got him into the emergency room, and a doctor soon diagnosed the man's serious, but not life-threatening injuries. In view of the nature of the injuries he suggested the police were called. The police came and took note of the incident, saying they would come back at a later date to interview the victim when he was conscious

The doctor assumed it was some sort of gang punishment. He guessed that whoever had carried out the beating, was an expert in knowing how to inflict the maximum pain and damage, without actually killing the man. The police and the hospital authorities went through his clothes, but could find no means of identification. The nursing staff gave him the temporary name of Mr C Park, *hospital humour!*

CHAPTER 49

After the initial relief at being rescued, Rachel became quiet and spoke very little as they drove along. Jack kept reassuring Rachel that she was safe and it was all over. He realised he was really trying to reassure himself as much as his wife. Rachel fell asleep. Jack waited until they were nearly an hour away from where they'd rescued Rachel, before starting to look for a place to stay. He'd taken the smaller roads west, and eventually found a place, a small, pretty .looking hotel called the Auberge de Luberon, near a town called Apt.

The receptionist said they had a room and that it was available immediately. They booked in. Rachel slept for four hours and it was late afternoon when she woke. He ordered tea from room service and Rachel gulped down two cups. She had some bruising on her face and Jack, as tactfully as he could, asked if she felt able to say what they'd done to her. She began to tell him what had happened, breaking down on occasion, but she said she always knew he would find her somehow. That he would get her back, and she held on to that thought throughout her ordeal.

I'd like to take a shower now Jack.'

'Yes of course, sorry Rach.'

Rachel took her time in the shower, and when she came out, she looked much better. She took her robe off and showed Jack the bruises and cuts she'd sustained at the hands of the Bosnian. Jack struggled to contain his anger, but reminded himself, that the person who'd inflicted these injuries was now dead. He found that of some comfort.

Jack broached the next question carefully.

'Rachel, they didn't do anything to you, they didn't....?'

'Rachel frowned and said,

'No, no the English guy wasn't interested in me at all in that way, he just saw me as a bargaining chip. The foreign man would have done some terrible things to me, but the English guy stopped him. But then he told him, he could do what he wanted to me, once he'd got his hands on the drugs. I had no doubt what he would've done to me then. Fortunately, that didn't happen. I never thought I'd be in any way grateful that someone had been killed, but I won't shed any tears over that man, he was pure evil.

But how did you manage to get Ramsay over here? I couldn't believe it when I saw him. I knew you wouldn't let me down and that you'd come for me, but I realised you couldn't rescue me on your own. I thought you'd have to go to the police, and then you'd have to tell them the whole story and then you'd go to jail, and maybe I would too.'

'It's a long story Rach, I'll fill you in later, just rest now, plenty of time to tell you afterwards, but I need to call Ramsay now.' Jack took out his phone and dialled.

'I'm in Nice Jack and it's beautiful.' said Ramsay, always upbeat.

'I've booked into a little hotel on the Promenade, the Hotel de Flore, a cute little place. We need to talk, and you need to decide what you want to do,' said Ramsay, 'but not on the phone.'

'When can you get here?'

'We'll stay the night here, then drive over to Nice in the morning. I think I know where the hotel is, so I'll see you about eleven.'

'See you then Jack'.

The euphoria of Rachel being rescued had dissipated, and left them both feeling exhausted, emotionally and physically. Neither of them had had much sleep in the last few days, so they had a light supper and went to bed early. Rachel fell asleep straight away, and once Jack heard her breathing change into sleep mode, he also allowed himself to sleep. The next morning Jack woke and Rachel was already awake. She looked refreshed. They made love. Their lovemaking was tender but intense. They had always loved each other, even when they occasionally argued and sometimes fell out, but Jack's experience of near loss had made him realise what they had, and how most of the time they took each other for granted. He was sure Rachel felt the same. They had a light breakfast in their room, checked out, and got on their way to Nice.

As they drove along, Jack told her about how he first got the call from the kidnappers and ho he'd thought it was her, as they'd used her phone. Then he told her about calling

Ramsay to see if he could help, and how Ramsay didn't hesitate, but jumped on a plane and flew to Marseilles.

Rachel wanted to know how they had managed to wrong-foot the kidnappers and how they'd pulled the whole thing off.

'The truth is Rachel, even I don't know all the details yet. One of the men went back to the UK, to the area where I'd hidden the drugs. I was supposed to guide him by phone to where they were stashed. They said once they'd got them, they'd release you.'

'But that didn't happen?'

'No, and it was never going to. Ramsay figured that when the man in the UK got his hands on the drugs, he'd let the man holding you know, by means of a code word or something. And instead of releasing you, he'd take you back to where they'd been holding you, and, well… Ramsay said they couldn't afford to let you go, you'd be able to identify them.'

'It's okay Jack, they'd made it clear they were going to kill me.'

Jack looked at Rachel then continued.

'There were bits of the plan that Ramsay kept to himself. He said he'd tell me all about it soon enough, but he never told me the whole plan, which was just as well in the circumstances. Anyway, no doubt Ramsay will tell us how he pulled it off, when we meet. I think we'll buy him a very good lunch, in fact, I've just realised how hungry I am, I could eat a horse.'

'Well, you're in the right country for that.'

'What? Oh yeah right.'

CHAPTER 50

Just after Jack had rung off, Ramsay got a call from Freddie.

'What's the latest Freddie my man?'

'Mr Malone says he was working freelance. Just him and his pal. I'm not sure I believe him. There's something not quite right about his story, but I can't put my finger on it. From what you told me, the whole pick up and drop off involving a helicopter needs an organisation larger than one man and a sidekick. Maybe he was double crossing someone. Anyway way, he won't be a bother to Mr Brandon, or his wife in the future. Neither will he be telling anyone about his little adventure.'

Ramsay told Freddie how he had parked the car with an 'item' in the boot in Nice. And that it should end up being attributed to Mr Malone by the French police. Freddie thought for a few seconds then caught on.

'Ah yes, well thought through Ramsay, I like that.' Freddie then said.

'By the way, you were wondering how they picked the tail up on the Brandons, Well I'm afraid it was the guardian at their apartment complex, a man called Jean-Pierre. Matey paid him five hundred Euros to call him if the Brandons showed, plus another five hundred if and when he did.'

Ramsay nodded to himself.

'And how did he know where their French place was?'

'It seems he has a contact in the police who was able to see Jack's statement. Apparently, it had all the details of his UK and French addresses on it.'

'Okay, thanks Freddie.'

They finished the call with Ramsay asking Freddie to let him know how much he owed him for his services and he'd sort it out. They said their farewells and promised to meet up sometime soon.

Ramsay had first come across Freddie some years before when they worked both ends of a missing persons case involving an English man who'd fled to Florida. The case was a no brainer, as the man left clues to his whereabouts like the proverbial breadcrumbs trail, but the real result, was the establishing of the firm friendship between Freddie and Ramsay. They were as different as chalk and cheese, but they clicked as soon as they spoke. Each sensed they had something bordering on mutual telepathy. They'd stayed in touch but this was the first time they'd worked on a case together since, and the results were once again very satisfactory.

CHAPTER 51

Jack and Rachel arrived in Nice a little after eleven and found the hotel where Ramsay was staying. They parked their car and went in. Ramsay was sat in reception. Rachel threw her arms around him and gave him a big kiss on the cheek. She stood back and said.

'Ramsay, you're an angel, I don't know how to thank you enough. You saved my life.'

Ramsay looked embarrassed.

'I couldn't let you down, after all, clients who pay up on the button don't come along that often. Got to protect my interests.'

'So you just did it for the money?'

Ramsay laughed,

'Of course I did. What else? Well that, and I'd heard great things about French food too.' They all laughed, and no more thanks were given. It was obvious that Ramsay was uncomfortable with such praise. Jack said.

'Why don't we go for a walk along the promenade, then find a nice restaurant and have a slap up lunch? They walked into the centre of Nice and found a suitable restaurant. When they'd ordered their food and were settled with their drinks, Jack asked.

'Okay Ramsay. Come on, how did you do it?'

Well, it was a team effort, and you played your part well Jack. I'm sorry I couldn't tell you what I had planned at the UK end. I thought it might make you hesitate, and the man at the other end might pick up on it and figure out that he was walking into a trap. I assume you've told Rachel about the set-up, with you guiding the man to the stuff in the UK?'

'Yes, I've told Rachel as much as I know.'

'Okay, well I planned for a number of events to happen simultaneously, and thankfully it worked. I figured that the man you were guiding to where the drugs were hidden in the UK, would also have an open connection on his own phone to the man holding Rachel in the car, so that he, the man in the car, would know precisely what was going on at the UK end.'

'Hence the repeating of my instructions,' said Jack.

'Yep,' said Ramsay, 'I assumed that once the guy in the UK had his hands on the drugs and checked they were okay, he would immediately let the guy holding Rachel know. Probably using a pre-arranged code word, so as not to alert you Jack. Then the man in the car would drive away with Rachel. And at best, dump you somewhere and escape, but more likely take you somewhere and, well, kill you, so as to leave no witness to the kidnap. Sorry to have to tell you this sort of stuff Rachel.'

'It's okay Ramsay. I'm over it now, please carry on.'

'Well I got Jack to draw a map of an alternative place where he might have hidden the drugs, and we used that location to set the trap, then I faxed a copy of Jack's map to Freddie and he and his man Albert, a very capable man by all accounts, lay in wait in the old farm building. And as soon as the man entered the building to get the drugs, Freddie, or more accurately Freddie's man Albert, flattened the guy. Freddie grabbed both of the phones he was carrying, and switched them off.

Freddie, who had an open connection to my mobile, was able to tell me the target in the UK had been neutralised, and his phone lines cut. That was the signal for me to go into action against the guy holding you in the car. You know the rest, well most of the rest.'

'And what about the man who went to find the drugs. You say he was 'neutralised. What does that mean in plain English?' asked Jack

'Let's just say he's been taught a severe lesson, and won't be bothering you again, ever, I can guarantee that.'

Rachel hesitated to ask but felt she had to.

'And the man, the man in the car, I assume he's dead. I saw you put his body in the boot. What's happened to him. Well, his body I mean.'

'Boot? oh you mean trunk,' said Ramsay. 'Well, he's still in the trunk, or boot as you limeys insist on calling it. But don't worry about that either, I'm pretty sure his death will be attributed to the other guy, the one who went to the UK to find the drugs. If not, there's no way the authorities could ever connect it with me, or you, so forget about it, okay? I don't normally go around killing people, but he chose the play, and I had no choice. As far as I'm concerned, all I'm guilty of is defending myself, and you.'

'You don't have to justify anything to us Ramsay,' said Jack, 'we're just grateful to you. We'll never forget what you've done for us. So where do you think we go from here?'

'Well, I've had some time to think about that, so here's what I've come up with. There were three parties looking for you, forgetting about the police, who might be irritated by you not keeping in touch, but don't represent any serious threat. Agreed?' Jack and Rachel nodded.

'Okay, so we have the guys who chased you to Florida, who we can reasonably assume were heavies hired by the brother of the first victim, Ezra. As far as they're concerned the trail went cold at Key West. And they have no idea where you are now, so they will have gone back home and my guess that the only practical thing they could do was to stand down, but keep their ears and eyes open for any sign of your return to the UK. Maybe they'll pick up where they left off. That is, if the contract is still on, which I doubt, but you never know. Agreed?'

Deferring to Ramsay's experience in such matters, they again nodded in agreement.

'Okay, then we have our friend Mr Malone, who kidnapped Rachel. We know he's out of the game for good. So there's one possible party left. But if there is another party, they've kept very quiet, and I've had Freddie try to find if there's any activity by anyone else in relation to you, and he's come up with zip. And Freddie's the best.'

'So what are you saying?' Jack asked.

'Well I'm not sure it would be wise to go back to the UK yet, but you could maybe have a more normal life at your home in Eze. Maybe tell your kids where you are but tell them to keep it to themselves, think of a good excuse. No one can keep on the run forever, it just doesn't work, and now we've pretty well neutralised any immediate threats against you, you should be okay staying at your apartment over here. That would also give Freddie time to look into this contract thing and see if we can find some way of bringing pressure to bear to get it sorted.

In time, people do calm down. Things blow over, and I'm sure you'll be able to go back home eventually.'

Jack looked at Rachel.

'What do you think Rach?'

'Well it all makes sense to me, and Ramsay hasn't been wrong so far, so I'm in agreement.'

'What about you Jack?'

'That makes two of us then,' he said.

'Now, before they serve our food I think I need to tell you something.

Rachel and Jack looked at each other, and Jack could tell they were both thinking the same thing - *what now?*

'There is one little problem that needs sorting, so you can go back to live at your apartment in Eze.'

'Oh?' said Jack wondering what was coming now.

'Well, I'm afraid your good friend Jean-Pierre? the Guardian at the complex - is not really a very good friend.'

'What?' Jack said looking thoroughly confused.

'Well, it looks like your so-called "Guardian" sold you out for a thousand Euros. Although he only got five hundred in the end.' Ramsay added.

'What are you saying, I…' Jack ran out of words and looked at Rachel. They both looked shocked. Ramsay went on.

'I couldn't figure out how the kidnappers picked up your trail, but it turned out to be simple enough. The man visited your apartment complex some time ago, when you first skipped. He paid your guardian five hundred Euros to call him in the UK, if and when you came back to your apartment, plus another five hundred when he did.'

Rachel and Jack had the same reaction, total disbelief.

'You mean Jean-Pierre sold us out, put Rachel's life at risk for a lousy five hundred Euros? All the years we've known him, and he's done this to us? I find it so hard to believe, are you absolutely sure?'

'Yes Jack I'm sure, but in fairness he probably didn't know what the guy's intentions were. He could have told him you owed money, gambling debt, anything really, so I shouldn't be too shocked. People will do all sorts of things for money if they can be made to justify it to themselves.'

Rachel and Jack were silent, still trying to take the information on board. Ramsay went on.

'My plan was that if you decided to go back and stay there for a spell, then I'd come back with you, have a look at the place and see if there's any suggestions I can make with regards to security. Then I planned to have a quiet word with your friend Jean-Pierre. I'll put the fear of God into him, but I suggest that you never tell him anything about the men who followed you, and nothing about what happened. The less said about that, the better. In fact, I suggest, that for practical reasons, you carry on the friendly relationship you had with him before. Otherwise it's going to make difficulties for all of you.

I won't tell him you know anything about his betrayal. I'll tell him I don't want to upset you, and say how much you like him etc. But I'll make sure he knows that I know. And that if anything should happen to you in the future, I'll come looking for him. Believe me, by the time I've finished, he'll be the best and most reliable friend you could have. What do you say?'

Rachel and Jack looked at each other. Rachel spoke first.

'It'll be hard to look the little shit in the face without thinking about what he's put us through, intentionally or not. But I suppose on a practical level, what you say makes sense. What do you think Jack?'

'I'll find it hard as well, obviously. But yes, I agree. I'd been wondering how they found us and it all makes a lot more sense now.'

'Okay, we're settled then. When do you folks want to go back to Eze? Have I pronounced it right?'

They all laughed at Ramsay's pronunciation. The laughter provided a release from some of the tension resulting from Ramsay's revelation.

'Let's go back this afternoon Jack, I can't wait to see the Eze again.'

'Fine by me Rach. What about you Ramsay? what are your plans, I assume you'll stay with us for at least one night. But you know you're welcome to stay as long as you like. We can put you up in the spare room and show you the delights of Eze.'

'That's a very kind offer Jack, but I need to be getting back home. If you can put me up for tonight, that would be great. I've already booked my flight back home leaving tomorrow,' said Ramsay.

They finished lunch and went back to Ramsay's hotel to collect his luggage. The drive to Eze took them along the promenade, then through the port of Nice with fishing boats, luxury yachts and ferries moored there. They continued along the Basse Corniche. The views as they came into Villefranche were stunning. Cruise ships, sailing boats and smart private yachts shining in the sun. They carried on driving, through Beaulieu sur Mer, past the famous La Reserve hotel, and up the small winding road to the Moyenne Cornice, then right and on towards Eze Village.

A few minutes along the road, Eze mountain village emerged into view, precariously perched on top of a rocky outcrop. They drove past the village, turned left up another winding road for a few hundred yards until they came to the gates of their apartment complex, Le Jardin d'Eze. Rachel found the remote in her handbag and pressed it to open the gates. They drove through without encountering Jean-Pierre, or Judas as Rachel now called him. They drove up the steep road to the entrance of their underground garage. Once they were in the apartment, Rachel pressed the button to raise the shutters and the light flooded in. Ramsay wandered out on to the terrace and took in the view.

'Wow.' He said, and looked across at Eze village and the wider view below, of the Mediterranean sea, Cap Ferrat, Villefranche and the boats in the bays, The late afternoon sunshine glittering on the sea.

'Well, I've seen some seascapes in my time, but this really is something.'

They left Ramsay to enjoy the views and Rachel went to prepare his bedroom. Jack made coffees for them all, and they joined Ramsay on the terrace. They finished their coffee. Ramsay asked for a tour of the complex. They walked around, and it didn't take long. It was quite a small complex as such complexes go. Four blocks of twelve apartments of various sizes, one large communal swimming pool and one tennis court. They walked down past the tennis courts, and Jack pointed out the guardian's small office located near the entrance gates. Ramsay said he'd come back later to have a word with Jean-Pierre. As usual, there were very few people in residence, a fact that always gave Jack pause for thought every time they stayed there.

Jack left Ramsay to walk around by himself and went back to help Rachel unpack. About an hour later Ramsay came back and told us them he'd come across Jean-Pierre as he was strolling around. He'd asked to go to his office, and they had, what Ramsay described, as a man to man conversation.

'And how did Jean-Pierre react,' asked Jack.

'Oh as you'd expect, protesting his innocence initially, saying he hadn't told anyone anything. But after I told him that his actions nearly ended in Rachel's death, he cracked and said he had no idea he would be putting you in any danger. Anyway I think Jean-Pierre's got the message and now understands that his health is very closely connected to your wellbeing. Should anything happen to you when you stay here, he knows I'll be back. I told him that you weren't aware of his treachery, and that I was going to keep it that way. He got the message. Just put that issue out of your mind. I know, easy to say, hard to do, but you have a life to live, so live it. This isn't the worst place in the world to chill out while we sort out the UK end, so enjoy.'

That evening they had pizza and drank a few beers, chatted about lots of things.Ramsay told them about his father and uncle, who were two of the Navajos decorated for their part in the war against Japan in 1942, when they'd transmitted messages using the Navajo language, a code which the Japanese never managed to break. He told them he'd been in the army himself, Special Forces, then a cop in

New York for twenty years, at which point he was able to take early retirement if he wanted. He wanted, he said.

'Unlike most cops, he said, 'my marriage survived the force, and we moved down to Naples where my wife came from originally, and where she still had family, a sister, a nephew and a no good brother. We have two children, one boy, one girl. Great kids, all grown up now,' he said.

Jack and Rachel were exhausted by the events of the last few days. Ramsay was tired too he admitted, but he wanted to stay up and watch the CNN News and catch up with events in America. They said goodnight and Ramsay asked to use Jack's PC to email his wife and kids and to confirm his return flight to the US. They said goodnight. Rachel gave him another hug and thanked him again for all he'd done for them.

'All in the line of duty Ma'am,' said Ramsay, in a deputy dog impersonation.

Was he never serious? thought Jack.

CHAPTER 52

The next morning Ramsay told them he needed to be at Nice airport by one o'clock to catch his flight to Tampa via New York. He said he'd get a taxi, but Jack and Rachel wouldn't hear of it, so after breakfast Ramsay packed and they got in the Fiat for the drive to the Airport. Jack asked Ramsay to make sure he sent his bill as soon as possible, and he would send him a cheque from their French bank account as soon as it arrived. Ramsay said he'd need to wait for Freddie to tell him what his bill was, but he expected that would be on his email when he got back. They dropped Ramsay at the kiss and fly zone.

They said their goodbyes in the car, as there were lots of cars stacking up behind. As soon as Ramsay got his bags from the boot, they had to drive off, Rachel waving out of the window until Ramsay was out of site. Jack and Rachel drove back to Eze in a sombre mood. They were on their own again, and Jack felt they were a little more vulnerable now good old Ramsay wasn't there to watch their backs. Neither Rachel nor Jack had much of an appetite that night, so they decided to watch the television, ate a sandwich then went to bed early to read and try to get a good night's sleep.

CHAPTER 53

Over the next few days they got back into their old routine, playing tennis on most days in the morning before breakfast, then having a frugal lunch, then a sunbathe by the pool. In the evening they'd venture out to one of the local restaurants where the staff greeted them like old friends. *I wonder if it's anything to do with me being a good tipper*, thought Jack.

They emailed their children, mentioning nothing about their various adventures. As far as the kids were concerned, they were just the usual boring old mum and dad. *If they only knew*, thought Jack. Rachel called Mrs Anderson and checked everything was okay. She told her they were in Galicia, Northern Spain touring round and she told Rachel they should go to Torremolinos as she went there when she was a young girl and what a fabulous place it was. Rachel promised they'd visit if they went near there.

Now and then they would see Jean-Pierre as he carried out his duties, around the complex. He had always been very friendly to Jack and Rachel, which made it all the more shocking when they learnt of his betrayal. But if anything, they now found him overpoweringly effusive whenever their paths crossed.

'Ow are you Jack and Rachel,'

He would shout, waving at them from a distance, or if they were at closer quarters he would insist on coming over and shaking Jack's hand and giving a little courteous bow to Rachel, who always feigned a coughing fit or pretended to be looking for something in her handbag to avoid making direct eye contact. They managed to maintain the pretence of not knowing, as the alternative would be even more awkward. The truth was, putting aside his moment of treachery, Jack and Rachel thought he was a very good guardian. *Compromise Jack kept telling himself, life is all about compromise.*

Rachel avoided talking about recent events, most of the time. She told Jack she didn't want to let it take over her life, or indeed their life. But occasionally, she would talk about what happened when the two men held her. She said they made her drink this stuff which she assumed was some sort of sleep-inducing medication as most of the time that's all she did, sleep. She was kept in a cellar and tied to a chair. She told Jack about her failed attempt to escape, and Jack was proud of her and admired her courage.

She said she had been terrified of the Bosnian, the man called Kamal who'd told her he would do horrible things to her once they'd got their hands on the drugs. Jack found it too distressing, but Rachel had to talk it out of her system, so he listened patiently, but he told her to try to forget all that stuff now. Things had worked out okay, and hopefully, she could eventually put it all behind her.

Jack kept an eye on the UK news as they had Sky TV. About a week after Ramsay had left, an item appeared on the BBC news, about a body being found in the boot of a hire car in Nice, saying that the French police had contacted their British counterparts in Cheshire to help find the man who had hired the car. They thought the man had flown back to Liverpool the previous week. Jack went down to the local Newsagents in Eze and saw the headline in the Daily Mail "Body in the Boot Manhunt"

He bought the paper and took it back to their apartment. Both Rachel and Jack felt really strange knowing the true facts. They read the story in its entirety, and Jack went on the net to see if there were any more details available, but it was just the story of the body and the search for the man who'd hired the car.

It brought all the memories back for Rachel, but gradually she relaxed again. They wondered if there was any way they might be linked to the events on the news, but realised that it was unlikely that there would be anything to link them to the dead man, or his presumed killer. They got on with their lives as best they could, and agreed between them to only think only about getting by for the next few weeks, rather than speculating all the time on the long term situation.

anny was watching the TV when he heard Gloria's key in the lock. They'd met just a few months ago but got on well from the start. They soon decided to live together, and it had all worked out well up to now, *so who knows?* thought Danny, and wondered what his uptight mother would think about coffee coloured grandchildren. He kept the thought to himself, but couldn't help a little giggle escaping his lips as he pictured the look on his mother's face, should that ever happen. Gloria was from a Jamaican family who had immigrated to the UK two generations ago. Gloria had beautiful dusky skin, a figure to die for, and looks that turned heads wherever she went.

'Could have been a model' Danny often said.

'What and have to mix with all those coked up airheads? No thanks, I'll take real life.'

And she did. With her looks and obvious intelligence, she knew she could have chosen a much more lucrative and glamorous career, but she chose to be a nurse. Her mother had been a nurse, that was what the young Gloria had always wanted to be, and so she became one. She worked in the A&E and liked the unpredictability of the work. Danny had felt a little uneasy when she mentioned 'coked up airheads.' Danny was the manager of the IT department of an online betting company, Betright.com, owned by Tom

MacBride. Tom MacBride's other businesses involved security services, and it was strongly rumoured that there may be a connection to the supply of drugs as well. Though no one would ever say for certain.

Danny had recently taken Gloria to a garden party thrown by Tom MacBride, and MacBride had been the consummate host.

Tom was immediately captivated by Gloria and took her away from Danny, walking her around the party himself, introducing her as his new mistress. Gloria had joined in with the joke, hanging on Tom's arm acting like a tart. Some of the party were horrified as MacBride, with a deadpan face, introduced Gloria as his mistress. Momentarily some people were fooled and embarrassed, especially as Tom's wife was only a few feet away, then everyone had fallen in. They had a great time at the party and Gloria said she really liked Tom and Danny thought, the feeling was definitely mutual, *but who wouldn't fall for Gloria?*

Gloria was still in her nurses' uniform as she handed Danny a cup of coffee.

'I'll just go and take my uniform off then we can think about what we want to do this evening.'

Danny said 'how about you keep your uniform on, I'll go and get my stethoscope and we can play doctors and nurses?'

'No, you mucky perv, anyway this uniform's seen too much blood and guts today. I need to shower and change.'

'Spoilsport' said Danny as she flicked his hand away from her bottom.

'By the way,' Gloria shouted from the bathroom, 'we had a guy in a few days ago, badly beaten, quite serious, broken bones, no ID. He was abandoned in the A&E car park. Anyway, as the swelling in his face has gone down, I'd swear it's one of the guys we met at Tom MacBride's party.'

'Really, who?'

'Would it be the one called Malone? I remember his name because he introduced himself at the party as Tony Malone and I said it would be funny if he'd been called Tony Maloney, which he'd obviously heard before and didn't seem to think was very funny. Anyway, I'll swear it's him. Do you know why he might have ended up in such a state, and without any ID?'

'I don't,' said Danny, 'but keep it to yourself for now and I'll ask MacBride.'

'Well we're supposed to tell the fuzz if we find out who he is, but as I don't really know for sure, so...'

'That's the girl, d'you know, I'm feeling quite dirty myself now, is there room in that shower for another one?'

Tom MacBride made the call to Malone's replacement, John Mercer.

'John, one of the lads in IT has just told me that his girlfriend, who works in A&E at Waterfield hospital, thinks they may have Malone in the high dependency ward there. Broken bones etc., a beating comes to mind. Apparently, he was dumped in the car park and had no ID on him, so apart from the girl, no one knows who he is yet.'

'That sounds a bit weird, what do you want me to do?'

'Organise a private ambulance and get him out of there pronto.'

'Where do I take him to Tom?'

'I'll call you and let you know, just get him, then call me when you're well away from the hospital.'

'Will do Tom.'

*S*o here we are, thought Jack, *hopefully, free of being followed, kidnapped, beaten or murdered even.* The last few weeks had changed his perspective on life, and Jack knew that Rachel felt the same. Ramsay called them when he'd arrived back home in the US, and they thanked him yet again for all his help. He said it had been a pleasure and hoped to see them again, but in happier circumstances. Jack was impressed by Rachel's resilience and her ability to bounce back from her ordeal. Though she had been lucky in some respects, it had been pretty rough experience by any standards.

As they grew in confidence, they started to get out of the apartment, and Jack would walk down the steep hill to get his croissant for breakfast in the morning. Sometimes he'd stop for a coffee at the Cafe Gascogne, greeting any of the locals he knew. Jack found the French very friendly in this part of the world, more like Italians he thought.

After lunch at the apartment, they would occasionally drive down to Beaulieu sur Mer to do some shopping, or go to Nice and spend the day on one of the private beaches where they found the restaurants were more than acceptable. Once in a while they would drive along the A8 to Lac Cassien, about an hour away on the road to Fayance, hire a boat and Rachel would read while Jack fished, very occasionally, he actually caught a fish.

In the evening they would sometimes barbecue on the terrace, and eat al fresco, listening to Classic FM on the radio. The nights were balmy and the views at night were arguably even better than those during the day. Sometimes there were firework displays on Cap Ferrat, or in Villefranche when cruise ship departed.

Days turned into weeks, and both of them felt all the bad memories beginning to fade. They knew they had to deal with the problem of going back to the UK eventually, but for the moment they both felt content to put that aside and enjoys their lives in the sun.

CHAPTER 56

They'd been back in Eze for a while and were well into their previous pattern of dining out twice a week. It was Wednesday, so Jack called the Café de la Fontaine in La Turbie, a village just a mile or so along the road from their apartment complex, and made a reservation for that evening. They arrived and were greeted effusively by the head waiter. He showed them to their table, and after they were served their aperitif. A couple on a nearby table spoke to Jack. The man said they heard Jack and Rachel's English accent, and wondered if they could help them out and translate a couple of the dishes on the menu. Jack obliged.

'I think that couple were hoping they could join us,' Jack said to Rachel.

'You don't know that, and if you ask them, it might embarrass them, if they don't want to.'

A few minutes later, the man came over to their table and said.

'Look I know this is very forward of me, but are you on your own, I mean is anyone coming to join you?'

'No, we're on our own tonight,' said Jack, 'would you and your wife like to join us?'

'Well if you don't mind, that's very kind, I realise I'm being a bit forward, but we're new to the area and as you seem to know your way around here, we thought you might be able to give us some pointers, best restaurants, places to visit and all that.'

'Yes please do join us,' said Rachel, 'we'd be happy to tell you about the area, well as much as we can.'

'That's very kind. My wife said I shouldn't ask, but then she has much better manners than me.'

And with that, he went to collect his wife and their drinks. His wife apologised for her husband as they sat down, saying he was always embarrassing her doing things like that, and she hoped they didn't mind them imposing.

'Not at all, after all, it's us Brits against the rest,' Jack joked, and they all laughed.

It turned out they were from Willersley near Manchester, quite an upmarket area and not very far from where Jack and Rachel lived. They were a similar age to Jack and Rachel and found they had lots in common. They chatted about French food and how it was much superior to English food and the service so much better.

It turned out that they had a place in Spain, so the two couples swopped stories about their experiences there too. They'd been chatting for a while when Jack realised they hadn't introduced themselves to each other, and so did the honours.

'By the way, I'm Jack, and this is my wife Rachel.'

'Very pleased to meet you both, my name's Tom, Tom MacBride and this is my wife Esther.

'Very pleased to meet you both too' Jack and Rachel said, almost in unison and they all shook hands.

They carried on chatting throughout their meal, then Jack and Rachel realised it was very late and said they had to go, but they hoped to bump into Tom and Esther again sometime. The other couple said it was past their bedtime too and got up to leave.

'Do you have a place here or are you staying at a hotel?' Jack asked, as they left the restaurant to go to the car park. The two women were chatting away on their own.

'Neither' said Tom MacBride, 'we're renting an apartment in a place called Le Jardin d'Eze,'

His pronunciation left something to be desired, but there was no doubt they were staying on the same complex.

'Lovely place' he added.

'Amazing,' said Jack, 'that's where we live, I thought I'd seen your face somewhere before.'

By then the girls had caught up to them, and Jack told Rachel where the couple were staying. What a coincidence they all agreed. Tom MacBride asked Jack if the tennis court in the complex got busy.

'It never gets busy Tom, we play nearly every morning, to get a bit of exercise you know, but we never see anyone else there, and it's a really good court.'

'Well' said Tom MacBride 'you must be good, it's just that Esther and I love a game, but we're crap players, so wouldn't be up to your standard.'

'Listen Tom, we're rubbish as well, but we just enjoy a knock about.'

'Fancy a game tomorrow morning then?' asked Tom.

Jack looked at Rachel who smiled an expression of why not, so Jack said

'Great, but not too early.'

'Suits us,' said Tom, 'we're not what you'd call early birds. How about ten?'

They agreed to meet on the tennis court at ten thirty.

'We'll look forward to it,' said Jack.

And with that, they all bid each other goodnight and went to their respective cars.

'What a nice couple,' said Rachel when they got into their car to drive back to the apartment.

'Yes, I can see we'll get on with them,' said Jack.

'Hope they're not good at tennis though.'

They met the next morning, and as luck would have it they were fairly evenly matched. They had a great laugh and agreed that with having had all that exercise, they needed to cool off and relax. So they went to their respective apartments. Jack said they'd see them at the pool in a while. When they got to the pool, Tom and Esther were already there, Tom MacBride swimming up and down the pool, splashing most of the water out of the pool, and Esther on a lounger reading a book.

They'd saved Jack and Rachel some loungers next to theirs, so the two couples chatted about this and that and variously dozed, had a swim and read. They all seemed to feel at ease with each other. Jack felt that Esther and Rachel were getting on really well, and they would make great friends. Pity they were only on vacation, he thought. He liked Tom, who seemed a pretty straightforward guy.

There was none of the tension where they felt they needed to keep chatting. They also seemed to have a great deal in common. Tom MacBride had a number of business interests, betting shops, security business and a waste recycling business, which was suffering a bit in the current recession he said. Jack told him all about his business interests, and they swapped stories and jokes, occasionally indulging in a bit of one-upmanship, but all in a spirit of friendliness and gentle mickey taking.

Lunchtime came, and Rachel said.

'Come on Jack, we need to eat, and I'm sure Tom and Esther want their lunch as well. Jack could see that neither couple wished to appear "pushy" by suggesting they meet up again, but finally, Tom spoke.

'We've really enjoyed our morning, haven't we Esther?'

'We certainly have.'

'So why don't we meet up again tomorrow evening, we were planning to go to the little place in Eze village, the Café Gascoigne I think it's called. Unless you tell us it's no good?'

'No it's okay, we eat there a lot.'

'Well, why don't you join us, say about seven thirty?' Rachel looked at Jack who was nodding in agreement.

'That would be great,' she said, 'we'll look forward to it.'

They met the next evening, and Jack thought it went well. They all got a bit tipsy. Tom and Esther were going back to the UK on Sunday, so Tom suggested they have one more game of tennis the next day, Saturday morning.

'But not till eleven this time, give us all time to recover.' he said.

The next morning dawned bright and sunny but with a pleasant cool breeze coming from the east. Jack knew this usually signified rain, but there was no trace of clouds, nothing to get worried about anyway he thought. They met Tom and Esther at the tennis courts, and after they'd played tennis, they all went to the pool again to cool off. Rachel said,

'As it's your last day before going back to the UK, I'll make lunch for us all at our place if that's okay with you?'

They agreed enthusiastically and went off to change.

Rachel prepared a big salad Nicoise, followed by some pasta and when they'd finished Rachel and Esther said they'd like to top up their tan and sunbathe by the pool for a few hours. Tom suggested to Jack that they go for a walk down to Eze as he'd promised to get some perfume for Esther from Fragonard, the perfume showroom in Eze.

Tom asked Esther for the details of what she wanted him to get, and she wrote it down for him and gave him the piece of paper.

'Could this generous offer to get me my perfume have anything to do with you and Jack going for a snifter Tom?'

'Nothing could have been further from my mind,' he said, 'but now you mention it...'

Esther laughed and told him not to lead Jack astray.

'As if,' said Tom, and pecked Esther on the cheek.

They all laughed. Jack asked Rachel if she needed anything from Fragonard, the perfume factory shop in Eze, and she said not really, but surprise me. Okay said Jack, and off he and Tom went to walk down to Eze village.

They chatted as they walked down to the village square. They found a table at the Bar Collette and ordered drinks.

'You know, we'll miss your company when you leave Tom,' said Jack, swirling his cognac around in his balloon glass.

'Yes, we've had a great time too. Esther's very fond of Rachel, they seem to get on like a house on fire.'

'They do seem to, don't they' said Jack.

CHAPTER 57

Gloria had been on an early shift at the hospital so she'd been home a while and was doing some ironing when Danny came in. The front door of the apartment opened up on to one large open plan room which served as both dining room and sitting room. He hung his coat on the back of one of the dining chairs, loosened his tie then took it off, walked behind her, put his arms round her, hugged and at the same time fondled her breasts. Gloria put the iron down, turned and pushed him away.

'Randy git' she said smiling, 'Don't think you're going to get your evil way with me just like that, dirty bugger.'

Danny feigned a hurt look.

'What's for dinner then?' He asked.

'You tell me. You're taking me out. If you think I'm cooking after the day I've had at the hospital, you're badly mistaken, and anyway, you said you'd take me to that new Italian.'

'Okay,' said Danny, 'but I may have to be persuaded, know what I mean?'

Rachel looked at him, then took him by the hand and walked him to the bedroom.

'Wow, that was easy' he said.

'Don't flatter yourself, it's just that I'm hungry.'

They both laughed and fell on the bed. Later, as they were getting dressed to go out Gloria said

'I knew I'd forgotten to tell you something. That man who I thought was that Malone who worked for Tom MacBride, remember?'

'Yes, I remember' said Danny.

'Well you won't believe this, but the day after I told you, he disappeared off the ward, and we all assumed he'd been moved to another ward. He wasn't my patient see. Anyway, it turns out he'd been picked up by a private ambulance service and taken away. But then today, he was found dumped in the car park again, and then brought back into the ward. He wasn't in a much better state than he was when he left, and no one seemed to know what was going on.

The ward manager is going apeshit. Anyway, this time he still didn't have any normal ID on him but he did have a note in his pocket saying who he was. I was right, it was that Tony Malone. The manager called the police, and the next thing is, he's been moved into a side ward and given a police guard. Someone said he's a suspect in a murder case.'

Danny said nothing. He knew it was better not to speculate on such things. *None of my business* he thought, and anyway, he had more important things on his mind, such as what a great wife and mother Gloria would make.

'Come on Gloria he said, they'll be giving our table away if we don't hurry up and I've got something important to ask you after dinner.'

CHAPTER 58

Tom MacBride looked down at his drink then up at Jack and said.

'Jack there's something we need to discuss.'

Jack was surprised by the sudden change of tone in Tom's voice. He suddenly sounded serious.

'Yes Tom, what is it?'

'Jack, I'm not here by accident.'

Jack instantly made the connection to recent events. He hoped he was wrong. Tom saw the anxiety in Jack's eyes and quickly answered the unasked question.

'No Jack I'm not a hit man, but I do have a serious interest in your situation, or predicament, as it might more accurately be described. I need your cooperation, otherwise ....'

Tom MacBride left the unspoken threat hanging in the air.

Jack's mind was spinning. He'd just gone from having almost forgotten about the nightmare, to being thrown back into it.

'Jack, have a drink, providing you help me, then maybe we can work things out.'

Jack found it difficult to readjust from relaxing with a new friend, to being in the company of your potential worst enemy.

'Have a good slug Jack, and I'll tell you a little story.'

Jack took a drink, and as he did the questions started to go through his mind. How could he have thought just a few short minutes ago that Tom was going to become a good friend, a great friend maybe, and now? Jack now realised how Tom had manipulated them in the restaurant when they first met. How the casual conversation had led to them sitting at the next table. Was it he who suggested the game of tennis the next day? No it was Tom, but he'd done it so cleverly. Jack realised how well he'd been played.

Tom MacBride looked Jack in the eye.

'Look Jack, I'd like you to focus and listen to what I have to tell you. Don't worry about Rachel, she's not in any danger, so relax. Esther knows nothing about your situation, or this part of my business activities. Come to that, there's no one who knows everything. Now Jack, by necessity, I'm going to have to tell you some confidential things about some of my business activities. Things other people don't know about. So if anyone else finds out, I'll know who's talked, and that, my friend, would have the most serious consequences for you, understand?'

'I understand.' Said Jack, thinking to himself *that 'serious consequences'* can be a two way street Mr MacBride. But he kept his mouth shut for the moment.

'Well I hope you do. The good news is that if you co-operate with me, I just might be able to help you with another problem you have, okay? Do you understand what I'm saying?'

Jack wasn't sure what he meant. *The contract on his life? Was this the man who'd arranged it and not the man's brother?* Jack nodded in agreement, *best to go along with this for 'till I find what's going on.*

Tom MacBride continued.

'What I told you about my various business interests is accurate. I just left out another business interest I have, a very lucrative one, importing drugs, well the raw materials to be more accurate. I figured out a relatively simple and fool proof way of getting the raw drugs past the authorities, and to where they're processed ready for distribution on the street. I won't go into detail but suffice to say that it involves dropping the stuff by helicopter into a field not too far from Manchester Airport. But you know all about that Jack, don't you?'

'So you're the...', Jack searched for the right description, 'you're the organiser, the person who owns the drugs, the raw materials whatever?'

'Yes, I am, as you so put it, "the owner", the rightful owner and I want my stuff back Jack, and I believe you have it.'

'Well believe or not,' said Jack, 'I've been trying to think how to get the fucking stuff back to whoever owned it. I don't give a shit about drugs. Couldn't care less. All I care about is getting on with our lives, the drugs mean nothing to me...' Jack had raised his voice in anger.

MacBride looked around then said to Jack.

'Look, calm down, we don't need to advertise here, let's discuss this rationally. If I get what I want then everything will be fine, okay?'

'Okay' said Jack, 'but answer this. If the drugs belong to you, then who the hell kidnapped Rachel?'

'We'll come to that eventually Jack. Now I honestly don't believe you intended to steal my goods. Otherwise we wouldn't be having this conversation in such civilised circumstances. And I don't know precisely what happened that morning, but I assume you have no objection to telling me all about that? Then we can all move on.'

'Okay' said Jack and he had another sip of cognac, cleared his throat and began. He told Tom MacBride how Ezra had demanded his phone and threatening him with a knife. How it subsequently turned out that Ezra's phone had run out of battery. Tom MacBride nodded, and it seemed to answer a question in his mind. Jack carried on, telling MacBride how he kicked out at Ezra, missing his head and accidentally kicking him in the throat.

He told him about cutting Alfie and sending him off with Ezra's money. Jack thought he saw a look of grudging admiration on Tom MacBride's face when he told him that bit. He went on to describe how afterwards, he'd taken the rucksack and hidden it, so that whoever owned the drugs would assume that Alfie had stolen it, after he'd killed the man who'd attacked him, and whom he now knew was called Ezra. MacBride stopped him at this point and asked if anyone else knew where he'd hidden the drugs. Jack said no one else knew, not even Rachel. MacBride gestured for him to go on.

He recounted his interviews with the police and how at one point they'd told him that someone may have put a contract out on him, they said probably Ezra's psychopathic brother. They'd him that he was still in jail but nevertheless, had contacts outside that he could use to have him hunted down.

'I was worried that my story wouldn't hold up once the police found the other man, Alfie someone. I can't remember his surname. I knew that he would be able to contradict my version of events, but as it turned out, he'd been beaten senseless by some thugs, and apparently is unlikely ever to recover enough to give any evidence. So his bad luck and my good luck, poor sod.'

Then Jack told him about going to Florida to escape the people who had been hired to harm him, but that they had been followed to Florida nevertheless, but managed to lose the men in the end and had flown back to France.

Jack went on to tell him about being followed to the Luberon. About Rachel being kidnapped, and how the people who'd kidnapped her wanted to know where he'd hidden the drugs, in exchange for releasing Rachel. He stopped telling his story and asked Tom MacBride a question.

'So if these are your drugs, but you didn't arrange the kidnap, then who did?'

'I'll clear all that up shortly' said Tom MacBride, 'just carry on with your story.'

So Jack continued and told him how Ramsay had come to France to help him and that they'd managed to get Rachel back. He didn't mention that one of the men was killed in the process.

'We managed to get Rachel back, without revealing where the drugs were hidden. So the kidnappers ended up, empty handed.' He said.

'Obviously, there's more detail, but that's pretty much it.'

Tom MacBride sat in silence for a while. Then he said,

'Right, first things first. You can still remember clearly where you hid the rucksack I assume?'

'Yes'

'And it wouldn't have been too far from where all this happened?'

'No, it's actually down a manhole that my dog Bess fell down once. It's on a farm, Meadowcroft, by a farm track. You'd never find it in a million years. I only discovered the place, because of Bess falling into it and howling until I found where she was. It's quite deep, behind a big hedge, near a pond and all overgrown with weeds and stuff.'

'So if I get my man on the phone and get him down to the general area could you guide him to where it's stashed?'

'Yes, I don't see why not.'

Jack was more than glad for the opportunity to tidy up this very dangerous loose end.

In any event, if he didn't co-operate, Jack had the feeling that Tom MacBride could arrange whatever he thought appropriate as punishment. And that would no doubt involve serious consequences for Jack, Rachel too maybe.

Tom MacBride wandered off and made a call on his mobile. He spoke for a few minutes then came back and sat down.

CHAPTER 59

'We've got an hour to kill while Charlie gets down to Briarley, so I suggest we go and get the perfume we came down here for. Okay Jack?'

Jack was a bit taken aback by the sudden change of tack, and he was still in a state of mild shock. Nothing seemed real.

They went to the Fragonard perfume factory shop, a large impressive building just behind Eze village. As usual, at this time of year, the place was busy, and all the smart young female staff were serving other customers so they had to wait their turn. Tom made small talk while they waited, which Jack thought a bit weird in the circumstances.

It was as though there were two Tom MacBrides, the amiable friend to be, and the ruthless gangster. Jack found it hard to contemplate that such different versions of life could exist simultaneously. Here we are, thought Jack, doing what tourists do, buying perfume and the like, while at the same time being involved in another very dark dimension, where people were killed and tortured, dealt in drugs and went on the run. *Bizarre doesn't come close.*

Tom MacBride ordered his stuff, and the girl started to get all the items together. Jack bought some soap, not knowing why particularly, they had plenty of the stuff already. Rachel had asked Jack to surprise her, but couldn't think about surprises at the moment. Anyway, he thought, there were going to be enough surprises, without taking any perfume back.

Tom MacBride's phone chirruped. Charlie had arrived in Briarley Village.

'Give us a few minutes Charlie, we'll go and get comfortable and call you back.'

Tom MacBride paid for his purchases and they went back to the bar. Tom MacBride called Charlie back and introduced Jack as someone who would tell him where to find the stuff.

'It's still in the original rucksack, in a hole in the ground apparently.'

He handed his phone to Jack.

'Hello.'

'Hello, Tom tells me you're going to guide me to pick up a rucksack from a hole in the ground?'

'That's right. Well, it's actually a concrete manhole without a cover, but it's well sheltered and covered over with grass and weeds. It's sort of under a big hedge, and you'll have to be careful not to fall down it when you get there.'

'Okay, let's do it,' said Charlie.

'Tell me where you are exactly.' Said Jack.

He said he was at the Greyhound Pub car park.

'Okay, you're about as near as you can get in terms of parking your car. So, park your car, you'll need to walk from there.'

Jack gave him directions and kept the phone open. Charlie gave Jack a running commentary on his progress, and corrected him when necessary.

It got a bit tricky when he got to the immediate area, and it took a bit of explaining by Jack, before Charlie found the manhole. Despite Jack warning him previously, he nearly fell down it. Charlie disappeared from the phone while he lay on the ground and leaned into the manhole. The only way to get hold of the rucksack would be to lower your upper body down the hole, and it was not a pleasant experience, *although not nearly as difficult as trying to get hold of the scruff of a dog's neck as I'd had to do.*

At last Charlie confirmed he'd recovered the rucksack. Jack passed the phone back to Tom MacBride. Tom grunted a couple of times into the phone,

'Right yeah, okay. Now get it to you know where and pronto, but don't get caught speeding okay?'

Tom MacBride turned to Jack and beamed.

'I think that calls for another drink don't you? Now Jack, why don't you phone Rachel and tell the girls we're running late? They'll be wondering where we are.'

Jack called Rachel but they were obviously having a drink or two themselves and seemed to have forgotten all about them.

'Okay Jack,' fresh drinks had arrived, 'now I'll tell you what *I know* about what happened that morning.

My so called right hand man, Tony, had got himself into a bit of bother. Gambling debts of all things, and me owning a bookies. I don't know. Anyway, he was up to his neck in debt, and they were calling in his bits of paper.'

'I assume this was a Tony Malone?' Jack asked.

'It was,' said MacBride. He carried on, 'the people he owed money to are not known for their tolerance or patience, so they told Malone he had two options, and the other one involved a wooden box. He decided that the solution to his problem was to swindle me, to get the money to pay them. A major error of judgement. All he had to do was tell me, and I'd have worked something out somehow, anyway that wasn't to be. He decided to wait for a big shipment and lift the lot himself, sell it, then do a runner. He'd have to get rid of it to someone with their own processing plant, so would have to go south somewhere, but he assumed he would get enough for the gear for him to get lost in luxury for long enough, South America, South Africa, the USA who knows? Anyway, he knew Ezra was a mug for a deal and talked him into believing that he'd cut him in for half, if he brought the stuff to Malone instead of delivering, as planned, to the processing plant courier. Same plan, just a different ending.

His plan was that Ezra would collect the gear from the helicopter, as normal, but call Malone, instead of the courier, to confirm he'd got the gear and meet Malone who was waiting in a car on a side road not too far away from the drop zone. Then he and Malone would drive south sell the gear, the sale already arranged by Malone, and off they'd go to who knows where? Poor old Alfie was expendable, and Ezra was supposed to get rid of him, permanently. But of course, unknown to Ezra, Malone planned to get rid of him as well, as soon as he'd delivered the stuff to Malone. Are you following all this?

'Yes I think so,' said Jack.

'Okay, so when Ezra didn't call, Malone waited, then eventually realised something had gone wrong. He knew all the details of the route Ezra and Alfie were supposed to take so he went to find them.

Sure enough, he came across Ezra who was, shall we say, not very well.'

Did he mean Ezra wasn't dead or was this just Tom MacBride being sarcastic?

'You don't mean Ezra was still alive?'

'Yes he was, but in a pretty bad way apparently.'

'Are you sure?'

'Yes I'm sure, you thought you'd killed him, but you hadn't.

Jack took another drink of his cognac. MacBride carried on.

'Anyway, Malone couldn't get Ezra to talk. Problems with his throat. But you'd know all about that. So without Ezra being able to tell him what happened, Malone drew his own conclusions. It seemed obvious to him that Ezra had tried to off Alfie as planned, but he assumed that somehow Alfie had got the better of Ezra and done him a nasty, then buggered off with the gear. Malone couldn't leave Ezra, as he might recover and tell someone – me for instance, that he had planned to lift the gear himself. So Tony, being Tony, thought he'd put an end to that problem, took off his jacket, rolled it up and held it over Ezra's face until he suffocated.'

Tom MacBride must have finally seen what effect this information was having on Jack and gave him a minute to take it in, and had another sip of his drink.

'Malone then had to cover up his involvement and simply told me that Ezra and Alfie had collected the goods, then gone missing and had never made the call to drop off the drugs. He figured this would give him time to retrieve the situation.'

Jack could hardly believe what he was hearing, but the last weeks and months had been so far removed from anything that he might have considered normal, that he just sat there in a stupor.

Tom MacBride went on.

'So, when it became known that the police had found Ezra's body, we all went chasing off after poor old Alfie. My boys, the boys that Ezra's brother had hired, and Malone, who already knew Ezra was dead, but had to wait until it was public knowledge to avoid being caught in a lie.

Unfortunately for Alfie, Jay's hired hands found him first, tortured him and beat him senseless. But what they did discover, beyond doubt, was that Alfie hadn't done Ezra in, but you had, or they thought you had, because Alfie thought you had. I found out subsequently, that they had no idea who you were, but they concluded you'd nicked the drugs, and so they thought you were maybe a player. Jay then put out a contract on you, which I found out about a bit later. I wasn't bothered about you being knocked off. No skin off my nose after all. The problem for me was, that if Jay's men got to you first, they would probably get their hands on my drugs, and consider it a huge bonus. Not to say, a serious poke in the eye for me on a personal level. Jay and I are not what you'd call best friends, lots of history there.

Malone on the other hand, knew that you hadn't actually killed Ezra, but that was just a minor detail to him. It was obvious to him that you had attacked Ezra, and as such you must have been the one that had lifted the drugs. So he needed to find you before anyone else did, otherwise the opportunity to solve all his problems would disappear.'

'Malone had a mole in the police and was able to find out details of where your place was, over here in France. He also spoke a bit of schoolboy French, so I agreed to send him over, to talk to the locals and see if he could get a line on you. He actually came over to Eze but told me it was a dead end. No sign of you having been here, and no indication you'd been to your place lately. He said he spoke to the guardian at your apartment complex and gave him a few quid to let us know if and when you went there. Well, it later transpired that the guardian did call Malone, but Malone kept that to himself.'

Jack didn't tell Tom MacBride that he knew this bit of the story. Tom MacBride continued,

'A week or so went by with no sign of you, so it looked like we were all in for the long haul. Malone came to me and said he needed some R&R, and I had to agree he was well overdue for a holiday, then the cheeky git said he was a bit skint and could I sub him a couple of grand for his trip? As usual, being a soft touch, I lent him the money. He disappeared off on holiday but called in now and then to see if we'd found you, when all the time the tricky bastard had found you himself and kidnapped your wife.'

'How do you know all this in such detail?' asked Jack.

'All from the horse's mouth. That's Malone's mouth to be more precise.' Tom MacBride said

'When Malone didn't show after a couple of weeks I realised I'd been had, and asked the boys to see if they could find him. I had a missing load of expensive drugs and a missing senior member of my team. Doesn't take a genius to make a connection. But I wrongly assumed he had done a runner with the drugs, and that I was at least two weeks and a bit behind him.'

'Then, as it happened, one of the lads who works for me in another business, has a girlfriend who's a nurse, and she told him about a man who was dumped outside A&E with no ID, badly beaten and unconscious for days. But as his face mended, she thought she recognised him and told her boyfriend she thought it was Tony Malone, who she'd met at one of my parties. Her boyfriend told her to keep shtum, then he told me.

We then heard that the police were looking for him in connection with a body found in the boot of a car in Nice. I have to say we were a bit confused by that particular development. But I thought we should get him out of hospital before anyone else could find him, which we did.

We put him in one of our staff apartments, got him a private doctor, very private, and very expensive. As soon as he was fit enough, we had a sort of question and answer session, you might say. Malone spilled his guts. He wasn't feeling very tough after the beating someone had given him. All he wanted, was to put an end to his nightmare.'

Tom MacBride went on.

'Malone cracked wide open and told us the lot. Everything, all about his plan to steal my drugs, his plans to kill Ezra and Alfie, then when it all went tits up, and he found out it was you who'd messed up his plans, and more than likely had the drugs. So he took the Bosnian nutter with him to kidnap your wife so that you'd tell him where the drugs were etc., etc.

Tom MacBride stopped talking and ordered another round of drinks from the waitress. The drinks came, and Tom MacBride picked up where he'd left off.

'So Malone told us how you'd promised to lead him to where the drugs were hidden, in exchange for your wife's release. He was convinced that his plan was fool proof, and

I have to admit, it seemed pretty sound to me when he told me. Kamal holding your wife in France while he went to the UK to get the drugs. But obviously, he badly underestimated you. He told me how you walked him, well more like talked him, into a trap, and that he was slugged, then taken away and worked over, very professionally it seems. And that's how he ended up in hospital with broken bones and all.'

Tom MacBride took a swig of his cognac, then said,

'You must tell me how on earth you pulled that off sometime. Blindsiding Malone and the Bosnian? I mean these boys were pretty good, yet you managed to get the better of them, and lined Malone up for murdering the Bosnian to boot. Unbelievable!'

'I had help' said Jack, 'a guy called Ramsay, the PI we hired in Florida, he came over to help when I told him they'd kidnapped Rachel.'

'Was it this Ramsay guy who killed the Bosnian?'

'Yes it was, but it was self-defence. Ramsay attacked the Bosnian to get Rachel away from him, and he pulled a knife on Ramsay, which was a big mistake.'

'So,' said Tom MacBride, slowly working out the sequence of events, 'Ramsay dumped the Bosnian's body in the boot of the car, which was presumably the one that Malone had hired. Then drove it back to Nice, abandoned it, waited for the police to find it and let them draw the obvious conclusion! Brilliant, absolutely fucking brilliant.' He took another swig of his drink.

'Well well. Anyway, to continue. Tony couldn't really remember that much after meeting your friends, but he was clear about the threat they made to him regarding your future wellbeing, underlined by a good old beating, It was clear that Malone had seriously underestimated you, so we didn't want to make the same mistake and had to re-think our plans.

I now knew that you had the drugs, or at least you knew where they were, but you obviously weren't a pushover, so I had to find out exactly what you were, and what your angle was. I was a bit concerned when I found out that Jay's men had followed you to Florida, but I couldn't do anything about that. I just hoped that they wouldn't get to you, and more importantly, as far as I was concerned, to my drugs. I figured that if they didn't find you, that you'd eventually turn up in Eze, once you thought the heat was off. So I arranged for one of my female security staff members to rent one of the apartments in your complex. She loved the job, sunbathing and swimming in the pool every day. She was a bit disappointed when you arrived and she had to go home, nearly didn't tell me, she said.

So once I knew you were back here, I thought I'd come across myself and see what the score was. Make my own judgement, hence the "chance" meeting in the restaurant.'

CHAPTER 60

'So where does that leave me now?' asked Jack.

'Well, as you've been so co-operative, and it looks like I've got my stuff back, I'd say things are looking up for you Jack.'

'But what about Ezra's brother and the men looking for me?'

'Yes well, I've been thinking about that. Malone is still, how can I say, detained at my leisure I think is the correct term. I could let it be known to Jay Madaki, that Malone is the one who did for the poor unfortunate brother Ezra, and not you. But I'm not sure he'd believe it, especially coming from me. So, you'll have to leave it with me and I'll see what I can do.

'And what about this Tony Malone, said Jack.

'Yes well I'll give him a sporting chance of course and let him go just before I tell Jay Madaki. But I wouldn't bet on Malone's chances of outrunning them, that is if they accept that he's the one who killed Ezra. Even if they don't, Malone has the little problem of the police looking for him in connection with the "body in the boot murder", not forgetting of course the original people Malone owes the gambling debt to, so I don't rate his chances of a long and happy life, too highly, poor sod. And even if the police get to him first and he goes inside, the other people who are after him won't find that a problem. So things are definitely looking a bit grim for poor old Tony. But, as the bible says 'as ye sow, so shall ye reap.'

Jack sat there, still not quite able to take in all that he'd heard. Tom MacBride on the other hand was acting as though they'd just been discussing a football match or something, rather than a tale of double-dealing, murder and mayhem. Jack was still taking in the fact that he hadn't killed anyone. It was slowly started to sink in.

I haven't killed anyone. But just as important, the brother who wanted revenge might be persuaded of that too. MacBride had his drugs back, I'm off the hook with him. One kidnapper dead and one going to jail.

Jack felt he should have been jumping up in the air, and although he felt a great weight had been lifted off his shoulders, he still had the psycho brother to worry about.

Jack was thinking so hard about what had just happened that he hadn't heard Tom MacBride speak.

'Jack, don't you think we'd better get back to the girls? They'll think we've found ourselves a couple of dolly birds.'

As they walked back, Tom MacBride was talking,

'Esther and I need an early night Jack, don't forget we're flying back to the UK tomorrow, and we need to be up nice and early.'

'Yes, yes of course' answered Jack, and they walked back the rest of the way to the complex mainly in silence. Jack was trying to decide what he thought about Tom MacBride. On one hand, he was a self declared ruthless drug dealing gangster. Of that there was little doubt. But on the other hand, he'd promised to get the contract on him removed. When they arrived at the pool, they found their wives lying on their sunbeds, still chatting away.

MacBride had made Jack promise that he wouldn't tell Rachel anything, until well after he and Esther had left for their flight back home. Jack was going to keep that promise, on the basis that Tom MacBride was the only person in the world who could get this Jay person off his case. Tom had said that it would take a while to sort out, but he'd call Jack once he'd spoken to Jay's man Mickey. If that didn't work, then he promised he'd think of some other way to sort it.

Rachel asked if they wanted a drink, but Tom said they'd better leave as they had to be up early the next day and they still had to pack. They all said their goodbyes and told each other how much they'd enjoyed meeting each other.

As they made to leave, the women hugged, then Esther gave Jack a hug and Rachel hugged Tom MacBride.

'Well, goodbye Rachel, goodbye Jack, we've really enjoyed meeting you and who knows, maybe we'll meet again. And Jack, I promise to sort out that little problem we discussed.'

The day after the MacBrides had left for their flight back to the UK, Jack told Rachel about his conversation with Tom. She was horrified and found it hard to believe they'd been so easily taken in. He told her about Tom's promise, to try to convince the man who'd put the contract out on him, that this Tony Malone was the real killer of his brother, and not Jack. But McBride had said, he wasn't sure the man would believe him.

Jack watched the news avidly, and sure enough, a Tony Malone was eventually arrested for the "Body in the boot" murder. Rachel found the news disturbing, but was grateful in that it brought an end, that particular chapter of their life.

'Funny.' she said reading the news report.

'What's funny?' said Jack

'Well, how justice works sometimes. I mean here's a man going to go down, for a crime he's not committed. But he hasn't been caught, for at least one murder he did commit. Not to mention, that he and his friend also planned to kill me. A sort of justice in the end, I suppose.'

Tom had asked for Jack's mobile phone number, and said he'd let him know if there were any developments, but he'd never called. Jack just assumed he'd got nowhere with the "psycho brother" as he now thought of him.

Some two weeks later Jack walked down to Eze, as usual, to get his croissant for breakfast, and pick up the Daily Telegraph from the local newsagents in the village. He sat down at one of the tables outside the boulangerie, ordered a coffee and began to read his paper. He enjoyed these solitary moments in the morning. He began to read the main story. Another scandal involving government ministers. Then he noticed another, smaller headline, in the bottom right hand corner of the paper.

"Prisoner found dead in cell" then a sub headline "Police corruption uncovered." He continued reading, and just as he was raising the cup to his lips, he read "Convicted killer Jay Madaki was found dead in his cell yesterday...." at that, Jack nearly spilled his hot coffee in his lap. He put his cup down and read on.

"The prison authorities are still investigating the cause of death, but initial reports indicate a possible drug overdose. The prison service has been plagued in recent years by an increase in the amount of illicit drugs in prisons, and the government have promised a crackdown in this area. A white paper will be produced this autumn with recommendations for ministers to consider etc etc.,.

Jack speed read down to the next details.

"Ironically, in another twist, Madaki's death has triggered a full scale investigation into corruption in the Greater Manchester Police Force. Photographs and MP3 sound files are said to have been found in the deceased prisoner's cell, which may have implications regarding corruption involving a senior officer in the GMP. This is another area which the government has said it is ...."

Jack put the paper down and sat there trying to absorb what he'd just read. *Happenstance, or the work of Tom MacBride?* Jack decided he'd rather not know. He knew he should feel great relief, that finally, the source of all that fear and worry no longer existed. He thought of how Rachel would react. She'd been finding it increasingly difficult staying away from their home in the UK. She missed her friends and the animals. She was homesick, and it showed.

He began to tally up how many people had died since that fateful morning walk. There was Ezra, then his mate Alfie, who if not yet dead was as good as. The man who'd helped kidnap Rachel, whose name he found out later to be Kamal, the "Body in the boot" corpse. Tony Malone, who according to Tom MacBride, wouldn't stand much of a chance in prison. And now Jay Madaki. And all because Jack had got up early and gone for a walk that morning.

He took another sip of his now cold coffee and comforted himself with the thought that they would probably all have come to a sticky and untimely end in any event.

Nevertheless, how different their own lives would have been if he'd just stayed in bed that morning ....

Jack finished the dregs of his coffee, left a big tip, got up from the table and walked quickly back to the apartment to tell Rachel the news and to start packing for home.

CHAPTER 62

'Call for you Sammy.'

'Put 'em through George.'

'Hello Chief Inspector, Sergeant Carter here sir.'

'Hello Carter how are you?'

'Fine sir, thought I'd give you a heads up in case you hadn't heard. Our esteemed Assistant Chief Constable Neale has just been nicked. Alleged corruption charges apparently.'

'Bloody hell, Colin Neale. Well I never. No, I hadn't heard. When did all this happen?'

'Well, Jay Madaki, remember him sir?'

'I certainly do Carter, what's he got to do with it?'

'Well sir, he was found dead in his cell, drugs overdose according to the prison doc, but when they searched Madaki's cell for the drugs, and any other evidence, they found some other stuff hidden away, photographs and sound files on a memory stick.'

'Oh, and?'

'Well sir, the photos apparently show Colin Neale meeting with Jay. And the sound files are apparently a recording of a conversation, which strongly suggests that Neale was on the take.'

'What, from Madaki?'

'Yes sir. Bit of a surprise isn't it?'

'It certainly is Carter. I assume Neale's had a visit from Internal Affairs?'

'Yes sir, I believe that's already happened, and now the brass are trying to figure out how to deal with the corruption fallout with the press.'

'Hmm, rather them than me. Mind you, does none of us any good, this sort of stuff, one bad apple Carter.'

'Yes I know sir.'

'And Madaki. Is there any doubt about the cause of death?'

'Doesn't seem to be sir, obviously there'll be a post-mortem, but by all accounts, it'll be a formality.'

'I suppose you should feel some pity for him, but it's difficult, when you think of all the damage he did to others while he was alive. No doubt had a bad start in life, and all that sort of stuff. Still, no excuse.'

'Yes sir, I suppose so sir.'

'Funny isn't it, first Ezra Madaki and now his brother Jay, just months later, then there was poor old Alfie who mercifully died, poor sod. All connected in one way or another to that killing out in Briarley.'

'Yes it does seem a bit of a coincidence, but they do say things happen in threes.

'Yes you're right they do say that, but I've always thought it a load of old codswallop, no offence meant Carter.'

'None taken sir. Wasn't it Jay Madaki that was said to have put a contract out on the guy walking the dog, the witness, Brandon?'

'Yes, well that was a rumour at the time, but we never really knew if that story was true. And anyway, we couldn't ever figure out why he would do such a thing. I personally couldn't ever see that Brandon would have been involved in the death of his brother. But I did feel I had a duty at the time, you know, to tell Brandon about the rumour. So, I suppose I'd better tell him that, if there was any truth in it, Jay Madaki's death will have put an end to all that. Well, goodbye Carter thanks for letting me know. Keep well.'

'Will do sir, and you too, goodbye.'

Chief Inspector Pownall sat at his desk and thought about Colin Neale being on the take. He never liked the man, and for some reason, he wasn't too surprised at the news. Unfortunately, there would always be bent policemen he supposed.

Then he turned his mind to the news of Jay Madaki's death and the circumstances surrounding the unsolved case of his brother Ezra's death. There were inconsistencies and coincidences and lots of loose ends. He was sure that Jack Brandon wasn't mixed up with the likes of Alfie and Ezra and neither was he a killer. But the story about the spray still niggled in the back of the inspector's mind and the frustration of not having been able to interview Alfie Campkin irritated him. Alfie, probably the only person that could have told him what really went on that spring morning in Briarley. Other than the killer, assuming that wasn't Alfie himself? *Ah well, he's dead now* he thought, *so I suppose I'll never know.*

Pownall turned his attention to the latest case to arrive on his desk. *This is a bit more like it, plenty of circumstantial evidence this time.* Body left in the boot of a hire car, found near Nice airport, cause of death stabbing. Main suspect, one Anthony Malone, UK resident, who hired the car but according to the French police, dumped it in Nice then flew back to the UK. Suspect subsequently found hospitalised in Manchester having been badly beaten, and saying absolutely nothing.

Pownall sighed, picked up the phone and asked if someone could check with the hospital to see if Mr Malone was fit enough to be transferred to the cells for a more formal interrogation.

CHAPTER 63

Some months later

The static crackled in Martin Brown's earphones as he struggled to hear his co-pilot's voice over the noise of the engine. He adjusted the dials, and Bob's voice became clearer.

'Please repeat, over.'

'Looks like we've got something Martin. Three o'clock, over.'

Martin looked at the heat sensors on the dashboard. They were only supposed to be testing and tuning up the equipment, prior to a sweep over south Manchester, but it seemed they might already have a result.

'Strange pattern though, not the usual. Can we go round again? Over.'

'Roger that.'

The police spotter plane banked sharply to the right as it turned to take another pass over the farm.

Chief Inspector Pownall was at his desk. It was a crisp late January day, and the weather had been unusually warm for the time of year. He could actually feel the sun on his face as its rays streamed through his office window. As usual, he had lots of work on, mostly run of the mill stuff, with the occasional unusual case that brought that extra buzz to the job. He loved excitement and the latest report to come across his desk from the drug squad showed great promise in that regard. He read it again.

*

Confidential report – 19th January 2011

On the 15th January, the Manchester drug squad requested the assistance of the police spotter plane to conduct an aerial sweep of south of Manchester, and using their thermal imaging equipment, locate and identify any potential cannabis factories.

Prior to a sweep of the designated area, they flew over an area of north Cheshire to test their equipment, and by chance came across an unusual heat pattern reading, while passing over a large barn which forms part of the Byecroft Farm buildings near Briarley. The readings are consistent with a large cannabis factory operation, or similar. The imaging sensors also indicate a number of people inside the building, circa ten in number, but subsequent, on the ground observations, showed no obvious movement of this number of personnel, into or out of, the farm on a daily basis. There were regular vehicle movements, but non suitable for carrying people.

A subsequent sweep of the area was conducted two days later to check the data, and a reading similar to the previous one was recorded.

The tenant farmer, a Mr Harry Antrobus, lives in the farmhouse, from where he also runs a marquee hire business. Mr Antrobus used to operate raves on the farm some years ago, but transferred that business to Manchester, using old warehouse buildings. He is said to be quite wealthy, and on the face of it, a respectable businessman. Harry Antrobus is a big contributor to local charities etc., including the police charities. In this regard, he is known socially to the Chief Constable, so investigating officers should take note of this. Should the investigations uncover anything untoward.

The Chief Constable has been made aware of the investigation. The drugs team subsequently obtained access to the utility bills relating to the farm and found usage to be in excess of what might be expected as 'normal'.

Recommendation; We feel that this data, together with Mr Antrobus's connection to the Rave business, provides sufficient reason to justify a raid on the premises in question at the earliest opportunity.

The report was signed by the drug squad chief investigating officer, Jim Parkinson. Never a dull moment thought Pownall, and penned his response.

I approve the team leader's recommendation.

Made in the USA
Columbia, SC
22 July 2018